Seeds of My Field

Vic Topmiller Jr.

authorHOUSE®

AuthorHouse™
1663 Liberty Drive, Suite 200
Bloomington, IN 47403
www.authorhouse.com
Phone: 1-800-839-8640

© 2008 Vic Topmiller Jr.. All rights reserved.

No part of this book may be reproduced, stored in a retrieval system, or transmitted by any means without the written permission of the author.

First published by AuthorHouse 3/10/2008

ISBN: 978-1-4343-5779-3 (sc)
ISBN: 978-1-4343-5780-9 (hc)

Library of Congress Control Number: 2008900512

Printed in the United States of America
Bloomington, Indiana

This book is printed on acid-free paper.

This Book is Dedicated
First to my wife.
Dona
and then to all of those special people along the way that provided the inspiration and characters for this book.

Introduction

This story is set in the beautiful Tampa Bay area of west central Florida. It begins in a village a few miles north of Tampa called Lutz - in the 1950's.

This is not an entirely true story. It is emotionally true. You should read it as though it is true, you will soon believe it is.

Be one of the characters – be Bud or Albert or Junior or Moses or Junebloom or Amy or Dawn.

Above all, visualize the trees, the swamps, the dogs, Bud's old cut down Plymouth, the school, the trips home from school in the school bus, Albert's new green GMC, Fort Desoto. Live the book in your mind as you should all good novels and be a better person because you read it.

Thanks,
Vic.

Part 1
"BUD"

Chapter #1

Which has the most vitality in your mind, the memories of the past or the dreams of the future?

So often, when I'm pondering over subjects to discuss, especially when I'm sick and tired of writing politics, I come upon visions of times past. So many things I remember from the past seem to have a special priority across the events that make up a person's story. Is it that in our memory we can't remember the sharpness of pain, the pungency of smell, the dejectedness of sorrow or the weariness of body? Possibly, it is that in our memories we magnify the highlights of a happening and minimize low-lights.

I'm going to tell you a story, a story retrieved out of the memories of my heart and mind. It will begin in the innocence of youth, that period when in a young man's life when the pricks of thorns teach suspicion, the commitment of friendship teach trust and the thrill of laughter teach confidence. It will be this period that we will recognize the cultivation of spirit and personality that we each will look back at in our own circumstance and vainly try to understand ourselves, our fears, our secret pains, our low esteem. It is here, in these years of adolescence, not even understanding at the time, that a happening is happening in our lives that will plant the seeds and begin the momentum that is nothing less than the foundation that all of our impulses and meta-motivations will originate. Those strange influences, buried deeply in the recesses of our psyche, that our subconscience uses to evaluate and justify every action and reaction, every right, every wrong, every hate, every love from that early time until the time the circuitry discontinues. These are the times and places that Freud dared to trespass.

I want to tell you a story of a boy trying to understand love, hate, joy, sorrow. How a young man dealt with them.

A story of passionate love, of fiery hatred, the devils Satan. It begins in the life of a boy beginning his teens.

FROM THESE ROOTS THE TREE GROWS

Years ago, in a little town on the outskirts of Tampa, Florida called Lutz, there was a unique setting non-typical to any area that I know except the deep south. The little town, mostly orange groves on the higher ground, which wasn't much higher than the low ground, with lanes running from the pavement through the trees to houses and barns hidden deep within the orange tree forests, small lakes here and there surrounded by tall cypress trees, dense ferns and thick swamp growth. Every so often around the lakes the undergrowth would be cleared away by the people living close by, exposing the white Florida sand, making a swimming beach in the back yard. The local grass, I'm not sure it was native, was St. Augustine, it grew tall and unruly if unkept, but dense and soft if mowed. From the back of each house, sometimes it was the front, the grass was mowed to the lake's edge, making a lovely and secluded Eden of sorts. Late in the afternoon, it was my pleasure, more than occasionally, to be in the backyard and watch the red-orange sun set over the tree canopy horizon on the far side of the lake framed between the cypress trees on either side of our beach, the Spanish moss hanging mysteriously like loosened tresses swinging slowly back and forth in the light evening breeze, the welcomed cool evening breeze coming from the lake, the first calls of the Whippoorwill, supper smells hanging heavy in the damp air.

Between the groves and the lakes, on land not deep enough for lakes and not high enough for groves, were the swamps called cypress heads. The water stood shallow in them not over knee deep. Although the trees were fifty-feet or more tall, the Spanish moss hung from their high limbs nearly to the ground. Where the water was shallow, ferns grew making little islands of refuge for the non-aquatic creatures like snakes, lizards, rats, possums and coons (opossums - raccoons.) Vines hung down from the trees attaching their roots into the swamp floor (or maybe they hung up). Cypress knees protruded up from the water a few feet high like stunted stumps that wanted to be a tree but didn't have the oomph to get up there. All in all, the swamps, though eerie, were at the same time enchanting and beautiful.

The swamps were full of possums and coons, during the day that is, because at night they ventured out of the swamps into the groves and melon fields to sinfully gorge themselves on the choicest and sweetest of the fields. One old fat coon could take out a dozen melons a night by himself. Now consider what a dozen or more coons could do to the farmer's field.

Naturally, most of the farmers were coon hunters in self-defense, or possibly only in pretense, but nevertheless, a jolly group who were never understood by their wives. One such farmer - hunter was Albert Newsom, a successful and well-off farmer who successfully hid his success under his dirty overalls and knee boots. Albert, as he was called, would not let anyone call him Mr. Newsom, didn't own the first coon dog, he seemed to have little interest in dogs except during the hunt. What he had was orange groves and swamps and permission to hunt on everyone else's.

Albert had taken a liking to me, maybe because I had a hounds and would rather coon hunt than eat. He enjoyed teasing me about my girl friends knowing in advance that I would smart back. I hated girls, even more so when he teased me about them.

On Friday evening I put an extra emphasis on getting the chores done early. Hopefully, supper wouldn't be too late. Along with the sunset, cool breezes and smells from the kitchen, there was the restlessness of my two hounds. I always had a couple of hounds when I was growing up. I failed to realize that sophisticated people weren't coon hunters and high school boys dated on Friday nights and that whooping it up was throwing a party, not encouraging the hounds. But no matter what, nearly every Friday night I'd load my hyper-hounds in my old Plymouth cutdown and head for Stiekies to meet Albert, Junior and Junebloom.

I told you that Lutz was an unusual place, but not so unusual except to city slickers, because most of the little towns of the south had a "Stiekies". Stiekies was a garage in the center of town on the main highway, US 41. It wouldn't be fair to leave with calling it just a garage for it was much more. It was a big, old-fashioned wood building, painted white, mostly, sometime in the distant past, it had big double opening doors in the front and rear which were always open except during a storm, two red gas pumps in the front, regular and ethyl - inside, a mechanic shop, always cluttered with parts and tools, baskets of fresh vegetables setting on milk crates lined the front of the building in the shade of the porch that covered the gas pumps, milk, bread, drinks, cigarettes, cakes and candy bars. Everybody met there for everything and Mr. Stiekie sold something to everyone who did. It was the male social center for bad jokes and the spreading of tales. Women were seldom there except to get gas or check on their husbands. Everything was sold on credit, there was never a question about paying, there was no other place in town to socialize.

It was going to be a good night for coon hunting. The dew was settling early, the sky would be clear, partially moonlit and no breeze at all.

I finished supper before the sun had completely set, I never went hunting without eating first. Suppers in Florida, more often than not, consisted of either black-eyed peas or white rice or both with pork of some nature, cooked in. What was ironic about this was, although I would not have made it through the night without supper and a snack for later, the dogs weren't fed until after the hunt. I guess if they were hungry, they were supposed to be more aggressive hunters.

I backed my Plymouth cutdown around to the back of the house where the dogs were tied, Plymouth cutoff was more nearly correct, the only thing original about the old truck was the hood and front fenders. There were long planks that ran from the front to the rear that formed the driver's seat as well as the bed, even the windshield was cutoff which was alright for rabbit hunting in the orange groves but the swarm of evening flying bugs was rough on the eyes and you'd better keep your mouth closed. They knew it was hunting night, they were bawling and jumping against the end of their chains. Ole Blue and Lee. Blue was on his hind feet pushing against the chain with all of his might, his forefeet thrashing in the air, his funny-looking torn and scarred ears flopping around from front to back. He would extend himself as high as he could, then bawl ferociously. Just as it appeared he would fall over backwards, he would drop to all fours, take a few steps backwards and go through the whole routine again.

Maybe Lee thought it too undignified to carry on like this.

After all, he was only half hound, the other half American Pointer. He always stood at the end of the chain. Only a slight wiggle in his rear end gave away his excitement and the whining that he couldn't conceal.

This routine had been done so many times I didn't need to direct the hounds to the cutdown, they knew we were going hunting. I only needed to release the snap on their collars and almost in a single bound, they would sail over the wooden tailgate, no sooner getting their footing and turning about to face me, their heads hanging out over the tailgate, tails thrashing dangerously, "come on, come on", they seemed to say.

Sometimes hunters would come out from Tampa or nearby Sulphur Springs and bring their dogs to throw in with mine for the hunt. This always made Albert happy but I didn't like it much. They were always bragging and giving credit to their dogs for what I knew full well my dogs did. Besides, Ole Blue and Lee didn't need any help treeing coons. The other dogs may have made the swamps ring with music, it was Blue and Lee that were always first to tree.

There was never a coon hunter alive that didn't love to talk about his dogs. I never bragged much, why, I was too young, nobody ever listened. But I'll tell you, Blue and Lee could do it all, all by themselves.

Blue was an old bluetick hound. He got around pretty good for his age, but I'm pretty sure there were nights when his bones ached and his feet were sore, but he had what all good coon dogs have, a love of hunting more than life itself. He was an ugly dog as dogs go, but beautiful in the realm of coon hounds. His eyes were always bloodshot, his long floppy ears were scarred and ripped from too many coon fights and too many miles through the palmetto underbrush. Besides all that, he wasn't very fast, but that didn't matter, he was a trailer, nose right on the ground. Every now and then, as the scent got stronger, he would throw up his head and let out a bawl that would echo back and forth across the swamp. He could go right into the middle of a whole swamp full of trails and work out the freshest scent and stay on it until he had the coon lined out in front of him. That's what Lee was waiting for.

Lee was half bird dog and Treeing Walker. He was bigger than most hounds. He seemed to develop the hunting instincts of the bird dog. Like all good bird dogs, he never put his head to the ground to trail, rather, he kept it high, running from here to there, head held high in the air, winding for scents to drift his way. It didn't take him long to figure out that Blue would do the work and he would have the fun. Lee would never bark while Blue was working out a trail. It was like he was honoring a master trailer. Sometimes he would hang around close to me, head pointing, ears straining to capture any messages in Blue's bawling.

It was never long until Blue would get the trail straightened out, you could tell by his rapid bawling.

The coon would quit criss-crossing back and forth as Blue began to push him and begin to move rapidly through the cypress head. Lee would stand taller and taller, his eyes and attention fixed on the direction Blue's voice was coming from. Then with a bolt he would lunge into the dense underbrush to intercept Blue. Lee would run out ahead of the direction Blue was trailing, then criss-crossing back and forth, his head high, he would wait for Blue to drive the coon right toward him. When Lee would first see the coon or get it's strong scent, he would make this strange barking noise, as only a bird dog could, but barked little as he bore down on it. This was the signal for Blue to leave the trail and run for Lee as fast as he could. If the coon was real smart, Blue would have to help Lee stay with the trail, but more times than not, it was only a few minutes until Lee was chopping out a machine gun tree bark all the while tearing off tree bark strip after strip. I always waited for Blue. Sometimes it took him a little longer to get to the tree, but he was almost foolproof. If Blue said he was in the tree, go ahead and bet your pocketknife.

Coons frequently marked a tree, run up it a few feet and then jump down on the other side, sometimes a rangy old ringtail would climb all the way to the top, run out on the longest limb and jump as far as he could trying to deceive the hounds into believing that he was still in tree. But Blue was never fooled by these tricks. He would go to the tree and smell where the coon went up, then he would make wide circles around the tree trying to cut a trail if the coon had jumped. If not, back to the tree he would go, climbing as high up it as he could, sniffing the bark all the way. If he liked what he smelled, he threw his head back and "Yaw-yaw-yaw, Yaw-yaw-yaw, Yaw-yaw-yaw.

"Come on let's go, Blue's treed.

*   *   *

The dogs were hyper-ventilating with excitement. Blue was jumping from one side of my cut-down truck to the other picking up scents along the roadside. Lee, as usual, was standing behind me as erect as he could, his big head over my right shoulder, looking straight down the road. I would get an occasional lick in the ear. They knew full well that we where headed to Stiekie's station to meet Albert, Junior and Junebloom.

Thank goodness it wasn't but a quarter mile to the station. Everything about my cut-down was illegal, no top, no windshield, only one tail light. I was always on the back roads except to cross the main highway one time, and besides, this was in the good old days (I didn't know it then) when the law was a little more tolerant than today.

I pulled in beside the station, shaking my finger in the dog's noses, "Stay," I said several times sternly. Though I should have, but I loved them so much, I almost never tied them in because I was afraid it would hurt their feelings.

I looked over towards Albert's house just in time to hear his pickup start and back into the drive way on his way over. He always insisted that we take his truck. It was okay with me. I didn't have much money for gas, and besides, it was a brand new green half-ton GMC, the first pickup I ever saw with an automatic transmission. Plus, I think Albert felt more in control that way. After all, he was a lot older.

I walked on in to the station, "Hi Mr. Stiekie, (his name was Bill, but he seemed to prefer Mr.) I need a new battery". I didn't need to say a new six volt lantern battery for my head light, he already knew. The batteries were eighty-six cents, a lot of money I thought. I could get a few nights out of one battery. I even found that one additional night could be had if I heated the old battery in the oven for thirty minutes before I left. So, don't look so curious, for one additional night I could have a strawberry Nehi before we started hunting.

"Hi Junior, Hi Junebloom. It's going to be a good night," I said as they walked into the station together.

The world is full of characters and the ones that don't fit the normal mold are usually the most interesting and curious. Junior was only about two or three years older than me, much more mature, not as tall, but stout and agile. His skin was dark from years of being a woodsman, one of the best I've known. His hair was dark to match his burnished skin, usually a little long and always unkempt except when he had a romantic impulse. He was considered unkempt. Now, he would either look normal or he would be making a statement. His folks were grove caretakers. That meant they were poor which in turn meant that they didn't have the time or money to teach junior the niceties of life and pretty much left him to grow up by his own devices. Even with all of his freedom he never did anything seriously wrong. I expect that he knew that if he got into trouble there would be no one to bail him out. He was an excellent hunter who had forgone a normal lifestyle to be just what he wanted to be, a fellow who worked to the degree necessary to provide his basic needs and spend the rest of his life hunting and fishing. He was still a good citizen, fairly law abiding, so it's okay isn't it? One thing Junior always hated, I could run faster and could beat him to the tree.

Junebloom, now that's the other side of the coin. Junebloom was always in trouble. He couldn't stay out of the bars in Sulphur Springs and was constantly getting beat up. I guess he was a good hunter but a lousy fighter. He was always a gentleman with us, but then, we didn't drink like fools and we didn't allow him to. Albert may have had a nip before he left the house. I often thought that if we had hunted both Friday and Saturday nights, possibly we could have helped Junebloom avoid some bruises.

Junebloom was one of those mystic characters that no one knew where he came from or where he finally went. We only knew him as Junebloom because that's what he instructed us to call him. I have no idea how old he was, maybe in his forties. He was a black man, medium build, worked for one of the orange grove companies as a tractor driver and lived alone in a small shanty in the middle of the grove. He didn't drive anything but a tractor, so he walked in to go hunting.

There was a lot of protocol and traditional bias that went along with socializing with a black man during that period, but you'd never know it with this group. When we all showed up to hunt, he seemed as white as the rest of us. Besides, we all just liked him a lot and he kept us in stitches all night with his funny jokes. He seemed to not resent being black and I for one didn't care if he was.

Unfortunately during those days white people seemed to think it was a God-given privilege to call black people by a lot of demeaning names, names like Boy or Nigger or Coon or Jig. Looking back it's no wonder they were offended. Although we would have never called Junebloom by these names, I have to tell you about the time that the difference slipped through.

I'll never forget that first night when Junebloom showed up to ask if he could go hunting with us. Sure, why not, we all agreed and he could have the coons. He went in and asked Mr. Stiekie if he could charge a flashlight and some batteries. Mr. Stiekie consented after Albert nodded that he would be responsible for the bill. We headed for Albert's pickup.

Albert had already transferred the dogs to his truck and they were jumping around and barking at us as we approached. I always rode in the back with the dogs on the way to the swamps. That way I could stand behind the cab and shine my light into the trees and maybe spot a coon's eye shining out from the Spanish moss.

I vaulted over the side, the dogs greeted me with licks on the face and uncontrollable barking. They loved hunting so much and hated waiting at the station. Albert and Junior got into the front. There was never a question where Junebloom would ride. The only part of a pickup he had ever seen was the back part. "C'mon, you can ride back here with me," I said to him.

I'll tell you how the ice began to break between us and our new hunting partner. Lee had been raised around colored people. He thought no more about Junebloom being there than anything. Blue had not. Junebloom grabbed the tailgate, put a foot on the bumper and was about to step into the truck. Blue met him with a challenge, his head out over the tailgate, teeth showing, hair raised on the back of his neck, a vicious growl coming from deep down in his throat, daring Junebloom to put one foot in his private mode of conveyance. I shouted, "Blue, no," as Junebloom jumped backward in a state of shock. "Bad dog, Blue. C'mon Junebloom, it's okay now." I grabbed Blue's collar and drug him to the front of the pickup bed. "Maybe so," Junebloom said, "But I'm riding up front." Junior realized what was happening just as Junebloom grabbed the door handle. He stepped out to let Junebloom slide into the middle. I thought it was kinda cute, Junebloom sitting between Junior and Albert so they could protect him from Ole Blue. I hated the thought that I may have to punish Blue further. Yes, he was spoiled.

It was plenty dark as we drove north out of town, maybe a mile, then on to a sandy road through a grove of overhanging grapefruit trees to the other side where it opened up into a clearing between the grove and a densely treed cypress head. The cleared area was about two hundred yards wide. The grove owner had leased this area out to a farmer who had planted about twenty acres of cantaloupes. They were about ripe and the coons were beginning to invite themselves to dinner. I'm pretty sure Albert had received a call earlier to "Please bring the dogs to my cantaloupe field."

As we pulled into the clearing, I flashed my light over the field to see if I could shine some eyes. "Must be too early," I said, "No coons out yet, they might be waiting for the moon to get a little higher."

We decided to sit tight and wait for the moon and maybe, if we could catch a coon out in the field, we would get a longer race before he headed back into the swamp which was blessed with some of the tallest trees around.

We were standing alongside the pickup looking across the field at the cypress head, quietly talking about what we thought the coons were going to do when they finally came out to feed. I had lead ropes on Blue and Lee and was holding them close. Otherwise, you could bet your life they would hit the cypress in a flash. About that time Junebloom decided to venture out of the pickup and join the conversation. He didn't see Blue as he came around the back end of the truck. Blue jumped up on him, putting his forefeet as high as he could on Junebloom's chest and began barking right in his face. I neither knew what Blue or Junebloom were going to do. Just as I was about to respond by jerking Blue down by his lead rope, Junebloom grabbed one of Blue's ears in each hand, "What are you doing dog? I ain't no coon," he hollered. Blue was so taken aback by this unusual treatment that he quit barking. I looked around at Albert and Junior.

They were about to blow the corks out of their ears trying to hold it back. We broke out in spontaneous laughter.

If Junebloom had any idea why we laughed so hard, I don't know. I expect he did but decided to ignore it. If he did, he never let on. But from that night forward he had gained a lot of respect from Ole Blue.

It was not very likely, after all the fuss Junebloom and Blue had made, that any coon in his right mind would be coming out of the swamp anyway soon, so I suggested that we load up and go to a different area. We all agreed and decided to go down the road a ways where there were some cypress strands bordered by small lakes and slews.

There were always a lot of coons in this type of swamp, it was just a natural habitat. But these coons, not like the coons that gorged on watermelons, oranges and cantaloupe, were all rangy and lean from a diet of crawdads, frogs and mussels. This meant that you usually jumped just one coon and that coon ran nearly all night long. He could run through the cypress head for awhile, across a palmetto ridge, swim a pond, jump from log to log across a slew and tiptoe across a tussock that the hounds might break through. And, they could do these things over and over without getting tired.

There are other things that reside in these swamps besides the coon, things like wild hogs. They are truly wild, although not originating from wild hogs. These were feral hogs that had gotten crossed with razorbacks and developed into a pig with a fighting propensity. They spend most of their nights feeding on grubs and worms around the edges of the swamps in the grassy fringe between the water and the palmetto border. We were careful to keep the dogs away from the wild pigs because if they decided to catch one, it could be trouble. A wild boar grows large tusks protruding up from his lower jaw. These tusks can be six or seven inches long and be as sharp as razor blades. A wild hog can throw his head against the dog and rip his body open.

The other problem living in these swamps was the alligator. There was plenty of these. They seldom were a problem, as they preferred to eat things like rabbits and fish, but a large alligator would gladly dine on a dog if one got close. Whenever we were hunting around the ponds and slews, I swept the pond with my light regularly in search of a pair of deep red eyes set wide apart on the surface of the water.

There was only one way to hunt this area, drive as close to the edge of the swamp as possible, drop the tailgate and let the dogs work up a trail.

There was a fair moon by now, probably pushing midnight. The coons would already have been out feeding, walking along the edge of the water, scratching out little meals, holding them in their agile paws, biting open the shells, pulling out the small pieces of meat and rinsing it in the water, throwing down the shells and dropping to all four feet and ambling along, checking here and there for the next meal. By now the trail could be long and zig-zagged and probably crossed by other feeding coons. The swamp could be a maze of trails not over a couple of hours old. "Ole Blue" could work it out, you could bet on that.

As we always did, almost in ritual fashion, we, Albert, Junior, Junebloom and myself, left the GMC up on the palmetto ridge, shushed the dogs to be quite, and walked down to the edge of the pond to ascertain if we could see any fresh tracks in the soft mud. If so, it was usually Junior that saw it first. "Schish," he would say, "I see a fresh one right here." He would reach up and jerk his headlight from his head and hold it close and parallel to the ground making the light beam cast a shadow in the outline of the track. "Big Ole Boar - pretty fresh. Bud, go for the dogs." They all called me "Bud" because I was a Jr. and I didn't want to be called Junior. Junior was not a Jr., He didn't mind being called Junior.

I'm here to admit that Ole Blue could have found that track easier than we could with one smell, but he had also learned that when we took him to the pond and he dropped his head and bellowed like an old bull, we would turn him loose whether there was a coon in the area or not.

When I would come running back to the GMC alone, the dogs knew that a fresh track had been found and it was time to go.

They were jumping against their leads hard enough for them to make a snapping noise. They were straining so hard that their profuse barking would often come out as choking sounds because their wind was cut off. I would release Blue first. He would dash headlong to the water's edge where the other three were waiting motionless to avoid messing up the track.

Poor Lee, I held him tight as he lunged against his lead to follow Blue, but he must wait, wait until Blue had had time to work out the direction of the trail. Blue would only bark once at the intersection of the trail and then run in silence up the trail and down until he could determine which direction the coon was traveling. When he was sure he was trailing in the direction the Ole Ringtail was traveling, he would lower his head to the trail and begin bawling. This was my cue to release Lee. Lee respected Blue enough to not cross the trail in front of Blue and mess up the scent.

Instead, he would run along a little behind and then back to me, his nerves not allowing him to stand idle.

We would encourage Blue, taking turns, we'd holler silly things like, "Work it out Blueee." "Hoowee". "Go get him Boy." "Straighten im out, Blue."

I was so proud of Blue I could almost burst. I wouldn't have been happier if I had had a new car.

Every time Blue would get the trail straight and pick up speed, Lee would get hyper out of his mind. He would charge forward and then return knowing better than us that Blue was still working out the kinks and had not gotten the coon on the run yet. Finally, Yaw - Yaw - Yaw, Blue would let out. His bawls would echo from the cypress heads. I could hear that he was holding his head up and running faster. Lee knew the same thing and charged through the palmetto fringe toward Blue. "Get im Blue, get im Lee," We would all bark out almost simultaneously.

Hot dog the chase is on.

"Yah, Yah, Yah," the music of the hounds in hot pursuit came echoing from across the pond. The hounds were sure that they could put this old rangy ringtail up in a hurry and they pushed hard. But the smart of some coons seems to transcend the genes of natural instinct and this was one of those boys. He would hear the hounds gaining on him and he would know that it was time to reach in his bag of tricks and lay out some trails that would test the skills of even the most seasoned and savvy coon dog.

"Hoowee - Hoowee," I yelled.

Knowing full well that this smart old coon might line out and run clear out of hearing, we began pushing through the sludgy marsh trying to keep in earshot of Blue and Lee. The coon was laying down trick after trick trying to evade the hounds. I could tell by listening to Lee. It was obvious that the coon was running straight out for a hundred yards or so and then he would crawl logs or mark trees and confuse the dogs for a few minutes. I could tell because Lee would run hard and ahead of Blue on the straight trails only to get confused and fall behind Blue letting him untangle the coon's latest diversion. Soon Blue's steady bawling told us that he had figured out the trick and away he and Lee would go, neck to neck in a race.

We kept after the dogs, pushing through the dew-laden brush until our clothes were wet to the skin, never a comfortable feeling your clothes wet and clinging to your skin, but it was one of those things that you have to get used to if you're going to hunt coons in the South. And wet feet. Albert wore knee boots. I bet they were always full of sticks and debris plus I'll bet his feet got just as wet from perspiration. Junior and I wore plain old high top sneakers, you know, those black things with a white patch on the inside ankles. The water ran in and the water ran out again. Junebloom wore some old leather shoes, probably the same shoes he wore every day. Every time we stopped to rest, he and Albert would sit down, take off their shoes and pour them out like a bucket.

Albert was sitting on a big pine stump, his foot in the air, pulling on his last boot. It made a rub sound and a whoosh as the heel sank into place. "Well boys, I'm ready for another run," he said, "Can you still hear the dogs?"

Junior had his hands cupped behind his ears funneling the sounds in. "Listen close," he whispered out, "it sounds like they're turning. What do you think, hear im? Yah, they're turning alright. Hotdang, they're coming right this way."

Albert climbed up onto the flat-topped pine stump, straining to hear the sweet music of the chase coming directly at us. Had the coon forgotten about us? We kept our lights off and stared out across the pond into the silvery haze of the moonlight. Soon, unless he changed directions, the coon would be across the pond from us not more than a hundred yards away.

It was during these high tension times that we all began to second guess the coon's plans.

"When he hits that pond he's got no choice, go right, go left, or go up," was Junebloom's offering, "And he's gonna go up."

It got quiet. We could hear an occasional splash across the pond. The dogs barked sparingly as though they had come upon a barrier that they couldn't handle. I could hear the sounds of the dogs splashing in the edge of the water, their barking was directed towards the middle of the pond.

Albert, "We've got a problem boys, that dang coon has walked the tuscuss right out to the middle." - I don't know where the term tuscuss came from, I suppose it was an easier way to say tussock, which you know is a grass island. "Yesssir, that coon is walking right out on that tuscuss. If those dogs go after him they'll fall through that tuscuss and he'll drown 'em for sure. Hear ole Lee fighting the water, falling through the tuscuss? He's trying to get out there now. We'd better do somethin before that coon does or he'll be atop Lee's head."

A quick shot of emotional pain surged through my body as I imagined the possible fate of Blue and Lee. I'd heard how a smart old coon would entice a hound to chase him out into the water where he would be vulnerable and then crawl right up onto his back and hold him under the water until the dog would drown. Even as good a swimmer as Lee was, he would not have a chance trying to swim through the thick tuscuss with a coon on his back. And Blue for sure.

I could hear Blue now. He had caught up to Lee at the edge of the pond. He was barking like a cur dog would, making a choppy erratic bark showing his frustration as he leaped to the edge of the water and then backed out. Lee was pushing to get to the coon. Some of the time the tuscuss was thick and he would climb up onto it only to fall through it in a few steps.

"Come on Albert," I pleaded almost sounding like a cry, "We can't let that ole coon drown Lee!"

"Let's go guys," said Albert, "Maybe we can do something from the other side. We can't do much from here, too far away."

About that time Lee screamed. I could hear the thrashing of the water and knew that the coon was taking advantage of his superiority in the water to attack Lee. Lee was strong enough to throw the coon off but then he would attack again as Lee would try to swim through the grassy slime.

"I'm going out to help Lee," I called back as I broke into a run.

"Go to the far side and come in from over there," Albert hollered. "Let's all try to get out to Lee from different sides and maybe we can find a place in the tuscuss thick enough to hold us up."

I was running as hard as I could go, I could hear Junior behind me. "I'm going in here," I shouted over my shoulder to Junior, "Come in from the other side."

I was half swimming, half crawling on my stomach trying to make it across the lake on the wet slimy tuscuss. Sometimes it would be thick enough for me to crawl, then thin and I would fall through and have to kick and pull myself back up to the top. I was several yards out into the lake when my light picked up Lee and the coon. The coon had crawled almost to the top of Lee's head, his claws slashing at his nose and eyes. Lee was fighting hard to get his feet on top of the tuscuss to pull himself out but the weight of the coon was too much and he fell back into the water. I could hear him coughing, a sign he was giving out and taking in water. "Hurry, help, help, he's going to drown Lee."

I heard Junebloom scream, "If dat damn coon drowns Lee, I'll kill 'im wid my bare hans."

It seemed like an eternity of time until I reached Lee and the coon. The coon was so confident of his victory he hardly cared as I slid up on my belly only a few feet away from him.

His weight was beginning to win over Lee and he began to sink into the water. I was unable to get to my feet to knock him off. My heart began to sink as I saw Lee begin to give up from exhaustion.

I laid as long and stiff as I could out over the cruel grass toward Lee, I could reach his tail without falling through. I grabbed with all of my grip and tried to pull him towards me.

Lee felt my pull and began to struggle again. I was pulling him to me, but as I did I was losing ground and sliding into

the water hole. I wasn't going to give up. As long as Lee could fight, I would too.

I didn't know if I would have the strength to swim out if I fell into the hole. Maybe this monster coon would even attack me. What would I do?

"Don't give up Lee, don't give up," I cried.

Laying prostrate on the tuscuss as I was, pulling poor Lee to the edge and out of the hole was about as impossible as impossible could be. I couldn't raise up on to my knees because the concentrated weight would cause me to sink through the grass. By holding his tail, I could pull him to the edge of the water hole but I didn't have enough strength to lift him up. Then, he would thrash with all of his might and his fighting worked exactly against my own.

"I've got Lee, I need help, hurry," I shouted over and over.

"We're coming, hang on," I heard Junebloom respond.

I was surprised to hear Junebloom; he was so afraid of alligators. It was probably not true at all, but folklore had it that gators loved to eat dogs, babies and colored people. Junebloom bought it "hook line and sinker."

Alligators, like most carnivorous animals, hardly ever pass up an opportunity to attack an animal in distress. I knew in my mind that at any moment a gator might explode out from the water below Lee, tear him out of my grasp and thrash him back and forth with his gigantic head, his huge teeth penetrating his body like tiger fangs, then carry him silently away to his underwater den to be devoured. The many criss-crossing trails through the marshy grass were an undeniable signature of their presence.

Blood was flowing profusely from Lee's head from the many wounds inflicted by the gashing and biting of the needle-like claws and teeth of the raging coon. The open pool of water was nearly covered with blood as well was the surrounding grass. Any gator in the area would surely come to the smell of fresh blood like bees to honey. He was beginning to cough and choke on the water he had ingested. Neither Lee nor I could hold on forever. The clock was running, I knew we were running out of time.

Something struck me sharply on my outstretched heel.

"Take this stick," Junior yelled, "beat the coon off with it."

Junior had enough coolness to grab a dead limb from a low-growing cypress tree before lunging into the swamp. It was a good-size limb several inches in diameter and about six feet long. His adrenaline flow must have been at a peak to have broken off such a limb. I reached behind me and grabbed the limb. It was dead and smooth for the bark had already fallen off. It was dry which made it light and rigid. I didn't even take aim. When I felt that I had a firm grip on the limb, starting from the position of my arm and limb stretched out behind me, I came immediately with a full swing only a few inches across the top of the grass. I could hear the swooshing sound of the limb as it gained speed and momentum around the passage of the great arc. Whop!! Somehow, surely by the grace and guidance of a higher power, the limb caught the startled coon broadside and sent it hurtling through the air, landing on his back several yards away on the grassy tuscuss. He lay stunned for a minute and then jumped to his feet in preparation for another attack. He looked at Lee still struggling in the water, then looked at me and the limb, then eased off into the darkness swaggering to and fro from the lingering dizziness of the shock.

I reached the stick out to Lee who no longer had the strength to fend for himself. "Grab hold," I called to Lee, "take the stick in your mouth, Boy."

I don't know whether it was instinct or it is that dogs have more intelligence than we give them credit for, but Lee immediately took a death-grip on the end of the limb all the while coughing through his open teeth. I pulled him in close enough to grab his collar with both hands. "Pull me, Junior, I've got Lee." Junior pulled hard. In a minute we had slid Lee out of the water and onto the grass beside me. Exhausted, he lay on his side, his eyes looking into mine as though they were trying to communicate something he was incapable of saying, his chest heaving as though his heart might burst.

I lay on the tuscuss beside him for a long moment searching his back and face for deep wounds and cuts that might be dangerous. I looked back into his wet eyes that traced my every movement, great tears began to appear in my eyes and then began migrating down my cheeks and I saw little circles as they dropped into the water we were lying in. I felt in my heart how much this dog and I owed each other, the price we paid to hunt together, the commitment to our sport, the dedication to excellence - the bonding of a boy and a dog.

"Over here," Junior called to Albert and Junebloom, "we're over here."

"How's Lee?" Albert called back.
"He's okay, he's gonna be okay."

* * *

There's something crazy about the way people risk life and limb during an emergency to help someone or save someone. It really never occurred to me how dangerous and daring going out onto this tuscuss pond to rescue Lee from the coon was. More than once has a man slipped out of sight through the deceptive layer of grass never to be seen again. Lee's blood on the water could have sent an old gator into a feeding craze. It could have been Lee or me, or any of the others as far as that is concerned, that he would have dragged below the water and tore apart, but as I saw the lights of the other hunters making their way to us, I knew it didn't matter. For the moment we were a team, a team of comrades, ready to take whatever risks had to be taken. If it were necessary that all should be lost in the effort to save Lee and me, so be it, that's how it would be. In war or in sport, that's how good men are.

* * *

Blue had made it out to us and was licking the blood from Lee's head and muzzle. Junior had slipped up alongside and was patting Lee on the flank, I guess trying to give him reassurance that all was okay now. Junebloom was sitting there with his back resting against mine frantically tearing apart his wet package of cigarettes trying to find one that wasn't wet and falling apart. We were all soaked to the core, totally exhausted, death warmed over.

Albert, who was still fifty yards away, stood up. "Look guys, I've found a firm place, try and come towards me."

We just looked his way too tired to move at the moment. I wasn't sure how strong Lee would be or even if I would have to carry him out.

"Hold the spot," Junior called back, "we'll be heading out directly."

In a hushed voiced Albert said, "Quiet boys, I think I hear the coon coming this way."

In a moment, out of the dead silence, a commotion that sent shock waves across the tuscuss, "Here he is, he thinks I'm a tree, he's climbing my dammed leg."

I flashed my light in Albert's direction in time to see his gold-crowned teeth shining like fireflies in the darkness and his six-cell light catch the coon in the belly and hurl him out into the darkness.

As you can imagine, Junior and I were choking with laughter at the comical predicament Albert was in.

"You okay?" Junebloom called out.

"Biggest coon I ever saw, thought I was a cotton pickin' tree. Let's get out of here, it's getting cold, don't ever want to see that 'Son of a Gun' again."

We made our way across the tuscuss pond to the clearing at the edge of the receding water. The moon had completely set. It was coal black, our weakened lights were our only eyes.

In less than an hour we were back at the GMC. Albert sat on the running board and poured the water and debris out of his boots. We were too tired to joke about the hunt as we usually did. Junebloom had found a pack of dry cigarettes and lit up. Blue jumped into the back and was sitting down leaning against the cab. Lee was sitting on the ground looking up at the tailgate either too tired to jump or taking advantage of his condition. Junior and I helped him make the leap up.

We loaded up, Albert, Junior and Junebloom in the front. I sat in the pickup bed with the dogs, down low out of the wind. Blue had his nose resting on the side-rail of the truck still winding the smells along the road. Lee curled up in a ball beside me. He pushed and squirmed until his head was laying in my lap and then fell asleep.

The eastern sky was turning whitish-pink as the GMC hit the pavement.

Chapter #2
"THERE'S OWNERSHIP, YOU KNOW"

Well, it'd been about three weeks since I'd seen Albert, Junior or Junebloom. It had taken most of that time for the wounds on Lee's head to heal over. He had gotten an infection in his lungs from ingesting so much swamp water. The Vet had given me some medicine to clear it up and some smelly stuff to daub on his wounds. After the second week he began to mend real fast and by now he was as good as new, except that he had put on some weight.

A late summer afternoon rain had just stopped, the puddles were standing everywhere, the air was cool and had that great clear, clean smell. The clouds were breaking up but the sun was low enough that it would have no chance to heat the ground and the atmosphere before the cool of nightfall. If you've been through many summer rains in Florida, you know what a steam bath it can be after the sun returns.

As a matter of fact, it was so pretty and fresh I decided to walk down to Stiekie's garage instead of driving my cutdown. It was only little over quarter of a mile.

"HI Mr. Stiekie, It's kinda quiet this evening."

"Lo Bud, there'l be a few in after this rain I magine."

"Did those Strawberry Nehi's come in?"

"Yep, there in the box already."

"Think I'll have one, and a bag of peanuts too please."

"If you like those Strawberry Nehi's so much how come you dump those salted peanuts in it?"

"I don't know, seems like it makes the peanuts better."

"Want me to put um on your folks ticket?"

"Better not, there gonna get a bill from the Vet they're not gonna like already."

"Well, twenty five cents."

"How's ole Lee anyhow, heard he got beat up pretty bad by that big coon the other night."

"Yeh, exactly three weeks ago tonight." "But he's fine now." "I don't guess Albert or Junior has come in yet?"

"Haven't seen Junior in a few days, Albert's got some pumps runnin in that low section of grove, trying to get this rain out. Told'm it was to low. He'll be in directly I suppose."

I was leaning with my back to the counter looking out the big double front doors of the garage. Albert's GMC came in angleing off the highway down the ramp by the gas pumps and pulled up at the side of the station.

Albert came in, still wearing his rubber knee boots, grinning from ear to ear displaying his fortune in gold crowns.

"Give me a Miller's, Bill." How's it going Bud, How's ole Lee?"

It was obvious that his real concern was about Lee's health and not mine.

"Oh, he's fine, he could go hunting any day now."

"That's good, real good." "We're going tonight, let me run home and get some grub and we'll go get Lee and Blue."

"You mean Junior and Junebloom?"

"They may be going, but Moses is coming out from town with his dogs." "We ought to have a good run tonight."

"Moses!"

"Moses Wilson."

"But he got two to ten didn't he," I replied sounding both surprised and concerned.

"Yep, but after sitting in the slammer for eight months he got weak and told where he hid his still. After the Revenue boys chopped it to pieces the judge let him out for good behavior."

I need to stop and tell you about Moses Wilson. Mr. Wilson seemed to be well past middle aged. He was a black man, bigger than the rest of us, hair was mostly white. He always spoke in a deep, serious voice. If ever a man looked the part of the Ole Deacon down at the Baptist church, it was him. As a matter of fact, he was a deacon down at the Baptist church.

If you want to know how to rationalize the deacon at the Baptist church getting two to ten for moon shinning, ask someone else. To me it's a paradox of paradox's.

I guess it wouldn't have been such a paradox if I hadn't been early raised my early years by my real Mom, an austere baptist woman, who was fully convinced that all deacons where fully filled with the Holy Spirit and that alcohol was the spirit of the devil. Poor Mom and her rigidity, if she'd known Moses Wilson the conflict of characteristics would have broken her down.

But let me tell you, I learned a lot of spiritual wisdom from that old man, he had a parable or example to cover about everything. He loved his church and when the hounds weren't hot on a trail he always talked about it.

"Now you see," Mr. Wilson would start, "Lot O church's get's into trouble because they pick the wrong preacher."

I knew he was mad at his preacher tonight.

"Now you see that ole redbone there?" He was walking down the trail under foot. "He done nothin all week but lay around the pen an be lazy. He ate my grub and done nothin. Nows friday night comes along and he gets all stirred up to go huntin." He don't do nothin all week to be nothin, but when the big hunt shows up he's ready to go." "But when you gets im out to the woods, he still don't do nothin, he jus hangs around and waits for the workers to get the coon up the tree and then he wants to run in for the fun." "He don't deserve no fun, ought to leave im here in the swamp."

"Lots a preachers the same way, they don't do nothin all week long, they tells us deacons and the wives to go out and bring um in, they preaches to go into the highways and hedges and they ain't never even seen one, after we done did a days work already, but he don't, he ain't got time, to busy meditating, he says." "Why, if it was up to him, I wouldn't even have time to go coon huntin. They's jus like that sorry ole dog there, ain't never leading, always followin." "Gonna leave im in the swamp."

"I'll tell you another thing," he went on, "They's always saying, Bring all the tithes into the store house." "And so, we bring the tithes in and put them in the store house, but when the poor ole widows and hungry folks show up to get something out of the store house, the store house is bare." "Now who's store house is it, and who's gettin all the tithes."

Well, if Mr. Wilson was mad at the preacher about something, he would go on like this all night. But the next hunt he may be happy about something the preacher did and that's what we would hear all night.

One night Mr. Wilson erased any doubt I may have had about the integrity and sincerity of his faith with a little example that I was neither prepared for or able to completely understand until years later.

I guess I being a little smart alec. Every time he would talk about religion I would think about his moonshine still. "Mr. Wilson, what color do you think Jesus is?"

"Well, son, I thought about that a lot of times when I was your age, I hated white folks so bad that I didn't think I could ever love a Jesus that was white." "But I want to tell you a good lesson, one I figured out while I was out coon hunting alone one night." "You hear them dogs, they's after that coon." "They ain't nothing in this world they likes better than putting that ole ringtail up a tree."

"No sir, there's not," I agreed.

"Hear how happy they are, they're work'n hard in mud and water up to their bellies and it's hotter'n all get out, but they don care, cause they know if they works hard and long and they hunts with all their hearts, that sur-nuf they'll put that ole coon in the tree."

Mr. Wilson went on, "Now listen to this, I've seen different kinds of coons, some is as black as can be, so black you can hardly make out the rings on the tail or the mask on the face, I've seen some so sun burnt that they was almost solid yellow, and do you remember that albino coon, white a she could be, jus barely make out the grey where the black was sposed to be. Now boy, when them hounds gets that smart ole coon up the tree do you think they's gonna care whether he's black, yellow or white?" They's gonna be so happy, they won't care what color he is."

"That's the way it's gonna be with Jesus, Boy, you wait an see."

You may have sensed that there was more to Mr. Wilson's coming than the fact that I didn't think his dogs were much good and always got the credit while Blue did the work. There was. When Mr. Wilson was sentenced to serve time, he farmed his dogs out to different hunters to keep for him. He had told Albert that I was the only one good enough to keep Lee for him.

Albert must have noticed my melancholy that night, "Bud, you not feeling good tonight?"

"I don't know, hunting's not fun anymore, I don't think I'll ever hunt again."

Albert knew the source of my despondency, "Well, what about Ole Blue, aren't you going to take him hunting anymore?" "You'll still have him you know, and besides, Moses will be out nearly every weekend."

"It won't be the same." "Do you think he will take him." "Won't he want to leave him with me?"

"I don't think so," Albert said. "I think he's planning to take him tonight."

"But why?" "He doesn't love Lee as much as I do, and I know Lee loves me more than him, I can tell, and he's got so many dogs." "Why should he take him," I blurted out?

Albert stopped for a second, looked at me like he wanted to say something and then started walking on. "There's such a thing as ownership, you know."

That night when the hunt was over and the dogs were being loaded up, it seemed to me to be the worst night that a boy could ever have. There was this big knot in my throat that pounded with my heart beat, it choked me so that I couldn't talk. I know the tears in my eyes were easy to see so I always looked at the ground. It seemed that Lee knew as well as I that the time had come for him to return to his owner, Mr. Wilson reached down and jumped him into the truck with his collar. A jump Lee had made a thousand times by himself. Blue automatically jumped into the GMC and was looking inquisitively at Lee. I believe there is more emotion in a dog's mind than we understand for Lee starred at Blue and me for the remainder of the time there, forsaking his heart because he was owned.

"Come on, Bud," Albert said, "Maybe we can find you another dog like Lee."

I couldn't respond, and even if I could have, Albert didn't know how empty his statement was.

As I watched Moses Wilson's pickup leave the grove and turn onto the pavement the moment seemed to bear down with excruciating finality. The pain of every soldier boy and his sweetheart when it is time to go, every slave sold away from his own, every boy and girl divided in a broken home.

So, what if the heart does break? So, what if the soul does yearn? There's such a thing as ownership you know.

Chapter #3
COMING HOME

Yes, a lot of time has passed since Moses Wilson took Lee back to his kennel in town, and yes, it was almost like Albert had said, that Mr. Wilson would bring Lee out on the weekends and we would still be able to hunt together just like old times.

The first Friday night afterwards was like the reuniting of old friends. Blue ran up to Lee as he jumped out of the pickup, his curled up tail wagging like a run away metronome. They lunged at each other and bumped chests, one would drop down to his knees giving the "let's play" sign and then other. They would jump back and forth, dodging each other's playful lunge and take off in an explosion around and around the pickup, each taking turns nipping at the other heels. Finally Lee ran to me, jumped full force on to my chest. I went sailing backwards, falling to the ground, instantly being pounced upon and mauled by two old friends. We wrestled on the ground rolling over and over. With my hands I would push one away and then the other in an attempt to protect my face and ears from the gouging wet noses and the laps from frothing tongues. I could hold one dog temporarily in a hammerlock around the neck but I soon had to release one hand to push away the flailing tongue of the other. Then, they would both get free and the roll and tumble started all over. This went on until I was panting like the dogs and soaking wet from perspiration and rolling on the dew-saturated ground.

It was this way for a few weeks. The spark of friendship glowed strong, but then I began to notice and then Blue, that the excitement was wearing away and Lee seemed less and less spontaneous to Blue's advances. I noticed a diminished spark in his eyes and his playfulness seemed only half-hearted. In the past he had always hunted right with Blue no matter what the other dogs were doing or even if they were off on another coon, but more and more Blue would come down treed and Lee would not be there.

Didn't Lee like me and Blue anymore? Was he forgetting who we were? I had a sinking feeling in my stomach as I considered the possibility that a friend I loved so much could become apathetic toward us. Maybe, with some, a relationship that isn't fed is soon dead.

One night when Mr. Wilson showed up with the dogs, Lee was the last to leave the pickup bed. Blue and I rushed to him, as we always did. He just stood there, lethargic and non-responsive. "C'mon Lee, what's the trouble Ole Boy," I said as I stroked his head.

Lee's coat, usually slick and glossy, was dull and stiff, his eyes were matted and where I used to see spark and flash, I saw dry and dullness; he wheezed slightly as he breathed. He looked at me as if he were trying to tell me, but I couldn't understand. "C'mon boy, aren't you glad to see me anymore? You haven't forgotten me and Ole Blue have you?" He looked at me, but didn't respond even as Blue nudged him and licked him across the nose.

It seemed that Mr. Wilson was avoiding me.

I made him look at me, "Mr. Wilson, something's not right about Lee. Did you give him some bad food or something?"

"Naw Bud, wuddent bad food that's making him feel so bad, tuwoosh it was."

"Well, dangit Mr. Wilson, what is it?"

Too many times we have to answer questions that we'd rather not, the reason being is that even in truthfulness a taint of guilt will fall on the teller.

Albert, who had been watching me examine Lee, was now propped against the pickup within hearing but out of the way of a dialogue that was eminent.

Mr. Wilson answered, busily looking here and there, avoiding my stare, "Bud, I figured as many dogs as you've raised you'd know what was wrong with Lee."

"Well, what?"

"Got distemper."

"No, Mr. Wilson, you're wrong. It's not distemper, it can't be," I cried out. I grabbed Lee's head and held it close to my chest.

Mr. Wilson went on, this time looking at me and Lee, "Bud, you know it is. Look at his eyes, hear that infection in his lungs. Distemper, that's what it is."

"No, it can't be. Didn't he have his shots?"

"Nope, never did need no shots before, my dogs wuz always healthy, never got sick or nothin. One guy that wuz keeping a dog for me while I wuz doin time had a whole mess of distemper in his kennel, must have brought it home, might lose most of my dogs over it. Ole Blue's got his shots, ain't he?"

I grabbed Blue around the neck and pulled him over to be near me and Lee, "Blues had shots," I responded defiantly.

Junior and Junebloom had moved over by Albert and were standing quiet and observant. Mr. Wilson was staring at me cradling the two dogs in my arms.

Spontaneously I blurted out, "I told you I should have kept Lee, now look at him, he might die. Why didn't you give him his shots like you're supposed to?" my words becoming fluid and vicious.

Albert responded to my harsh remarks, "Hold on Bud, you can't blame Moses, he don't won't to lose Lee either. After all, he's his best dog."

I turned inward, "Don't you worry Lee, I won't let you die, me an Blue will take care of you, yes we will," already I was entertaining ideas of stealing Lee and running away.

It had gotten melancholy, everyone was somber as they watched the tears streaming down my face. I was still on my knees hugging Blue and Lee, neither dog made an effort to get free. I could feel the fever in Lee's neck and the pulse of the big vein.

Mr. Wilson walked over and knelt down beside us, "Bud, I know you must hate me and I don't blame you a bit, but I never wanted this to happen, I promise. I had no idea that these dogs would get distemper from that kennel, and Lee, I sure don't won't him to die, why, he's too good a coon dog, smarter than the rest. It'd just be a terrible shame for him to just up and take all his smarts away so soon. Why, he's just barely starting to hunt as good as he can."

"He won't die," I choked out.

"Well, what if he does?"

"He won't go and leave me and Blue."

Mr. Wilson began to sound like the Old Deacon, "Just the same, if he does have to go, I know he'd won't to spend whatever time he has left with you and Blue. If you'll take him and care for him, he's all yours."

"Forever, no take backs?"

"Yessiree boy, forever, however long that is."

"Don't you worry Lee, it's gonna be a long time," I said confidently.

"Albert," I said, "S'pose you could take me and the dogs home now, Lee's not feeling too well."

Chapter #4
HOPE SPRINGS ETERNAL

And so it is with a young boy, "Hope Springs Eternal, Life is Forever, There's Always Tomorrow." I knew in my heart that Lee would live, by some magic he would live, after all isn't magic what the life of a kid is made of? There's no reason to believe that life is any other than eternal if you've never experienced death.

It was only nine o'clock, barely dark, a light tint was still showing on the west horizon as Albert wheeled the GMC into my folks driveway. All the way home, sitting in the back of the truck, Blue with his head hung over the side rail, Lee, his feverish head in my lap, I felt a sense of power, a strength that said that I was in charge, I was in control. I had Lee back to keep and even though the distemper was advanced by now, and even though I had no idea how to treat it, I would win, I would be victorious, I could conquer all. That's how young boys think.

Lee was already in the advanced stages of distemper and unbeknownst to this young lad, if not beyond saving, certainly beyond recovering to be the dog he once was. Even if I had known these things, I would have blocked the facts from my mind and continued in blind faith anyway. In my heart, I believed that everything would finally be alright and we would live happily ever after.

For as long as dogs have been in existence, distemper had been a devastating disease literally capable of killing whole communities of dogs in a matter of a few months. It is a highly contagious virus infection, similar to the measle virus in humans. You would think by observing the symptoms of a dog with distemper that he may merely have a cold, but the fact is that dogs don't have colds and if the symptoms appear to be cold- like, the dog is probably in the first stages of distemper and should immediately be taken the a veterinarian for treatment. At this early stage, proper treatment may save the dog from permanent disorders or death.

Some dogs are immune to distemper, by fortunate genetics, their bodies produce enough antibodies naturally to destroy the distemper virus and as long as the dog continues to produce these antibodies, the immunity will continue. It is not permanent, if even in the dog's latter years, his body fails to maintain the necessary antibodies, he will most likely become affected as would any other dog.

The only other natural immunity is the immunity passed to the puppy in the mother's milk. Although we have always believed that the mother's milk was sacred and protected all offsprings from all communicable diseases, the fact is, it isn't true. The fact is that the mother's milk passes into the offspring the immune antibodies in direct proportion to her own antibody count. In other words, a mother, not vaccinated, may have no immune antibodies to pass along at all. And even if there were magic in the mother's milk, passive immunity is not permanent and at the age of twelve to fourteen weeks the immunity is gone. Distemper is the result of a persistent, contagious virus. It is usually spread from dog to dog. The trying thing is that no contact with an infected dog is required for the virus to be transferred. It can drift in the air currents, be left in bedding or reside in food and food receptacles. It would be almost impossible to seclude a dog well enough to guarantee that it would not come in contact with the virus.

The problem is most dogs that contract the disease will be permanently damaged. The damage may manifest itself in several ways. Neurologically, the brain is damaged causing the body to jerk while at rest. A mild condition may result in a slight twitch, or the whole body may jerk. Finally the dog may develop epileptic-like seizures. Permanent respiratory damage usually occurs stymieing its physical activity. Often the dog dies after three or four weeks of suffering.

With careful attention from the veterinarian, it is possible that the dog can be saved.

Nowadays, it's fool hardy to suppose that a dog might live to a ripe old age on the basis of its own immune system. Frankly, dogs have been cared for and coddled until its own immune system has been shut down and rendered inactive. There is only one proper approach to owning a dog. You must have it vaccinated. As a matter of fact, your dog should visit the vet once every year for a checkup and examination just as you do (at your doctor.)

I know, shot's, vaccinations, checkups, he's just a dog you know. But that's not true. He was just a dog when he was born, but shortly there after he became a soft, bouncy, cuddly bunch of personality. Thereafter, he becomes very much, a separate personality, adopting and adapting to its surroundings and environment even to the degree that he takes on the qualities and characteristics of his adopted family. So, he's not just a dog, dang it, he's a member of the family. Get his shots, or you'll be sorry.

* * *

There was an old shed at the side of our house, a wooden thing with no floor, but big enough for me to care for Lee in. This would be the place of my occupation for the next couple of weeks.

For the next couple of days I was as busy as a beaver fixing up the old shed. I put fresh sawdust on the floor, chinked up the cracks in the walls, put a latch on the door and made a pallet in the corner away from the door out of a piece of rug for Lee to convalesce on. I placed it where there would be the minimum draft, as though it was the flu that he had. I fixed it up for the long haul because I had extracted any notion from my head that he might not live. Most of my spare moments I spent sitting on a little stool in the other corner talking to him and giving encouragement like you would at the bedside of an old friend. I watched him wheeze as he breathed. I watched mucous run from his nose and his eyes mat shut. I even believed when he had involuntary jerking spells that somehow it meant he was feeling better. I was serious about this thing. The vet had given me some medicine to try. He didn't, however, give any encouragement with it. He just said take it and try it and see if it helps. I had described Lee's symptoms to him; he said he knew the ailment, don't spend the money to bring him in, and gave me some penicillin pills to give him, and some other stuff, maybe sulfa drug.

All the old-timer's had remedies to offer. I'm sure they meant well but probably none of them ever worked, like tying a towel around his neck saturated with camphorated oil, kerosene and hot pepper sauce. His eyes were always matted, so I went through several bottles of eye drops trying to clear this up to no avail.

Not only had he become apathetic about everything, he also was rapidly losing his appetite. He was no longer interested in dog food even if I stirred in hot water to made it gravy-like. I would hold his head up and slide his bowl under his nose so that the steam from the hot gravy would drift into his nostrils. I would spoon up the food into his mouth. He would chew a little and let most of it run out the sides of his lips. I started stealing pieces of meat from the supper table, wrapping them in my napkin and sneaking them into my pocket. I would slip out while the meat was still warm so that it would be aromatic and soft. Lee wouldn't get up to eat, so I would hold his head up and slip small pieces of the meat into his mouth. He would chew very little but I would rub his throat and he would swallow.

Although I would not admit it to myself, each day he became less and less interested in my appearance at the door. He was slipping away gradually, day by day and I wouldn't see. I was driven to do everything in my power to bring him through this crisis, but the truth is, except for the fellowship and the attention Lee received, I'm sure that all I was doing was increasing his agony and prolonging what I was not willing to accept as inevitable. I now wish I could have asked Lee what his preference would have been, to have endured the suffering to extend the days or to have gone to sleep when the options were obvious. To me, there were no options; I was still relying on some juvenile magic. In the end there would be only one acceptable conclusion, I never doubted it for an instance.

My step-mother would periodically appear at the door and look in. She would shake her head, "How's Lee today?"

Oh, he's gonna be up and around soon."

It was as still as a tomb, as quiet as a cavern in that little shed where I faithfully nursed Lee - hot and humid that September afternoon. Little droplets of sweat had formed on my forehead - I didn't notice. I sat on a little wooden stool, my elbows planted on my knees, my chin cradled in my hands. I stared at Lee lying on his side as he had for days, legs stretched outward, his head turned slightly backwards in an angle that mimicked looking upward into the eyes of a treed coon as I had seen him do so many times - if he had only been on his feet.

He was listless, unaware, motionless, except for the constant involuntary jerking in his hind legs.

His eyes were closed, maybe in resolve, maybe in pain or sorrow, I don't know.

Sitting across the small, stale-smelling rectangle from Lee, close enough to reach out and render an occasional stroke of encouragement which he no longer acknowledged, my mind roared with desperate questions. What to do next, what other remedy, what old wive's potion? Anything, if I could only think, my mind was blank from days of stress, I'd run out. But, wasn't there one more thing I could do, even one more?

It was obvious that I had passed the point of considering Lee's goodwill. I was now thinking only of my own, mistakenly assuming that they were one and the same. How much loss, how much pain, how much sorrow - for me?

I sat there hoping, looking for any sign of progress.

Momentarily Lee began to move, his front feet stretched backward to meet his hind feet. His head jerked up over his shoulder in a motion to move the center of gravity to the center of his body. He struggled absentmindedly to move his stiff body over on to his feet.

"Lee," I cried out, certain that this was the long-awaited sign of victory over death.

I leaped to his side, prepared to help raise him to his feet and steady him - "C'mon boy, you can do it," I rendered confident encouragement.

He staggered to an upright position, his legs jerking under him. I fell to my knees in front of him, my hands outstretched like a father encouraging a child's first steps, "You can do it fellow, come to me."

I immediately noticed that Lee's gaze was blank; he neither saw my hands reaching out for him or heard my excited cries of hope. What energy or hidden force it was that caused this final movement I don't know or understand. I only suppose he was trying to say I want to live, I love you, but no more.

He dropped back to his side, his head lying flat on the floor, his partially-opened mouth spotted with chips of sawdust. His eyes closed and remained closed, until moments later they reopened, glazed, fixed in an eternal stare. One last gurgling sigh and it was over.

* * *

And so, in our innocence and maybe our ignorance, we lovingly prolong the agony of the final transition hoping beyond hope that by some magic we can beat the eternal system. So, what have we done? Have we denied the dignity of death with the apparatuses of life extension? Or, have we acted out the role of a seemingly sane society? If in error, are we exonerated by well-meaning?

* * *

One would have thought, considering the intensity and emotion I had maintained during these days of watching Lee pass, that the moment of his death would have been a time of hysterical release. Maybe for the story it would have been so, but it is that that was not the case. Instead, there came a great draining of emotional anxiety, a release of contained stress. The anticipation of various unpredictable potentialities no longer viable, it was disconnected from the circuitry, so to speak.

So, in opposition to the release of life's tether, mortals contest with life's infirmities, the victory over biological temporality - I became nauseated, helpless, defeated.

Death had won - I had lost. How many times has the score been the same?

* * *

At death we react, not to death itself, we don't understand death, what it means instantly, what it means eternally. We've seen death, we've been near death, we've heard death. We've never experienced death.

We react to death according to our own predispositions, by whatever experiences we retained, physically, emotionally, spiritually. What we gain in death, what we lose, is how it affects us personally.

Is it truly death we fear? Or, is the fear of death only a motor response necessary for the perpetuation of mankind? Peace, sweet peace, a soul no longer encumbered with frail limitations.

No more hunger, no more sorrow, no more pain, always tomorrow.

Chapter #5
A FITTING FUNERAL

There I stood over Lee. He was cold and dead, gone forever. His death, a matter of fact now, no more mystic possibilities, what to do now, can't stand here forever, only a few hours left of daylight, could I wait until morning, is it too hot to wait, will he stink by tomorrow, should I wait until my stepmother gets home and ask, will some eerie disease get on me if I handled something dead?

There was only one thing to do, Lee was dead and I had to make a decision. It had to be my decision and I had to carry it out not only when to bury Lee, but where. I needed to talk to someone.

I covered Lee with the remaining gunnysack up over his head, like they do at the movies, and walked out of the shed. I walked to the other side of the house to where the dog pen was. Blue was standing by the fence to greet me, probably wondering where I had been all this time. His tail was shaking, his head extended up towards me. I reached over the fence and rubbed the depression in his forehead with my fingers, "How've you been boy? Guess you know Lee didn't make it, died a few minutes ago." I looked down at him, he was still looking up at me. I assumed, in his own perception, that he knew and understood what I was saying. "I'm going to miss him a bunch, aren't you?" His face looked sad and melancholy. Again I assumed that he was responding to Lee's death. Actually, he was only responding to my own sad countenance and had no idea what I was talking about or why, but it didn't matter, it was my stage, the actors would act out my script.

"Blue, I think Lee wasn't no ordinary dog. He was about as good as they come. He was a good hunting partner and friend, don't you think?" I had not missed a stroke on Blue's head and he had not budged an inch. I interpreted this to mean that he and I were joined in sorrow and reverence. He, of course, thought it felt mighty good.

I became more magnanimous and forthright as I went on, "Just ain't no ordinary carrying off gonna be good enough for Lee', no sir. He's got to have a super good burying. Everybody's got to know that he wasn't just an ordinary dog that you carry out to the dump in a sack. Do you know where we're gonna bury him? See that little cypress tree over there? Remember how we used to sit and lean up against it and watch the sun go down over the lake and you'd lay your head against my leg so I could scratch your ear and we'd say, 'God, won't you send us another dog so Blue won't always have to hunt by himself.' Then one day he sent Ole Lee and you remember how the first thing Lee did was tree our stepmom's cat up this very tree and we thought she was going to make us take him back and then you remember how Lee laid into our neighbors mean ole tomcat and run him off for good and then everything was okay and he could stay and how Lee was always climbing out of the pen, like I couldn't build one high enough for nothin and I chained him to this very tree until he agreed to stay in the pen from now on? You remember all that, don't you Blue?"

"Well, we're going to bury him right there under that ole cypress tree. That way we can still come out every afternoon and sit on Lee and watch the sun go down, all of us together."

"C'mon Blue, we got to hurry, Stepmom gets home she'll never hear to it."

I ran to the shed to get a shovel. I didn't know that digging at the base of a tree, especially a cypress tree, that I would encounter so many roots. After a lot of exasperation and a little deliberating, I moved the grave about ten feet away from the tree toward the lake, telling Blue that we could sit against the tree and look over Lee at the sunset, which would be just as reverent and respectful.

One nice thing about Florida soil is that it is about six inches of grass roots and below that, gray sand all the way to China, so it only took a few minutes to complete digging the grave. Albeit, the grave should have been deeper I'm sure. Just the same, I dug it with care, shaved the edge of the walls to make them vertical and smooth, then scooped out the bottom of the hole until it was flat and hard, only the grooves of the shovel edges marked it. The spades of dirt were carefully mounded along side the hole so that it could easily be returned without much loss. The grave was completed in record time for a lad that age. I attached Blue's lead rope to his collar and led him to the cypress tree and tied him so that he could participate in the liturgy.

The hibiscus bushes were in bloom around the house - whites, pinks and yellows. I gathered a bunch quickly and brought them back to the grave and stuck their long woody stems into the soft mound of dirt which seemed to me to enhance the gravity of the ordeal. This was not just an ordinary dog funeral.

Blue was sitting up on his front legs, backed up against the tree as close as possible trying to avoid the angle of the sun coming through the limbs overhead. His eyes were following me as I moved here and there trying to figure what the devil was going on.

"Well Blue, everything looks pretty good here. I might as well go get Lee."

I went to the blistering hot shed where Lee was lying between the two gunnysacks. I pondered about how I was going to move him without picking him up. It finally occurred that I might be able to drag him by tying a knot in the end of the sack and pulling. It worked. I slid him the one hundred or so yards to the edge of the grave. I looked in, there was Blue, stretched out on his side in the bottom of the hole on the cool, moist sand looking like peace personified. I looked down onto him. He opened one eye and looked up but the remainder of his body never flinched.

"Blue," I said harshly, "That's Lee's grave, don't you have any respect?"

Blue remained stiff as a board, his one eye open, monitoring my reactions. As it was, he had no intentions of moving from such a cool, comfortable spot.

"Blue, get out of there," I scolded, "Right now." I reached to the ground in a motion indicating that I would pick up a stick to throw at him. He jumped to his feet and climbed out over the mound of fresh dirt dragging some back into the hole and leaving the flower arrangement in disarray.

"Oh Blue, did you have to do that? Are you jealous because Lee's getting all of the attention?" as if Blue knew what was going on or even cared. "Now get over to the tree and stay while I shovel out this dirt you kicked in."

I had the hole and the flowers back in order in no time at all. I drug Lee up to the opposite side of the grave from the mound and drew back the gunnysack that covered him, "C'mon Blue, let's show our respect one more time before we put Ole Lee in the grave. C'mon Blue, C'mon boy." Blue meandered over. To my disappointment he showed no emotion, just lowered his nose down over Lee, turned around and walked back to the tree and laid down.

"Dang it Blue, you sure seem a little coldhearted. I bet if that was you in there you'd show more sorrow."

I eased Lee into the hole and covered him with the second gunnysack. I was going to say some beautiful words like noble hunter, loyal friend, but Blue's nonchalant attitude had thrown some cold water on the solemnness of the occasion and I decided no one but me wanted to hear them anyway. So, I gathered the hibiscus flowers from the mound, gently laid them across Lee, two at a time, making little crosses out of them, took the shovel and began filling the hole. I patted the rounded mound down with the back of the shovel to make a respectable presence then went back to the tree and sat down with Blue. He pushed up against my leg reminding me to scratch his ear. I looked at Lee's grave confident that due respect had been shown, then down to the edge of the lake and then to the top of the tall moss-laden cypress trees just as the evening sun was disappearing behind them.

All in all, it was a nice, adequate burial. Due respect was shown by all, or at least me anyway. I would not have to feel any regrets or remorse because I had done all the right things, after the fact. That's what funerals are all about anyway.

"Blue, you remember that time when you ran that ole possum in that hole in the bottom of that big cypress down in Hathaway's swamp? You just stood there howling and made Lee stick his head in there and pull that possum out? That possum stuck on the end of his nose. I don't care if you did grab him and pull him off. Don't you feel a little ashamed about that now?" Blue was sound asleep, apparently he could deal with it.

I was sitting on the ground, my back resting against the cypress tree that I had buried ole Lee under. It had been thirty or so minutes since I had thrown the last shovel of dirt onto the grave mound and firmed it down with the back of the shovel. Blue hadn't budged an inch, curled up on the ground beside me, sound asleep. I was facing down towards the lake behind the house. The sun had sunk deep behind the cypress trees that fringed the lake. The sky behind them had changed to a dark orange with rays of yellow spraying upward and disappearing into the gray sky overhead.

"Sure is pretty here, Blue. I think Lee would have liked being buried here if he had known. We can come out here every afternoon and sit by Lee's grave and watch the sun go down over those trees. He'd like that, I'm sure he would."

"Won't be able to sit here much longer, mosquitos are starting to get up. Guess I'd better put you away for the night and get on in. Doesn't seem too right, Friday night and not going hunting. Think you're gonna like huntin' with Mr. Wilson's dogs without Lee to help you?"

I had stopped scratching Blue's head while I was talking to him. He pushed my leg in a punching fashion with his nose to remind me to continue.

I was just beginning to hear the first calls of the tree frogs sounding up from the lake and an occasional roar from the belly of an old bullfrog on the far shore. A whippoorwill landed at the edge of the water on the narrow beach. Whip-poor-will' - whip-poor-will' it called, reminding of the many nights that his call had marked the beginning of our hunt.

Chapter #6
EVERY VOID MUST BE FILLED

"Listen Blue." I cupped my hands to my ears and directed them towards town. "I think I hear a vehicle coming." There was about a quarter-mile of straight away on the road before it got to our place and on a quiet afternoon you could hear the cars for the whole stretch. "Listen Blue, I'll bet anything that that's Albert pickup." I had heard Albert's pickup coming so many times and it sounded so unique with its automatic transmission that it was not hard to recognize. I was right. Soon I heard the engine rev down and the scratching of the wheels as the GMC turned into the driveway.

Blue and I stood up between the cypress tree and Lee's grave just as Albert, then Junior, then Junebloom and finally Mr. Wilson came around the corner of the house toward us.

Usually Junebloom was talking all the time, but in matters serious, talking was delegated to Albert. "Your stepmother stopped at Stiekies to get gas earlier, said Ole Lee finally gave it up. We sure were sad to hear it. Moses here is taking it pretty hard too. He feels pretty bad about the whole thing. You know, the distemper and all."

"Yes he did," I said nodding toward the fresh grave. "Blue and me gave him a right nice funeral, buried right here where he can be close to Blue."

"Sure was a fine dog, that Lee," Albert went on, the rest nodding agreement in the back ground. "We're sure going to miss that fellow an awful lot. They didn't come any better, you know," the rest of the group continuing to add emphasis by looking at me and nodding positively.

It was obvious that the group was letting Albert test the waters to see how I was taking Lee's death.

I looked back at them blankly, "Yep, I'm going to miss him awful bad. But you don't need to make a big deal out of it, I got Blue here," I gave him a slap on the head. "I still got the best dog in the swamp." They all motioned in the affirmative whether they agreed or not. "Me and Blue are gonna keep right on hunting just like always, just as soon as we get over the mourning. We think that's what Lee would want. It'll still be Ole Blue you'll hear at the head of the pack."

"That's right, you can count on that," they all chimed in.

There was a long silence after that statement. I had no idea what was on their mind, maybe they just felt self-conscience and didn't know how to keep the conversation going. I stood there looking at them for a spell, their eyes moving back and forth avoiding any contact with mine. The silence was repeatedly broken by the shuffling of nervous feet. I didn't realize it at first, but these were special people, the men that I spent time with, doing the thing that I loved most of all. Their eyes were misty with compassion. They, too, shared in my pain for Lee, my love for silly ole hound dogs. I watched them fidget, at their loss for words, at the fact that they had not recognized that I had put the thing away, and sure there would be times that I would slip away and remember Lee, my courageous fighter, my funny friend. And I did, many times, many tears, a funny kind of tears, tears that didn't come from sorrow or grief, but from somewhere that their coming made me feel good.

There they stood, four grown men, one a successful farmer and businessman, one a skilled hunter and outdoorsman, one a scamp whose love of drinking, fighting and chasing women was surpassed only by coon hunting, the other a fatherly deacon, a convicted bootlegger. Two white, two black, each at a loss to find words to console a young lad over the loss of his hound dog. It was funny. I bit my tongue to keep from laughing - I loved them so.

A screeetch, crash and banging of chains against metal jarred us out of our melancholy. Yip, yip, yip and a great crying noise screamed out from the direction of the GMC; more intense again came the clanging of the chain. "Oh lawdy me," Junebloom cried out as they all broke in a dash for the GMC.

"C'mon Blue, let's see what's going on," I hollered.

I caught up to the GMC just as Moses Wilson turned to face me. He and the rest were grinning from ear to ear, almost unable to maintain their composure. Mr. Wilson was holding a little round, fuzzy ball of fur that looked a lot like a white with brown spots hound dog. He was holding him around the chest with both hands and pointing him at me. "Here, he's yours," he blurted out, and stuffed him into my arms. "He's Lee's pup. We ran to town and bought him off that other hunter. Looks just like Lee - see that brown ear and the black tip on his tail? Lee'd want you to have him, won't be long he'll be huntin jus like Ole Lee did, you'll see, you'll be glad, sides, Blue don't want to be all alone, he'd be proud to learn Lee's pup."

I never heard Mr. Wilson run on so; he was beside himself. Every word he said was appropriately confirmed by the body motions of the others. Me, I was speechless, not for a loss of words, I was so choked up I could hardly breath. I was standing there with the pup cradled in my arms, tears running down my cheeks like a silly ole girl that got stood up, the pup reaching up from my cradled arms licking my cheeks as fast as the tears flowed.

"Gonna keep'um, ain'tcha," said Junebloom. "We done paid a lot."

"I don't know, maybe so, but Blue has a voice in this you know," I replied resolutely.

Blue was already pushing against my legs reaching as high as he could to get a smell of the little critter.

"C'mon Blue, let's put this little fellow over on the grass so you can check him out for a few minutes," I said.

We all moved over to the lawn in echelon as though some great thing was to be discerned. I stroked the pup's head a few times and gently set him on the ground, "Okay Blue, check him out good."

Blue would stick his nose under the pup's belly and roll him over. The pup would lay on his back for a moment as Blue ran his nose up and down sniffing him from head to toe. Then the pup would jump up and run full steam in a puppy waddle around Blue stopping at his nose. Blue would again roll him over and sniff his belly, and again and again and again. Just as Blue was preparing for another cycle, the pup ran to his head and lunged for Blue's long floppy ear and got a vice grip on it in his mouth. We were all in stitches as the little pup squatted backwards on all fours and pulled and tugged in a great tug-a-war with Blue's ear. Blue's face was in a painful grimace as the tiny razor-sharp teeth penetrated to the nerve. I was waiting for Blue to react against the pup in retaliation, but instead he walked along in the direction of the pull trying to reduce the pain.

"Well Blue, what do you think, we gonna keep him?"

Through the stress on Blue's face it looked like his response was affirmative. "Good boy," I said.

"Think your step mom will care?" Albert asked, sounding a little concerned that he might be in questionable territory.

"We're keeping this pup even if we have to keep it under my bed and feed it half my supper, huh Blue?"

I grabbed the pup up and held him up close in my arms. He was wiggling and lunging, trying to get at my ear. I stood quiet for a few minutes before I spoke again, "You know, I may not be able to keep this pup after all. I know he must have cost a lot and I've only got three dollars to my name."

Junebloom jerked his head up, "Mannnnn, we don't wont no money for that pup. We jus wanna see a mighty sad boy happy agin."

"You mean it, you don't want any money?"

"No way, he's all yours, right this minute forever."

I ran to them like I was going to hug them all at once. The fact is I couldn't get my arms around Mr. Wilson, let alone the whole bunch.

I backed off a step, "I've got an idea - it's not quite dark yet. Let's load up and go hunting tonight and break this pup in right."

"How you gonna take that little thing huntin?" quizzed Junior. "He can't see above the grass."

"Tell you what," I went on, "let's all meet at Stiekies in thirty minutes and I'll show you what a real huntin dog is made of. While we're hunting we'll think up a name for this little fellow."

"Okay," said Albert, "that's just what we wanted to hear."

"See you in thirty," shouted Junior from the back of the GMC as it sped out of the driveway.

Life, death, life. Can either be defined without the other? So, is life before death, or is death first? Can there be death without life? Then, doesn't death make way for life? Then, is death an end or is death a beginning? Is there any man that is not kin - any man who doesn't carry the genes of the very first man? So in death, isn't a man relived in the genes of his offspring? So, as certain as birth and death are equal parts of the contract of life, if that, death is not the ultimate sorrow but the epitome of eternal life, as one man, after planting the seeds of his own dreams and character, removes himself from center stage to relive his own life from an enhanced platform, undergirded, reinforced and elevated by the legacy of his own transcendental wisdom.

So, if the first die, then the second will be better. He will begin with the accumulated wisdom of the first. The second will also be part of the first. Hence, the fusion of the second and the first creates a counterpoint. There is not one, nor two, but three. If.

Death is not an end, nor is death a beginning; it is a continuance of God's master plan.

* * *

Chapter #7
BOSS COON

The agreed thirty minutes had passed in a heartbeat, I had rounded up my headlight and was standing by the gate to the driveway with Ole Blue on a short leash and the pup stuffed into a rucksack. The little guy looked a lot like a puppy commercial, his head barely sticking out the top of the sack and laced in around the neck to prevent him from climbing out. He was squirming and scratching at the bag with his hind feet trying to push upwards but to no avail. Blue would look up at him when the scratching became intense, sometimes raising up on his hind legs to smell his nose and see what the commotion was all about. From time to time I issued a light command, "Take it easy boy, you can't get out of there."

I pulled the cutdown off the edge of the highway and down the slope to park at the side of the station. I pulled the straps of the rucksack tight securing the pup to my back and made a fast gate to the front of the station where the rest of the group was standing side by side under the canopy waiting.

"Thought you wuz bring'un that new pup," chided Junebloom, "did he chicken out?"

I abruptly spun around revealing the pup in the rucksack.

"Bless my bones," roared Mr. Wilson, "Don't that beat all?"

Albert pulled the GMC around to the side of the station where Moses had parked his truck. He carried his dogs in a wooden box that sat in the bed of the truck. It had screened over windows cut in the sides and barred doors on the back for the extraction of the hounds. He had only brought three dogs out from town with him which rendered the box not all that heavy even with the dogs in it, we easily slid the box from one truck to the other.

Mr. Wilson deciding to leave his pickup and ride with the group in Albert's pickup necessitated a new arrangement in the seating. Junior's position by the window with Junebloom in the middle next to Albert had to subordinate to age and Mr. Wilson took the window seat. Junebloom, after having such a bad experience with Blue wasn't about to give up his position in the middle so Junior had to sit in the back with me and the dogs.

Albert dropped the shift lever down a notch and the pickup eased out onto the road. Destination? I expect it had been decided before I was picked up.

I expect we looked a little funny driving through town all piled into the pickup like we were, but by now everybody was used to it and hardly turned an eye.

Albert drove the pickup down the road toward the chosen coonhunting territory as deliberate as if he had done it a thousand times and I suppose he had. He seemed to transition through all of the corners and wandered along the road center as if he had a vested interest in it, and I suppose he did. From time to time a wheel would catch a puddle of water and cause a spray to suck in behind the pickup cab where Junior and I were resting our backs. Blue, his head hanging over the side as usual, trying to wind a scent along the roadside, would catch it in the face. He would shake his head for an instant and lean back over the side.

Both Albert and Mr. Wilson were pressed against the doors of the GMC, their arms resting on the sill, elbows turned down trying to entice the breeze to blows into the cab. I could see the cab light up with a yellowish glow from time to time as Junebloom attempted to light a cigarette in the wind to no avail.

It was a typical hot muggy August night. It rained that afternoon as it always did making everything I touched doused me with water droplets. The wind coming into the pickup felt warm and wet, not so much as one degree of cooling did it render. My shirt was wet already, it felt sticky, especially the long sleeves. But long sleeves was better than having the mosquitos eat my arms up or having to rub on that terrible smelling mosquito repellant. I don't know how we stood it or why. It was pretty miserable this time of the year, sleeves down as far as they would go, collars buttoned and turned up, caps pulled down over our foreheads. The call to hunt must have been very, very strong.

Albert eased the GMC off the paved road and down two wheel ruts stopping at a gate in the right of way fence. I could see him hand a key to Junebloom. Mr. Wilson opened the door and slid out stepping back to make way for Junebloom to pass by and open the gate. Since Junebloom was sitting in the middle it seemed it would have been just as easy for Mr. Wilson to have opened it but I guess that would have breached the bounds of status and protocol.

The lock was jerked open, the gate swung back easily and the pickup eased through coming to a halt just far enough in to allow the gate to return to the post. Mr. Wilson stepped out of the pickup again to let Junebloom slid back into the middle and we were off.

Immediately we were driving down a seldom used road under an umbrella of giant grapefruit trees. It appeared that the trees could have been fifty years old or older. Probably one of the oldest groves in the area. Citrus trees grow in groves while apple trees grow in orchards. I don't know which has the most status.

I had never hunted in this area before. We had always avoided it for some reason. It should be a good area, the grove was sitting high on a gentle sandy hill, about eighty acres in total and abruptly fell off and was completely surrounded by cyprus swamp except along the highway.

Albert brought the GMC to a stop at the bottom edge of the grove. I bailed over the side and landed abruptly on both feet hard enough to give the pup in my rucksack a good jolt. He whine and renewed his scratching effort trying to get out. "Sorry boy, I forgot you were back there."

"Stay in the pickup," I scolded Blue who had both feet over the side rail waiting for an opportunity to bail out.

Mr. Wilson's dogs were beginning to raise a fuss to get out of the box, barking and whining and chewing at the door.

"Easy boys," Mr. Wilson shouted into the box at the same time pounding on the top with his fist,"You'll hav dim dang coons scared over into the next county."

Seeds of My Field

Mr. Wilson's dogs were named in keeping with his beliefs-Matt, Mark and Luke. Three of the few left over from the distemper epidemic that ravaged his kennel.

Albert was leaning against the hood of the GMC looking straight ahead toward the black outline of the cyprus swamp. "What do you think, Moses," he finally replied, "shall we drop the dogs out right here and see what they can work up or just let out one for the time being?"

Albert was using a tact that he had refined to a fine art. I knew that what he was wanting to do was let Ole Blue out to work a trail because no dog could do it like Blue could, and then let Mr. Wilson's dog out then, but he wanted to be careful not to insinuate that Mr. Wilson's dogs might be inferior.

"Sho nuf," Mr. Wilson responded, Ole Blue ain't been on a trail for a while now, might be only trail he gets to wurk all night." Meaning, I'm conceding but not admitting.

"Okay, Bud, get Ole Blue down to the swamp there and see if he still knows what a coon smells like."

I was anxious to get Blue out of the pickup, it had been a couple of months since he had been free to run and since this was a spontaneous trip I had not even had an opportunity to exercise him in the least. Besides, he had put on several pounds while he was laying around the kennel.

When Albert gave the word to put Blue to "working up a trail" and Mr. Wilson agreed, tension relaxed from the anxiety of not knowing where Blue stood in the echelon of priority.

I hooked a lead rope into Blue's collar, snapped my fingers and Blue sailed out of the GMC bed jerking my arm nearly out of it's socket as he drove hard to get to the swamp. "Hold on Blue, you'll give me and the little guy a case of whip lash."

"Over here," I heard Junior call. He and Junebloom had already been scouring the soft sand at the edge of the cyprus head searching for fresh tracks. "Over here," Julior called again, "Cmme over here and see what you make of this."

I held Blue up tight against my side to keep him from lunging ahead and eased over to where Junior and Junebloom were hovered over and invisible object on the ground between their feet, their heads only inches apart, their lights shining straight down.

"What you got," I asked?

"Look what a foot," Junior responded," Big - great big."

He was right, big a coon foot as I have ever seen. It could easily have gone four inches.

"Hold Blue back there Bud, I want Albert to see this before it gets all messed up," Junior cautioned.

I called to Albert, "Albert, come on down here and look at this track."

"What you got boys," Albert asked as he approached.

I swung my light around to where it beamed directly onto the track so that Albert could see what had fixed our attention.

"My God," Albert blurted out, "Never seen such a track in these parts." "C'mer Moses, look at this track."

Moses came down in a rather rigid, matter of fact gate, "Boys' we gonna go huntin or what?"

About the time he got the last word out he saw the track, "Lawdy me, what a foot that thar coons got."

"You want to know something else a little strange about this track?" Junior asked, "There's not another track in this whole area, me an Juneblooms done looked."

Mr. Wilson broke in,"Not a nuther track in the whole swamp, you say?"

"Not a nuther track that I could find," Junior replied with Junebloom nodding in affirmation.

"Then I tell what we got here boys," Mr. Wilson said as he drew the group in close as if a major discovery was about to be unveiled, "We got a old "Boss Coon" here, shor as the world."

"Come on Mr. Wilson, what do you mean Boss Coon," I asked in a skeptical tone?

"Shor as we's all standin here, that thar's an old Boss Coon if I ever saw one," Mr. Wilson went on, "Yezzsir, it sho nuf is, an a mighty big one. Ever seen one Albert?"

"No, don't think I have, we don't ever hunt this swamp you know."

"Well then, this might be our lucky night, might not be lucky a tol," Mr. Wilson said. "Only seed one other Boss Coon in my life, lucky to get to see two. They's the biggest and meanest coon in the parts, they's usually real smart, real old and got's a real bad disposition. What they do's, they picks out the best swamp to their lik'n and then they whips up on any coon that tries to move in on'um. Don't no other coon mess with'um in his swamp. Now that's what we got here an you can brag mighty big on a pack'a dogs that puts a Boss Coon up a tree, but if he decides to come down on'um before we gets to the tree he might give'um a good whupp'n. Sides, he ain't gonna go up no tree no way less he just gets good'n ready." "So, what's it gonna be, Boss Coon or a nuther swamp."

I looked down at Blue with a little sneer on my face, "What's with you Mr. Wilson, Blue's not afraid of no coon, even if you do call him Boss Coon."

Albert looked over at Junior and Junebloom, "Well, what ya'll think."

"I never heard of a Boss Coon," Junior said, "I say a coon's a coon and he'll be in a tree before the nights over."

Our eyes all turned to Junebloom, "I'm wit Blue."

It would have been an interesting study for a psychologist, there we all stood in the pitch black of the night, the majority, equipped with youth and optimism - on the other side, the minority, cautioned by age and wisdom, drawn into groups by the magical force of common thought.

Albert looked at Mr. Wilson, "What do you think Moses?" "You know that we don't like to get to scattered out in this swamp."

It seemed there was something peculiar about this swamp and it was something that Albert and Mr. Wilson shared together. It seemed as if Albert was trying to get Mr. Wilson to take his side but Mr. Wilson was not getting the message.

"Lawdy me, Mr. Albert, mighty seldom that a man gets to see a Boss Coon twice in one life time," Mr. Wilson moaned. "Id be mighty fine if'n I could."

"Well dang it Moses, what if that coon comes down the tree and tears up the dogs real bad? No point in getting a good dog torn up just so's we can brag."

Moses stood up straight like he was going to tell us something out of the bible, "Two things, Mr. Albert, one is, if that Boss Coon comes down out of that tree an them dogs act like they's afraid of him and don want to fight, well, we'll jus call um off and go to the house. But on the udder han, if they's brave like I spec, we'll jump right in thar widdum."

Albert gave a quick glace to each of us, "Well, okay boys, I hope we know what we're getting in to.

I must have seemed a little hesitant as I stood there gripping Blues' lead rope up close. I may have been, it had been some time since I had turned Blue on to a track to work up.

"C'mon Bud, you're not changing your mind about letting Ole Blue have a run at that Boss Coon are you," Junior teased.

I don't think that I was as concerned about the Boss Coon as I was about the fact that Blue had not trailed a coon in months and I worried that he may have forgotten some of his skills that I had bragged about so profusely.

"Get back away from the tracks," I said to the bunch, "No need of covering the coon's scent with your scent, although I doubt that Blue would really care."

"Okay Boy, get that Boss Coon," I admonished Blue as I unsnapped the lead from his collar.

Blue dropped his nose to the ground and curled his tail high over his back. His actions were exactly as they had always been and would have convinced anyone that he hadn't missed a weekend hunting in years. Of course, that is how it should be and would be. It's not a learned or taught skill that makes a hound dog trail a coon, or work up a cold trail, it's instinct pure and simple. Never the less, I bragged on the fact that even after months of not hunting, Blue was as smart and sharp as ever, proving that his intellect was superior to the average hound. I think it's so neat the way we give Fido's instinct credit as intellect. Animals are lucky that way, they don't have to spend much time learning and training, they're only taught to do what their instincts have already prepared then to do. All that a dog trainer does is reinforce the instincts that he wants the dog to use and it's off to the races. A very smart dog trainer has the insight to discover the instincts that are most dominate and outstanding and trains the dog to take full advantage of these, not so unlike the wise teacher of children. As a matter of fact, if you want to have fun just try and teach the pooch a trick that's not in his instinctive bag of tricks. As a matter of fact, you can teach a hound dog to hunt quail, but you would be well advised to get a bird dog.

Blue dropped his nose to the ground and curled his tailed up high over his back and began a stiff legged jog back and forth along the edged of the swamp. It was a thing of beauty watching his black outline moving back and forth and up and down the coon's trail, darting forward, jerking to a halt, his nose pushed into the ground, then charging forward, sometimes letting out an anguishing bawl as though calling up hidden resources or simply reassuring me that he was still hard at work.

"Work him up boy," I'd respond.

We kept our lights turned off so that the flashes would not distract Blue from the business at hand. It was so black and so quiet that we could hear each others breathing. Even the occasional flare as Junebloom relit his damp cigarette caused me to squint my eyes.

I wondered what Blue was doing, I could hear him pushing through the palmettos at the edge of the cyprus and sometimes the splash of water.

"Yah," Blue bawled a single time.

"What's he doing," I asked spontaneously?

"Spect he's back trail'n," Mr. Wilson replied.

"Back trailing," I responded sarcastically. "I've never known Blue to back trail."

"Course he's back trail'n," Mr. Wilson let out a little disgustingly, "You think he looks at them coon foot tracks an figurs out which a way the coons go'n. All dogs back tracks some. Jus giv'm a fuw mo minutes and he'll get it straightened out."

I knew that dogs back tracked when they were working up a cold trail, I just wasn't willing to admit that Blue wasn't perfect.

"Yah, yah, yah," Blue screamed.

"Sounds good, don't you think," Albert said?

"Shur do." "Any minute now."

Junior let out a cry that sounded like a modified hog call,"Hooo-eeee, get um Blue'."

Blues' bawling became more consistent, he had the trail straightened out now and was pushing hard right toward the center of the swamp.

Junebloom was so excited that his draws on his cigarette were lighting up the palmetto bushes in front of us.

"C'mon Junebloom," Moses said, " We'd better get them other dogs out there with Blue or that Boss Coon will turn on him for sho."

The dogs in the truck knew that blue had the trail straightened out and were screaming at the top of their lungs and tearing at the bars on the cage.

"Get Ole Matt out fust, he's the fastus, needs to get out der wit Blue fas as the dickuns," Moses blared out at Junebloom.

There was not much of a chance that Junebloom could select which dog would burst out of the cage first, the GMC was bouncing from the commotion the dogs were making. Junebloom threw open the cage door and sure enough, it was Matt that emerged first. Of course the other dogs fell on top of him as they piled up on the ground.

"Hooo pee," Mr. Wilson called out as he watched Matt, Mark and Luke disappear into the swamp.

Junior, you and Bud had better get in there after those dogs and stay close, I don't have a good feeling about a coon that size," said Albert.

Junior and I raced for the swamp, plunging through the dense thicket of palmetto and saw grass that fringed the perimeter. We were no sooner into the interior of the swamp than it opened up into a forest of tall cyprus trees, towering high making umbrella tops, our lights barely able to reach the lowest limbs. We were pushing and running in water up to our knees, the boggy bottom reluctant to release our shoes.

After we had run a couple hundred yards into the swamp we came to a halt, side by side, peering off into the darkness in the direction we last heard the dogs.

"What do you hear," I asked Junior?

Junior cupped his hands behind his ears and rotated his head in sonar sounding fashion trying to pick up the sound of the hounds.

"There they are," said Junior, nodding in the general direction of the middle of the swamp. "Blue's up ahead, Matt'l be caught up in a minute, so'll Mark and Luke."

"Bout out of hearing, better keep a moving, never gonna catch up, they'll be plum out of hearing in no time."

Junior was stocky and stronger than me and could out run me in this muddy bottom. The pup in the knapsack gave out a periodic yelp from all the pounding he was getting bouncing off my back. "Hang in there boy," I called out reassuringly.

We had run hard for a ways when suddenly Junior held out his hand in a gesture to stop. "Don`t hear a thing." "How bought you"?

"Not a thing," I replied.

"O crap."

We both cupped our hands to our ears searching for a sound in the darkness over the heavy breathing noises we were making.

"O crap," Junior said again. "Either that coon has took them dogs out of the country or he's done laid a big trick on um." "We'd better go like hell," Junior exclaimed using one of his rare curse words.

I reached back to give the pup on my back a reassuring pat on the head, "You'd better hold on good, it's going to be a bumpy ride for a while."

I fell in behind Junior and we ran full out through the boggy swamp trying to keep our feet under our bodies as the mud and water tried to pull us down. We ran and ran until I began to wish Junior would stop before my legs gave out. He came to an abrupt stop, I pulled up a long side of him. A hundred yards ahead a dog screamed out. "That's Blue," I shouted. "That Boss Coon must have him down."

Blues' cries were cries of pain and anguish. Over his cries I could hear the growling and scowling of the coon as he tore at Blues' head and neck.

"We`ve got to get there fast," I hollered at Junior.

Junior knew and was pushing through the swamp as fast as humanly possible. We had to help Blue.

The other dogs were racing to Blue like hell was after them. As we drew closer we could hear the water in the swamp churning from the thrashing and swinging back and forth Blue was doing futilely trying to throw the huge coon from his back. Matt got there first. With out hesitating he threw himself into the coon dislodging him from Blues' back causing him to release his death hold on Blues' neck. Blue rolled over several times from the impact of Matts' blow. While he was trying to recover his balance the coon attacked Matt going under his belly and fixing a vise like grip on his throat with his powerful jaws and digging the claws of his four giant feet into side. Matt screamed out in pain as he dragged the coon through the water and debris trying vainly to dislodge him. Mark and Luke came charging in from the side. One grabbed the coon by the back, the other apparently catching Matt because poor Matt screamed profusely.

Knowing he was vulnerable in this position, the coon released Matt and fought off the hounds until he reached the base of the nearest cyprus tree. He bounded at least five feet into the air and dug his vicious claws into the tree bark. Blue leaped for him but in an instant he had reached a low limb and was hidden in a clump of Spanish moss.

I flashed my light across the dogs until I found Blue. His head was bleeding from the gashes the coon made but when he saw that I was there he threw his feet high up on the tree and began barking tree. Soon the other hounds followed suit. Matt and Luke were circling the tree, Blue never stopped barking tree and never took his eyes off the spot that he saw the coon disappear into the Moss.

"Gall dang, Bud, I never seen such a coon in all my life." "You suppose Ole Moses knew what he was talking about- Boss Coon?"

"I don't know about that, but if we hadn't been pretty close, we'd had some bloody hounds to haul out of here. I sure would have liked to have gotten this club on that coons head," I said gesturing my intentions waving the club over my head.

"Hey Bud, you still got that pup in that knapsack back there?"

I turned around so that he could see.

"Sure nuf," Junior said as he reached over and tapped the pups' head. "Look at the little feller trying to get out of that pack, he ain't no more scared than nothin. C'mon Bud, let's get him out of there and let him smell were that coon went up that tree.

I drew an arm out from the pack strap and swung it around in front of me, the pup was lunging and straining to push the rest of his body through the hole that his head protruded from.

Junior took him and sat him at the base of the tree, "Look, Bud, he's smellin up that tree already, s'pose he knows what he's smelling."

I took the pup up and cradled him over my arm and began to scan the tall tree with my light. "Dang it, Junior, that coons to smart to even look so we can shine his eyes."

"Bud, c'mer," Junior called. He was standing at the base of a nearby tree.

I shined my light were he was pointing. About six feet up the tree was damp bark and claw marks. "Know what, Bud, that coon parked hisself on this tree and waited for Blue to catch up so's he could jump right onto his back as easy as pie and weren't nothin Blue could do about it. Bud, that's a smart ole coon, you can bet."

Junior came over and helped me stuff the reluctant pup back into the pack.

"Bud, here's what we're going to do, let's turn our lights out and I'm going to squall like the devil, then flip your light on and see if you can pick up an eye."

Junior hung on a squall that echoed back and forth across the swamp. I fanned the tree with my light but not an eye shone out.

Squalling was supposed to sound like two fighting coons on the ground. Some old timers could squall so good that a treed coon would jump right out of the tree.

"What do you think, Bud."

"There's no coon in that tree, cause with a squall like that he would have either looked out of fright or fallen out from laughing so hard."

Blue had dropped down from the tree and was beginning to make increasingly larger circles around the tree suspicious that something had gone wrong.

Junior had pointed up to the limb where the coon had disappeared. "Look there, see that little limb coming out from that other tree, it just touches this other limb. Bet that smart sucker has crossed over to that other tree and is hauling tail across the swamp by now."

"You could be right," I responded, motioning toward Blue. "Look how Blue's left the tree and's circling, he thinks something funny's going on. If he's come down, Blue'l pick'm up."

Junior responded with concern, "Think Blue's crazy nuf to try'm agin?"

I responded defiantly, "Till one of them's dead, put your money on it."

We turned out our lights and leaned back against the cyprus tree, I had turned the pack around to the front, Junior and I were taking turns stroking the pups head as we listened for Blue to open up on a trail if the coon had actually come down from his safe haven high in the branches. The darkness was over whelming but we could trace Blues' location by the splashing of the water and the sounds of air being drawn in and across his olfactory cells as he matched his instinctive wit against the cunning and cleverness of this exceptional creature.

It took Blue nearly ten minutes to cut the trail where the Boss Coon came down from the tree and slide off into the darkness. He had set his course on a line that projected from the line of the two trees keeping as much timber between him and the dogs as he could. A line that would carry him deeper into the center of the swamp.

Mr. Wilson's dogs, Matt, Mark and Luke, were still milling around the original tree trying to figure out what the coon was up to, believing him to still be up there, when Blue let out his first bawl. The swamp became dead still as the other dogs focused there attention on Blue. Then another bawl and another as he moved out onto the trail of the coon. A scramble of noise told that the other dogs were on there way to fall in on the trail. Soon it was Blue and Matt. Then Blue, Matt and Mark. Then all four in a scramble to be the lead hound on a trail fresh and easy to follow.

"Might as well listen from here awhile," Junior said, "they might run a ways and circle back or he might be looking for a hollar tree to go up right now."

Junior was right, soon the hounds were beginning to make a wide turn to the left. "Bet he's hit the middle of the swamp and is turning out to find some deep water or a pond. Dogs wouldn't have much of a chance against a coon that size in deep water. "Okay," Junior went on, "we'd better head this direction and see if we can cut them off, least be closer." "Let's make tracks," he said and began a slow jog in a direction that would quarter the hounds if they continued in the same direction.

As we were passing close to the center of the swamp, it opened up because the water was to deep for the low brush to grow. The clearing was about one hundred yards across with no trees or fern growing. It was so dark that nearly everything in the swamp was indistinguishable except the black outline of the trees, but I was almost certain that I could see a black outline of something square like a building or a shed. "No, that can't be," I thought to my self as I pushed on to catch up with Junior.

The coon, unaware of Junior and me being in the swamp and trying to cut him off, continued to circle in a wide arc.

"Hey Bud," Junior called back to me, "better come on, if that coon keeps turning he'll be heading right back to the GMC."

It's not all that uncommon for a seasoned coon to pull this little trick. The trail usually begins in an area that he's familiar with and after he leads the hounds away from his favorite trees and territory he will try and shake them from his trail and return to were he probably has a tall hollow tree with a cozy little nest of dried leaves and twigs. The Boss Coon, thinking he had left the hounds "barking up the wrong tree," was on his way back to familiar turf.

Yes, Junior was right, the coon had turned full circle now and was headed straight as an arrow back to where this chase had begun. No doubt, the coon had in his mind a safe and secure haven where he could sit out the night and listen to the hounds tree at the tree where he had left them, and then as they tired of the impasse he would listen to then drift away home as it had happen so many nights before as the town dogs would come out for a romp in the swamp. Then he would come down from the tree and finish the night feeding along the edge of the swamp, breaking open the little mussel shells for the tasty bite inside and maybe if he's quick get a paw on a hapless frog before it leaps into the deep water and security.

But what this coon had not experienced before in this sanctuary that he assumed his private domain, that these were not your ordinary town dogs and they were teamed with hunting partners possessing manipulative intellects, and neither were accustomed to leaving the swamp without a coon in Junebloom's gunny sack.

"Might as well stop now," Junior called, "Coons headed straight to where Blue first picked him up and I'll bet you anything he'll go up a big tree to set the night out. "Might as well set back and let the hounds work it out from here."

We found a fallen tree resting horizontally a few inches out of the water.

"Come on over here Junior, here's a good log to sit on."

The Boss Coon had a good jump on the dogs and it would be several minutes before they caught up to the coon, assuming that he had gone to a tree. I took the pack off and laid it on the log between us.

"Might as well take the little critter out and let him play on the log," Junior said.

I took him out of the pack and held him out over the water with both hands. No sooner had he felt his freedom than he began to pee in a parabolic arch. I held him high and Junior and I laughed as the little golden fountain arched out and into the air making a trickle noise as it hit the water.

"Looks like you had a mighty close call there, that pup being bounced around in that pack like he was," Junior blurted out in laughter."

I nodded my agreement and laughed even more as the pup squirted little spurts in a final effort to purge his bladder.

I sat him on the log between Junior and I. He acted comfortable and accustomed as though this was the place he wanted to be. Running from my release down the log and raising up on his hind legs and licking Junior in the face, then returning to me in a repeat performance. Then stopping between us, turning crosswise to the log, straining to hear the hounds in the distance.

The pup perked up his ears and aimed his stare in the direction of the GMC. In just a moment we began to see a light flashing and hear the splashing of water. Junior flashed his light in the direction and called with a "Who, there."

"That you, Juner, " came the response.

"Yeah, over here."

Junebloom made his way on over to us and sat abruptly down on the log between us, the pup jumped into his lap and began to lick him in the face. I guess no one had told him that in this era a black man didn't get the same respect and affection as a white man.

"Glad to see me, little feller?"

"Glad to find you fellers, must nearly be to the middle of this here swamp."

"That ways just a little," Junior responded gesturing with his hand as he talked. "Where's Albert and Moses?"

"They's cummin," Junebloom replied. "They's say I'd better get in here fas and catch youse boys for youse done went clear cross da swamp an den de coon cum right back. They say, no way let youse boys foller dat coon cross de swamp, da say."

"Guess they were right, Junebloom, that coon turned just like they said he would."

We began to see the lights of Albert and Mr. Wilson. "Who, there," Junior called out. There was no response but the lights turned and were now heading our direction. Soon they walked out of the darkness and I slid down to make room for them to sit on the log. As they sat the pup greeted them in kind in like manner leaving Albert and Mr. Wilson shaking their heads and wiping the saliva from their faces.

The silence was broken by Albert, "You boys get to the middle of the swamp?"

"Yes," I replied, "that's where the coon finally circled."

"Sho nuf, you did," Mr. Wilson questioned? "What's the middle of dis here swamp like," he asked?

Junior responded to Mr. Wilson's question, "Couldn't tell much chasing those dogs." Cleared up a little, I think."

"Yes, that's what I remember too, cleared up and got a little deeper. I bet that's why the coon headed that way before he turned. You know, looked like something in the middle of that clearing, couldn't tell for sure."

"Must have been a shadow or something, can't imagine anything being in the middle of this big-ass swamp," retorted Albert trying to make emphasis.

"Naw sa, nuthin," Mr. Wilson confirmed.

We were all silent for a minute, then Albert threw out a question, "Did you get a look at that coon?"

"Sure did," Junior replied. "Big son-uv-a-gun, biggest coon around these parts, I'd lay a bet on that."

I jumped in to the description of the coon, my voice excited and shaky, "Sure was big, mean and smart to. Like to have torn Blue's head off then got Matt in the throat, took Mark and Luke to get him off. I'm just hoping those dogs can handle him. Sure wish Lee was here."

Mr. Wilson responded, "See, wha di tell ya, sho nuf Boss Coon- Lawdy me."

"Junior figures that the coon is heading right back to where Blue picked up his trail, I do too," I said.

"Shh," Junior whispered, "The hounds have passed us now and there moving out. That coon must have left a trail as straight as an arrow."

He was right, the hounds were neck and neck, pushing hard and fast, bawling at every step.

"Who-eee'," Junebloom yelled out, "lissin to dat music."

Albert stood up, staring into the direction of the chase, "We might as well get headed that direction, the hounds'l be coming down treed here before we get there."

I grabbed the pup and stuffed his squirming body back into the pack and positioned his little head back out the hole in the flap. I threw the rucksack on over my shoulder and the pup gave out an "Uff" as he banged against my back. We fell into a line behind Junior and headed for the hounds, hollaring unnecessary encouragement to the hounds as we went.

As we made our way the dogs became silent. Junior threw out his hand in a signal to stop.

"Listen," he said, "Not a sound." We might as well stop here and wait for the hounds to work that tree out."

"You so sure it's a tree," Albert quipped, "Might have lost the trail, mightn't they?"

"Come on, Albert," I said, "Blue wouldn't loose a trail that easy."

All lights off, all silent, straining to hear any sound the hounds would make. How dark and foreboding the swamp had become.

"Yah, yah, yah." "There's Matt." "Yah, yah, yah," he barked again.

"Matt thinks he's found the tree, let's give Blue a little more time. Be quiet now," whispered Mr. Wilson, "Don't make no noise that gonna mess up Blue, he's makin shor dat coon ain't laid down no mo tricks."

We turned off our lights, the darkness seemed to intensify the stillness. We stood side by side facing the direction we last heard Matt bark. I couldn't see a thing, not even my hand as I held it up in front of my face. But still, in my mind, I could see Blue circling the tree as he had done so many nights before. Then coming into the tree and reaching up as high as his legs would push him, taking a deep breath of the scent where the coon went up. He would bark once confirming the smell and then begin an even larger circle around the base of the tree. Then unexpectedly, I would see Lee, standing off to the side as he always did, waiting for Blue to give the signal, "Okay Lee, he's up there." A lump came in my throat and then a tear in my eye. I pulled the ruck sack around to the front where it was resting on my chest and began stroking the pup across the head. He whined a little and began licking the tears as they flowed in rivulets now, "Sorry pup, I guess I'm not so tough."

Blue came down treed on this tree as solid as I ever heard him. There was no question from the other dogs as they raced to the tree and began barking in chorus. The swamp literally echoed with the music of the treeing hounds. Our own hollering, nearly drowned out, as we whooped up encouragement to the dogs and screamed meaningless instructions to each other. This was it, I half screamed with joy, half in fear of this monster our dogs had put in this tree for us. In my own mind I knew that in an even fight that neither the dogs nor the coon was going to be the winner. In a fight with stakes this high, nobody walks away not bleeding. The mother of the winning war who lost her only son.

We all gathered around the base of the tree, first examining the tree for marks where the coon climbed, then flashing our lights into the tree branches high above our heads trying to get the coon to look down so that our lights would get bright eyes and reveal his location.

"Whoo-boy," Junebloom called out, "Lawsy me, I wish you'd looky dare at dim eyes, looks lika allygator. Lawsy, don b'lieve they's a pot in da quarters big e'nuff for to parball dat sunna-gun."

Albert followed suit, "My word, that's the biggest spread of eyes I've ever seen on a coon." "Why, Junebloom, you could parboil that coon from now till christmas and you wouldn't get a fork in him."

The old coon sat on a big horizontal limb high above the swamp. A huge tree, no limbs until nearly the top. He sat there defiantly staring down at us, seemingly amused at our antics, enjoying the safety of his perch.

The hounds were beginning to get restless, and milling around the base of the tree and coming back and rearing up onto it and baying, almost in harmony. Blue didn't, he never took his feet from the tree, his eyes always fixed on the limb where we had our headlights focused. He may have seen the coon in the lights, but whether he did or not, there was no question in his mind, this coon was there.

"Well, what do we do now," I asked? "Did anybody slip a gun out tonight?"

"I sure didn't," replied Albert an looked at Junior inquisitively.

"I didn't," Junior replied, "I never figured the tree would be so high. I can try to climb it."

"Sure," I said, mockingly, "Try your luck. You'd better dig your toenails pretty deep."

Junior walked over to the tree and gave it a half hug reaching as far around it as his arms would reach. Which was not very far.

Junior backed away from the tree and traced his light up the trunk, "Not me," he said, "It's almost like climbing a wall."

I chimed in like a true smart aleck before anybody else could say a word, "Let's let Junior call him down, he'll have him laughing so hard he'll fall right off the limb."

"Don't laugh at me, plenty a coons has been jumped out of the tree by a good squaller. Ain't that so Moses?"

Mr. Wilson nodded in agreement.

"Well, I've got a big Nehi strawberry loaded with salted peanuts back at Stiekie's that says it ain't so."

"You're on," Junior snapped back.

Junior went back over to the tree and got in the thick of the Hounds. He cupped his hands over his mouth and began making horrible sounds. Like a dying calf or something. He hollered and squalled and splashed the water until he had the hounds in a frenzy.

"Shine your light up quick," Junior called out.

We all shined our lights simultaneously.

"Lawsy me, Juner, I b'lieves dat coon is laffun," Junebloom teased. "C'mon now, let me try it, Cain't do no wuss."

Junebloom walked out into the swamp an stood along side Junior. He first looked up into the tree and then at the swamp floor. He performed this exercise several times seemingly not sure how the first line of the script began. When he finally got his act together it was hilarious beyond description. He cupped his hands over his mouth as he had seen Junior do, but he raised his right leg into the air, then with a horrendous squalling bellow he began stomping the water with his raised leg. Soon he was squalling and splashing the water in syncopation and dancing and turning trying to keep his balance on his leg that wasn't splashing the water and causing such an entertaining sight that we soon found all of our lights were shinning on Junebloom.

Albert shouted to Junebloom over the squalling, "Keep it up Junebloom, I think he's about to say uncle."

About that time Junebloom turned and fell backwards into the water.

"What's da holler'n, cant fool no coon wit youse holler'n."

"Get up out of the water, Junebloom, You'll catch a cold."

I looked over at Mr. Wilson, "Is it true, can a coon really be called out of a tree like they were doing, I asked?"

"No sa, and dats a fact." "You can call a coon out a da tree, but not lack dat."

"Well sa, my daddy could sho nuf do it. Ain't no slave had no gun and to a slave man, coon was purty good eat'n, my daddy would have'm walk right out o dat tree right in amongst dim hounds. I seen im do it a bunch o times."

"Well, Moses," Albert cut in, "Looks like you'll have to call this one out, look at'im, hasn't budged an inch since we started all this commotion."

"Can you do it, Mr. Wilson," I asked enthusiastically.

"Don no," he responded, "try to member how daddy done it."

Mr. Wilson walked a few feet away from the group towards the tree, "Turn off da lights and don make no noise," he called back in a whisper. "We'll jus try it an see."

Even the hounds seemed to know that someone special was about to take control of the situation as Mr. Wilson looked up into the huge eyes of the Boss Coon. The hounds were soon circled around him, watching his movements as he prepared to try and talk the coon out of the tree. It seemed that part of the plan was to allow a period of absolute silence pass before the talking began. I wonder how the hounds knew.

The hounds knew, they knew that a master had walked into their midst, they looked up at Mr. Wilson as if to say, We submit to your superiority, we form in columns behind your guidance and lay success or failure in your hand.

Just as I turned my light off I glanced at Mr. Wilson, his large outline framed against the black shadows of the swamp, his white beard, his white hair protruding from the edges of his weathered felt hat, produced a powerful grace that commanded respect, even provoked deep consideration of the significance of a black man. Yes indeed, what ever it was that the hounds felt and sensed, so did I.

In a moment the last light was out. I stared in the direction that I had last looked. Silence, black silence.

"Squeeee - sha-sha," the first sounds from Mr. Wilson.

"Squeee-squeee - shulush-shulush", over and over in rapid succession. Than Mr. Wilson began growling and squealing in ever increasing volume and cadence, his hands cupped over his mouth directing the noise toward the water. Now he was screaming and thrashing at the water putting the hounds into a frenzy. So skilled was he in talking to the coon that it sounded as though many coons were in the water crazed in orgy.

Junior moved over close to me touching my shoulder, he cupped his hand over his mouth to conceal the sound and began to whisper into my ear, "Bud, it's so noisy under the tree that Moses can't hear a thing, but I think I can hear that coon stirring around up there."

I directed my attention toward the top of the tree and strained for a sound. I could hear scratching noises and limbs rustling. I tugged on Junior's arm and stuck a thumb up close to his face in a gesture of affirmation. I tapped Albert and showed him a circled thumb and forefinger.

Albert pulled me over close and whispered directly into my ear, "Is he coming down?"

I nodded yes and motioned the same signal to Junebloom.

Mr. Wilson hadn't let up his theatrics at all. Anyone who had ever heard a pile of coons scrapping over a female or a prize toad would swear they were hearing the real thing.

Junior must have had the best ears in the bunch because it was always him who would hear the first noise from the woods, "Listen," he said in a whisper.

The scratching and clawing had increased. The excitement of the orgy was beginning to tear at his nerves compounded by the invasion of his sanctuary.

"He's coming, he's coming now!"

Mr. Wilson must have sensed the same because it sounded like several more coons joined the orgy.

Then - WHOP!

We snapped on our lights in time to see Mr. Wilson thrown with a huge splash broadside into the water, and the huge coon leaping from his shoulder and head. Blood was flowing from open gashes left from the coons vicious claws. Matt was at the coon in a heartbeat, but alone was no match for this monster as the coon turned on him and slapped him away. Then Mark and Luke dashing in together only to be repelled by the deadly slashing and clawing of the powerful forearms. The dogs backed as the coon hissed and growled and lunged at them keeping them from regrouping and attacking as a force. Mr. Wilson was recovering from the smashing blow of the coon and was struggling to get his feet under him. As he began to move the coon recognized a foe from another direction and just as Mr. Wilson was raising up the coon leaped at his head. Blue came sailing out of nowhere and knocked the coon away from Mr. Wilson, but before Blue could regain his balance the coon was attacking him, clawing at his head, re-opening the cuts and slashes he had inflicted at the previous tree. Blue was screaming for help. Mr. Wilson's hounds attacked the coon in force showing the grit of true hounds in life or death conquest.

Even as the hounds tore the coon away from Blue the coon never quit ripping and tearing flesh from their heads and faces. The swamp water had turned crimson from the blood as this seasoned coon made attack after attack slashing at their heads and eyes trying to render the hounds defenseless.

A reasonable man would have retreated by now to re-examine the worth of the booty but good hounds are not bred to be reasonable in a fight and were not inclined to give ground. I ran into the swamp still gripping the club I had secured from a willing tree. I ran with intentions of running in and working the coon over for the dogs but as I approached I discovered that the formidable opponent was not just a big coon but in fact was a vicious fortress of power and weight and no one, not even a boy with a club was going beyond the circle of dogs.

"Hold it," Albert called out over the noise, "That coons mad to crazy, he'll attacked anything close, stay back."

I could see that the flesh on the dog's heads and shoulders was torn back to reveal bare muscle and bone.

Blue made a lunge at the coon and it lunged back, but as though orchestrated and by design, Matt leaped at the same instant grabbing some coon rear. The coon folded over backward and bit Matt's nose with a solid hold causing him to release. Mark and Luke saw this as an opportunity to counter attack and leaped at the coon. The coon dashed away from their attack and backed into shelter of two tall protruding roots at the base of the cypress tree where the hounds could only attack one at a time from the front because of the constrained opening. Each dog in turn would run at the coon and try to drag him out to expose him to help from the others but the coon was to powerful and vicious. Each time the hound would release, torn and crying for help.

"Aren't they going to stop," I cry at Mr. Wilson? "He's going to tear them to shreds."

"No su," he said back, "These here dogs ain't quiters." "I sho hopes we ain't made a big bad mistake."

I pushed in as close as I could. Blue knew I was there close and attacked the coon again. The coon grabbed him with his claws and held him, Blue couldn't back out of the narrow opening. He was wedged in to tight for Blue to drag him out and he was making deep penetrations with his dagger like teeth. I could see that Blue was in deep trouble and I grabbed his tail and began to pull, "Help, I screamed, He's killing Blue."

The others got holds on me where they could and together we pulled Blue far enough out of the hole so that the coon had to release.

I was sickened by the blood and opened flesh of Blue's head. He looked up at me, whimpering from the pain, eyes of stress, saying I'll go in again if you tell me to.

I became wild with rage, "I'll kill the son of a bitch," I screamed not aware of what I was saying. I raised my club high and ran for the coon's haven. I could see him from above and I was determined to bash his head until it was pulp in revenge. The coon saw my light as I stood over him. Blinded by my light, he raised up on his hind legs, growling and slashing the air with his claws. I tensed, every muscle in my body charged with adrenaline, poised to smash the coons brains against the tree roots. I came down with all the power that rage could muster. My arm wouldn't move. It felt as though it had been locked by immovable anchor.

"What?" I cried out.

I turned my head to my arm, it was Mr. Wilson, his great hand gripped my arm with a force I thought not human.

"What, Mr. Wilson, let go, kill'im!"

"No Bud, not this time," Mr. Wilson replied in such and even steady tone. A stern sincerity fixed his expression.

"Look what he did to Blue and Matt, let go so's I can kill him."

"No Bud, not this time," he replied in the same soft tone. "Not this time, don deserve ta die, he gots rights to live."

I had dropped the club to my side unaware that I was in the midst of a vicious coon and the hounds. The fight stopped, it was quiet, except for my sobs of frustration. "Why, Mr. Wilson?"

"Why yo ask? I'll tell yo why, Dis ain't no ordnary coon boy, he got's pride, he b'lieves he got's the rights to live in dis swamp all he wants, he's gonna die fo dim rights if yo says so, white boy. Which man God give da right to say who got rights and who ain't? I don wanna see no mo dying ova rights, thas why."

To this day I don't know what it was about hounds and black people, they seemed to understand each others thoughts. I stood there with tears streaming down my cheeks and watched the hounds back away from the tree and line up beside Mr. Wilson and me. Our eyes were fixed on the coons hideout at the base of the tree. As if the coon himself understood, his head appeared over the top of the root. Tired, hair matted and swirled from dog saliva, he eased out over the root and un-hurriedly slide into the water on the other side. I was amazed, as were the others, that he neither ran or showed any fear of impending attack. The dogs stood motionless and watched.

"I swear," Albert exclaimed, "What the hell's going on here?"

I had forgotten all about the pup in my knapsack.

Splash. He had freed himself from the packs confinement and fallen to the water. I reached down to grab him but he slid away from my grasp and made a beeline in the direction of the disappearing coon. With all the yipping and splashing his little body could muster, he fell in on the coons trail. I ran for him thinking the coon might turn and attack such a small foe but to my amazement, he swam away through the darkness of the swamps mysterious door.

"Lawsy me," Junebloom exclaimed in disbelief, "Never see'd such a pup in my life."

I grabbed him up into my arms and held his little head up close to my cheek. "Good boy," I whispered into his ear.

"Next year that coon'd better stay in the tree," I said gleefully.

"Yes su," Mr. Wilson joined in. "An I got jus a name fo dat pup that ain't fraid of dat Boss coon."

"Okay," I said, "Just what have you got in mind and we'll vote on it." He sorta belongs to all of us you know."

"Samson, we'll call'im Samson caus he ain't scared'o nobody and tinks he kin whup anybody."

"Samson," I said and let the sound drag out slowly, "Samson, I could call him Sam for short."

"Sho nuf, boy, We'll call'im "Bud's little Samson" and youse jus call'im Sam."

I held him up in front of the rest, "How's Sam sound to ya'll?"

Everybody nodded in agreement, I was relieved, I was sure that Mr. Wilson would fight to name him John to finish off his apostles and I didn't want to hurt his feelings.

We gathered the dogs in close, I gave Blue a hug and praised him for doing a great job. I snapped a short lead rope to the ring in his collar and began working my way towards the GMC. The rest took a dog in turn and fell in line behind me. We were soon standing at the tailgate of the GMC and jumped each dog into the cage.

Junebloom broke the silence, "Wuz dat a coon or what?" "Bigga coon I's eva see'd, his hide cova da whole doe, fo sho t'wud." "Ain't it so, Albert?", as if to say if Albert confirmed it, it was so.

Yes sir, Junebloom, a coon that size is even a little scary, I'd say.

Then Moses broke in, "Mighty proud a dim dogs, da hung in der til the las, sho nuf woulda killed that coon o died try'n, days no doubt bout dat."

"I tell you what," Junior cut in, "Let's get those dogs up in good shape an bring'm back out here. Maybe I'll bring my old "Twenty-Two" along."

"No," I said, "I guess you didn't hear what Mr. Wilson said, he said that coon had rights and shouldn't have to die until he get's ready, I guess I agree with him, I don't think he ought to die either."

"No sa," said Moses, "dat coon is da biggest, smartest, meanest critter in dis country, don't never wont to kill him." "Been think'n," Moses went on, motioning with his hands for strict attention, "dat coon could o done one o dim dogs in, if he'd a mind ta, and dim dogs jus mighta done him in, but day agreed to a fair and square stan-off. I say we leave it dare. As a matta o fact, I been mo think'n. I say, les say dis here swamp belongs to da Boss Coon and les don never hunt dis swamp no mo. We'll call dis da Boss Coon Swamp an we wont never hunt here no mo, an never tell nobody. Who say yes?"

Albert jumped in with his yes almost before Moses had a chance to finish. Junior complained about not being able to brag on a coon that you didn't take in to Stiekies, but finally consented. Surprisingly, Junebloom just muttered something about not having a pot that big anyway.

"Load up fellows, we'd better get these dogs in for some stitches and a tetanus shot. I know you can't afford a vet bill, Moses, but this'l be on my ticket," Albert said as he drew the door to the GMC shut. And maybe we'd better get you some stitches while we're at the Vets."

We all responded with chuckles, but the the truth was, it was a little hollow, for we all knew that more than once a black man with cuts from a saturday night fight or joints swollen with rheumatism and little money to pay, would tap on Dr. Brown's back door and quietly ask for help that was never refused and then return later to dedicate a Saturday or a Sunday to Dr. Brown's orange grove.

The sun was breaking the horizon as we reached the highway, it's water color orange and yellow would lead us to Vet Browns office, he'd be finishing his first cup of coffee.

Chapter #8
BEYOND DNA

 From start to finish, life provides a lot of cuts and scars. Some have said that these are the tempering of the steel, testing the gold by fire, the preparation for adulthood. But in each a lesson is learned and somewhere down deep in the psychic or the sub-conscience, a condition is set and a marker is positioned as a spontaneous warning when these scenarios of danger are re-encountered. A lighthouse, so to speak, not arbitrarily set at the peninsulas' point, but set because a ship has lost it's way in the dark and been driven by storms and gales until its life was beaten out by an angry sea against the boulders along the shore. The sailor learns and the sailor knows, that the light on the shore isn't a beacon of safe haven, but rather a warning of peril.

 And such as this it is in every normal life, your's, mine, that unbeknowings to us, forces deep in our minds are pushing and tugging us away from learned dangers and snares.

 I guess you could say that the next few years of my life were somewhat that way. Hard lessons learned by trial and error as a boy tries this and that searching for the path to manhood. Oh yes, you and I know that most boys, and girls I suspect, have tempted rationality trying to prove something strange about themselves, trying to be unique, trying to establish identity, flirting with self-destruction, thinking in terms of power. Without the guidance of a properly positioned light, self-destruction is often the result.

 You can't say that I had no guidance or lighthouse, sure, like a lot of homes nowadays, guidance was a token, but after all, I was fortunate to have other sources of wisdom. Albert was a businessman, very successful by most standards, he knew how to take a dollar and make two. He owned houses and land and groves and was always ready to share his secrets of success with me. Mr. Wilson was as fine as gentleman come. He was a master of brotherly love, a giver of compassion and a teacher of bible matters. Junior, who knew more about hunting and woodsmanship than anybody, was my good friend and guide and often chauffeur until I got my drivers license. And then there was Junebloom, an exhibition of low estate. Humbled by tradition, calloused from labor, content with his status, unaware that another option was on the horizon.

These were my teachers and mentors during these growing years and as the body forms according to the regimen that life requires of it, so does the mind.

If you really want to know, before learning comes bonding. The greatest teacher of all times was loved by his disciples. As he taught they clung to him, tasting his words, savoring his wisdom. As he taught he put self aside and revealed in his own life style, so that none could doubt, the truth of life and living. Teaching is a combination of explanation and personal example. You can decide for yourself which ex is the most important in the combination. I for one, believe them to be inseparable and would propose that any person striving to teach, first master the mystical skill of bonding with the pupil.

Isn't bonding a curious phenomenon? One person bonding to another. A person to a dog. An adult to another's child. Why don't you explain bonding? Is it mystical, chemical, spiritual, coincidental, accidental, orchestrated, pre-destined, genetic or just convenient? I dare not say, but I will give you a funny example of an inappropriate bonding. Once upon a time, in truth, a mother cow refused to accept her calf. I don't know why a mother cow would do this, considering that a mother cow is supposed to be bred to genetic perfection, but in no way would she give this little brahma bull calf the time of day. So, as I rode into the pasture to see what was to be done, the little calf ran under my horse and began to make like there was food there. My horse didn't like this routine but I calmed him down and made him stand steady. The calf, looking for a mother, adopted the first thing that would stand still and not kick it's head off. Between that place and the pasture gate, a complete bonding took place and no amount of fancy riding could shake the little critter from the horses side.

Who then, should be the guide and shaper of a child's life, the birth mother who would abandon the baby and seek it's return in the future or the adopted parent who yearned and cried in the night for a child. Strange, isn't it? The birth mother versus the adopted mother. If you were to judge, would you look into the heart for love and bonding or into the blood for a common DNA?

I mused over the wisdom of great King Solomon and I tried to understand all of the implications of his beautiful rendering of the child's fate who was claimed by two mothers. One must wonder if King Solomon was sure of the outcome of his ploy? "Bring me a sword and divide the baby into two parts so that each may have a half." Surely he sighed a sigh of relief as the one mother exemplified a parental perfection and cried, "No, don't kill the child, let the other have him."

There's more to life than DNA.

Now Sam, devilish and bold as a pup, grew to meet or even exceed the expectations of the bunch. Except for me, I was never amazed at his progress or surprised by his mastery of the sport. It was just routine as far as I was concerned.

You may have thought that Blue would have been a little jealous of the attention Sam was receiving, but he took it in stride, even to the point of showing pride in "his pup" so to speak, as though the teacher were presenting the student. But really I think that Blue missed Lee a lot more than a dog can show and was happy to have a cocky partner to hunt with.

Me, well, I thought he was the greatest thing that had ever hit the swamp and I was never hesitant to say so. By his second year, Sam had become the dominant hound in the pack. The other dogs, including what had become known as Mr. Wilson's apostles, Matt, Mark and Luke, had conceded the head dog position with little more than a few growls and snarls. Mr. Wilson didn't seem to mind, probably because we all thought we had some stock in Sam. But then, no wonder, Sam had grown to weigh eighty or ninety pounds and stood far above the average hound.

Seldom a weekend passed that we weren't in the swamps treeing coons and an occasional bobcat. I bragged a lot down at the station and soon Sam's fame was spreading in ever larger circles.

Seeds of My Field

It was nice that Sam had grown older so soon, but then, Blue had also grown older, gray hairs began to show around his muzzle, and I had grown older, too.

The august rains hadn't let up in several weeks. Everything was wet to touch and even wetter if it touched you. Hot? Yes, and humid of course. It was that time of year when the rain turned to steam and there was no reprieve from it's constant torture. About the only way the rain could be endured was to stand in it, face up. Clothes, how terrible clothes felt. They clung to you like greased wrappings. They stunk a little from hanging in the closet and stunk progressively more as the day continued. Everyone wore them but nobody wanted to. They were soaking wet within minutes after being put on, either by sweat or by the humidity, that the fabrics absorbed like a candle wick. And sweat, why did I sweat anyway, there is no evaporation when the humidity is ninety five to one hundred percent. The bodies cooling system was rendered useless. The sweat just poured from my body from the top of my head to the bottoms of my feet. It ran into my eyes until they burned from irritation, it ran from my legs and feet until my shoes sloshed as I walked. And, there was no earthly reason to shower, you couldn't smell the difference, you couldn't feel the difference and when it was all over, you couldn't dry off. And that's the kind of day it was.

I had worked the day in one of Albert's groves. We were digging trenches here and there trying to drain the standing water away from the orange trees. It only took a few days of standing water to either cause the soil around the feeder roots to sour, or worse, to drown the roots of air and causing the tree to die of starvation.

I would hope, on one hand, that the rains would let up and allow the ground to drain and dry, while on the other hand, the only way I could stand to work in the heat and humidity was for it to be raining.

I had finished a cold shower which felt good as long as I was in it. Still un-comfortable, I took a swim in the lake. Finally, I had to go down to the station because a big event was to take place tomorrow, and I would need some support. Moral and otherwise. It was still raining so I decided to walk the quarter mile.

Because of the heat and rain, we had decided to put off hunting for a few weeks. It's almost impossible for the hounds to trail in the rain because the scent particles are washed away almost instantly and besides that, the coons seldom came out of their hideouts in a downpour. So, I needed to find Junior and see if he would give me a lift into town tomorrow.

I was dripping like a colander when I walked into the station. "Hi, Mr. Stiekie, dang sure is raining a lot these days."

"Not anymore than normal this time of year," he replied.

I instantly, as though by habit, reached into the drink box and pushed the drink bottles around in the watery ice until I found a Strawberry Nehi. The icy water felt good on my wrists and I left them there for a while until they began to ache from the cold.

I was already pouring salted peanuts into the bottle, cupping my hand around the top to make a funnel. Mr. Stiekie looked up from the counter, "You want me to put those on your folks ticket?"

"No, better not, my step mother's been saying things about not having to much spare money these days. Besides, I've been working for a few weeks now and I've got some money to pay for my own stuff. How much is it?"

"Twenty cents."

"Been working, have you? Where bouts?"

"I've been working for Albert, he's been needing my help pretty bad with this rain and all. Spect' I'll work right up til time for school to start. Maybe then I'll have enough to carry me up to Thanksgiving break."

"Albert pay you pretty good," Mr. Stiekie asked?

"Pretty good, I'd say. Dollar an hour."

"Yes sir," Mr. Stiekie came back, "That's pretty good pay for a young pup, alright. Albert think he's taking you to raise or something?"

"Albert said, if a man gets to work on time, works hard and tries to make the boss some money, he ought to get a share of the profit."

"A boy too?" said Mr. Stiekie under his breath.

"By the way, have you seen Junior lately? I need to see him," I said, getting to the purpose at hand.

"Yep, sure have, he's walking in the door behind you."

"Hi, Junior, you're as wet as I am. You walk over too?"

"It's the only way to get cool, seems like. Unless you're rich and have air conditioning."

"Guess what, Junior, I got paid, got a pocket full of money, let me buy you a Strawberry Nehi and some peanuts."

"Well, it's like this Bud, I'd rather have a Miller's, but Mr. Stiekie won't sell me one, and if I can't have beer I'd rather have a coke."

"Well, what ever you want, I owe you one, remember?"

"C'mon, Mr. Stiekie, give Junior a Miller's, nobodies going to come in this down pour."

"Be just my luck they would. And don't you ever say something dumb like that again."

I guess by today's standards a sixteen year old would respond to Mr. Stiekie's command with something smart aleck, but then the standards were a little different. Adults all seemed to band together in a cult of a sort and if one adult said spank all the kids in the neighborhood they all got a whipping. Good judgement said to pay for the coke and keep my mouth shut.

"Did you want to see me about something, Bud," Junior asked?

"Yeah, I did. Tomorrow I've got to get into Tampa to get my drivers license and I'll need a ride."

"How come your old man don't take you?"

"He's not home and my step mother, well I just don't won't to ask her."

"Well, who's gonna sign for you?"

"What do you mean, sign for me? I'll just sign for myself. I got the money."

Mr. Stiekie was propped up against the counter intently entertained by our exchange of dialogue.

Junior gave me a stern look with his hands propped on his hips, "It takes more than money to get a drivers license. You've got to have a birth certificate, and you've got to pass a written test, and then a driving test and if you pass all of those, then you've got to have a legal guardian sign for you. So that means you've got to get your step mother to go down or else."

"Well, that's not the only problem," I hung my head a little, "the real reason I can't ask my step mother is that the car is broke pretty bad and she's waiting for my dad to send some money to fix it."

"Sounds like you've got a problem," Mr. Stiekie broke in, "You may have to wait awhile. How long you think before your dad sends the money?"

I shrugged, "Don't really know, can't tell."

They all knew and didn't pursue it any further.

"Look," I responded, "It seems like after a guy is sixteen and has driven as much as I have, they ought to just go ahead and give him a license. Don't you think?"

"Sorry, Bud," Mr. Stiekie said, "It's just not so simple, besides making you take all those tests, they're going to check all the lights and brakes on the car to make sure it's in good shape."

My heart sank a little, it seemed that I had come to another one of those hurdles that was a little higher than I could jump.

"Well dangit, I may never get a license if they test the car, too. We don't own any perfect cars."

I guess I looked a little dejected as Albert came in shaking the rain from his hat. "Hey Bud, you look kinda down in the mouth. That check I gave you bounce?"

I just stood around as Junior and Mr. Stiekie explained to Albert the crisis I was having. He listened intently, already aware of the circumstances. First he would look at Junior as he talked and then glance at me. Then he would listen to Mr. Stiekie and glance at me. I was beginning to feel smaller and smaller, getting caught up in the remorse of the moment.

"Why hell, what's the problem," Albert blurted out?

"Don't you see, I got no car, got no body to sign. I'll never get to drive to school," I was almost in hopeless tears.

"What do you mean, got no car? We can take mamma's Caddy or the GMC and I'll sign. How's that for a plan?"

"Hold it," Mr. Stiekie responded instantly, "Let's don't get silly about this thing. You could get in big trouble signing as Bud's legal guardian."

"Oh, well who's to know the difference if nobody ever tells," Albert said with a twinkle in his eye and a golden grin. Just what's the worst that could happen?"

"They could fine the hell out of you, for one thing," said a serious Mr. Stiekie.

Seeds of My Field

"Now really, do you think that ole Judge Harris is gonna fine me and take a chance on me telling everybody that it was him that got thrown in jail with me that night for stealing watermelons. I don't think so."

Mr. Stiekie replied as if the secrets of the universe had just been divulged, "So that's been your ace in the hole all a long."

"A good businessman always keeps some aces in the hole."

Once again Albert used an opportunity to put a puzzle to rest by using a half truth to end the speculation and satisfy the curiosities of the neighborhood. He knew that soon, all those who had wanted to know the curious relationship between Judge Harris and Albert would be saying, "Oh, they stole some watermelons and got caught." But that was not true at all.

"You mean I could take my driving test in the GMC," I blurted out. To me, the GMC was the greatest vehicle in the world. Mrs. Newsom's Cadillac wasn't even a close second.

"Well, why not," Albert said grinning, "Lord knows you've drove that pickup all over these woods enough to get a feel for it."

"What time we need to be at the court house in the morning?"

"The lady said nine o'clock if we wanted to go right in."

"Okay then, get down here at seven in the morning and get the junk out of the GMC and we'll head for Tampa. Haven't been there for a while, might pick up some things."

Albert looked around at Mr. Stiekie and Junior, "Well, think I don't know how to get things done? We'll still have time to get the water out of that Prichart grove before dark tomorrow."

Seeing Albert in action, causes me to understand why he was successful. His philosophies for managing his groves and real estate would have worked equally as well and been equally successful if he had been managing a large corporation. He made decisions as soon as he had all of the facts, and executed them at the very next available instant. When he decided what needed to be done, he applied all of his energy and resources toward it's conclusion. If Albert had made a decision that couldn't humanly be executed, I suppose he would still be working at it.

I knew that by noon tomorrow I would have my drivers license because that was how Albert planned it and it always happened. I also knew that Albert never did any idle planning and somehow his effort and investment would have a multiple dividend.

I was to choked up and excited to say thanks, or anything else for that matter, so I grabbed Albert around the waist and squeezed hard and ran out of the station before he could respond.

"Albert," Mr. Stiekie broke in, "Are you sure you know what you're doing? You've got a lot of money and assets and if anything was to go wrong in this deal they'd come after your loot like bee's after honey. You oughta reconsider, at least get Bud's step mother to sign off on something."

"Now Bill, I'm going to go over this with you one time and I want you to hear me out and then keep your damn mouth shut." "That boy's got a right to have a drivers license, his step mother's not his legal guardian and her signature wouldn't count for nothing, his daddy don't care about it for a minute or he'd be here to do it. That boy's kinda like a boy I'd want for myself and I think he's worth the risk. Besides, all I've got's a couple a little girls, they're not going to be much help around the grove. Albert looked Bill sternly in the eye, "Bill, don't you or Junior, either one, forget what I said."

By eight o'clock the next morning the shovels and scuffle hoes were out of the GMC bed and into the barn. The gloves and rags were gathered off the seat and thrown into a box for future use. The mud was hosed off the floor board, the dash dusted clean.

"Hey, Bud, this the same old truck or we got a new Jimmy here?" said Albert as he came up to the GMC.

"Hasn't been this clean for a while, has it Albert?"

"Well, hop in under the wheel and let's head for town."

"Under the wheel?" I responded to Albert, "I don't have my license yet."

"You're going to need to get a little warmed up before we get there. Maybe we'll do some parallel parking practice, too."

I pulled the GMC into a parking place reserved for license applicants and stepped out.

"You know where to go," Albert asked?

"Oh, sure, all the guys from my class have already been here."

We climbed the steps side by side, it felt good having Albert there. Through the door and up to the counter. Albert let me reach the counter first, there by letting me have first contact with the stern looking, gray haired lady looking over the counter at me.

"You look like a boy that needs a drivers license."

"Yes ma'm, I do."

"Well, let me help get this form started. Now, what's your full name?"

Everything was going along fine until we got to the end of the form.

"Now let me see your birth certificate. Says your old enough by a couple of days. Now, all we need is for your father to sign right here."

I got a lump in my throat, I didn't have any idea how Albert was going to get through this one.

Albert spoke up, "I'm not his father, I guess you'd say that I'm his guardian."

"Legal guardian, are you? Well then, I guess you've got the original guardianship certificate?"

"Well, no, actually I don't, you see, I'm Albert Newsom and.."

"Oh, so your Albert Newsom, Judge Harris said you'd be in this morning. Sign on this line here where it says "Legal Guardian."

* * *

"Part 2"
"AMY"

Chapter #1

It was a couple of weeks into the new school year. I had no use for school, but I tolerated it since I didn't have any options. I thought about asking Albert for a full-time job so that I could quit, but I knew Albert would never hear of it. As a matter of fact I would probably get a good lecture. I especially didn't like riding the school bus every morning, so many of the kids had cars or buddies with cars to ride with. Each morning I would take a seat at the rear of the bus and try to be as obscure as possible.

About a mile from where I boarded the bus each morning was another pickup stop. Several kids would board and find seats. The driver would draw the door closed and ease back out onto the highway. I tried not to notice the other kids on the bus and I tried not to be noticed by them. There was one particular girl who got on at this stop each morning, I always noticed her. She looked a little out of place with the other kids, a little more mature, as some girls do at this age, especially more so than the boys.

I tried not to notice her, although I did anyway. I tried harder to not let her notice that I noticed her.

She was a pretty girl, physically developed more than the average early teen. She had shiny blonde hair pulled back into a pony tail and very blue eyes. She seemed to choose to sit by herself or if with someone, she seemed to be uninterested.

After a few weeks our eyes began to meet and shift away. Then as she would enter the bus she would look to the rear to see if I was there.

One day I had finished lunch and was sitting on a bench in the school patio staring at my shoes, minding my own business for a change, waiting for the bell to ring. I looked up and she was standing in front of me. Bold and confidently she reached out her hand gesturing a diplomatic handshake, "Hi, I'm Amy, Amy Brooks. Don't we ride the same bus to school every day?"

Of course we did, we had looked each other directly in the eyes just about three hours ago. "Girls are silly," I thought to myself.

"Yes."

Not knowing for sure what I was supposed to do, I stood up and clumsily shook her hand.

"May I sit with you a minute - until the bell rings?"

"Sure."

"Did you tell me your name?"

"No - Bud."

"Is that all?"

"Isn't that enough?"

"I mean do you have a last name?"

"Olson"

"Is Bud what you're usually called?"

"Yes."

"I thought it a little silly for us to ride the same bus to school every day and not get to know each other. Don't you?"

"Yes."

"I noticed that everyday you're sitting at the back of the bus all alone. Do you like people very much?"

"Yes, most people."

"I thought maybe we could sit together from now on. Okay?"

"Okay."

"Maybe you'd rather I didn't."

"No, I want you to," I said quickly, amazing myself.

"Okay, I just thought that maybe you didn't want me to, you know, since you don't seem to talk too much."

"No - yes, I want you to. I mean if you want to."

"I want to."

"Maybe I could sit by you now instead of standing?"

I scooted over on the concrete bench to make room. The bench was plenty wide, but I nearly fell off the end as I scooted over as far as the bench would allow.

It felt like heaven had just moved in and sat down on the bench next to me. I smelled the fragrance from her soft shiny hair and thought I felt the warmth from her body even though she was sitting at least a foot from me.

My poor head was so stunned and stressed with Amy sitting so close that I couldn't think of a word to say. Conversation was completely out of the question. What I did manage to say was usually in response to a question. Everything else was mostly irrational, or at best uninterpretable. The only thing that saved me from a total washout was that Amy seemed to be amused at my mumbling and pressed on with the introduction.

Finally Amy began to show a little pity, "Bud, am I making you uneasy? You really don't seem to want to talk much. If you're waiting on another girl, I can go on to class."

"No! No- I'm not. I mean I'm not waiting on a girl. Don't know any."

"Are you really that bashful that you don't know any girls?"

"No, I mean I don't have any girl friends."

"Well, I bet you're nice enough."

I think I would have choked on my tongue if the bell hadn't rung just at that minute. We stood instantly together.

"I'm going that way," Amy said, gesturing with her hand. "Which way are you going?"

"202, I guess the opposite direction."

"Oh well," Amy said with a little sigh in her voice. Do you want to sit in the front of the bus with me or do you want me to sit in the back?"

I shrugged a little, "In the back?"

"See you later," Amy called back over her shoulder as she walked away. I noticed her prissy little gait that made her ponytail shish back and forth in rhythm.

I woke up to a bump on the back, "C'mon Bud, you'll be late for class. Who's the doll you're talking to? Just move up from Junior High?"

Thinking about school the rest of the day was hopeless, not that I would lead you to believe that I ever did anyway, but this afternoon I wasn't thinking about hounds and hunting.

I was already in my seat at the back of the bus when Amy stepped up the steps to the aisle. She had a small, white purse and some books cradled in her arms. I fully expected her to go to her regular seat and ignore me. My defenses were already in place to protect my ego from the hurt and embarrassment.

She looked until she saw me, "Hi, Bud, save me a seat?"

It never occurred to me that someone as pretty as Amy Brooks could like me. What she would see in a lanky kid that had spent most of his time hunting and participating in various out of doors pursuits, whose concept of beautiful was long ears, a curled up tail and a voice that would echo through the woods, was eluding as well as confusing. But, the relationship was steady and Amy entered the bus each day with a smile and a "Hi, Bud," and made her way to the back of the bus and the seat that I had reserved.

One day as the bus made its way down Highway #41 the fifteen or so miles to Lutz, (that was becoming a shorter trip as the days passed by), I was leaning back against my seat studying the cars and people along the roadside as Amy talked about school, "Bud, are you listening?"

I jerked my head around pretending that I was, at the same time trying to remember what the subject was when I drifted out of it.

"Oh, I'm sorry," I said, "I just saw a pretty car. See, that blue and white Chevy?"

My heart made a little surge as I noticed that our hands were within a few inches of each others. We both had placed our hands on our knees in a pushing back position. Amy noticed at the same time and let her hand slide to the side of her knee until our fingers were touching. My first impulse was to jerk my hand away in fear that somehow it may appear that I was being too forward and familiar. My heart was skipping beats and nothing intelligent seemed to come into my head to say.

"Don't," Amy said.

"I'm sorry, I didn't mean to."

"No, I mean don't take your hand away."

"You mean."

"Don't you want to leave it there so we can touch?"

"You mean you don't mind?"

"Well, I think we could touch a little or maybe even hold hands a little if we like each other a little bit. Don't you? Maybe you don't want to."

"I don't know, Amy, it makes me feel good and nervous all at the same time."

Amy turned and looked at me with interest, "Bud Olson, are you telling me that you've never held a girls hand before?"

"I don't think so. I know I haven't. Have you?"

"Well, yes, not girls, at parties I have and sometimes in the hall between classes. But not very much. You know, I never did really like anybody that much."

"Oh?"

Amy looked straight to the front of the bus with a bit of a determined smirk on her face and slid her hand over until it was cradled in mine, "I'm going to leave my hand there until we get to Sulphur Springs and if you don't like it we don't have to hold hands anymore."

The bus reached Sulphur Springs in no time. Amy seemed to be amused at my speechlessness but maintained her stare toward the front of the bus. The bus stopped at a red traffic light and began to roar up through the gears. I made no movement or motion to move my hand away as we approached the far side of Sulphur Springs. Just as the bus was passing out of town Amy gripped my little finger and squeezed. "I like to hold your hand, do you like to hold mine?" Amy asked.

"Yes."

"Let's hold hands every day. Want to?"

"Yes."

"And sometimes at lunch?"

"Okay."

Amy seemed to know that our holding hands was the breaking of the ice that would lead to a broader relationship. As a matter of fact, I was no longer intimidated by her looks and outgoing personality and we began to communicate with shorter periods of silence. She would tell me of her girlfriends and parties and her activities on the week ends. She even seemed somewhat interested, even coaxed me into telling her about Blue and Sam and Albert and Mr. Wilson and Junior and Junebloom. She squeamished as I detailed with all the graphics I could command the dogs and coons fighting with superlatives like the coon screamed as Sam and Blue tried to pull him apart. And, the blood from Blue's ears covered the water as the coon stripped the hide away. It made me feel big and strong as she made noises and expressions of horror at my stories but always seemed interested and attentive to the end.

"Mr. Wilson and Junebloom are Negro people, aren't they?"

"Yes, how'd you know?"

"I just thought they were. Your parents don't mind you hunting with Negro people?"

"I don't suppose they even know. But it wouldn't matter, they're the best friends I could have."

"Even me," she responded with a little chill in her voice.

I knew that it hadn't come out exactly right the instant I said it. "You know, Amy, they're a different kind of friend."

Amy grinned, "I know."

Amy squeezed my fingers between hers. Her hand had a little twitch which always meant she was meditating about something at hand, "You know, maybe someday I could go hunting with you, as long as my parents didn't know that Negroes were along."

"You mean Mr. Wilson and Junebloom?"

"Well, my parents don't believe that blacks and whites should mix."

"I sure do like Mr. Wilson and Junebloom a lot, almost like kin folks."

"Sure, I know, I'm just telling you."

"I'd like that too. You'd like Blue and Sam. They'd like you too. And I'd like for you to meet my friends, especially Albert. He's almost like my own dad. But, I don't call him dad, I call him Albert. That's what he said to call him."

"Okay, Bud, it's a done deal. One night I'll go hunting with you and you can come to my house for a picnic down at my beach house. I want you to meet my parents."

A chill went through me at the prospects of meeting someone's parents.

Chapter #2
AMY'S WORLD

Our basic instincts and inclinations must still be appended to the genetic evolution that carried man across the ages where from the beginning of mankind he was a hunter and gatherer and the strength of these two qualities determined who would survive and who would not. Today, it seems that these traits are not so very important, as few have to hunt, fish or gather for survival. However, these characteristics still seem to be dominant in most of us even though the importance of hunting, fishing and gathering has been supplanted by electronics, automation and technical skills.

Just the same, most males and some females, find themselves regularly departing from the boring repetition of modern pursuits to replenish the spirit by employing the arts and skills of the primitive wanderer.

Should we be so surprised at a phenomenon as this, considering that man has rehearsed, refined and fine tuned this life style for millions of years while it's only been a few generations that he has had to perfect the technical skills of modern innovation.

I suppose that a logic of this sort could be used to justify a vocational agriculture class in a school in the middle of a town as big as Tampa, Florida. And also, why most of the boys in school took the class and why it was one of the few classes that I cared much for. That's right, I can't think of a lad in that class that lived on a farm.

Ag class was the last class before lunch and I was settling down at my desk, preparing for a lecture on watermelon blight or blossomend rot on tomatoes or something when I heard a whisper at the doorway.

"Psst, Bud".

I looked around and saw Amy standing half hidden behind the door motioning for me to come over. She handed me a note and headed down the hall. "I'll be late for class," she called over her shoulder as she left.

I went back to my seat and laid the note flat in my text book so it could be read while I was appearing to be reading the textbook.

In her neat and correct hand writing,
My Dear Bud,
I'll meet you in the patio at lunchtime at our usual place. I've got something to tell you. If you have enough money get me one of those things you eat for lunch. Bet I beat you.
Your Amy

This was the first time Amy had something so important that she couldn't wait until after school. But I guess I really wasn't so very surprised because Amy seemed to always have something important to talk about. Sometimes I think it was her leash.

The lunch bell rang and I shot out of class like a bullet. I went out the back door which went through the shop and out into the parking lot and down to the street where everyday at lunch time a street vendor would have his bicycle parked against the curb. It was retro-fitted with a square box and lid for holding deviled crab sticks which were prepared just that day and were still hot and steamy when he lifted the lid to retrieve an order.

"Hi, Bud." "You in a hurry today?"

"Give me two this time," I said.

"Hungry too?"

He cradled the crab sticks in a napkin and handed them to me. Then he handed me a bottle of hot sauce so that I could sprinkle them well with the fiery red mixture. It never occurred to me that Amy may find these a bit hot.

Amy was sitting on the bench watching me approach, "See, I told you I would get here first."

Of course she did. I had to walk two blocks after the bell rang. So what, I never made an issue of her little inconsistences.

"Oh good, you got cokes."

"Yes, I'll trade you a coke for one of those things."

"Here, take the one on top. Be careful, it may be hot."

She slipped it out of my hand, "No, doesn't feel hot at all. What is it?"

"Deviled crab stick."

"Yuck, doesn't sound so good."

"I like them just fine."

She took a bite from the end of the crab stick, trying not to get to much on the first bite. I had let the hot sauce run to the end as I was carrying it from the vendor, "Gosh, Bud, hand me the coke quick. This thing is awful and hot."

"Here, you eat it," and she handed it back to me.

I felt a little more than dejected, thinking that finally I was going to share something with Amy that was uniquely me.

"Don't you want it?"

"No, you can have it. I'll get something after awhile. You eat and I'll talk."

"Now listen," Amy said, and scooted over close to me like a great secret was about to be shared, "My parents aren't having any friends over or parties this weekend, and they said that I could invite some friends over for a party by the lake. We could swim for a while and have hot dogs and watermelon. " And," she drug out the and for emphasis, "I told my parents about you and they want to meet you."

Amy was holding my hand and I guess it must have started feeling a little clammy, "Don't you want to have a party?"

"Yeah, I do, but meeting your parents and all of your friends makes me a little scared."

"Oh you scaredy cat. It's our party, yours and mine, so we'll just have mom and dad there. If they get bored they'll go to the house and we can go swimming by ourselves."

"Is this Saturday night okay?"

In just an instant, less than the time it takes light to shine across the room, all of these thoughts flashed through my mind - Did I fix the hole in my bathing suit - should I walk to Amy's house or drive my cutdown - if I left my cutdown parked around the corner would anyone know - should I take money to help pay for the food - do rich people talk like everyone else?

Although Amy's parents weren't rich, they were very well-off, much better off than the environment that I was accustomed to and the thought of going there for a party left me chilled and awkward like a fish on dry ground.

"Now, Bud," Amy said drawing out the "now". "We made a deal. Are you going to back out?"

"No," I blurted out, surprising myself with my spontaneity.

Amy turned until she was facing me. She took her free hand and laid it over the top of mine so that my hand was firmly clasped between hers, "You know what? Sometimes I don't think you like me. Do you?"

I would never have had the nerve to ask a question like that in a hundred years, but it seemed to come as freely from Amy as reciting a verse.

"Yes."

"How much?"

"Oh, Amy, it's not that I don't like you. I like you a whole lot. It's just that your so rich and I'm so poor. Don't you see? I've never been to a rich persons party."

"Bud Olson!!, I am not rich and don't ever call me rich again," her voice was demanding, her fists were firmly planted on her hips.

"A lot richer than me."

"Well, maybe a little, but that's not what's important. Being richer doesn't make you better, and it doesn't make you bad. Besides, if being richer made anybody better, why would I want you at my party more than anybody else that I know?"

"Well, I hadn't thought of it that way. Do you really want me there more than anybody?"

"Yes I do, Bud Olson, and don't you forget it. I promise, I will always be there to make you feel comfortable."

Amy had successfully eliminated any option I may have used to beg out of the party, but I don't know that I was feeling much more confident.

"Since you put it that way, how can I say no?"

Chapter #3
BEING RICH DOESN'T MAKE YOU BAD

The dreaded night of Amy's party finally arrived. I was rummaging around my room looking for the most appropriate clothes to wear to the party. It never occurred to me to ask about dress. Should I wear regular slacks and take my bathing suit or just wear the bathing suit? After much agonizing deliberation I decided to wear my bathing suit under my slacks. I found that I still had a clean tee shirt in my drawer. That was enough to finish my attire.

"Bud," my stepmother called from down stairs, "Amy's on the phone.

I descended down the stairs in two leaps and picked up the phone from the counter, "Hi, Amy."

"Hi Bud, I wanted to call you before the party so that you wouldn't be surprised. Mother thought that I should have some other friends over for our first party. I hope you don't mind. I just invited two."

"It's OK," I replied.

So I replied. But it was in no way OK but far to long done to do anything about it. I tried to hide my apprehension but as always Amy saw right through my charade. Apparently I had not been socialized adequately enough at this point to be a convincing actor.

"Oh, Bud, I'm sorry, It's just that mother didn't think at my age I should be having swimming parties for just two people. After she knows you I'm sure she'll change her mind. Besides, when we go hunting I'll meet some of your friends."

I parked my cutdown just before the last curve to Amy's house and walked the remaining quarter mile or so. As I walked the apprehension built and I wondered why I didn't just turn and go the other way, toward surroundings and people that I would be at ease with.

Their house seemed immense and costly. Like most Florida houses, it was built low to the ground and gave an appearance of being long. Great Live Oak trees spread massive limbs covered with hanging Spanish moss to shade nearly the whole roof top. A concrete sidewalk divided a manicured lawn and led up to three wide shallow steps. I ascended, one after the other, methodically acknowledging each one. I walked the fifteen or so feet across the covered porch until I stood in front of a large, white door that was closed. "Why is the door closed on such a warm evening?" I asked myself. It never occurred that some people had airconditioning. There I saw it, a button with a brass plaque over it that said "The Brooks". I pushed it.

From the inside I heard, "I'll get it, Mom," and the door swung open. She was the prettiest, brightest, happiest looking thing I had ever seen. White shorts, red belt, white blouse with ruffles trimmed in red hanging from her shoulders. She even had on a tiny tinge of red lipstick and a touch of red on her cheeks. She reminded me of a little girl who was all made up for a party. It made me feel like I was at the wrong place.

"Hi, why are you staring at me?"

I hadn't realized that I was and when I did I couldn't think of anything to say.

"I know, you can't talk again. Well, do you think that what I am starts with U, a P, or a B.

"B".

"Okay, you've said the magic letter, come on in."

Amy closed the door behind me. The interior of the house was spacious. I was standing in the entry way. To the left was a large living room which looked as if it were only for looks. Straight ahead was an activity room or possibly it was a social room because it seemed to have comfortable furnishings. Beyond it was glass doors opening onto a beautifully decorated patio with hibiscus and holly shrubs growing around its perimeter. Beyond was a beach, seemingly carved out of a tropical paradise. Beyond, a quiet lake. To one side of the beach, built on pilings, so that nearly all of it would be over the lake, was a beach house. The beach house was mostly open. Screen windows let everything in and out but the bugs. It had a long bar-type serving counter with stools, a refrigerator and small grill. At least half of the lake house was porch whose floor was only a few inches above the water. I couldn't see how anybody in the whole world could have enough money to have a place like this. I knew I was in the wrong place. I wished I was back at Stiekies with Albert.

"Mom," Amy called out, "Bud is here."

Oh god, couldn't this have waited a little while, at least until I had a chance to see if I could talk.

Amy grabbed my hand and dragged me off into a kitchen area that looked so clean and white that I assumed that it also was only for show.

Mrs. Brooks turned around from her busy work. She didn't look all that rich. I checked her over for big diamonds and jewelry and stuff, but she didn't seem to be wearing any. She did have a look of correctness, but pleasant.

"So you're Bud? Amy's been anxious for me to meet you."

Instinctively and stupidly, I stuck out my hand. Realizing that that might not be appropriate I immediately let it fall to my side.

"Oh, it's OK to shake a women's hand," Mrs. Brooks said, "Usually you let the lady extend hers first." She raised her hand and we shook. How much she was like Amy, never at a loss for the right thing to say to recover my fumbles.

"Ya'll go out to the patio," she continued. "I'll bring you some cokes."

We sat on the patio steps looking out toward to lake, "Where's the rest of the party?" I asked.

"They'll be along in a minute. I wanted you to be first so that you could meet mother. Besides, I only invited two."

The door bell rang, "C'mon to the door with me and I'll introduce you as they get here."

Amy opened the door, a boy and a girl standing together.

"You came together," Amy said as a greeting.

"I rode over with Ronney. He has his own car."

We were introduced. I knew Ronney Harper. He was a senior, a jock, well off family, had his own car, didn't ride the school bus. He didn't know me.

Peggy Waylan - nice friendly girl, some freckles, brown hair, Amy's age, Amy's bosom buddy forever. No secrets.

Amy closed the door and gathered us all up in a herding motion and began directing us towards the lake. "Let's go down to the lake house. Mother said she would bring down hamburgers after a while."

You could jump right off of the lake house porch into the lake and climb up a short ladder to get out. We swam a few minutes until Mrs. Brooks came onto the porch carrying a large tray of hamburgers and things.

"Come get it while the hamburgers are hot," she called, "There's ice cream for later."

We were more or less finished eating, Amy and Peggy were talking like long lost friends. Ronney and I weren't saying much.

Finally he broke the silence, "You out for any sports?"

"No, I'm not much in to sports. I hunt my dogs on weekends and work some."

"Ought to go out for football or something, everybody does."

"I thought about it. But if I did my dogs wouldn't get to hunt and Albert needs me to work some on weekends."

"Well, If you decide to, I could help you get on the team."

I felt uncomfortable with Ronney. It seemed that what he said wasn't at all what he meant, as though he was looking down at me, trying to be nice to a poor, unfortunate person. Condescending, so to speak. Not only that, but he wanted to put me in my place so that I would not contest his superiority.

"Oh, by the way, Amy," Ronney went on, "Did you see that cutup junker parked down by the curve?"

I cringed at the subject and knew that Ronney was going to make fun. He had probably guessed who it belonged to.

"No, I didn't," Amy said, "What did it look like?"

Ronney went on to describe my cutdown, right down to the boards that made the seat. He must have deducted that it was mine and was ready to have fun at my expense. If there had been a hole in the bottom of the lake I would have swam through it on my way to China.

"Oh, that must be Bud's hunting truck," Amy said looking quizzically at me. "Did you park it way back there and walk?"

My expression was apparently enough of an answer.

"I wish you had driven it up, I've heard so much about it, I would like to see it."

She pulled me over close and cupped her hand over my ear and whispered, "Maybe after everyone leaves we can take a ride, mother might like to go."

Amy didn't slow down, "Guess what, Bud bought his hunting truck with money he earned all by himself and remade it to carry his dogs. He says it goes through the swamps real good."

Amy was trying, but I was only feeling a little better. The only thing that would have made me feel good was to be somewhere else. Telling her about my cutdown in private seemed to make me proud but now it sounded ugly and dumb.

Ronney knew he was being put down. It was also obvious that he was attracted to Amy and was disturbed that she appeared to be taking my side. He no doubt was used to being the center of attention and wasn't likely to forget the embarrassment.

"I can believe that," he said in a superior tone. "Why'd you leave it parked down there? Hiding it?"

Now my feet really wanted to get up and get out. What would Amy ever see in me with nothing to drive but an old truck?

Mrs. Brooks came in with the ice cream and sat it on the table, "If you want more, just holler."

The rest of the agonizingly long evening was spent listening to Amy and Peggy talking incessantly and Ronney making remarks calculated to make him look good in Amy's eyes and me look out of place. On that I would have agreed. Besides, he had all of the things that a girl would be interested in. All I had was a cut down truck, two hounds and four friends. At this point I was to intimidated to know for sure that Amy was still a friend.

Not long after sundown I saw Amy whispering something in Peggy's ear. I assumed it was about me. But, a few minutes later Peggy was explaining to Ronney that her mother had told her to be home early and could he take her home now.

Amy walked them to the door, "Thanks for coming over. Come back sometime."

"Maybe I'll be back after I drop Peggy off," Ronney said.

As soon as the door was closed, Amy went into the kitchen to talk to her mother. Her tone was too low for me to hear. When she came back out to the patio she was grinning a sheepish little smirk, "Mom and I want to take a ride in your famous hunting truck and cool off. Would that be alright? Too bad if Ronney misses us. Let's walk up and get it now."

"Mom, we're going to get the truck, pick you up in a minute."

Amy moved over close as we walked towards the cutdown. She slid her hand into mine and locked her fingers into my fingers. Our arms made a swinging motion as we walked down the road. I began to feel happy again as I usually did when we were alone together. Everything seemed to be perfect now.

There was a brightness over the black outline of the cypress swamp straight ahead of our walk. A full moon was about to emerge. There were a few long slender clouds above it. The reflected brightness coming from them made the sky behind all the more black. There was an occasional break in the otherwise dense trees and eerie white light would shine through.

Amy pulled my hand back, "Let's walk slow. Maybe if we go slow enough the moon will be all the way up when we get to the truck. It's nice that we don't always have to talk."

The moon was up full when we got to the there. It was fully illuminated.

I reached under the seat and found an old rag that I used for checking the oil and cleaning the headlights. I wiped the evening dew from the seats.

"Amy, you're dressed up awfully nice. Are you sure you want to take a ride?"

She slid into the seat closer than I had expected her to. I pulled the knob that I had replaced the ignition switch with. I pushed the button I had mounted on the dash for the starter. It started instantly. I pulled the next knob and the lights came on. Although they had never failed me, I felt a sense of relief as we pulled up onto the road to pick up Amy's mother.

Mrs. Brooks was standing at the edge of the road waiting for us. A light spread was draped over her arm. "So this is it," she said as I pulled away from the house. "Do you call it any thing special?"

"I just call it my cutdown."

"I think it's so clever how you guy's can make just about anything into a vehicle. I brought a blanket along in case it gets cool or damp. Amy, I bet you didn't know that I know a lot about these things. Your dad picked me up in a cutdown a lot like this on our first date. We went rabbit hunting, of all things." Then her voice changed to shallow and melancholy, "Oh, how I miss those days. I'd trade my Cadillac in an instant to just have that old truck to park in the yard. I'd sit on the porch and look at it and relive every minute."

Amy reached over and took her mothers hand, "I love you, Mom. Some day I want you to tell me all about it, when you and dad were young."

It was at that moment I remembered what Amy had said, "Being rich doesn't make you bad."

"Thank you Bud, that was such a nice ride. What if I fix us all some hot chocolate before we call it quits?

I was smart enough to know that that meant staying late was not on the agenda.

Amy walked me out to the cutdown, "Thanks for a nice evening. I know you didn't like it at first, but I hope it ended well." She pulled my head over, I thought she was going to whisper in my ear, but instead placed a light kiss on my cheek, "Someday I'll do better."

She waved. I watched her until the front door was closed. My heart was beating like a stamp mill. Oh, was I in love.

Another boy and girl ascend to another plateau.

Is it LOVE?

What fool would even try to define or quantify those emotions that cause the body and soul to malfunction and run out of control.

One could raise a case for biology, sighting the hormonal secretions of various glands.

Another would surely reference the spiritual unity of the inner soul.

And still another would point up the divine gift of the creator when he ordained the oneness of Adam and Eve.

But me, I'll not take sides in the matter. Nor do I even need to. Come with me and journey back in time to when that one person, the first person that we felt our life would end without, said, "I feel that way too."

It defies rational debate.

Chapter #4
A SPECIAL PLACE

I don't need to go into a lot of dialogue describing the next few months. Every man and woman who has experienced the wonder of first love as a boy and girl can relive each feeling and sensation at any moment the lights are low, the fragrance soft and the air quiet.

Why not do it now? No reason not to. Eyes closed, softly - quiet. The sight of the person first appears - see her, see him? Now a hand reaches out - you take it in your hand, feel it? Something special. Is it electricity? Is it radiance? Or magic? They're closer to you now, see the sparkle in their eyes, smell the fragrance of their hair. An arm goes under your arm, a hand against your back draws you close, your heart beat accelerates - nothing in the world is so important as this moment.

That's about how it was as Amy and I began to learn about each other. The heretofore shyness gradually melting away, giving license to more personal questions, sharing of secrets and assuming duality.

Do I remember? Absolutely. I feel great sorrow for anyone who doesn't.

It became automatic that Amy and I would meet in the halls between classes, our affection was obvious, our handclasp became a trademark, or maybe a hallmark. It seemed that nothing could challenge the thrill I felt when Amy popped out of the school door to meet me at our bench at the far corner of the patio, beneath the arms of a loving live oak tree, where everyday for the whole school year we shared lunch and Amy chattered away about the events so far and the plans for the rest of the day.

It was only a matter of time until the little time we had together at school and the short trip home from school on the bus was not near enough to satisfy my need to be with her and apparently not for her either. I found myself getting off of the bus at Amy's stop and walking her home and then walking the mile or so from there to my home. In a couple of weeks I got smart and began to drive my cutdown to the bus stop and cut about three miles off of my daily walk.

Mrs. Brooks was usually sitting in the porch swing when we arrived at the front walk. I greeted her and she responded as though she was glad to see me.

On the days that Mrs. Brooks was away we sat in the swing together. We sat close in the center, our school books on either side. I was tall enough that Amy could sit close and I could lay my arm on the back of the swing and slowly let it slide down to her shoulders. I did it as though not to be presumptuous, but I know she expected it and would have insisted that it be so.

Only the coldest days of December and January kept us from swinging together.

It was early spring now, maybe March or early April, a little breeze was blowing, not much, just enough to cause a tingle in our cheeks, and just enough to give justification for sitting so close. I had laid my jacket over our legs, we were holding hands under it. Amy's fingers began to twitch and her grasp became tighter as it always did just before a new and delicate subject was about to be broached.

"Bud," Amy looked at me with a great deal of thoughtfulness in her demeanor, "Do we really share all of our secrets?"

"I don't know? I share most of mine."

"But not all, you mean."

"I don't guess so. Do you?"

"Well, I know there's personal things like, well," she paused and thought a minute as if debating with herself how personal we should be, "You know, why you never talk about your dad and why you live with your stepmother instead of your real mother - but other things." She paused again and seemed to be gathering up confidence, "Do you have a secret place?"

"You mean a secret place to hide things?"

"No, you know, a secret place to go be alone, like a place where nobody can find you and you can hide for a while."

"No, not really a special place. I can do that just about any place I go hunting.

"Not even one special place?"

I thought a minute. I did have a special place, but it might sound foolish.

"Well, I guess I do have one special place, it's where Blue and me buried Lee. You remember me telling you about Lee."

"Go on, tell me about it. What makes it special?"

"Mostly it's special because I loved Lee so much. He was special. When he died Blue and me buried him next to a little cypress tree. We made a mound out of the dirt so that we could sit on the mound and talk about hunting and make believe Lee could hear us. Little Sam sits there with us, but he doesn't know what it's all about."

"Do you really think Lee knows you're there?"

"No, he doesn't know. I was a lot younger then. I like to sit there just the same, it makes me remember all the good hunting we had together and what a good friend he was."

"Bud," Amy said reverently, "could I sit there with you and Blue and Little Sam some time?"

"Sure, the tree has grown a lot since then, it's fairly comfortable to lean against and you can watch the sun set down across the lake."

"Can we sit there real soon?"

"Promise you won't laugh, it's real solemn to Blue and me."

"I promise. You can tell me all about Lee and I'll be real solemn too and we can watch the sun go down together.

A couple of minutes passed as I pondered Amy's questions about having secret places. Then I asked, "Do you have a secret place?"

"Yes."

"You have a big house and another house down by the lake. Why do you need a secret place?"

"I found this place when Peggy and I played with our dolls. We made believe we were hiding from Indians and robbers. I still go there sometimes just to be alone. I think it's okay to be alone sometimes, don't you?"

"Does anybody else know about it?"

"No. I bet Peggy doesn't even remember where it is."

"Then, are you going to take me there sometime?"

"Of course, silly, that's why I'm telling you about it, because we have to share our secrets. Let's go now."

Amy jumped up from the swing and pulled me along. "It's not very far, just a few rows over into the orange grove where Dad thought the trees were too old to cultivate anymore."

Amy led me through the sandy grove between several rows of trees and to a dense clump of uncared for trees whose limbs had grown down to the ground and entwined giving the appearance of being absolutely impenetrable. When we reached the back side of the clump she motioned for us to kneel down and crawl, "Follow me on your hands and knees, you're going to be surprised."

I followed Amy through an opening in the limbs on the hidden side of the tree. Once inside I found that the whole clump was made by a single tree. Inside the tree had formed a large umbrella high enough to stand up and so dense around the edges that the light from the outside could hardly be seen.

"Boy, Amy, what a hideout. I would never have guessed this in a hundred years."

"Do you like it?"

"Yeah, it's swell."

"Then from now on it's our secret place. We can sneak out here whenever we want to be alone."

"Your mother doesn't worry when your not at home?"

"Oh, Bud, Mother has to let me be alone sometimes. Besides she thinks I'm safe when I'm with you."

"Bud, we've only got a few minutes before I have to go in." She took my hand and turned me around where I was facing her, she looked into my eyes, "Do you think it would be alright if we kissed once? Just a little kiss? I don't think I'm old enough for a big kiss yet."

As I remember, and I remember well, we didn't touch anywhere but lightly with our lips. A light peck. We kissed as though we were expecting an electrical shock. Even though our mouths were firmly closed and our eyes rigidly shut, I remember, as I always will remember, that no one could have been more wonderful than Amy.

She pulled her head back slightly, her blue eyes fixed on mine. Our lips came together again, gently, softly, lingering. Here am I, my lips are yours.

She reached my head and pulled it down to whisper in my ear, "This is our secret place, whatever we want to do or say in here will be our secret. Will that be our promise? Will you promise?"

"I promise."

"I promise too," Amy said sounding as if a she was making sacred vow.

"We've got to go now. You can leave from here and I'll walk back alone. See you in the morning."

It should have been no surprise to me that Amy would have been the first to suggest that our devotion be sanctified with a kiss. She was aware that I was much too bashful and insecure to suggest becoming this personal and probably knew that my insecurity would cause me to fear rejection. Amy, on the other hand, because of the consistency and security of a stable two parent home, could reference the interfacing of a male and female bond and as Amy always did, when she felt like something needed to be done she did it.

I always had two feelings about the poise and confidence that Amy had. One that her consistency abated my reoccurring doubts, but yet, she seemed so perfect, that I often felt inferior. I was sure I was. After all, I had never lived in a house with a mother and father. Certainly not a house where a man and women demonstrated affection. As a matter of fact, I always felt more like a guest than a resident where ever I lived and it haunted me when I wasn't with Amy, that surely sometime in the future she would lose interest in me because she brought so much to our relationship and I brought so little.

I spent the next few days agonizing over the right or wrong of kissing each other. I'm sure that Amy didn't, she would have thought it over before hand and when she decided that it was time to kiss there would be nothing left to decide.

Amy seemed to know this. She spent hours with her mother talking. I expect that I was often the topic and more understood than I realized. How much would I know if I had someone to talk to?

Friday night, while we're hunting, I'll tell them that I'm in love with Amy. Maybe they can help me understand.

Chapter #5
THE LIGHT'S ON

It seemed so perfect, Amy had it worked out to a tee, I hardly ever had to think. We had agreed that Friday night was for me to hunt and be with my friends and for her to be with her mother or busy about school things. Saturday night was our night, without fail.

Every Saturday afternoon when I had finished at Albert's I showered and made tracks for Amy's. Sometimes we would swim. Sometimes Mrs. Brooks would have supper on the table and make a big deal about me eating with her and Amy. She had learned my favorite dishes, especially pork chops and white rice.

Amy would always meet me at the door or be sitting in the swing when I arrived. It made me feel important that someone never failed to be anxiously waiting. I kept expecting that one day she wouldn't be there. It took many times before I finally accepted that Amy and her mother were truly sincere.

Amy would take my hand and lead me through the door, "Mom, Bud's here."

"Hi, Bud," Mrs. Brooks would say. Have fun hunting last night?"

"Bud, Mom has fixed supper for us. Hope you haven't eaten yet."

And you could bet I hadn't.

After supper, Mrs. Brooks and Amy would put away the dishes together and then Mrs. Brooks would disappear into another part of the house. Amy and I would always walk down to the lake house and sit on the porch. We would tell each other of the many events that took place during the long period that we were apart. Twenty hours.

If the water was warm we would swim and laugh at the clumsy pond birds that flew up in fright or make believe that alligators were swimming after us.

We would sit for hours on the cushioned couch and whisper, muffling our voices below the soft sounds of the aquatic creatures, making jest of the secrets of the tree frog and making "Who" jokes about the eerie call of the night owl. We quietly laughed and teased and let our bodies innocently cherish the excitement of touching.

Slowly, gradually, one touch at a time, each time we were together, we became more familiar and close. Amy's closeness became more and more a need. As we sat together, she would lean firmly against me proving the oneness, the mutual need, the consent. Our kisses were longer, our lips lingered softly on each others, experimenting, exploring, sharing our emotions as young love does.

After a while I began to notice that about midnight a light would come on at the porch. After a few minutes Amy would begin to close down our night and I would go home. One night when it came on I said, "Amy, the lights on."

"Oh, you noticed it, too."

"I've noticed it several nights, what's it about?"

"Well, since it's not a secret any more I might as well tell you. It's mom's way of letting me know that it's time to come in."

"You mean, like a curfew or something?"

"Well, sort of, but not exactly. It's different from a curfew because we agreed on when she should turn it on."

"You mean that you were the one who decided."

"Well, yes and no. What we did was, Mom told me what she thought and then let me decide. That's how we do everything."

"I think that's funny. If Mrs. Brooks is going to let you decide, then why doesn't she just let you come in when your ready."

"Because she loves me."

"Amy, I just don't understand that."

"Oh Bud, don't your parents have rules for you to go by?"

"No, none that I know of. Besides, I probably wouldn't pay any attention to them anyway."

"You mean you wouldn't obey your parents?"

Seeds of My Field

"Well, I don't know. They're never around to make rules for me, so I don't know."

"Well, your stepmother is there, isn't she?"

"Yeah, she is, but what right has she got telling me what to do. You can't just go up to somebody else's kid and say, "Now I'm the boss.""

"But what if you loved them and they loved you?"

"Well, I hadn't really thought about that."

"Don't you love your real mother?"

"Sure I do. But she doesn't have enough money for me to live with her."

"How about your dad?"

"I don't know. It would be hard for me to tell if he loved me and I don't know whether I love him or not."

"I guess that's why you love your silly ole dogs so much."

"You know Bud, I have never thought about loving my parents before. I think it would be very lonesome if I didn't love my parents and they love me. I would be so sad. I love my mom so much that I would never let her down. Nor would she let me down."

"Yeah, it must be nice to love somebody that much."

We stared out across the water. Our moods had turned to melancholy. I had slumped down into the couch as my body posture seemed to mimic my mood. I had become sad, a little confused as to why.

Amy laid her head on my shoulder and turned it so that she could talk in low whispers. Her hand was holding mine, by the fingers. There was a slight nervous jerking as she squeezed, "Bud, do you sometimes wonder if anybody loves you?"

"Sometimes. Except I'm sure Mom does. I'm sure she would want me home if she had the money. And I've got Albert and Mr. Wilson. I paused for a few minutes, not certain if I should go on or even if I would be rebuked if I said what was on my mind. I whispered almost unaudibly, "You said you did."

"And I do. Can you say that you love me?"

"I love you more than anybody."

Amy abruptly raised up to a straight position and turned to look directly at me, "You know what Bud? I'm going to tell Mom that she can love you too. She would like that very much. Is it alright, can I tell her?"

"Oh, Amy, I don't know. It might be embarrassing for her and besides, she probably won't want to," I said thinking more of protecting my fragile ego.

"You just don't know my Mom."

Chapter #6
LOVE DEFINED

"Hey, Bud," Albert let out in a surprising yell in an effort to emphasize my mental distance, "What's going on in your world? You've been all glazed over for the last few weeks."

"Yeah, I've been noticing the same thing," Junior said as he walked along beside me and laid a hand on my shoulder.

I guess tonight would be the night that I would get it off my shoulders and share my new experience with my best friends. Why not? The moon was still on the other side of the world and the night was as black as coal. The coons weren't likely to feed until dawn and Junebloom was picking up wood like he had a fire on his mind, and probably a cigarette.

"Well, let's help Junebloom get a fire going and I'll tell what's going on. I kinda need somebody to talk to, anyway."

In no time Junebloom had found enough liter'd wood to get a nice, pitchy fire dancing into the dark sky.

"Well, okay Bud, let's hear what you've got on your mind. What have you been up to that's got your tongue?" Albert questioned looking at me first and then the rest.

"I'm in love."

Albert jumped to his feet and threw his hands into the air as though he was scattering dry leaves into the wind. "Well, of course. Am I so damned old that I can't recognize a boy in love anymore?"

"God Almighty," he went on, "Bud, that's great news. Hurry up, tell us who with."

"Amy Brooks."

"What Amy Brooks?" Albert asked.

"She lives over on Bonita Lake road."

Albert looked a little quizzical as he looked straight back into my face, "You mean you're in love with Madge and Eddy Brooks' daughter. Isn't she just a baby yet?"

"Sixteen."

"More years passed than I thought," Albert went on. "How come you picked such a rich girl?"

"I don't know, guess I didn't know she was so rich. Do you know her parents?"

"Sure, everybody in these parts do."

Albert remained standing at the fire's edge, the yellow flame from the pine wood caused his face to look more dark and brownish than usual.

Albert kept the floor, "Well, what do you guys think about Bud being in love? Ever been in love, Junior?"

"No, not me, I'm a hunter. Girls don't usually get attracted to hunters, and if they do, they usually cause him a lot of grief. I don't need no women. Mom said as long as I stayed home and helped her and dad, she'd keep my clothes in good shape and keep the food cooked up. Don't need no woman, not for a while, least ways. Besides, got a draft notice the other day, probably heading for Korea before long. Mon'l have to get along without me for awhile. Maybe she'll need somebody to look in on her sometimes.

"I'd be glad to, Junior, you know I would," I said.

"Cause you like Moms watermelon jelly."

Junior looked over at me with a little smirk on his face that was a little cynical and yet approving, "That young girl that comes in to the station with the Brook's, if that's Amy, I never seen no prettier girl in these parts. I might could fall in love too if one that pretty came along."

"Well, Junebloom," Albert gestured toward Junebloom. Junebloom was staring listly into the fire." What do you think about it?"

Junebloom drug a stick out of the fire and was lighting his cigarette, "Well, Sa, I don kno much bout luv, cep un ting, I get's in luv evur satdy night an cant member hu name sundy mon. I don tink I'd call dat luv. Not da real ting. Not many black boys gets to know da real ting. You know, ya goes to da bar wit jor money and drinks it up wit a women and tomar da both gone. Dats about all fo a black boy. Couldn't ford feed un if'n I had un, besides, who'd wanna liv in dat shack o mine.

I knew that next it would be Mr. Wilson's turn. I automatically looked over toward him. His snow white beard was now yellowed by the smokey, brownish-yellow flame dancing up from the pitchy pine wood. He looked into the fire, not looking up to see if he had the attention of the audience for he knew from experience how the system worked. There was a little sadness evident in his voice, a melancholy that revealed a hurting inside. He had listened deeply to the hopeless plight of Junebloom, knew that it was the plight of many young black men, and felt the empty acceptance in his voice. I wanted him to be happy and excited about my love, but as usual, there was an agenda buried deep in Mr. Wilson's bosom, burning coals of sadness that continually burned away at his soul but tempered by a gray rain cloud that never allow them to ignite and rage out of control. He laid his big hand on to Junebloom's leg like a gentle father would as an unspoken signal that his attention was required. He never looked from the fire, "Junebloom's rite as rain. Black boys mostly don't never get true luv cause da tink da ain't good nuf. Da been told to many yers, da only gets satdy nite. Da don nevur meet da good womans. God's got da good woman fo evur good man. I's one dim lucky uns, s'pose. I gots da good woman. Mighty good. Didun fin er at no bar, she's wukin in da feel wid us mens. I try make out like da yung buck. She dun say I wasteing my time wid er, gonna get a good man at da church, don need no trouble maker have ta support."

"I's down at da church da nex sundy. Fins da Lawd an a good woman all same day. Sings da good ol songs. Sounds mighty like da angel singin. Lawd, she don take no crap offin nobody but she stay right dar wid er man. She big'n stout, knows jus what I needs when I coms home nights. God knows I'd be lomesom black man wid out er. Yessir, I's a mighty lucky Moses. When I dies, she'll be rit dar by my side. Man don min gettin ol if'n he's gots a good woman t'home.

No sa, ain't gonna fin no good woman at da bar. How's a man gonna know da good woman if evur satdy nite he dun drunk on is face? God knows, black folks gots to pull'm selves up. Ain't nevur gonna rid dis curse."

We all stared into the fire for a moment, we all sensed the pain in Mr. Wilson's heart as he seemed to feel the pain of every black boy. I felt sorry for Mr. Wilson, I guess we all did. He wanted so much to rid the stain of the blackman's skin, but anything he would do would just cause more grief and it ate his guts like a cancer.

"How about you," Junior asked Albert, What do you think about love and getting a good woman?"

Albert meditated a little while, I don't think he really wanted to respond, he reacted like a man who had spent most of his life avoiding a direct confrontation with the subject and was content to leave it lay. I had never seen Albert and Mrs. Newsom show any affection toward each other, but then, I only assumed that older people didn't have any affection and was not surprised.

Mr. Wilson, who hadn't taken his eyes from the fire suddenly looked at Albert, as if expecting, almost demanding that Albert respond.

"Well, you know what? I've never really given love much thought before," Albert said in a matter of fact tone. "I don't think being in love was all that damn important when I got married. When you got about the right age you just kinda looked around and if you found a girl that was attracted to you, you jus got things started. Being in love, as I remember it, was kinda like keeping house and having babies and washing clothes. I don't think you had to be so all fired in love as much as you just needed a woman to do the things a woman does. That's about how it is at my place. Don't think I'd want to ask Mrs. Newsom about love. I just work most of the time, we adopted those two girls so's she'd have something to do and that's about it. I believe I got a good woman, but I'd use a different measuring stick than Moses.

"Do you know Amy's folks, Albert," I asked?

"Oh, sure, I expect about everybody around here does. So you're going with their daughter. Bet that girls just like her mom. I'll tell you about her Mom and I bet's it's just like your girl, Amy. Ole Eddy and Madge moved down here from up north somewhere. Bought a piece of ground and decided to raise chickens. Mostly they sold eggs but some pullets. They had great pullets, real pretty, guess that's why your Amys so pretty."

"Amy's no pullet," I shot back.

"Just funnin, Bud."

"Then Ed decided that all that chicken manure ought to be good for something so they started planting orange groves. That's how I got to knowin them. Bought their trees from me. Madge worked right along with Ol Eddy like a man. We all wondered why such a pretty thing should have to work so hard. Might near over did it. She just about pulled her guts out lifting all that heavy farm equipment. Doctor made her quit. Almost to late."

"They were making good things happen on that place and was making money hand over fist. They decided that since things were going so good they might as well get a family started. The doctor said Madge had hurt her self to bad and having a baby might be to much for her body to stand. But, Madge knew Eddy wanted a family and when Madge decided that something ought to be done, she done it. Well, they had a baby alright, Madge died two times before they finely brought her around. Laid in the Tampa hospital for months in a coma before they brought her out. First two months, Eddy raised that baby. So guilty when Madge came around he wanted to kill himself - we wanted to kill him too. Madge just told him that baby was worth it all and he didn't need to feel bad. She'd just do it all over again if she had to. Course she couldn't, that was gonna be her last baby. But Ole Eddy, just never was the same from the guilt. Got to drinking a little, made sure he had a lot of business out of town so's he wouldn't have to face Madge so much. Had a problem with drinking after that. Guess he wanted to cover up how bad he felt."

After a pause Albert continued,"Madge just took over. Always knew what to do to make things work. Always said the right thing to make a person feel good about themselves, nobody ever minded helping. Prettiest girl in these parts."

"Holy Cow, Albert, that sounds just like Amy. I bet that's why Amy and Mrs. Brooks are so close."

Mr. Wilson hadn't looked up from the fire in all this time. He was sitting on a large log, staring into the flame, sometimes stirring the coals a little with a stick he held in his right hand, aimlessly moving a red coal back and forth while gently stroking the head of his Black and Tan bitch, Ell. "Boy, you dun ask't our pinions so I's gonna tell ya da truth. God done made jus da right women fo eva man, jus like he done for Ol Adam in da gard'n. It's a smart man that takes da time ta fin'er. Maybe ya done did. Maybe not. Ain't no hurry. But lemme tell ya, da man dat goes on over an he still gots da women he's in luv wid, he's gonna leave a happy man."

One by one the dogs came in. Tired and wet from the heavy dew and somewhat subdued from the lack of even an old trail to follow. We jumped Mr. Wilson's dogs into their cage in the back of the GMC. Though usually they're reluctant to load until the last hours of night, this time, aware that the coons weren't going to cooperate, loaded without encouragement and promptly laid down in a curl to sleep on the way home.

Behind the cage, between it and the cab of the GMC, was a remaining space just large enough for Sam and Blue and me.

"Ready, Bud," Albert called out as he revved the engine and we pulled back onto the road leading out of the orange grove.

My mind drifted to Junior and then Junebloom, then Mr. Wilson and Albert. They really didn't seem to understand how I felt about Amy and her about me. It was different how we felt. Was I the only one who ever felt this kind of love? It didn't seem like they ever loved at all. I felt sorry for them at first, then realized that maybe Mr. Wilson was right and I had found the "good woman." I was disappointed in their responses and confused all at the same time. I thought of Amy, I wanted to be close to her.

Chapter #7

I decided not to spend a great deal of time deliberating on the topic of love that I had had the night before with Albert and my hunting partners. Each had such a differing point of view that even as a composite they would have had no practical or logical rationale. So, as the logic of a young lad runs, I laid the whole matter aside and decided to go on instinct.

It was Saturday, and as the events of every Saturday had found me for the last year or so, I was working in one of Albert's groves.

There was not too much to do to groves at this time of year, the fruit was already set waiting for a winter picking. We mostly cleaned, chopped out weeds, made sure excess water was drained away from the roots and made light applications of fertilizer.

Now that Albert had learned that I was going with the daughter of one of his wealthy peers he determined that in exchange for cleaning out, washing and servicing the GMC, I could drive it to Amy's on Saturday night. To most people the GMC would have been just another truck, but to me it was the best thing on wheels. I didn't, however, tell Albert that Mrs. Brooks insisted that I drive the cutdown periodically so we could continue to take those cool afternoon rides in the style she remembered from the days that her and Mr. Brooks were courting.

This evening I arrived at Amy's in the GMC. As I came to a stop at the front gate Amy waved from the swing and came out to the gate to meet me.

"Hope your Mom didn't want to go for a ride tonight," I said glancing at the GMC.

"Nope, I've got another idea. Want to hear it?" Amy replied with a rather curious quirk in her voice.

"Well, tell me. I'm always curious."

"Okay."

Amy led me to the swing and sat where we would be close. She held my hand in hers and was raising them up and down hitting my thigh like someone trying to drive a nail in it. "Okay, I'll tell you. Let's go to the movie."

"Really? "I responded, revealing a little surprise and a little concern at the same time. I've never asked your mother if we could go out by ourselves."

"Well, would you like to?" Amy asked.

"Yeah, I sure would if you don't mind going to town in the GMC. Albert doesn't care if I drive into town."

"Can you guess what Mom said when I said we would like to go. She said it was a great idea and since we always went riding in your cutdown that we could just take her car. And do you know what? She's already got supper on the table."

"Amy, great Mom."

Amy jumped from the swing pulling me after her. Mrs. Brooks was standing at the stove retrieving a plate of food when she saw us. "Hi, Bud, did Amy talk you into going to the show?"

"Mom," Amy responded, "It was by mutual agreement- wasn't it."

"Well, I sure want to go. Mrs. Brooks, Amy said that we were to take your car. Are you sure? it's a very expensive car."

"Oh, Bud, you know if I had a neat cutdown I'd let you take it, but the caddy's all I've got."

During supper Amy asked me about last night's hunting. I explained that there was no moon last night and most of the time the coons wouldn't come down to feed until early the next morning. I went on to tell how we built a fire and just talked a bit until the dogs came in and that was about it.

"What did you talk about?" Amy asked.

I was a little surprised that she asked. I wasn't really anxious to talk about our conservation since it was a little personal.

"Do you know what," I said in a serious, concerned tone, "I don't believe that any of them are happy unless they are hunting."

"My goodness, what did you talk about that made you feel that way?" Mrs. Brooks asked leaning into the table looking deeply into my eyes for insight into what I was thinking.

"It's kind of embarrassing to tell, but we were talking about love."

"Isn't that just like a bunch of men to get together around a camp fire and talk about love," Amy laughed.

"But do you know what? I don't think they even know what love is all about. They even seemed embarrassed to talk about it, except Mr. Wilson."

"Is Mr. Wilson your colored friend?" Mrs. Brooks asked.

I nodded in the affirmative and she continued, "Bud, there's a lot you still have to learn about love. I expect that each of your friends knows a lot about love but has a hard time dealing with it. Some men are afraid of love. It can hurt you very much if you love to much. Some people would rather never be truly in love and avoid the possibility of being let down or cheated. But I bet they have loved and life caused them to become tired and weary and they allowed the fire to go out. "Bud," I received a look of seriousness from Mrs. Brooks that was unusually deliberate," Love isn't a perpetual flame, if it isn't fed it soon burns out."

I must have looked up in shock as several moments passed before the conversation was continued.

"Love isn't a perpetual flame, if it isn't fed it soon goes out. Love isn't a perpetual flame, if it isn't fed it soon goes out. Love isn't a perpetual flame, if it isn't fed it soon goes out."

"That's it," I thought to myself, "That explains why Albert didn't want to talk about it and Mr. Wilson did. To Albert the flame was replaced with work and success, but to Mr. Wilson, his wife was all that there was and their flame would never die because they needed each other and their need fueled the flame. Junior wasn't going to take a chance on love because his love was hunting and Junebloom could never love because he believed that a black man wasn't worthy of love. And Mrs. Brooks seemed to speak as a person of insight.

"Come on, Bud, let's eat so we can get going. We haven't even decided which show to go to," Amy spoke out dragging me out of my trance. We'll decide on the way."

We no sooner finished supper than Amy jumped up to start clearing the table and help Mrs. Brooks with the dishes as she always did.

"No, not this time Amy, I'll have plenty of time after you're gone," Mrs. Brooks said as she motioned us out of the kitchen.

"Are you sure, Mom, I don't mind being a little late?"

"Out you go, you two and remember to be home by the time the porch light goes on."

Mrs. Brooks handed me the car keys and winked.

"Ya'll have a good time. This is your first date to town together without me along so don't get into any fights because I won't be there to referee," Mrs. Brooks joked.

"We won't fight, I promise," Amy laughed back.

"Thank you, Mrs. Brooks, if you would like to go with us it would be alright with me."

Amy grabbed her little purse and then took Mrs. Brooks by the arm and lightly kissed her on the cheek, "Love you, Mom."

As we went out the door Mrs. Brooks held her head turned slightly away from us to conceal the tear that forced it's entrance. For so many years she had prepared Amy for this day, the day that she would become a young women. Amy had been her life, her only life, all in life that had meaning. Now the moment had come, a lengthening of the tether, soon to be severed. Was she overwhelmed with joy or broken in fear and sorrow? A mother would know, I wouldn't.

Amy slid across the car seat and was next to me. As I drove she was dealing with the air conditioner controls and running the radio needle indicator back and forth across the dial searching for the right station. She finally leaned back against the seat, we were listening to the current top ten, "A white sport coat and a pink carnation, I'm in a mood blue mood. Once you told me long ago, to the prom with me we'd go, now you changed your mind it seems, some one else will hold your dreams. A White Sport Coat and a Pink Carnation, I'm in a mood blue mood."

Amy leaned forward and turned the radio down low, "Bud, could you wear a white sport coat and a pink carnation when we go to the prom?" There was a little silence. "Would you take anyone else?"

"No." I put my arm around her and pulled her close, "I guess if you didn't go, I wouldn't either."

"Good, I'll go."

We arrived at the theater along with everyone else in town. Equipped with popcorn and a large coke to share. We made our way to a seat that was as private as private could be had in a crowded theater.

It was the Wizard of Oz. I was doing pretty good until the Great Oz declared to Dorothy that he had no powers to send her back to Kansas. "I'll never see Auntie Em again," as Dorothy burst into tears.

"Bud, let me have your handkerchief. You mind if I cry, I can't help it."

Amy turned to take it at the most inopportune moment as a tear that I had been suppressing burst forth. "Oh, Bud, your crying too."

We made it through the movie, sliding low in our seats, leaning shoulder to shoulder, leaning head to head, un-consciously feeding each other popcorn.

I opened the car door for Amy, "Bud, let's stop at the Spinning Wheel before we go home. I'd like a shake, how about you?"

The Spinning Wheel was one of those wonderful places where a boy could take his girl and get prompt curb service. It was a simple system, if your car lights were on it meant you needed service, if they were off you were left along. The carhops were usually the popular girls in town, we all considered them special and lucky to have the job. I'm sure that their short-shorts, white go-go boots and other anatomical considerations played some part in the consensus.

Before long they knew all about you, down to the songs you liked on the jukebox. The jukebox was inside the restaurant and fed music to the parking lot via speakers on the roof. Your carhop took your selections to the jukebox and inserted the nickels for you. Six plays for a quarter.

If you stayed at the Spinning Wheel long enough you would probably see about everyone you knew. It wasn't far from the school and a lot of boys came there for lunch. But for most of us it was a special treat.

The carhop delivered our shakes in a few minutes. We leaned back against the seat and watched the other young couples come and go as some drove in for refreshments and others drove through to see who was there.

As usual, Elvis was singing in the background. Amy reached up and turned off the radio so we could listen to the jukebox, "Let's talk," Amy said breaking the silence.

"Okay, what about?"

"Guess what they want me to do at school."

I shrugged to show my ignorance.

"They want me to try out for cheer leader."

Immediately I thought of football games and Ronney Harper. I was jealous of Ronney already for no reason. No reason except that I knew that he would like to have Amy for his girl friend and with out me there he would be flirting with her all the time. I choked this thought back and responded with the first positive thought that came to mind, "Well, if you go out you'll get it for sure."

"I talked to Mom about it. She said that I would only be young once and if I passed everything up I'd regret it some day. I told her I would talk it over with you. If you don't want me to I just won't."

My insecurity screamed out to say no, but I couldn't, I respected Mrs. Brooks greatly and if she said do it then it was the right thing to do.

"You know what, Bud, we'll still have Saturday nights to ourselves and sometimes Sundays and if you continue to hunt Friday nights there won't be anything different."

She was right and I knew it. I must overcome this silly emotion.

"Well, if your Mom thinks it's the thing to do, then I do too."

Amy swung around and grabbed me around the neck, "Oh, Bud, I love you so much."

I knew she knew.

"And maybe I won't get it."

"No, Amy, if you want it I want you to have it and you will."

We kissed lightly, "You know, Bud, I'll never love anyone but you. Tell me you know that."

As usual my first thought was that no one would love me for ever and my response was not spontaneous enough.

"Tell me, Bud."

"And I'll never love anyone but you, Amy."

Amy pulled away. She reached into her pocket and pulled out a chain looking thing that was indistinct in the dim light. "Mom and I went shopping and I bought us something. I hope you will wear it."

She held up two chains, each having two pendants attached. "See this one? It's a St. Christopher metal. I didn't know what it was, but Mom says some people believe that St. Christopher has power to watch over people when they're away from the ones they love. I thought that was a nice thought."

"See this one?" holding one of two mates between her fingers. It looked like a little heart that had been broken into two parts.

She held the two pendants together so that they made a single heart. "See, you wear one and I wear the other. If you put them together they make a note "Our love is forever."

"I'm going to put this one around your neck and you put the other around mine."

We did in the form of a little ritual.

"Bud, I'll never take it off. Will you?"

She knew the answer.

There was a squalling tires coming from behind us as a car made an dangerously fast turn from the street into the Spinning Wheel parking lot. Amy and I turned just in time to see the flash of the headlights as the car bounced over the incline from the street.

"Dang, I said, Who could that crazy driver be?"

"I don't know," Amy replied in amazement.

"Oh yes I do," She continued with consternation. "That's none other than Ronney Harper driving like a fool. I hope he doesn't see us."

Ronney brought his pretty little yellow chevy to a halt at the rear of the parking lot and was obnoxiously flashing his lights for service. "If he keeps up flashing his lights like that he could make someone mad," I said. No sooner had the words come out than the manager came out the door. It was his usual performance to go to the car causing the disturbance and saying something like, "You got a problem I can help you with?" That was warning number one. The second was by a leather clad cop who was never patrolling many blocks away. We could hear a rowdy exchange coming from the encounter and then saw the manager make a hand signal to someone inside the restaurant.

"Oh-Oh," Amy said still straining backwards to see what was happening, "Ronney's going to get into trouble."

"He sure is," I said adding emphasis, "I know. The cops will be here in a minute."

I grabbed the door handle, "I'd better get back there and see if Ronney needs help." As if there was something I could do.

"No, Bud, don't get mixed up in it."

"Bet cha Peggy's with him."

"Well, okay, go see if Peggy's got trouble."

I ran back to Ronney's car and sure enough Peggy was with him. I approached the manager as an arrogant teenager who thought he was older than a teenager. "Hi," I said to the manager, "my name is Bud Olson, this guy is a friend of mine, can I help out in any way.

I looked into the car and Ronney, slid way down in the seat as though he was trying to slide under the steering wheel. It was the first time I had ever seen him looking pale and meek as a kitten. Peggy was sitting on the other side leaning firmly against the door, her head hidden in her hands.

"Just stay away from the car and don't cause any trouble, unless you want to deal with the cops when they get here," the manager said showing a great deal of contempt for the situation.

"Could I ask what's going on?"

"Your friend here has his head running on alcohol. The law better get him off the streets before he kills somebody."

I ran to the other side of the car where Peggy was still hiding her face in her hands, "Peggy, it's Bud. Is everything alright?"

She didn't look up or even acknowledge that I had spoken.

"Peggy," I continued trying to emphasize the urgency with the deflection in my voice.

She turned her head away and began rolling up the car window.

I ran back to Amy, "Ronney's drunk and they've called the cops on him. I tried to get Peggy's attention but she just ignores me. You better try or she's in big trouble."

"And even bigger trouble if her parents find out," Amy blurted as she sprung from the car.

Amy ran to Ronney's car, "Peggy, it's me, Amy."

Peggy looked up from her hands and saw that it was Amy and quickly buried her face again turning her back to the window.

Amy began beating on the car window, "Peggy Waylan, you open this window or you're going to be in more trouble than you want."

And then with her hands on her hips. "I said open that window, right now!!"

Peggy looked up at Amy with the expression of horrified anguish. Tears were flowing uncontrollably as she sobbed.

"Peggy, open that door and get out of that car this very minute!"

The door opened without hesitation and Peggy popped out into Amy's arms.

"Look, manager, this is my sister and I'm going to take her home to Mother before this creep kills her in that stupid car," Amy half shouted at the manager.

The manager was about as dumbfounded as I was and stood speechless as we led Peggy to the car.

"Bud, pay up and leave a big tip and let's get out of here before the manager wakes up."

On the way home, between Peggy's sobbing, she explained that Ronney gets hateful and mean when he drinks and she was of afraid of him when he was that way. He had been grounded by his dad for drinking, but he begged and promised that it was his first time ever and he would never drink again and his dad gave in and let him have the car back.

Some of Ronney's close buddies on the football team knew where they could buy bootlegged whiskey without a ID card. When Peggy tried to discourage him from drinking he assured her that he could handle his booze and one drink would be all he needed. But as is usually the case, one drink started the bragging and the showing off for his teammates until he had carelessly drunk to much to be reasonable or safe. Peggy cried, "I tried to make him let me drive but he just got mean and said I should mind my own business."

"Well, it was your business," Amy interrupted with a large measure of sternness. "Why didn't you get out of the car and call your mother?"

Peggy sobbed, "I didn't want to get Ronney in trouble and he could get kicked off the team for drinking and he promised his dad and he would be mad at me for telling on him and I want him to like me."

Peggy's choked speech became inaudible in her sobbing, she leaned her head over on Amy's shoulder and cried like a baby.

After a moment Amy lifted Peggy's head up so that they were looking at each other, "Peggy, one of these days you and I are going to have a long talk before you get yourself into trouble or worse."

"Do you think Ronney will get in a lot of trouble?" I asked.

"I doubt it. His dad will probably blame the whole thing on the Spinning Wheel manager," Amy replied in disgust.

We drove the few miles from the edge of town to Peggy's house in silence, each seemingly emersed in our own thoughts. I pulled into Peggy's drive, "I'll walk to the house with you, if your mother has any questions I'll explain that some of Ronney's friends got to drinking and you decided to ride home with us," Amy said.

In a minute Amy was back, "Did Peggy's mother ask any questions?, I asked.

"No she didn't, I don't really think she cares. Poor Peggy."

I wheeled the big caddie into Amy's driveway just as the porch light came on. "Was that good timing or not," I said to Amy. "But shucks, I wanted to sit and talk for a while before you went in."

"It's okay, Mother doesn't expect me to come right in. I bet she still remembers sitting and talking to Dad."

"Oh, by the way, she continued, It's alright if you kiss me."

"Then I will, but first I want to tell you how proud I am of you."

"Bud - we've only got five minutes."

I'll be darned if Amy wasn't right. Mr. Harper blamed everybody but Ronney for being drunk and getting in trouble with the police. He blame the cop, the school, the Spinning Wheel manager, why, he even blamed Peggy.

Boy, was Amy furious about that. She was especially furious when Mr. Harper convinced the police that Ronney had never drank before, and wouldn't have this time except for the influence of the crowd he was thrown with and that being the star runningback on the Terrier team had him under a lot of stress and that he would be ineligible to play with a drinking conviction and that from this point on he would take charge and he would guarantee that there would be no more drinking. "Take my word," he said.

Before we sneer at Mr. Harper, I suppose that we would first have to deal with our own short comings in this area. Far to many parents find some sort of self edification in the athletic successes of their children. It must be akin to the manifestations of some unfulfilled fantasy of their own, for what else would cause them to encourage a young lad to sacrifice himself to demonstrate physical and mental domination over another kid? I guess we would find the answer in the hereditary genetics of evolution called "The survival of the fittest." Some others would find it's rooting in Little League baseball. It's little wonder that the world is bent on killing off the homo-sapien since a mild form of the game is acted out everyday with parental encouragement by our kids on the playing field. Kids, allowed to have the aggressive emotions and passions of the ancient gladiator, taught by adults who should know better, beginning as the nymph emerges from the cocoon.

But if that wasn't enough, he even insinuated that Peggy wasn't good enough for Ronney and that he should find a nicer girl that wouldn't be getting him in trouble. This absolutely infuriated Amy and more than once she had taken Peggy aside and told her as you would a sister, "Peggy, you don't deserve to be treated like a secondclass citizen. You'd better stay away from him before he gets you in trouble."

Peggy usually listened to Amy and took her advice, but this time was different. Something important was missing in Peggy's life, a reason to feel important- that others thought she was important. Bright, smart, and not bad looking, but she lacked the self-esteem that's planted early on in the wee life, and being known as Ronney's girl friend was a way to deceive herself.

Chapter #8
STUPID IS AS STUPID DOES

The school buses were lined up along the sidewalk in the front of the school. Some were already loading, others had lines of kids waiting to get on. I was already loaded, I saw Amy coming. Her little white purse was lying on top of her usual school books, she was holding these cradled in her arms in front using them to guide herself through the mingling groups with an "Excuse," or "Hi."

The kids in the front of the bus saw her loading. We had been going steady for so long now that everyone thought we were automatic and we only needed to get the ringing of the graduation bells out of the way and soon the wedding bells would be ringing. I must admit, the few times I attended the little community church there in Lutz, I visioned myself standing at the alter, watching Amy, dressed in a beautiful silk and linen dress, her arm locked in Mr. Brooks', a crimson red rose lying across a small white Bible, her deep blue eyes barely visible through the shear veil fixed on mine, coming step by step to be mine forever.

As she stepped onto the bus step the heads all turned to see if I was in position.

She sat down heavily and flirtingly slapped me on the leg, "Guess what," she said with excitement in her voice. She went on, "Saturday night, they're going to have a hayride for the cheerleaders and we can invite whoever we want to go, and I want you."

Amy knew that I had trouble getting excited about going to parties with her friends. She was so very popular and correct and I figured in contrast that I looked all the worse. But then, a hayride

Seeds of My Field

was one of those few things that we could do together and it was silly for me to make her feel bad about asking me.

"You mean a truck loaded with hay, a big fire on the beach, hotdogs, potato chips, hot chocolate and all that stuff- well count me in."

"Oh, good - It leaves from the school parking lot at seven this Saturday night. Can you pick me up?"

Let me tell you about these famous hayrides. There was a meat packing company in Tampa, I won't mention its name for obvious reasons, that wasn't as yet caught up in the current liability conscious syndrome that we find our corporate contemporaries in today. I guess doing things for the kids made sense. So this wonderful company furnished a flatbed truck, hay and two drivers and the only requisite was that the party bought the hotdogs from them.

Our hayrides usually went to the beach along the Courtney-Campbell Causeway, the route across Tampa Bay between Tampa and Clearwater. The area was relatively secluded at that time and the beach was first come first serve. Now you will find a park with tables, restrooms and paved parking plus parking meters.

The truck would angle in off the road and come to a stop between the highway and the soft sand. We'd bail out the back, the girls would begin setting up tables and carrying the boxes of food while the boys scoured up and down the beaches searching for boards and driftwood for the fire.

Soon the table would be set and laden with boxes of food. A huge fire lit the area. We splashed in the sparkling phosphorus water, played games and ran the beach while waiting for the fire's reduction to glowing amber coals.

The cooling of the firelight signaled the group to come in and gather around the fire. We roasted, we drank, we sang, we told stories and jokes until at eleven o'clock sharp, the driver flashed the truck lights, the familiar alarm clock.

The tenor of the party changed as boys huddled with their girl friends on the soft hay. The trip home was always quiet.

I wish this dialogue could end here. It would be an easy matter to make a happy ending, to close the book on young love, to assume that they lived happily ever after.

But the seeds of life are not that way, and there is no happiness except that it be offset by sadness, and no love unless it be balanced by hate. And I would that I need go no further, but no, that would not be fair to me, or to you, or to the truth. So I'll go on. Not without great pain for I have no desire to relive the rest, to re-feel the heartache, to see the haunting picture. But I promise to you, I will faithfully bring you to the end. There will be many smudges on the manuscript where tears have been wiped away. There will be great pauses where strength from a greater source had to be summoned. But I must harvest the field that was planted. Not necessarily a harvest of the seeds of my own planting, but never the less, <u>The Seeds of My Field</u>.

I'd bet almost anything that Amy would have won a cheerleader position without my help. She said I was the reason she won. I didn't take any chances. I made posters in art class, signs in ag class and buttonedholed everyone I knew for their support. She won easily-she would have anyway.

I'm not prepared to understand why one person can feel totally accomplished in another's success, but I did. So happy I was that I drained my savings to buy Amy her cheerleader jacket. Bright white background, HILLSBOROUGH HIGH SCHOOL, in bold red and black letters across a tough looking Terrier. Amy's folks could have bought it for her. Amy could have bought it for herself, she always had plenty of money, but she didn't, she let me buy it, then acted like it was the most wonderful thing in her life.

It was Saturday night, the night of the hayride. I wanted Amy to wear her new jacket. She resisted because the others might call her a showoff. I said I wanted to show her off, so she consented. It was pretty easy to locate Amy that night because of the bright-white jacket.

I picked Amy up in the GMC, the hayride was to begin at the school parking lot. As we drove along I noticed that for the first time I wasn't tense about being in a group with her. I had always in the past been anxious and uncertain, even to the point of being timid and stand-offish. But not tonight, I finally had worked myself through the silly shyness and was actually beginning to have fun.

It seemed that Amy was to wise and understanding for a young teenager. From the very first she recognized my shy nature and dealt with it as her re-construction project.

Seeds of My Field

The parking lot was already full of screaming, dancing kids when we pulled in. A box had been placed on the ground behind the truck for us to climb into the trailer. The truck was half loaded already. It was a flatbed semi type thing with wooden sideboards that went up about chest high. Some of the kids were throwing hay at each other, others were hanging over the sides waving and carrying on as you'd expect teenagers about to embark on a hayride to do. The adult sponsors, parents of the cheerleaders probably, were running around loading sacks and boxes of the hayride condiments, the truck drivers were shouting instructions about the do's and don't's of hayride etiquette over the shouts and screams of the excited participants.

Amy had no sooner gotten out of the GMC than Peggy came running up, her arms outstretched toward Amy as though they hadn't been together in years.

"Oh, Amy, is that your new jacket? It's gorgeous. I want one just like it."

Amy spun around so that Peggy could admire the Terrier on the back, and then with one arm on her hip and the other high over her head in an abbreviated cheer stance, she shouted, "Go Terriers, Go". Soon the truck load of kids were stomping and shouting in rhythm "Go Terriers, Go." That became the theme from the parking lot to the beach.

"Oh, Bud, get that blanket out of seat and bring it. It will probably be a little chilly on the way home and we can snuggle under it."

I gave Amy a hand for her to get onto the trailer. It was still a good size step from the box to the bed. A hand reached down to help her the final step. I looked up and was about to say thanks when I noticed it was Ronney. I should have known that Ronney would have been there with Peggy. I resented that Ronney had even touched Amy but before either of us were aware, the chivalrous act of courtesy had already been perpetrated.

"I'll be a good boy tonight, I promise," Ronney said to Amy searching her face for an expression of forgiveness.

Amy gave him a quick glare, "You'd better," she said abruptly.

"I will, I will," Ronney replied with pleading overtones.

"You'd better be good to Peggy if you know what's good for you," Amy snapped back leaving no margin of question about her statement.

Ronney shrugged away with the expression of the mis-understood kid that had only made one mistake in his whole life.

The truck pulled out of the parking lot and onto the street with the throngs in the back chanting "Go Terriers, Go, Go Terriers, Go, Go Terriers, Go."

The driver demonstrated great skill in handling the hayride crowd. He could monitor both sides of the trailer through his rearview mirrors. If he saw anyone standing along the sides of the trailer or leaning over the racks he would honk once. There was not a second honk, at the second offense he would pull the truck to the side of the road and sit there until a kangaroo court was quickly assembled and court was held in the trailer until the offender promised to behave. The driver was unemotional and emphatic and would have sat there until the parents came to pick everyone up if discipline had not been restored. At least we thought he would have.

What a great night for a hayride. Almost all fall nights were great in central Florida. The air was low of humidity, the temperature around the mid seventies, a three-quarter moon was already high over the bay waiting for us to arrive.

The truck pulled off the road and angled down the embankment the short distance that was available before the sand would become open and soft. It came to a halt, the lights and motor were shut off which signaled to the sponsors that the driver had completed his part of the undertaking and now all procedures were turned over to them.

The chains began to rattle on the tailgate and soon it swung open. Some boys jumped down and were taking boxes from the truck and placing them in the general area of the picnic spot.

Amy jumped to her feet and stood looking over the trailer racks toward the Bay, "Bud," she said with excitement, as she reached for my arm and pulled me over to her, "Oh, Bud, it's so beautiful. See how the ripple in the water makes the reflection of the moon turn into so many shapes? It just sparkles like a billion diamonds." She put both arms around my arm and leaning against me without turning from the water, Oh, Bud, I'm so happy."

A burly old backwater coon scavenging for food around the picnic site looked our way long enough for his yellow eyes to flash and then arrogantly ambled off into the mangroves.

Seeds of My Field

I was happy too, I was always happy when I was with Amy. But not just me, she was so kind and thoughtful, there was no doubt- in her eyes I saw kindness, in her smile I saw kindness, everyone did, when she was near the air breathed a magic fragrance. Even me, a sack of raging insecurities, felt an unusual and strange peace as long as our eyes or our hands were touching.

"Bud, Amy shouted, don't let me be standing around here day dreaming while everybody else does the work. Let's get busy, you've got to go find some fire wood."

We laughed and bailed out of the back of the trailer and disappeared in different directions.

In hardly any time at all a large fire was roaring on the beach with a large pile of extra wood heaped along side for feeding. A tall, slender column of light colored yellow and blue flames were jumping into the air reaching high above any of our heads. The flame would settle down and someone would throw another board or limb into the blaze, the disturbed limbs and coals would send great showers of many colored sparks dancing into the air above the great surge of the flame.

"Bud, did you wear your bathing suit under your Levi's?"

"Yeah, and I brought a towel."

"Bet I can get into the water first."

"It's a bet."

We both darted to the un-needed shadows to pull off our Levi's and deposit them in a safe place. I rolled mine up and tucked them in the back corner of the trailer. I noticed Amy carefully take off her jacket and lay it in the seat of the truck. I waited for her and we ran into the water hand in hand screaming at the sudden shock of the cool water. Amy and I had become excellent swimmers because we swam together so much at her place. We swam out into the deeper water beyond the bright light of the campfire. She swam up to me as she had learned to do, we took a deep breath, creating an additional bouyancy in the water. We put our arms around each other and relaxed into a soft embrace, our bodies settled slightly into the water until only Amy's long blonde hair could be seen above the surface swirling and drifting with the push and tug of the surf. In our private world of speechless wonder we caressed and our hearts beat fast as we cherished and absorbed the spirit that moved between us. Only mine, only Amy's, only ours.

But life is based on fact and not fantasy and the heaving of our chests, starving for fresh oxygen, told us in emphatic terms that mortals lived above the surface and no amount of young love and pretending would change the facts of life.

Almost unaware of the rest of the party, we played in the water, splashing and carrying on like snowbirds on their first tour to the sea.

"Look," I held my arms outstretched and swung them around my body. The swirling action created small bubbles and the vacuum created as my arm moved through the water drew in the ever-present phosphorus particles and the moon playing off the bubbles and light glow of the phosphorous made the water come alive with fiery dancing gems.

"Watch this," Amy said as she rolled over on her back and settled deep into the water. She began to wave her arms back and forth from her sides until they touched at the top of her head. The glowing bubbles and the fiery phosphorous gave off the effervescent radiance of angel wings.

Soon others were in the water, splashing, shouting, screaming until any semblance of order was vanished.

An hour of great fun is like a day in the creation of time and before anyone could have guessed that the time had passed a noble sponsor with rolled up levi's carefully approached lifting to tiptoe trying to stay above the small rolling waves. "Alright you guys, you can't stay out here all night and expect me to keep the hotdog fire going," she yelled over the roar of the screaming teenagers.

Someone yelled back, "What happened, did you forget your bathing suit?"

Before the sponsor could realize that she's been set up the ritual was made complete and she was dumped headlong off my shoulders into the water. We yelled Hoorays and charged from the water to line up for the food.

There's a great transition that takes place around an open campfire when the evening lights are gone and the world shrinks to the radius of the firelight. From jubilant cries of joy to passive melancholy by the magic of the intangible flicker.

Amy and I atended to each other by devying up the hotdog, mustard and relish chores. It had become so natural, so automatic, and though not a word needed to have been spoken, she seemed to be in charge.

"Where do you want to eat?" Amy asked.

There were no park benches furnished along the causeway and it was necessary for everyone to spread out and find a rock or a log to serve as a seat.

"We could get on our dry clothes and sit in the trailer."

"Hmm, you trying to get me alone in the back of the truck, are you?"

I almost bit my tongue.

"Well, that sounds good to me, she said with a wink, go get the blanket and we'll sit on it."

I don't believe that anyone could have been closer than Amy and I were. As I consider, I see that there was a great deal of maturity in our relationship. We shared our deepest thoughts, a common respect and an understanding of each other that many spend a life time trying to achieve without success. You could have mistaken us for a married couple had we not been so young. I never hesitated to call Amy if I needed something, sometimes just to talk, nor did she hesitate. Anything we wanted to do was alright. To a point. Once when we were alone, swinging in the porch swing, Amy scooted across to the other side of the swing, "Bud, look at me, she said with a hesitant seriousness. There is something we have to talk about."

"Okay, I said, talk away."

"No, this is serious. Are ready to talk serious?"

"Yes, go ahead."

"You know how much I love you. You know that I love to kiss you and hold you. But we need to talk about sex," she hesitated before going on knowing that wasn't enough to establish the topic. " You know, going all the way."

Amy's voice became deeper and became softer, "Can we talk about sex or does that make you uncomfortable?"

I felt the temperature rise in my face as the flush of my body reacted to the topic of sex so bluntly presented. Sure, as boys do,

I spoke with great authority and confidence on the subject in the "Sacred Halls of the Boy's Room," but dealing with the subject in the presence of the subject rendered me nearly speechless. "It does in a way, I've never talked to a girl about that kind of sex before. But if you want to I'll try."

"Sometimes when we hold each other and we're kissing and making love I get these strange feelings, something inside get's to feeling funny and I have urges to not stop and I have to tell myself no, no further. Do you think I'm naughty or bad for this?"

"No, I have those same feelings and I know that you can feel sometimes what's happening and it's embarrassing and I want to draw away."

"I know, I can tell when you're doing it. Well, I wish you had someone like a dad at home to talk to about those feelings but I know you don't. I talked to Mom, she always tells me and I trust her so much."

"Yeah, me to. You're lucky, Amy."

"Mom says that we don't need to be ashamed or embarrassed about the way we feel. That it only means that we are normal, healthy youths, that will soon be young adults. You know what she said? She said that you and I were so close that we should talk about our feelings so that we would know how to handle them and we could help each other. She told me, and I think she was worried about Ronney and Peggy, that the minute a boy and girl go to far that the sweetness and purity of youth is swept away and the sweet joy of marriage is compromised."

"What do think of that, Bud?"

"I don't know, I'd never thought about it like that before. What do you think?"

She took my hand, a little tear was in the corner of her eye, a seriousness that was new crept across her happy face, "I think that someday when the time is right and we're mature enough, we'll know, and we'll give our bodies completely to each other. Until then, we'll know that the best is yet to come and we'll do it right. I know you're mine now, and I'm your's, it's just a matter time. Can we pledge this to each other?"

She probably already knew that I would say yes. She probably didn't know that I would have pledged her the moon if she'd asked me to.

* * *

The lights of the truck came on and began to blink. Time to go, nearly eleven, just enough time to return to the school and make it home by midnight. But no matter, didn't we all love those enchanted minutes as the monotonous drone of the engine succumbed to the noises of the world?

"Bud," Amy called, "I left our towels hanging on the bush by the fire. I'll tell the driver to wait."

The driver halted the truck at the edge of the pavement awaiting my return with the towels. It took a little longer than I thought because the moon had moved on across the sky and now the lights on the water were only the faint twinklings of distant stars in a black sky.

I gathered the towels and returned to the trailer, hands reached down out of the darkness to help me in, the gate was re-latched and at the sound of the truck's horn the driver began a wide sweeping turn to head it back to the east towards Tampa.

It would be no trouble finding Amy in the darkness, by now she would have put on her new, white jacket. I had asked as I got in where she was and someone motioned towards the back. I went that direction crawling over legs and arms of reposed lovers.

For those who haven't known the dark shadows that eternally dwell in the soul of a boy or girl whose hopes and dreams are founded on the insecurity and emptiness of an unloving, uncaring, uncommitted broken home, or no home at all, will find difficulty relating to what happens from here, for the senses of the child thus raised are senses of abnormal sensitivity, sharpened and honed to a fine craftsman's edge, and often, before the required moment of reason has elapsed, the agony of programmed insecurity has decided in err. If you've never felt unloved, you can never feel the pain of a kid standing on the outside of life, crying to get in.

Peggy, as her nature seemed to dictate, had gotten cold after the swim to the point of having chills. Amy, as you would have expected, felt a motherly caring for her and wrapped her jacket around her to break the chill. Had I only known.

I finally made my way to back of the trailer and I recognized Amy's blanket. There obviously was a couple laying under it, I raised it up to see who had stolen it. All I could see before my mind lost control was the girl wearing Amy's white jacket lying on Ronney making passionate love. My eyes and mind were totally blinded by the terrible passion that swept across me like the impact of a raging tornado.

Fortunately, the truck had just completed its circle and was just gaining speed when in hardly a step I vaulted over the side rails and down to the pavement. I landed perfectly on my feet but the truck had gained just enough speed so that when I landed my feet were jerked from under me and my head was slammed against the pavement. I remember the impact and the flashes of lights that shot into my eyes and the stunned moment before the pain struck. I didn't hear Amy cry for the driver to stop or her scream for help.

I jumped to my feet and in a moment the daze was shaken. I ran and ran until the life had left my legs and fell crying to the sand at the edge of the water. Blood was dripping from deep scratches in my forehead, it was burning with sharp pain as sweat began finding it's way into the crevices. I hardly felt the sting of the saltwater as I cupped my hands to dip water and rinsed the blood away. I lay sobbing, not knowing the truth, knowing only the truth as it pertained to my world, I wasn't good enough, I always knew I wasn't good enough.

Amy ran to Peggy, "Peggy, what happened to Bud?" She grabbed Peggy and spun her toward her, Oh, know, my jacket. What were you and Ronney doing?"

Peggy broke down, "I'm sorry, you know what Ronney makes me do."

"Oh, poor Bud, I have to find him, I've got to call Mom."

I lay on the beach half dazed. It was the morning sun that awoke me to another day. I made my way toward home.

Seeds of My Field

With a ride in the back of a flatbed farm truck, squeezed inbetween a horde of migrant grove workers, I got home by the middle of the day. I didn't bother telling my stepmother that I was home, she knew that I often stayed in the swamp with the dogs all night, and besides if I went in and confronted her, she would want me to explain about my head, and wash it and bandage it, and couldn't stand having anyone touch me.

I eased pass the house and down to the familiar mound where Lee was buried and sat so that I could lean against the tree and be alone. Except that Blue was there, Blue was always there. It didn't matter that I had neglected him since I started going with Amy. And Sam was there, too. But never showed much emotion or interest in my problems, he walked over to me, I stroked his head a few times and he walked away.

Had I gone to the house first I would have known that Amy had frantically called and come to look for me. But it didn't matter, I didn't know, maybe I didn't want to know.

I sat there blindly staring off into the trees, not knowing what to think or where to turn. My heart aching with pain as I fought to hold back the breath choking sobs. Little by little the defense of anger began to show up and would have cared well its purpose except that Amy's beautiful face continued to break through the defense and appear in my eyes.

I reached my hand to my neck and it rested on charms that Amy had placed there and I had promised never to remove. Impulsively I jerked and it fell loose in my hand, I held it, gripped tight in my clenched fist. If she had grown tired of me, why couldn't she have told me?

That feeling that I had felt so often kept saying, "I told you so."

I had sat there for an hour or so, I heard a vehicle pull into the drive way, I could hear in the distance a rapid knock on the door. Shortly I heard running footsteps approaching from behind the tree. It was Junior, I read in his face a matter of grave importance.

His voice sounded exhausted and airish as he confronted me, "Bud, your stepmother said I might find you here. C'mon, we've got to go fast, I'll explain on the way."

I had no idea what was going on but the urgency in his demeanor transposed to mine- I dropped the treasure I held in my hand and we ran full speed to his pickup.

"What the heck's going on, Junior?"

"Bud, you remember Boss Coon Swamp?"

"Sure, who wouldn't?", I replied with more curiosity than urgency in my reply.

"In the middle of Boss Coon Swamp, where you thought you saw a building, well, it was a building. That swamp belongs to Albert and he lets Moses keep his moonshine still there."

"Oh bull," I smarted back, Mr. Wilson don't make moonshine."

"Oh yes he does, dummy, everybody knows he does, just that nobody knew where until these white guys from town was trespassing in the swamp and they said they was going to tear it down to get rid of the nigger competition. Albert said Moses was headed out to stop um and when they finished tearing up the still they'd probably tear up Moses pretty bad."

"What can we do?" I shouted, becoming drawn into the situation and becoming more involved.

"I don't know, but I brought my Twenty Two rifle, maybe we can keep Moses from getting beat up too bad."

"Junior, I've heard that moonshiners are mean and bloodthirsty."

"I know they are," Junior responded, "That's why we've got to get there fast."

The tires screamed as Junior wheeled the pickup off the road and through the open gate. We pulled up alongside Mr. Wilson's truck. How far he was a head of us, who knows, but we bailed out determined to catch him before he got to the still.

I could hear the banging and crashing of the axes. The destruction of Mr. Wilson's still had already begun. There, also was Mr. Wilson, standing at the edge of the clearing, staring at the destruction, stress covering every inch of his dark face, holding himself from rushing in to restrain the perpetrators, yet knowing that the probable consequence could mean more than just the loss of his still.

Junior rushed up to Mr. Wilson's side, thrusting his small rifle in front of him, "Moses, it's Bud and me, I brought my rifle, we can stop them."

In the commotion the gun accidently discharged, the bullet shot aimlessly into the air.

"G'me dat gun boy. Wa chu tinks you gonna do here wid dat ting. Get yo selvs out'o here. Ain't no matter o yous to get hut oar. I ain't having no killun."

Mr. Wilson grabbed the gun from Junior and thru it to the swamp floor. In the same motion he slammed his huge hands into our backs and shoveled us away, "Now, get out o dis place, run fo all you gots."

Just as we turning to run I saw the faces of two ugly, mean characters running around the corner of the shack toward where they had heard the gunshot. They had all of the characteristics of trash low life, dark, greasy and un-shaven.

Our boldness instantly changed to fear. Over the loud thrashing of the water as Junior and I broke to run I heard one, "There's the black assed sonna- bitch, shoot'im Mac, he's got a gun."

A shot rang out from a large caliber gun, I heard it impact above the echoing through the swamp. I heard a heaving noise and gushing of wind, I saw Mr. Wilson fall against the impact, head first into murky waters of Boss Coon Swamp, his blood and body fluids mingling and staining and disappearing into the stagnant waters of the abode of the Boss Coon, whose life was spared by a giant hand whose tender heart could stand no killing.

Wouldn't it have been heroic if I had to turn to fight the scum and somehow avenge the blow to my dearest friend and wise counselor. But I didn't, fear and cowardice replaced every fiber of nerve and daring and camaraderie. We fell over logs and into deep pits, scrambling and swimming and dragging ourselves frantically to Juniors truck.

"Hurry," Junior cried out, "get in, let's get to a phone fast."

Junior broke every law of driving and reason getting to the station. We rushed through the door, Bill was behind the counter as he always was, "Hold it boy's, what's the big hurry?"

Gasping for breath between sentences we related the events that had just taken place. Bill ran to the back and called for Albert to come over to the station.

"My God, they got Moses you say? Oh, my God." Albert gasped, "get the phone, get the sheriff. Never mind, I'll do it."

Albert got the dispatcher and asked for a the sheriff by name. In an instant he had related the details as we had told him.

"Alright, boys, the sheriff said for you boys to go home and stay there. He said don't talk about this thing to nobody and that he'd come looking for you as soon as he needed a statement." Then Albert turned a threatening look at Junior and I, "Mind what the sheriff said, keep your mouths shut."

The sheriff did what sheriffs do. He made lengthy dialogue, questioned me about every detail, took Junior and me to his office and questioned me alone and then questioned me again with Junior and I together.

Finally, he came back into the room with a deputy that we could see him conferring with through a window in the hallway, Deputy Andrews and me have decided from the description you gave of these two killers that you've described Mac Maston and Lew Mabrey. These are mean guys, we didn't know they were killers. We've got to get'um now, that's for sure.

But in the meantime, don't be running around town, no telling what these guys are thinking."

The order was absolutely emphatic. Junior and I were to stay at home, out of sight. But didn't he know that Mr. Wilson's funeral would be happening in a few days. Didn't he know that I would be at Mr. Wilson's funeral? He had only a few days to catch these vermin, caught or not, nothing short of prison would keep me from that funeral.

Chapter #9
MOSES' FUNERAL

My imprisonment was about to drive me insane. I was not allowed out of the house, period. I could not walk out to the road, I could not have friends in to see me. I was not even allowed to sit in plain view at a window. The sheriff had phoned these instructions to my stepmother and told her to beware of any strange activity around or close to the house. I don't know what we could have done if someone wanted to enter the house and capture me, it was only a few yards to the orange grove in the back. Just the same, I could see that the sheriff had a deputy on a regular drive by routine and I'm sure the phone was monitored. Even after what had happened to Mr. Wilson, I had a hard time comprehending that anyone would take my life.

The solitary confinement I was to endure would not have been near so severe if I could have shut my mind off for the time. Two terrible blows - Amy, Mr. Wilson. Two terrible visions kept re-occurring, Amy with Ronney, Mr. Wilson falling into Boss Coon Swamp. Over and over they would appear. I would hurt and grieve, then become angry and militant. As darkness fell across my room, I would see Mr. Wilson, a firelight dancing on his face. I would hear him admonishing the hounds and then he would tell a story of growing up in white man's world, how much he loved his church, loved Jesus. Then I would see Amy, her eyes coming from the darkness. I could hear her, "Can you say that you love me, Bud? It's hard for you isn't it? I will always love you."

I wanted her so bad. But, how could I go to her now? it would only hurt me worse. Besides, I had convinced myself that she no longer wanted me.

It was Tuesday morning. I had called the preacher that Mr. Wilson had talked so much about, I didn't reveal who I was but found out that Mr. Wilson's funeral was to begin at ten o'clock this morning. When it would end? Nobody could predict when a Negro funeral would end. But it would always end at the cemetery as the brothers shoveled the dirt back into the hole. I knew from the beginning that twelve harnessed horses couldn't keep me away, I was going to see Mr. Wilson's face one more time, I wasn't going to remember him as I last saw him, falling face first into the swamp.

I could drop out of my bedroom window to the ground and be only a few feet from the orange grove at the back of the house. From there I could slip amongst the trees and work my way out of sight up to Highway #41. A bus passed there almost every hour on its way to Tampa, it would be easy enough to flag down a ride to Sulphur Springs and get off only a few blocks from Mr. Wilson's church.

I pushed into my closet looking for some clothes that looked appropriate for a funeral. I had no idea what appropriate was, but I at least found some pants that had a little crease in them, a cotton shirt that hadn't been worn yet. Hanging on the door knob was a tie. I didn't own a tie. I hadn't put it there. It could only have been there because my stepmother knew that somehow I would get to Mr. Wilson's funeral and had put one of Dad's ties there for me. It was undoubtedly her who had called Albert and told him that I had defied the sheriff's instructions and where I would be, knowing that I would not have taken the tie were I going anywhere else.

I did everything exactly as I have described. It was only a moment and I was hiding out of sight at the edge of the highway under a large orange tree waiting for the bus. My wait wasn't but a few minutes. I ran to the edge of the road, facing the oncoming bus, I waved my arm up and down. The driver recognized the familiar signal, the bus lights began to flash as a warning to the other vehicles on the road. It leaned forward as it came to a stop, the door passing only a few feet from where I stood. With a great hissing noise, the air was released from the brakes, the door opened simultaneously.

I stepped up to the driver with the seventy five cent fee in my hand. The driver released the clutch and handed me a ticket stamped Tampa all in one motion and the bus gained speed.

The driver took his eyes off of the road for an instant and glance at me, "There's a regular stop right here at the intersection, you know, next time let's get on there."

The intersection was at Lake Fern Road. I knew it very well.

"Sir", I asked,"I'm going to the funeral of an old friend in Sulphur Springs, if I tell you when, could you let me off?"

"Depends on the traffic. We'll see. This bus has regular places to stop, you know."

Lucky the traffic was light. When we reached the edge of Sulphur Springs, every few blocks the driver would look up into the passenger mirror for an indication. Finally I gave him a handsignal and he pulled the bus over to the edge of the street and I hopped off. I was only a few blocks from the church.

Long before I reached the church I reached the crowd of vehicles parked along the sidewalks, in the yards and in every available space. I could see from the distance, a shiny, black hearse backed up to the steps of the church, it's single rear door was opened wide. There were a few men standing by it, probably attendants from the funeral home. I glanced into it as I eased past the attendants. It was empty, Mr. Wilson had already been taken into the church, the service would be ready to begin.

I eased up the few steps into the church. It was jammed full of people. The pews that I could see from where I was standing were full, maybe I could just stand at the back.

I eased into the auditorium, the last pew at the back, on my left, one seat on the end. I dropped into it, I was sitting next to Albert. Albert gave me a light smile,"Saved this one for you, knew you'd be here."

I sat quietly, looking down at my knees, too uncomfortable and out of place to look around and be conspicuous. It seemed to me that looking around as though out of curiosity, would show disrespect for Mr. Wilson, and I knew enough about colored people that this was not only a very solemn moment, but also a very private one, a time when a white boy would be considered an outsider, a tolerated guest of the family.

Occasionally, I glanced around the church. It was not new by any terms, but well kept. The crowd caused it to be unusually hot, one rotary fan in the ceiling was the only mechanical means of stirring the air. It made a whirring noise and rocked slightly in it's orbit from a arm that was out of balance. Some of the men were working with the windows trying to get them unstuck and opened as a last resort against the stifling heat. Printed cardboard fans with advertising from the funeral home were going back and forth in the hands of most of the ladies. Some of the ladies, their eyes closed, their head tilted back, as though acknowledging the stress and pain as to much to pose normal, just the same, the cardboard fans were in a back and forth motion, responding to automatic instructions.

At the front of the church, pushed over to the side to make way for the casket was a communion table, I could barely make out the words carved into the side, "This Do In Remembrance Of Me." The table was covered with flowers, some may have been purchased arrangements, but most appeared to have been gathered and arranged by the one who brought them. Mr. Wilson was lying in the open casket, it was rather plain, in the center of the church just below the preachers lectern. He looked stern and magnanimous, his white hair set perfectly against his head contrasted against his black suit. I was surprised that he looked so different in a suit from his blue bib overalls. He looked so peaceful, the pain and sadness that I saw so often as we sat by the fireside and talked about the repression of his people was not there. Left behind, no longer his trial.

I made a quick glance for Mrs. Wilson, I knew she would be at the front with her family - daughters, no sons - but the press was to much and I couldn't see.

All the people were in black, the ladies wore black hats, some with veils pulled down over their faces, others left the veils up, pinned into the hat. The men, black suits, white shirts, black ties. Many wore shiny black patent leather shoes, others, work shoes.

There was sobbing, sometimes the bellow of a nose being blown, the lamenting cry of a stressed soul, "Jesus, Jesus."

How ironic, a call to Jesus, the white man's savior, the Jesus the white man taught them to call savior, as they were whipped to call others master.

A door at the front of the church opened, the man closed it gently behind him, he turned and looked towards the back of the church and moved that way until he stood looking down at me. "You, Bud?"

"Yes," I answered as my heart jumped into my throat. I looked him in the eye, wondering what he was going to say or do.

"Come wid me," he said in a hushed voice. He put his hand under my arm and half lifted me out of the pew and led me towards the front of the church. When we got to the front pew, there was an empty seat. He stopped and motioned for me to sit there. I was next to Mrs. Wilson.

I hadn't known Mrs. Wilson as well I as I knew Mr. Wilson. I had been to their house a few times. I had a terrible and unique passion for turnip greens and pork fat that fascinated Mrs. Wilson and she looked forward to me coming because that was a main dish on most colored folk's tables. Other than that, it was mostly a casual hello and goodby.

She took my hand and held it as if for strength. There would be none there, because strength was something I hadn't learned yet. But, on the other hand, maybe I should gain strength from her. She pulled me close to her to whisper to me, "Bud, you stay by me, Moses always said if I was to get him a son, he wanted him jes like you. He dun loved you s'much."

At that instant some invisible lance pierced my heart. I made little jerks from the throbs in my throat, the tears began to flow.

"Don't chu never fo'get," Mrs. Wilson said.

I got caught up in the emotion of the funeral and was struggling to hold back my tears. Mrs. Wilson was not. Her stern and stoic countenance seemed to belie the life of disappointment and hardship that Mr. Wilson had talked about. That if mourning and emotion were permissible, then mourning and emotion would have been a permanent lifestyle.

No way could I keep the tears from coming, I tried, but they came and dripped off of my chin. I tried to be inconspicuous as I eased my hand up to brush them away. I hadn't thought to bring a handkerchief.

It seemed that things were pre-arranged, the seat reserved for me by Mrs. Wilson and a seat was vacant next to me, at the aisle, as if it too were being reserved. Just as the service was about to begin someone slipped into the vacant seat. I didn't look up at first, but then in a heart beat, I recognized the dress, I recognized the hand as it reached over and firmly took mine. It was Amy. I wanted to grab her and hold her. I was ready to forgive her for anything, I didn't care, if we could just be like we were. I timidly looked up at her, not knowing what expression I would see. She looked at me. I had never seen her bright blue eyes red before. I had never seen her look tired and sad before.

I looked down again, she held my hand firmly as Mrs. Wilson did the other.

She handed me a note prepared earlier. It was a plan. It read;

"Bud, I will explain later, but it is not safe for you to be here. The sheriff has word that the killers are looking for you. I have Mom's car at the back of the church. As soon as the service is over we must slip out the back and get away."

I took a pencil from the back of the pew and wrote a response; "No, I won't go until after I go with Mrs. Wilson to the cemetery."

Mrs. Wilson was apparently involved in the scheme and knew as she watched me write the response because she firmly turned me towards her and spoke almost loud enough for the church to hear, "Bud Olson, Moses luved you to much to have you gets youself hurt at his funeral. Now you do whats dis girl says and I means it."

I hung my head back down and whispered a weak okay.

The door at the front opened again, a different man came out this time. He held a Bible and another book. He must have been the preacher, looked so much as Mr. Wilson had described him, taller than Mr. Wilson, but slenderer. His hair was also white, but it was mostly just a fringe around the sides. He was much darker, his eyes more piercing. He too wore a black suit. It had a vest which he had buttoned tightly to the top. Across it hung a large gold chain, maybe significant to his elevated position in the church. He was Mr. Wilson's friend, he talked about him frequently. How different each of the people looked, so common in color, yet so different in every other characteristic. Even in color, common in brown, yet the tone and shade was not. Actually, many races of brown people from far removed regions of the dark continent, but considered one race in the definition of chattel, in the land of the Anglo-saxon.

The pastor, the man in every Negro community who is chairman and moderator of every meeting and council, the man charged to find the right words, to find the meaning, to focus the mind and soul of his flock. The man with the awesome duty to remain in control of his being, even as the world falls around him, so as to give his people hope and guidance in the midst of the storm.

No time to cry now, Parson Brown. No time to show weak or unstable. Hide your broken heart, repress the curse on your lip, cover the hate in your thoughts, smother the rage in your bosom. Your day will come, but not yet. Today you must die a thousand deaths in your bowels but your spirit must speak peace, love, forgiveness. Oh, but how you say, how can the body contain such rage and fire and yet not be consumed. You and your God know, only you and your God know.

Parson Brown stood tall and forceful looking down over the lectern, sweeping his eyes across the audience, studying the faces, acknowledging the pain-struck lines on the tearful faces, choking back his own grief, searching his heart for the words to fill the empty void of the much loved "Brother Moses." He looked down into the face of his dear friend and Christian brother. He pulled a handkerchief from his pocket and made a light wipe under each eye. Finally his eyes came to rest on Mrs. Wilson. Another moment passed. It was obvious that he was petitioning a higher power for the strength to go on. Without taking his eyes off of Mrs. Wilson, he began. The first words faltered but than the power he was praying for arrived;

"My brothers and sisters, We's here to mourn the death of Moses Wilson, God's gentle man. Gone too soon cause we needs him. Ain't hardly made sixty yet and he dun gon home. Jesus dun called 'im, called 'im home.

Moses dun left a wider, Emmeline, two daughters, Mary and Esther. He dun left lots o friens and lots o broke hearts.

Why'd he go? Jesus knows, Only Precious Jesus knows."

Parson Brown turned to sit down, great heaving sighs and sobs rose from the auditorium. Some jumped to their feet throwing their hands into the air, "Jesus, Jesus, Oh save us, Precious Jesus." The sounds of defeat and desperation were coming from all parts of the church as the people begged and cried to a "Precious Jesus" that seemed to not care, had seemed never to have cared.

A choir stood in the background, wearing pleated white robs, gold scarfs were drapped around their necks. They began to sing, almost spontaneously, lamenting in tone at first, but as the songs began to sooth the souls, songs of grief and desperation, girded with a quiet spirit of hope, so very familiar, so much a banner, a solace, a balm.

"The earth shall be desolved like snow,
  The sun shall cease to shine;
But God, who called me here below,
  Shall be forever mine."
"And when this mortal life shall fail,
  And flesh and sense shall cease,
I shall possess within the veil
  A life of joy and peace."
"When we've been there ten thousand years,
  Bright shinin as the sun,
We've no less days to sing God's praise
  Than when we first begun."

*   *   *

"When I can read my title clear
  To mansions in the skies,
I'll bid farewell to every fear,
  and wipe my weeping eyes."
"Should earth against my soul engage,
  And hellish darts be hurled,
Then I can smile at Satan's rage,
  And face a frowning world."
"Let cares like a wild deludge come,
  And storms of sorrow fall,
May I but safely reach my home,
  My God, My Heaven, My all."

There was a great welling up of responses from the people as the singers continue to sing. The songs became more and more rhythmic and spontaneous. The people joined in, some in cadence others in overtones and harmony. Many were shouting prayers and crying

"Jesus, Jesus," while others stood with arms reaching heavenward, their grimaced faces projecting desperate prayers of hope.

> "Amazing Grace, how sweet the sound,
>   That saved a wretch like me.
> I once was lost but now I'm found,
>   Was blind but now I see."
> "Twas grace that taught my heart to fear,
>   and grace my fears relieved;
> How precious did that grace appear,
>   The hour I first believed."
> "Through many dangers, toils, and snares,
>   I have already come,
> Tis grace that brought me safe thus far,
>   And grace will lead me home."

* * *

The singing was repetitious, it began to be like chanting- powerful and penetrating. I found myself becoming uneasy and fearsome as the singers left the cadence of the song, they began rhythms and pitch as though guided by a strange force, yet the heart of the words and the tune were always familiar. My hand became clammy as I gripped Mrs. Wilson's hand. I began to feel foreign and closed in.

There was no indication that the singers or the congregation were waning, nor would it appear that they would ever have quit their chant had not Parson Brown stood and walked slowing, head bowed, deeply searching his heart and mind for words to put meaning to the meaningless in that short distance to the lectern.

The music stopped, a hush came over the church. Out of the quiet that seemed so unearthly quiet contrasted to the volume of the singing. From behind me I heard a sad cry, "O Jesus, we's didin wanna gib yo Moses yet."

Parson Brown stared out across the congregation for a full two or three minutes, not uttering a sound, occasionally fixing his stare on one person, then another. Finally the old face began to reveal expression, finally his lips were prepared to speak, the words began,

"My dear brothers, God ain't ner tol me why'd white man tinks he gots right to hut on da black man. God gonna tell me som da. He dun tellin Moses rit now."

Strength seemed to be coming to Parson Brown, his voice had lost most of it's quiver, his hand could release the lectern without shaking as before.

"I ain't gonna tell ya much, today; you dun sung out yous hearts, you dun tol Jesus yous gonna miss Moses. I dun cried fo two das wit da widder, I don tink I can cry much mo. But I know dis, dare wern't no kinder, gentler man in dis place din Moses wus, Moses wouldn't hut nobody, not evun his coon dog or is ole cat. He jus luv'd an luv'd. Don make no sense dat a man wid so much luv would get muddered fo no reason atol, no reason atol. Jesus dun tol us, 'Love yo nabor'. How long luv gonna go one way?"

He stopped for a minute, pulled his spectacles from his vest pocket, rested them on his nose and then with one hand and then the other, fixed the stems around his ears. He pushed a large book to the top of the lectern, not a bible, for as he opened it I could see the pages. I knew later that he was reading from Uncle Tom's Cabin, for here the Negro Christian had a hero.

"Deem not the just by Heaven forgot!
  Though life it's common gifts deny,-
Though, with a crushed and bleeding heart,
  And spurned of man, he goes to die!
For God has marked each sorrowing day,
  And numbered every bitter tear;
And heaven's long years of bliss shall pay
  For all his children suffer here."

He closed this book and slid it down to the bottom of the lectren. Looking up into the eyes of an invisable God that only he could see, his own eyes filled with burning tears, "O God, how longs we got's to live in Uncle Tom's cabin?"

He took another book, large, black, worn. Opened it carefully to a marker, he looked deeply into it and began to read, but only a couple of words, for the words were so familiar that the page was not required;

"And behold the tears of such that are oppressed; and on the side of their oppressors there was power. Wherefore I praised the dead that are already dead more than the living that are yet alive." Eccl. 4:1.

He then closed this book and opened the other again. Half reading, half quoting;
"Twas something like the burst from death to life;
   From the grave's cerements to the robes of heaven;
From sin's dominion, and from passion's strife,
   To the pure freedom of a soul forgiven;
   Where all the bonds of death and hell are riven,
And mortal puts on immortality,
When Mercy's hand hath turned the golden key,
And Mercy's voice hath said, Rejoice, thy soul is free."
With tears streaming down Parson Brown's face now, the shifting lights from the windows dancing sparkles from them, he raised his head and stared toward heaven; "Precious Lord Jesus, we gib you our dear, beloved frien, Brother Moses Wilson. "Heaven's done got to be a better place now."

Great weeping came from the people, Parson Brown returned to his seat and sat down heavily. Mrs. Wilson, who had shown little emotion through the sermon, cried out, "O Moses, I'm coming soon."

The men from the funeral home came reverently down the eisle and stood by the casket, one on either side. The one that appeared to be in charge took over the remainder of the service, "The family has requested the casket be left open so that all da friends of Brother Wilson can pass by and view him one more time."

He began to direct the crowd, pew by pew, to pass by. Toward the end Junior and Albert came. Junior kept his eyes to the floor, Albert paused to look at Moses for an instant, then put his hand on Junior's shoulder and directed him on. After the last had passed, the door of the church was closed, nobody remained but Mrs. Wilson, the two daughters, Amy and me. The family held each other, I could hear them trying to say words of comfort to each other but none came audible, except for the words of Mrs. Wilson. Amy stood to the side, Mrs. Wilson pulled me close, we all stood together looking at the body, "Don't you worry none about Moses," Mrs. Wilson said, "Moses dun a happy man now."

After this, Mrs. Wilson looked around and found Amy standing a little behind us, she looked at her and nodded with her head. Amy took a step toward me, took my hand and led me out the back door of the church to where the car was waiting. I could hear Emmeline and Esther weeping as we passed through the door, Mrs. Wilson had gathered them up into arms, they were pressing against the casket, tears dropping on Mr. Wilson. Esther reached and stroked his face lightly as to wake him from a sleep, "Daddy" she whispered like her daddys' little girl, but daddy wouldn't respond.

Chapter #10
HIDING WITH AN ANGEL

Amy jumped behind the wheel of Mrs. Brooks Cadillac, "Hurry, Bud, I'm nervous around here. The sooner we get down the road the better it will be," she said with a sterness I'd never heard before.

The big cadillac bounced across the drain ditch onto the road. We were soon at North Florida Avenue. Amy sped on to the highway heading north, out beyond Sulphur Springs, beyond Lutz and out away from the populated area.

I had slid down in the soft, plush seat of the car and I began to be aware of Amy's driving. She moved the steering wheel erratic at times showing her inexperience behind the wheel, but I made no comments. The traffic had declined and the steering wheel became less erratic and she began to relax.

"I'm going to pull over at this store, you run in and get us a coke. I don't think I've had a drink since early this morning. Got money?"

"Yeah, I've got that much."

I ran into the store, it was just a little roadside stand. The cokes were in a red coke box filled with ice. It felt good to reach my hand in and stir the ice feeling for a bottle at the bottom of the box. Soon little pains were running up my arm and I jerked my arm out. I paid the clerk for the two bottles and the extra two cents each for the bottle deposit which he needlessly and apologetically informed me that I would get back as soon as I returned the bottles.

I slid into the cadillac seat and handed Amy a coke. "Not sharing this time?" she said rather matter of factly.

"I didn't figure you wanted to - and maybe you can tell me what's going on."

"I will in a minute, as soon as we get a little further down the road. I've got so much to tell you, I don't want to be interrupted.

"Does your mother know what you're doing," I asked?

"Sure she does, you know she does."

"Well then, why did you come get me out of the church and just why did Mrs. Wilson seem to know so much about what was going on?"

"Okay, here's what. Whether you know it or not, the man that shot Mr. Wilson must have gotten a good look at you because he told someone at a bar that you were the only one that could identify him and when he got you the case would be closed. The sheriff called Albert and told him to keep an eye on you. When Albert called your step mother she told him that you were either at the funeral or at my house. Albert called my mom and when you weren't there they knew that you would be at the funeral. They were going to call for the sheriff to pick you up, but I wanted to talk to you so bad that I convinced Mom to let me do it. As soon as you see a phone, I've got to call her and let her know that we're alright."

"Your mom is something else to let you take such a risk, but I didn't think you would want to see me anymore."

"Have you forgotten already that mom said she would love you too? You just don't understand, do you?"

It was nearly sundown when we found a phone, it was sitting on the counter of a little roadside fruit stand. An old lady, hair mostly gray, held in place by a tightly pulled miniature fish seine, was lifting baskets of oranges and tangerines that she had placed along the front of the stand for tourist to see as they drove by. The baskets seemed heavy for her, so I jumped out to help. Before the last basket was carried in, Amy saw me out of the car. Without taking the phone from her face, she straightened her finger and made a strong pointing jester toward me and a second toward the car. I sat the last basket down and retreated.

Amy had gotten her mother on the phone and I could see her making gestures with her hands as she related the events to her. Soon she was back at the car, she reached forward to the ignition key, the engine roared instantly. The car pulled out onto the road but Amy no longer speeded away, she relaxed and drove casually.

Well, what did your mom say?"

"She said be careful and stay lost for awhile."
"Is that all she said?"
"She said call again first thing in the morning."
"That's it?"
"Nope, she said she loved us both."

Amy looked toward the sun setting, "It's about dark enough. Do you think we could pull down one of the old roads and hide out of sight with out getting the car stuck?"

There's one up here we could, ends at a lake, we hunted there one time.

Amy pulled the car off the road onto the lane and stopped. "You'd better drive, I'm not used to these kind of roads."

We changed places and in a few minutes we came to the end of the road. We were only a few feet from a quiet little lake in a clearing pocked with black ash piles and party litter. A place apparently popular for weekend parties. But not tonight.

When the big caddy came to a halt, Amy and I relaxed down into the seat as if relieved that we had made a great getaway.

"The sunset's pretty, don't you think, Bud?"

"Yes, I like sunsets." I hated myself, I wanted to act aloof to Amy but I could clearly remember the many sunsets that Amy and I had watched together. I even remembered the first sunset, at our first party, when Amy rescued me from the taunting verbal jabs Ronnie was making towards me. I could almost feel the excitement as she slipped her hand into mine as we walked from the her house to where I had hidden my cutdown in the trees several hundred yards before I got to her house because I knew Ronnie would be in his knew chevy and I would be embarrassed more than I could handle. It was like magic, the sun setting over the lake behind the house and moon rising full in the front.

"Amy, why?" I wanted to make the question bigger and more complex but that was all that came out.

"Bud, did you think that it was me wearing my cheerleader jacket at the hayride?"

"What else would I think?"

"I knew you did. But it wasn't, it was Peggy, she was cold."

I felt so stupid,"You mean?"

"Yes, you know how cold Peggy gets every time we go swimming. She was standing there shivering and I put my jacket on her.

"You mean.."

"Bud, I only love you, can't you believe that?"

I turned until I was looking straight at her, her eyes were red and moist with tears. She leaned toward me very slightly- my heart pounded. "Do you still want me," I asked in a voice that would have sounded like a plead for mercy?

She didn't take her eyes away from mine, her lower lip began to quiver, we leaned closer until our arms were around each other, I drew her next to me, we kissed and I felt the magic I thought would be lost forever. I could feel her tears dropping onto my cheeks as I'm sure she felt mine.

We embraced in such a way that neither wanted to stop. It was the emotional sensation of the return of a great lost treasure. We paused, spontaneously we said," I love you", and continued our embrace, feeling the regeneration of warmth and passion, feeling the peace and security of returning home from a trying journey.

It was into the night before our passion and excitement turned soft and quiet. My shoulder was wet from Amy's tears, she was breathing heavy, the rise and fall of her chest and the rhythm of her rapid heart beat was telegraphing through her young, firm breast.

Finally, under her breath, almost to low for me to hear over my own deep breathing, she whispered, "Bud, I was so afraid I would lose you. It hurt so bad."

"I'm sorry, Amy, I don't know why I did it. I know you would never do anything like that. I just panicked. I just didn't think I was good enough for you. All I can ever do is hurt you."

"Bud Olson!!, Amy blurted out almost in a shout, "If you aren't good enough, do you think I would have been crying day and night all this time!" Amy pulled me around until I was looking her straight in the face, "Never, ever again say that your not good enough. OK?"

"Okay, I won't.

"Promise."

"Yes."

"Seal it with a kiss?"

"Yes."

She raised her finger to her lips and then touched mine, "But first." She reached into her purse and pulled her closed hand out, "I went looking for you where I knew you would be. You weren't there but I found this." She opened her hand and grasped each end of the golden chain that carried my Saint Christopher medal and the half heart she had given me. "I'm going to pretend that this never came off. I think that should be alright under the circumstances. Don't you?" The chain snapped into the lock and she lightly placed her lips on mine.

I began to speak, "Amy, I won't ever-,"

Amy cut me off, "I know, but I don't won't you to have to say it. I know." Amy's words drifted off into silence as pictures of the past events scrolled before my eyes.

After a few moments Amy broke the silence, "Are the doors locked?"

"They are now," I said as I locked them.

"I'm so tired," Amy said in a half yawn, "But it feels so good to be with you. Like a place all our own."

"I guess for now it is all our own. No body's here but us."

"Oh, silly Bud, I've finally got you all locked up in a car to myself. I could be dangerous, you know," Amy said as she made a weak attempt to grin.

"Go ahead and be dangerous, see if I care. I'll call it my just reward and enjoy every minute of it."

It was quiet for a minute as neither of us had the energy to create a follow up.

Bud, I'm so tired and sleepy, move to the other side of the car and lean back against the door so I can stretch out and rest my back against you."

I slid to the other side away from the steering wheel. Amy leaned with her back against me, she kicked off her shoes and let them fall to the floorboard. I felt her body relax and become heavy against my chest. "Bud, I'm so tired and sleepy. I feel like I haven't slept in a week. You won't be hurt if I go to sleep, will you?"

"No, go ahead, it feels good having you close. Maybe I'll go to sleep, too."

We didn't speak for a while. We just listened as the night noises from the lake and the trees began to creep in above the soft sounds of our breathing. I could feel Amys' light movements as she played with the buttons on the front of her blouse. Soon she reached for my hand and guided it under her loose bra until it was resting on her breast. Chills raced up my arm, I felt nervous. I wondered if I was to leave my hand there or pull it back. Amy knew and held my hand firmly, "It's okay, we owe it to each other, you'll know I'm yours, no other hand will ever touch me this way."

I was going to say something romantic to complete the moment but when it was said and done I only said, "Amy, I will love you forever."

Just before sleep Amy whispered, "I just can't stay awake any longer. Good night, Sweetheart."

"Goodnight, Amy."

In the very faintest of whispers before she went to sleep, "Bud, I wish we didn't have to grow up. It seems like people have to hurt a lot when they grow up."

Her body relaxed as she slept. For one of the few times in my life, I felt like the Knight in Shinning Armor, protecting the fair princess. I was strong now, I was reborn, I was ready to defend my treasure from any and all of lifes' dangers. I drew strength from her strength, determination from her will. In only minutes, from a beat and broken lad to a fierce warrior.

Was it all because my hand lay on Amys breast. Was Amy so wise and beyond her teenage years in wisdom that she would know of the great power that passes from the breast of the one you love. But then, wasn't the babes first knowledge of this new and awesome world learned as it was lain by the nurses hand against it's mothers' breast. And was not the mothers breast it's source of strength and nourishment from it's very beginning. And, didn't the mother, seeing the darkness of danger, clutch her baby and hold it tightly against her bosom. And what young lad, having put his hand in adventures trust, drawn it back in hast to find blood oozing from a fingers cut, buried his head in the healing warmth of his mothers breast, extending his wounded finger for his mothers' magic kiss and the hurt stopped instantly. And when the black mothers' baby was stripped from her, under the guise of ownership, from where was the baby stripped?

Then, is it any wonder, and isn't it only true, that a man fills his emptiness and girds up his strength by the magic touch of the bosom of the woman he loves.

How sad and empty the soul of one who never knew this bond. And how desperate the life as it thrashes through jungles of torment, cutting trails with no possible destination.

* * *

I soon fell asleep. The interior of the car was a little warm and always humid, but I didn't dare lower the windows for fear of a mosquito attack. But it didn't matter, Amy and I were both so tired from the trying events of the past few days that sleep came despite the few physical discomforts.

"Whip O Willll", came the shrill call of the night bird, "Whip O Willll." How kin I'd become to the sound of his call.

I lay with my eyes closed listening, "Whip O Will." Between sleep and awake I wondered to myself, "Is this the bird I listened to so often in my backyard at Lee's grave?"

"Whip O Will."

No, I know now, it's not him, this bird's song is much more shrill and higher pitched. Besides, we're so many miles from where he lives. I slept on.

The soft rays of the early morning sun were beginning to warm my cheeks. I looked up to see the sun moving up above the trees, it's light dancing from the night dew.

Amy stirred a little, then drew her legs up to her, shifting her body to lie side ways in the car seat, her head in my lap. "It's not morning yet, is it?"

"The sun's up a little. Don't you feel it getting hot in here?"

"Yes, I guess I do. Can we lower the windows now?"

"In a minute, I don't think the sun's up enough to run off the mosquitos yet."

It was only a few more minutes until the direct sun light had the car unbearably hot.

"Okay, down come the windows, mosquitos or not."

Amy raised up from the seat and stretched her arms above her. She shook her head from side to side in a motion designed to straighten out her hair and then ran her fingers through her hair to finish the job. She was looking around the area while she was fixing her hair, "Lots of trees," she said, "Let's get out."

"Good idea, I'm burning up in here."

Amy threw open the door and jumped out, "Okay, you go that way and I'll go this way and I'll meet you back here in a minute."

I turned and watched her walk away, her church dress was wrinkled and ruffed, her hair disarrayed, bare feet, the most beautiful thing in the world.

In silence, we leaned against the car hood, side by side, hand in hand, looking out across the lake. After a while the silence was beginning to bug me and make me nervous. "Penny for your thoughts," I said.

"Really want to know?"

"Sure."

"I was thinking how good a swim would feel."

"Boy, would it. But we don't have any clothes to swim in."

"I know, but I have a plan."

"Oh, sure. You're not thinking about you know what?"

"You swim in your pants, I'll swim in my dress, then we'll walk around until we dry off and who's going to care."

"Okay," I shouted, "Head for the water."

"Not so fast, Amy said and grabbed my arm. You go over there and take off everything that's not required and I'll do the same over here."

The lake had a clean sandy bottom and it was easy to walk out into the water to chest deep. The water felt cold at first but it took only a few minutes to warm up. At first Amy's dress wouldn't cooperate and floated in a big circle around her, she spun making it swirl, but after pushing it down a few times it became water logged and stayed down. It was a small lake and in no time we reached the center, "Is it hard to swim in your pants?"

"Sure is, like pulling an anchor. How about you?"

"Yeah, but it doesn't make treading water any harder. Want to try our famous under water embrace before we head back?"

Without responding I rolled over and dove under the water. Soon we found each other and embraced, the water was clear enough that I could see small bubbles coming from her nose. We brought our lips together and held each other tight for as long as our lungs would allow and then we burst through the surface.

Amy rolled over on her back and began a back stroke towards the beach. I caught up to her and rolled over in to the same stroke. We could swim a long way in this position and we often talked, "Well, Bud, how did it feel to do our famous underwater thing with a fully dressed girl?"

"Not to bad, considering."

I dragged a log up to the edge of the beach for Amy and I to sit on, "Come on over here, I shouted, We can sit here and dry in the sun."

"I'll be right there, but first I'm going over here and wring the water out of my dress."

We sat for a couple of hours. For a change, I did most of the talking, it was the first time since the ill-fated hayride that Amy and I had been together. I told her all the details from the time I leaped over the truck rails and fell to the pavement, about Junior finding me sitting at Lee's grave, about the terrible shock when the villains bullet knocked Mr. Wilson into the water of Boss Coon swamp. As I related the story, Amy would grab my arm and gasp "Oh Bud, my poor Bud." Amy's response was just enough encouragement to keep me going. Finally, after telling how I had tricked the deputy sheriff by slipping out my bedroom window and catching a bus to Mr. Wilson's funeral, we just became quiet, buried in our own private thoughts, sitting on the log I had retrieved from the edge of the cyprus swamp, pressing toward each other, my arm around Amy's back, her head leaning onto my shoulder, looking out and across the lake at the cyprus forest that lined the lake on the other side. The sun was high enough now that the it was bearing down directly into the face of the trees, brilliantly lighting the white plumage of a dozen or so egrets that had chosen a long bare limb of one of the taller trees to spend the night. As the sun heightened, one raised tall, and in a moment, after stretching its tallest, as I frequently do at the side of my bed, spread his great wings and glided down to the shallow waters at the edge of the lake to begin his morning feed.

Life was at peace, as mornings so often are, before the toils of the day begin. Two hearts, two souls, so gradually, so im-perceptually, becoming one. So silent, even the morning chatter of the sparrows was missing, not even did the waters of the lake stir enough to make a ripple on the shore- "Bud."

"What, Amy?"

"Do you love me?"

"Yes I do, more than I ever thought I could love anyone."

"That's how much I love you, too."

"Bud, what time is it?" Amy asked with a start as she snapped from her daydream.

"Oh, about ten I'd guess."

"We must have been sitting here for over an hour watching those funny looking long legged birds over there."

"There Egrets. Not a bad idea to watch them if your bass fishing, they show you where the little minnows are, usually a big bass around feeding on the same minnows."

"Really."

We'd been sitting there for a while alright, but it didn't seem like it. It seemed like only a minute ago that we sat down to dry our wet clothes. That strange love magic was taking over, that yearning to stay close, the tugging in the heart that makes it beat faster, that emotion that a young boy and girl feel that tell them no obstacle is large enough to come between them or keep them separated. That not even poverty, hunger or even sickness is a consideration. That all is surmountable, even negligible, only to be together. Neither boy nor girl, ever having paced the long path of life, having no experience to build a foundation for decision making or measuring the possibilities, could ever believe that down the road of even the deepest, devoted love, that clouds and shadows often follow the brightest sunshine. That in twenty years or so the hormones that drive the early emotions will be beat and bruised and in only a few will the fire endure. But why tell them? May this not be the only experience of true and emotional love that some will ever taste? So why? Let's not. So, let the pure surge of love and adventure take it's course. Just tell them what Moses said, that God made a good woman for every man, and the man that takes the time and finds her, someday, will leave this world a happy man. Tell them that not even death has more power than their love.

Amy abruptly jumped to her feet, "C'mon, we've got to find a phone. I've got to call mom, she'll be worried sick if I don't."

We headed for the car, "You drive," Amy said, "It's more fun when your driving."

With a bump the heavy car caught it's footing on the pavement of highway #41 and we headed north again. There were few cars on the highway, we felt secure and made no attempt to hide or disguise our selves.

"I bet there's a phone just up ahead at that fruit stand. Pull in there and I'll check," Amy said motioning with her hand the direction of the stand.

I pulled up close to the front, Amy jumped out and disappeared through the door. I jumped out next and stood at the entrance. I could see Amy talking to the lady in charge. Soon Amy came back toward me, "I forgot that this is long distance, the lady is not sure about me making a long distance call."

"Well, that's silly, just give her the telephone number and let her give it to the operator and she can tell the her to reverse the charges to your mom's phone."

"Good idea. How'd you know to do that?"

"When I lived with my mom I used to run away a lot and I'd call her to come get me."

"Yeah, well, she should have left you there so you'd quit."

"You know mom's aren't that way."

Amy talked to Mrs. Brooks for a few minutes. I could tell by the gestures Amy was making that she was reassuring her that everything was going fine. The lady never moved far from the phone and was running her eyes up and down Amy's dress observing the wrinkles and droop. When Amy hung up the phone the lady moved over into the isle making an obstruction between her and the door, "Is everything okay," she asked?

Amy stopped and then realizing what prompted the question grabbed the edges of her dress in each hand and held then out from her sides, "Oh, sure, would you believe, I fell into the lake in my Sunday School dress."

The lady moved to the side and Amy was back in the car and we were off.

"Where are we," Amy asked.

"Oh, I'd guess we are about ten to fifteen miles this side of Brooksville."

"Brooksville, that's a pretty big town, isn't it?"

"Not as big as Tampa, but a lot bigger than Lutz."

"Think they'll have a good restaurant?"

"Sure. You hungry."

"Boy, I could eat a horse. I don't think I've eaten much in the last few days. Aren't you?"

"Bout the same."

"You have any money?"

"Didn't get to work for Albert last week. How much is in there," I asked as I handed her my wallet?

"Well, let's see. Hmmm, not to much. Let me check my purse."

Amy was rummaging around through the gadgets in the purse and then abruptly turned it up side down and dumped it on the floorboard. She snapped open her change purse and dumped it. "One dollar and some change in mine and two dollars in yours. Is that enough?"

"Sure, it is if we don't have to buy gasoline to get home."

"Do we?"

"It's between quarter and half. That's plenty if we don't drive around to much."

"Great, let's go eat, I don't care what I look like."

How curious, Amy, who always dressed the best, had no particular care or feeling about what someone else might think of her appearance. On the other hand, I seldom ever could find such luxuries, but was constantly intimidated about my appearance.

We had barely gotten into the city limits of Brooksville and found one of those good, old fashion, (not old fashion then) restaurants that served big eggs with yokes that were dark yellow, biscuits that were made by real hands that blended the flour, real lard, baking powder and salt measured out in the hollow of one of the hands. Bacon that was thick with a big strip of lean meat running down the center and it laid flat on the plate. The grits were cooked slow, the cook had flavored them by pouring bacon grease in the pot while they were cooking. They were soft, fluffy, firm enough to stand up and hold a big chunk of churned butter while it slowly melted and ran down the sides of the pile. Even the coffee seemed better than usual. I had learned to drink coffee early with Albert before hunting, but it was a new trick for Amy. But this morning it was a sign of growing up and we drank away. Oh how we thought we were growing up, just us together, sitting in a strange place, a long way from home, calling our own shots, making our own decisions, saying whatever came to mind.

We were sitting across from each other at a booth against a far wall, under the table our legs were locked together, we were only aware of each other, certain that no one was aware of us.

The waitress seemed to be overly attentive at first. She made sure that our glasses were full of water and our cups topped off. Finally, she sat her coffee pot down on the table with a thud. She looked at me in a hesitating concern and then at Amy, "You kids ain't thinkin bout running off an doing sumpin silly are you?"

Amy looked up at me with a quisical expression on her face and then we both laughed out simultaneously.

"Oh, heavens no," Amy said looking up at the waitress, grinning from ear to ear. Not this time, but maybe before to long." And then winked at me.

"Well, ain't so funny, lot's of dumb kids runs off now o days. Then they finds life is tuffer'n hell out there. Take it from me, you got's lots of time. Les of course you wants to be like me, work'n fore daylight servin coffee and flipping cakes so's you can feed your baby."

"Oh no," Amy responded, "It's nothing like that, were not going to do anything like that until we're old enough. We've promised each other that already."

The waitress paused a moment and seemed to be studying our faces to see if she could locate a flaw in Amy's story. She seemed to be satisfied and picked up the pot, "How bout me gettin you kids some more breakfast?"

"Oh, thanks no, I couldn't eat another bite," Amy replied.

"Then, how bout another biscuit, I got some fresh honey back there," she pointed toward the kitchen with the coffee pot.

"Oh, no," Amy started to say but I cut her off.

"Well, maybe I could eat another biscuit or two. They're about the best."

"Sure nuff, honey. See, sweetheart, there's a lot to learn bout men."

Amy laughed as she looked at me, "Well, I'm trying real hard."

A young couple, deeply in love is easy to spot. I guess we made just such an appearance because the waitress seemed to seat everyone that came in away from us. She came over on a regular basis to make sure that our water and coffee receptacles were full, even though we hardly touched them. There was a lot of hustle and bustle at the counter where ordinary looking folks came in for breakfast, some just for coffee. The cigarette smoke rose from a dozen or so cigarettes resting in the little grooves of the glass ash trays while they rustled their morning papers, folding them in and out exposing each section in turn while trying not to take up to much counter space nor overly disturb the one at the next seat.

Men with their wives were occupying the booths along the edge of the restaurant walls. In all it was noisy and busy and smelly, but not so much that Amy or me even noticed, nor did we notice the occasional glance from the occupants.

Amy gave my leg a strong squeeze with her legs. I looked up at her, "What you thinking?" she asked looking intently at me with a grin after studying my face a long time.

"Bout us."

"Tell me."

"You mean what I'm thinking."

"Yes. Is it going to be a secret from me?"

"I was thinking that it would be nice if today could last forever."

"You know what?"

"What."

"That's just what I was thinking."

We squeezed our legs together.

Amy extended her hands out above the table. I reached for them and held them between mine.

We grew silent again, I found myself studying her face and searching her eyes. They didn't look tired and red anymore, they were white and bright as they had always been. They were blue again, as blue as the northern sky on a clear winter day. Her flax blonde hair, growing lighter at the ends from the bleaching of many hours of sunlight, was all muffed and hanging to her shoulders in groups of unorganized clumps. Normally it was smooth, almost silky, with gentle waves, but the morning swim had done away with that and the waves were trying to make tight curls. She knew I was studying her, she didn't move or change expression, maybe thinking I should see her as I would some day in the future before the morning makeup. But that's not what I saw, at first, maybe it was. But then, all of a sudden, I did notice something, her round and puffy cheeks were not so round anymore, her eyes were becoming deeper and appeared to have a more serious set. Her nose, that had always had a babyish pug to it now seemed leaner and more defined. Her cheek bones began to appear and her cheeks were slightly recessed. I was looking into one of life's phenomenons as a young and precious girl began to display the first physical signs of becoming a woman.

It seemed she was studying me at the same time. I wondered what she was thinking, but it didn't matter anymore, I wasn't afraid anymore of being found wanting or unworthy. Amy had fixed that. It seemed only correct for her to study me as I studied her. I was trying to reach through the space between us and find the thoughts in her heart, a legitimate explorer, as legitimate as reading my own thoughts. The fear and intimidation of being two very different persons was no longer involved, we were now a step beyond that, an inseparable being, two personalities making one, a whole, a unit, complete.

"Hey, ya'll, let me get them plates out of your way. Don't worry bout rushin off, got plenty of tables left. Sides, be lunchtime in a few minutes. Welcome to stay for lunch."

I glanced at Amy before I responded, "Oh, well, thanks a lot, but I guess we won't stay for lunch, we're heading home right away.

"Ok, but ya'll come back now."

I couldn't tell for sure whether the waitress was wanting us to stay or go, just the same, we slid out of the booth as soon as she left. I reached into my pocket and pulled out the meager change I had left, I held it in my cupped hand for Amy to see, she nodded and I left it on the table, enough for two breakfasts and a few cents for the waitress.

We were holding hands as we walked from the restaurant to the car, I went to Amy's side and opened the door for her to get in as if I knew what I was doing. I got in from the other side and Amy had already slide across to meet me.

"You know what? I would just as soon get in from your side and I wouldn't have to slide across."

I scooted down in the seat and didn't start the car, "Amy," I asked, "What did your mother say this morning when you called her?"

"Oh, she said she worried about us, said a prayer, said she knew I was in good hands, said everything seemed to be clear, be home before dark, said she loved us so much that if anything happened to us she couldn't take it so be careful and don't take any chances."

"Boy, I'll say one thing, I'm for getting home before dark, alright."

"You are, how come."

"Cause, we don't have any more money to eat on."

"Oh, silly Bud. Don't you know that we can live on love for a while."

"OK then, where do we go from here," I asked.

"Can I choose?"

"Sure."

"Well, I'd like to go back to that lake and sit on that log for a while longer. Then, I'd like to sneak back home and spend the rest of the day together in our secret place."

"Boy, Amy, that's a great idea. Nobody could ever find us there."

I turned the key and the faithful engine roared. No place in particular to go so I eased the Big Caddy onto the road and let it cruise almost by it's own will back toward the turnoff to the lake. Amy spontaneously twisted her position in the seat so that she could lay her head in my lap with her legs stretched out on the seat, she looked up at me with that look that I'd seen before and I knew a serious subject was about to be proposed. "Bud, we should have a serious talk now that we're alone with some time."

"I'm not to good at serious, you know."

"Yes you are, sometimes you seem so serious I worry about you."

"Well, sometimes I am. But it's only when I can't get things figured out."

"Let's talk about marriage."

"Really."

"Well."

"I Mean."
"You haven't changed your mind, have you?"
"Not me."
"Do you want to?"
"I said I did."
"No, I mean talk about it."
"Oh, yeah."

Amy drew her legs up and held them with her clasped arms. "Do you think we should get married real soon or wait."

"I want to get married as soon as you want to. You know, sooner the better."

"I want us to go to college first. Can we wait that long, do you think?"

"That seems like a long time and besides, I'm not sure I'd ever make it through college. I'm not to good at books, you know."

"But you're really smart, I know you could."

"I dang sure would if that was the only way I could get you to marry me."

"We'd be in our twenties then. Do you think we could wait that long to?"

"To what," I laughed.

"You know what."

"I guess we could. But a lot of kids don't."

"If we couldn't wait any longer we could get married before we finished college."

"Sure we could. And I would work part time to pay the bills."

"Then is it a deal."

"Which, about going to college or getting married or waiting."

"All of it."

"You know what, Amy? If waiting would make it right for you, I'd wait a long, long time."

"I love you, Bud. It won't be as long as it seems now."

A short silent pause as Amy contemplated her next statement, "Well, I do know that boys are different than girls and if waiting begins to hurt you to bad we'll get married when ever you say. That's my promise to you."

"But what about your mother? Would she want you to get married before you finished college?"

"She probably wouldn't mind if we wanted to real bad, but this is just between you and me, mother will understand."

"But, would she think that I'm taking you away?"

"Oh no, it would be you that she'd expect me to marry."

"She really knows how we feel about each other?"

"Of course, silly. Do you think I could hide it from her?"

Impulsively I pulled her closer.

Amy went on in a quiet moving spirit, "Do you want to have children."

"Maybe, I'm not sure. Do you?"

"Yes."

"How come?"

"For one thing, mom gets so lonesome with just me, and me not being home much any more. It would make her so happy to have some grandkids. She deserves to be happy. Could we do that for her?"

"As many as she wants is fine with me. Besides she'll probably want to baby sit free."

Amy laughed, "My silly Bud."

I was pondering Amy's feelings for her mother's loneliness, "How come your dad isn't home more? That would be better for her, wouldn't it."

"I guess it would be, but dad just can't bare up at home. The responsibilities he has at work are different from the responsibilities at home. Mom says that over the years of being gone so much that he just feels guilty around us and is always anxious to get back to the people that he has no obligation to. That doesn't make much since, I know, but that's about the only way mom can explain it."

"I would love you and your mom so much. Does he?"

"Oh yeah, very much, I'm sure."

"Then why?"

"I really don't know. Maybe he feels that we don't need him, since mom is so good at things. But sometimes I just wonder if it's because he's afraid of getting hurt if he shares his heart with anyone. You know how easy it is to get hurt when you love people. Maybe that's selfish, I don't know?"

"I wonder if that's why my dad left. I always figured I wasn't what he wanted and it was easier to just leave than face up to it. I just wish he could have loved me. A boy sure needs a dad."

"Is your dad gone for good," Amy asked?

"I don't know about for good, but he's never around when I need him."

"You mean like now."

"Sorta, I guess like now. But sometimes I think I'm lucky that I get to make most of my own decisions about things and if I get in trouble there's not anybody around to punish me. But, you know, sometimes I wish there was. Sometimes I get so lonesome and embarrassed when I meet people and they ask me about my parents."

"What do you tell them?"

"I just tell them that dad works away most of the time and I live with my step mother. I just don't think it's any of their business."

"But your step mother and dad let you keep your dogs and drive your cutdown. That means something, doesn't it?"

"Sure, I guess so. I just think they do it because they feel guilty about not being there for me. Maybe I'm wrong."

"Is that why you have your dogs? Do they keep you company and make a family for you?"

"Oh, I couldn't say that for sure. But I love them a lot and they love me, too. They've been good friends. Especially Blue."

"That's why you go hunting with your dogs instead of going out for sports at school, isn't it."

"I couldn't go out for sports and leave Blue and Sam home with nothing to do. That wouldn't be fair to them, sitting there day after day thinking that nobody cared about them. If I went out for sports and did good, nobody'd care anyway. At least when I go hunting, I know that Blue and Sam care, and I care for them."

"I'd care."

"You would?"

"Oh, maybe not. I guess you'd just be another jock, then."

"I wonder if I'd be good at football, like Ronney?"

"Who cares. Your just what I want you to be. Promise you won't ever change."

We drifted off into silence. We'd said and thought about a lot of things in the last few minutes, now we'd think back over them and wonder if the things said were the right ones to say or if the other understood the feelings behind the words.

I turned the car off the highway onto the sandy road leading down to the lake. The car bumped a little and I slowed it down to a easy, steady speed.

Amy raised up with a jerk revealing that she had dozed off, "We're at the lake already? Boy, seems like we just left Brooksville."

"Guess we were having a good time talking. And you went to sleep, didn't you?" I got a sheepish grin.

I brought the big caddy to a stop a few yards back from the log. The lake was quiet and placid. Across the lake a lone fisherman was sculling a small boat into the area we had seen the egrets feeding in earlier. I wondered if he to knew the secret of the bass. Maybe not, but he was casting a lure into the exact spot where they were feeding, maybe everyone knows.

We left the car and walked to the log. I sat astraddle so that Amy could lean against me. The sun had passed over noon and was making a great glare off the lake into our eyes. Amy said something about wondering the name of the lake and if we were on private property. That maybe someday we could buy this spot and build a house here, and we could have a beach house just like theirs and we could sit in the beach house and watch the sun go down and remember our first night together.

I agreed with her fantasies as she made them, but in fact I never in my wildest dreams ever dreamed of having something as nice as a house on a lake. As a matter of fact, those things seemed to be blocked out of my mind and I never thought of house or cars or any other opulent conditions for that matter. I never saw my self as much different than what ever condition I was in at the time.

"Bud, let's go walk in the water and cool off a little."

We walked around the edge of the lake where the water was shallow and the sand was firm. Amy held her dress up to keep the hem dry, occasionally she would loose her balance and grab hold to my arm. We investigated the myriad of aquatic things along the edge of the water, a cypress knee that looked like a little brown elves face, Amy stroked it and said with a silly smirk, "Nice boy", a scooped out bed that a bass was preparing to nest in, an intricate web erected between some tall cattail stalks, coon tracks along a narrow trail where some coon had been feeding the night before, probably while we slept. A clump of hyacinths had broken away from the main clump in the center of the lake and had drifted to the shore. I picked some of the delicate violet and white flowers and handed them to Amy in the form of a bouquet. Small frogs leaped into the water ahead of our approach and swam quickly out of sight. A tall, grey pond bird slipped out of the cattail reeds and was startled by our approach. He soon put distance between us taking long awkward steps lifting one skinny leg high out of the water and then the other, turning his pointed head on his skinny neck so that he could keep a beady eye on us. Amy seemed to be amazed at every discovery we made and pretended to believe I was a master of the universe. "Bud," she laughed, "Did you get to help name all the animals?"

We laughed and turned toward the car, the shadows were getting long and the clock had continued mercilessly around it's course, "I think we'd better head toward home. It's going to be late when we get back."

The trip back to Lutz didn't take long and we'd soon be approaching Amy's house.

I broke the silence, "Let's hide the car down the road behind the grove and we can sneak over to our secret place."

I pulled the car over to the edge of the road behind a growth of wild fruit trees, hardly hidden, but any further would have probably resulted in a stuck caddy. We exited the car and dashed for the tree that was our secret place, weaving through the trees like seasoned commandos. Soon we were on our hands and knees crawling through the low opening at the base of the sprawling limbs and then up on our feet in the shelter of our imaginary Eden.

It had been some time since we'd been there. Over time we had equipped it with a little table and two chairs. A little rug was on the ground, irregularly laying to the form of the ground. A pillow was against the tree where we sat and leaned against the tree trunk and talked. There had been no rains recently so all was fairly dry for this part of the world.

"Do we have much time," Amy asked.

"Not much, I don't think. If you get in late your mom will be worried sick."

"Then, will you just hold me for a while before we go."

"If I lay on the rug you can lay on my shoulder. Will that be okay?"

"Yes, and hold me like you might not ever hold me again."

I can still feel the warm sensations that rushed though my body as we lay close. I can feel them, as a gift from another world, I can feel them, I can't find words of explanation that could do them justice or create the image in another's mind. But, I'm not naive, I know that you know, and would give most of your life to return to those moments one more time. But, was it really the electricity or the chemistry that created the sensation? I think that maybe, at least in my own case, that it was that someone more wonderful than life itself had dared to share that wonder with un-worthy me.

We kissed once, but not again.

"Amy, it's beginning to get dark."

The sun was low - long, lumbering shadows from the great trees were silently trudging across the grove floor.

"Can't we stay a few more minutes."

"I'd like to, but I don't want your mother to worry."

It was dark enough now that we felt confident that if Moses' murderers were lurking around that we would be unseen. We walked back to the car, I opened the car door for Amy and she slipped in. I reluctantly closed the it. She turned the ignition key, the engine caught. Amy looked straight ahead, staring blankly into the distance, letting the motor idle. After a few minutes she reached her arm out of the window, putting her hand behind my neck and pulled my head down. We exchanged a light kiss, "Call me when you get home. I'll wait up. I'll tell you what's going on."

She pulled the shift into reverse and backed out onto the road. I stood in the road and watched the tail lights disappear around a bend. Once again I felt this familiar empty feeling, a knot in my gut, a twisted pain in my throat, that reminded me that I was not in control, that if there was danger I could not protect Amy. I wanted to run for her, grab her and disappear into another world where we would be safe. But Amy said go home. Call when I got there. That is what I would do.

It took less than an hour to walk from our secret place to my house. Actually, I enjoyed the walk, it was cool and refreshing, as fall nights are. I cut through several groves and along some familiar trails that skirted the lakes that Blue and me hunted so often. We passed several huge cypress trees, I imagined that I could see two beady little eyes shinning out of the Spanish moss back at my light. I could hear the growling and the scuffling of the dogs as they lunged up the tree.

I was soon home. I eased through the front door, hoping, but knowing better, that my step-mother would have gone to bed, but don't be silly, it was to early for that. Just as I was about to put my foot on the first step of the stairs to my room, I faintly called out over my shoulder, "I'm home," hoping that I would be up the stairs before she responded.

"Bud," she called out with a rather stern inflection in her voice that meant that I had finally riled her up and had better not play dumb this time. "Come in here, we'd better have a talk," came the next command from the living room.

I came around the corner and leaned against the wall between the stairs and the living room, positioned to leap up the stairs at the first break in the dialogue. It wasn't enough, "Bud, come in here and sit down. Before this escapade goes any further, we're going to have an understanding."

She was looking me sternly in the eyes with a conviction that I'd not noticed before, "I've been talking to Madge Brooks these last few days." I shuddered at her and Mrs. Brooks talking because I knew I would be the topic of conversation. "She seems to think a lot of you. Strange, most mothers are pretty skeptical of the boys that come around to date their daughters when they're so young. Just the same, she does, a mighty lot, seems like. Whether you know it or not, she's not the only one. Now, your dad's going to be calling in a few days and unless I can count on you to stay home where you'll be safe until this mess is over, I'm going to have him come on home so's he can deal with you."

"Oh no," I blurted out, almost in a panic, "you don't need to do that. I'm sorry, but I just had to go to Moses' funeral. I couldn't have lived with myself if they'd buried him and I hadn't seen him one more time. Please, I'll stay home, out of sight until it's safe."

My step mother was no fool and knew that the threat of having my dad come home was about as big a stick as she would need. Over the years, especially in the early years, a lad makes substitutes for the lack of a dad. I had early on quit yearning for the sound of his car in the driveway or his voice at the door. As a matter of fact, I had become independent, self-serving, even defiantly so, and was not prepared to dismantle my barrier so that he or anyone else could enjoy the rewards of parenthood as though nothing had ever happened.

"Alright, Bud, if I can take your word there's no point in your father having to journey all the way home. Now, go call Amy, she called a few minutes ago to let me know you were on your way.

The phone at Amy's hardly made one ring, "Brooks."

"Hi, Amy, It's me."

We didn't talk long, Amy's mother insisted that she get to bed early and get some rest for school. She hurried through the message; the sheriff had an eye on the murderers and as soon as they came out of hiding they had a pick up order on them. He said he would put them in a lineup and if I could pick out the one that shot Moses that he would probably implicate the other and it would all be over like a bad dream. Also, since we had the car all weekend that Mrs. Brooks was going to be tied up and I was to ride home from cheerleading practice with Ronney and Peggy. Just this one time. Everything will be alright, Ronney's calmed down a lot, you know. Finally, Amy's voice softened," Bud, be careful, I couldn't bare to live if anything happened to you."

I promised I would.

The phone grew silent for a moment, "Bud, do you know what I'm thinking?"

"Yes, what I'm thinking I hope."

"I'll call as soon as I get home tomorrow."

She said goodnight and I heard her kiss the receiver before she hung up.

I went slowly up to my room. I sat on the edge of my bed, feeling somewhat sorry for myself. As natural for a young boy, I had very little sense of the danger around me, all that was smothered away by my thoughts of Amy. I lay on my bed, not bothering to take off my pants. From my window I could see the deputies car passing back and forth with fifteen minute regularity. I looked around the room, there were no pictures of trees, or cowboys or horses or circus elephants as adorn the walls of most boys rooms. No ball glove was laying on the floor or bat standing in the corner. No books, no radio, no record player. Just a bed, a small dresser and desk. On the desk, a picture of Amy in her cheerleading outfit, wearing the jacket I'd given her. How many hours, as I hid away in my room had I laid against my pillow, my arms locked behind my head and stared at the picture, and dreamed and relived the times I spent with her. I could still feel the warmth of her body, the tickle of her soft hair on my cheek from the few moments ago when she lay on my shoulder in our secret place. The thought was peaceful and I soon fell asleep.

Drifting up the stairs and into my room came the morning aroma of coffee and the makings of breakfast. I had slept deeply and sound and the smells from the kitchen awoke me as from only a few minutes after I'd lain down. I shook my head and looked out the window to see the bright light of late morning.

It crossed my mind that Amy was already on her way to school and here I was. I simultaneously threw back the bed sheet and rolled my body out and my feet to the floor. There was a lightness in my legs from the long rest as I sprung down the stairs. My stepmother met me at the bottom step, she swung a cup of coffee up in front of me, "Take this and don't come down until you've had a shower and changed from those dirty pants. I'll have your breakfast ready by then."

I said thanks and spun on the step and was at the top in a few bounds.

I wasn't used to this amount of attention, breakfast was usually not quiet so major. I suppose that everyone but me recognized how serious a dilemma I'd gotten myself in to. Or was she reaching out, trying to penetrate the shell that I'd built around my immature ego. Maybe she too felt trapped in a situation not entirely her doing. Maybe she too felt betrayed and lonesome.

I was soon sitting at the table, my stepmother had piled a layer of grits on the bottom of my plate, gently placed two eggs, sunny side up, on the top and circled the grits with strips of bacon. Instead of the usual toast, there were biscuits that were still hot. Beside my coffee cup was a glass of orange juice, freshly squeezed from tree ripened fruit displaying the sweet smell and rich color that we never see anymore.

As I began to eat, I noticed that she was fiddling around the kitchen making things to do and biding her time. When I was well into the center of the plate she turned and sat down across from me. She was holding a cup of coffee between her hands, sipping it occasionally then looking at me and watching me eat. Seldom did we sit across the table in such a manner and I felt a bit uneasy as I knew that sometime soon a subject would be brought up that I would have to address. I ate on trying not to show my suspicions.

"Bud," she finally said. Her head was tilted slightly downward, but still looking at me straight in the face, "you act a lot like you're just a resident here and not part of a family. Is that how you feel?"

"Oh no, I don't feel that way. I don't know why you'd think that."

That was exactly how I felt, but I had made inroads into my own lifestyle and I wasn't prepared to regress into anything different because it would probably mean giving up some freedom and surrendering secrets. If that was the direction this conversation was going, I had become a skillful diversionary player and would not easily be drawn into a serious discussion about what could or should be. But my step mother was still looking at me, on her face it was obvious that she hadn't concluded her talk.

She went on, the uneasiness in her voice was obvious, "You probably feel like you've been cheated because your dad left your mother and married me and broke up your home. That's probably why your so secretive, isn't it?"

She was right, I did feel cheated, I felt embarrassed, I didn't think a parent could love a kid if they were willing to do something like divorce so that a kid didn't know what to tell his friends. She was damn right, but to bad for her, I've got Blue and Sam and Amy. All I need from her and my dad was a place to sleep until I got old enough to get out of here.

"Oh, not really, It's not really all that bad, I guess. I'm doing all right, I guess."

"Well, you know that your Dad and me want the best for you and you can count on us if you have a problem."

I had learned to count on number one, I was self-sufficient and cunning. Often, I was suspicious of anyone or anything that tried to gain my confidence or pierce my cover. I had played so hard and long the role of rejection, I had become un-able to accept any kind of help or support without being suspicious of the giver's motives. Amy and her mother recognized this and dealt with it, few others did.

"Now, Mrs. Brooks told me all about your problem. It's not worth getting shot or hurt just so's you can go out and play. Whether you know it or not, these guys sound like they'd hurt anyone that got in their way, at least according to Mrs. Brooks. So you just stay out of sight until those guys are caught and if you need to talk about it or anything, you just let me know."

I thanked her and said I would and commented on how great breakfast was. I scooted out from the table with my plate in my hand and started for the back door. "Just where are you going," she snapped?

"I saved some bacon for Blue and Sam, haven't seen um for a few days."

"No sir, your not. You give me that plate and I'll see that they get the bacon."

"But dang, I haven't seem um, I bet they want to see me real bad. It's not right to leave your dogs not knowing what's going on. They just think I don't like um any more. They don't know the difference."

"Well," she said, standing with her hands on her hips in an expression that indicated that she was analyzing the situation, "if you don't get to see them, they'll probably begin to howl and you'll sneak out the first time my back's turned."

"Can I go see um, then?"

"No, but if you'll promise to behave, I'll let you take them to your room and they can keep you company."

"Really, that's great. When?"

"I'll go get the dogs. But mind you, when this is all over, your cleaning up the mess. I'm not cleaning up after no dogs and don't plan on living in a house that smells like hound dog."

In a minute I heard her holler "Okay, you'd better call them now, I'm turning them loose."

I stood at the back door and whistled and then called out, C'mon Blue, C'mon Sam.

Both dogs knew where I was and came in a race. Sam was ahead when they reached the door to the back porch but their momentum was so great that as Sam turned sideways to turn in the door Blue caught him in the middle and they slide beyond the door. Blue raced through the door and hit me with his forefeet in the chest knocking me backward in to the kitchen and over a chair and on to the floor. He was standing over me licking my face when Sam got there. I had an arm around each ones neck, holding them close as they licked away.

It was like a wrestling match when my stepmother came in, she grabbed the chair and stood it upright, "Get those dogs out of my kitchen, I mean right now. My lord."

I jumped to my feet and made for the stairs up to my bedroom. I had sneaked the dogs up to my room so many times they knew exactly where to go and we raced up. Blue jumped to the middle of my bed and sat on his haunches wagging his tail and watching Sam as he investigated under the bed and around the room.

"Now settle down, you guy's, or you'll get me into trouble."

I sat on the edge of the bed and watched out the window as the sheriff car made another routine pass by the house. I thought that if anyone wanted to know where I was they would only need to follow the sheriff's car.

I began to feel Blue moving around on the bed and then he flopped down into a comfortable position with his head pushed against my back. The bed bounced again as Sam landed on it with his full force, "Take it easy boy, were on thin ice up here, you know."

It was a long and terrible day, sitting in my close cubical. I studied the walls, I searched to see knew things out the window. I patted Blue and Sam and talked to them in the seemingly assumption that they not only understood but cared. Periodically, Sam would stand and walk to the door, stop and look back with an inquisitive look on his face, un-doubtably searching to find why we didn't get up and go out.

"Sorry boy, I know you want to go, but I can't. I'm sorry."

As I looked from my window the shadows from the tall punk trees in the yard were pointing long to my right toward the west. I watched as they grew shorter and shorter until they were a circle around the base of the tree. My thoughts drifted to Amy and our daily routine. I could have been with her right now if I hadn't gone with Junior to help Mr. Wilson. If Mr. Wilson hadn't been so stupid as to make moonshine. I thought a deacon in the church wouldn't do that. Did he just act like he liked the church so that nobody would know that he was making the stupid stuff. Maybe it's alright to make moonshine and doesn't have anything to do with the church. Maybe Mr. Wilson did both because he couldn't make up his mind whether it was right or wrong. Maybe he liked them both and just wasn't able to give up either one. Amy would be leaving the school patio about now, she'd wave at me and blow me a kiss before she turned the corner to the outside that led to the football practice field. I'd wave back and head for the bus to go home and wait for her call at six thirty. Sometimes I'd get my work done and be at her house when her and Mrs. Brooks turned into the yard. I re-felt the sick feeling that I had when they turned in, totally in fear that they would not be glad to see me or that Mrs. Brooks might reprimand me for being there to often. From the very first time, Amy would throw open the big caddy door and rush to me. Mrs. Brooks would wave and holler, "Hi, Bud, come on in for a coke." How dearly I loved them. How angelic and wonderful they were. How they could see beyond the flesh of my fears and self-worthlessness and find something worth while and valuable, I didn't know–I didn't care. The time to arrest the fears and quench the smoldering coals had taken place and I now assumed that I was welcome at any time. The shadows had moved beyond the trees now and were moving to my left to the east. It would soon be time for Amy to call. She would, she always did.

The shadows were long, reaching beyond the yard. I was sure it was time for Amy to call, but I could usually hear the phone ring. I went to the bedroom door. Sam jumped from the bed and tried to push past me, thinking that finally we were going outside. Blue at his side. "No, Sam," I said firmly while pushing him back with my hand. I called downstairs to my stepmother.

"It's not quite seven. No, Amy hasn't called. You can't expect her to call every night."

I did expect her to call every night. That's all I lived the day for. She said she would and she would, especially tonight.

The room began to darken, I felt sick and worried. I made the dogs stay on the bed and I closed the door behind me and went down stairs. "No call from Amy yet?"

"No. Why don't you call her? See if she's home yet. Never know what time if her and her mom went shopping. That's how girls are."

I didn't want to call her. I felt that calling her would reveal some insecurity or show a flicker of distrust.

"Go on and call," my stepmother repeated, "Get it off your mind so that you can sleep tonight."

The phone rang and rang, there was no answer.

I sat on the bottom step, my chin cradled in my hands. I was worried sick. It wasn't really all that late, not much after eight, but a good hour after Amy should have called. Thirty minutes passed and again the phone rang and rang.

My stepmother began to notice the stress that was obvious on my face. I was almost sick from worry. But it was only a few hours late. Maybe only a flat tire. But if I could be there, I could help with the tire. If she needs me I'm not there.

I called again at nine. Nothing.

"I jumped to my feet, "I've got to go to Amy's. Something's wrong, I know there is. She always calls."

"I know she usually does. But once in all these times doesn't mean anything."

"But I've got to go see that she's alright. I can run the back way to her house and nobody'l see me. It won't take long."

"Oh no you don't. You just take one step out that door and I'm calling the sheriff. That's for sure," she added for emphasis." You just stay here with the dogs, up in your room and I'll run over for you, so's you can get it off your mind."

It was well after nine when the headlights of the car turned into the driveway, I met my step mother at the door, I'm sure the anxiety showed all over my face.

"Wasn't home."

"Nobody," I responded, trying to keep my voice steady. "Had they been there."

"Didn't look like it. I left a note on the door that you had tried to call. You know, they may have had to run back to town after Amy got home. She'll probably call first thing in the morning."

"But what would have happened tonight?"

"Well, lots of things, like maybe they had to go pick up Mr. Brooks at the airport or something. Or maybe they had to go to the grocery and it's taking longer than they expected."

"How can I spend the night not knowing what's going on, they might be needing me."

"Well, Bud, if every time the phone doesn't ring or somebody does something irregular, you stay up all night worrying your self sick, I wouldn't want to spend the rest of my life in your shoes. I can tell you that, for sure."

If people only knew that this is the destiny of nearly every child raised in the insecurity of a broken, un-loving home.

Fear and un-certainity, the automatic response to every climax.

"Do you really think everything is alright?" I lamented almost in tears. My hardness was beginning to break down and I felt myself almost at the point of seeking comfort from someone I wouldn't even get close to.

"I'm sure everything's alright, go on up with the dogs and in the morning before time for Amy to leave for school, we'll jump in the car and run over."

Thank goodness morning finally appeared. I surely must have slept a little, it seemed I was awake all night. Something was wrong, I knew there was. I was much to young and un-pretentious to believe in something so mysterious as psychic transference of thought or circumstance and I'm not sure that I do even today, but something tugging at my heart and pounding my brain negated any possibility of peace until I had proven the premonition to be nothing more than anxiety.

Before the sun had lighted the yard I was putting Blue and Sam in their pen. I un-consciously filled their water bucket and dipped their food from the barrel. Usually, they would be jumping on me with excitement while I was feeding, but as great friends do, they knew instinctively that someone dear to them was emotionally broken, something they sensed revealed a deep tearing at the heart. They stood at my feet gazing up at my face, Blue tilted his head slightly, looking puzzled, for the buddy he had followed for so many years through the swamps and woods, laughing and screaming, wasn't laughing, wasn't happy, wasn't himself.

I noticed through the glaze of my stupor that they weren't interested in their food. I dropped to my knees, they pushed close, in turn licking my cheeks then resting their heads against my chest. I hugged them and held them close, "Sorry boys, it'll be better soon," was all I could choke out.

They stood side by side in puzzlement as they watched me pass out through the gate and head toward the house.

The sun was high enough now to light the yard and house. When I got in, my step mother was up and stirring around. She glanced at me as I came in. I was sure she'd make some statement about me going out with the dogs but she didn't.

"I'm ready to go if you are?" I said.

"No, it's to early and besides, you look a fright. Go wash your face and comb your hair. We'll have some coffee and toast and then we'll go. Give the people a chance to get up before we get over there."

I wasn't about to argue, to close to getting my way to take a chance.

I raced up the stairs to the bathroom, I threw water in my, face, the mirror revealed a great lack of sleep in the fallen lines of my face and I recognized them. I ran my wet hands over my head to moisten my hair so it would comb easily, my soft blonde hair lay flat from the moisture and I remembered that once a girl had said I would look better if my hair would stand taller like the other boy's.

"Bud." I heard my step mother call up the stairs.

"Ma'am"

"There's a pickup out by the front gate, I think it's Albert."

I ran to my bedroom window. I could see down through the trees that in fact it was the GMC. That's where Albert always parked when he wanted to see me. He seldom ever came to the house, but instead he'd park there and wait until someone noticed him.

"Yeah, that's Albert alright, I'll run down and see what he wants."

Before she could cut me off at the door I had bounded down the stairs and was on my way across the yard.

So many times Albert had parked just this way, often telling me of planned hunting trips, often looking for help on some small project that he needed a temporary hand for. I was half way the short distance from the house to the gate when the shear, stark, expression on Albert's face stopped me in my tracks. It wasn't the grinning, happy face with the cigar sticking out the corner of it's mouth held between it's teeth. Maybe I saw horror, maybe I saw disbelief, maybe great pain. He was standing rigid, he was holding a folded newspaper in front of him, it would be the morning "Tampa Tribune."

I paced myself until I was standing immediately in front of him, I never took my eyes from his, searching for some clue why the expression grimaced so.

"Albert," I said cautiously, "Is something wrong?"

"Amy," he choked out, nothing more.

"Amy, what?" I demanded.

"Amy," he responded again. He pushed the folded paper to me.

The Tribune had done it's usual good job of accurately and unemotionally dispensing the facts. Albert had read the paper early at Stiekies as he always did. Buried several pages in, the headline read;

"TEEN DEATH IN ONE CAR ACCIDENT. CITY CONTINUES TO IGNORE TEEN ALCOHOL PROBLEM."

"Around seven o'clock yesterday evening, a car driven at high speed careened off the embankment on North Florida Ave. and hit a tree killing one of the passengers. The other two passengers were taken to the Tampa General and released with only minor in-juries.

"The driver, a star running back for a local high school football team was sited for drunk driving and remanded to his parents.

"Names of the juveniles are

being withheld."

I grabbed Albert, "Not Amy," I shouted in his face, "They don't mean Amy!!"

Tears were streaming down his face, his lips were quivering but he couldn't speak. I knew, I knew. I fell against him, then to my knees. There was a moment of disbelief as the bodies defenses try to control the impact of great shock but soon the truth of the facts became overwhelming and I began to sob.

My step mother instinctively knew that something was wrong and was soon standing beside me. Albert took the paper from my hand and handed it to her. A glance was all she needed to know why Amy hadn't called. She dropped to the ground beside me, put her arm across my back and shoulder and pulled me close. Oh how the pain cut deep, how the wound demanded I cry out. But who does a lonely, defiant boy cry out to, "God?" Where was he when Amy needed him. To "Mother," who is my mother? To "Friend?" she was gone.

Tears flowed out of control, my face was buried in my hands. My step mothers caress, nor Albert's presence, could penetrate the loneliness of this young lad, bent in sorrow, alone without a bond, nowhere to seek refuge. I wept all alone.

* * *

Part III
"DAWN"

Chapter #1
THE QUIVERING PAIN OF A CRUSHED HEART

I seldom pass this juncture in the trail. I have for these years past recounted all that my memory affords except for this one intersection. I have, with fear and cowardice, blocked it from my mind. Almost to the point of psychological trauma, I keep this one memory bottled and caged and hidden and removed. But now, now I must deal with it, maybe never again. But I've been told that if a recessed burden is laid completely and fully out into the open that it can then be put away and left finally to rest in peace. But I guess I'm too sensitive, maybe even cowardice, for each time the door is left ajar and the shadow of this one moment peers through, I cry and cry more.

I'll just tell about Amy's funeral. I'll try. But before I do I will tell you that I've given a great deal of thought to the pain and anguish that attacks the heart. There is a plateau or a threshold that such pain achieves at these terrible moments. It's the point where the pain has reached such intensity, depth and duration that if it were not for the cushioning on the cell walls, a person would surely bash his brains in. The miraculous maker of the mind put in safeguards that precludes the breaching of this plane by introducing subtle, re-occurring personalities that fight for our sanity through the introduction a psychic fantasy. Otherwise, no mind could endure much of the trauma of life.

It could be said, and is often alluded to, that the grief and horror of the Jewish holocaust is the horror of all horrors. And maybe so, for there were many who took their lives and many who went insane as a result of the presence of such horrific suffering, sorrow, maltreatment. But then, the mind will only suffer so long and then it passes through the pain into insanity or suicide. Yet, I doubt that the horrific pain and anguish of the Jewish holocaust rendered any more pain to the mind and soul of the Jew at Krakow or Auschwich than the horrific pain and anguish that cut into the heart of Mrs. Brooks. This was especially true as we stood side by side looking into the pale, inanimate face of the most beautiful person God could have shared with earth this short while.

If it's in the mind and soul where we truly learn to love and not the body, no matter it's form, then why, I should ponder, at a moment such as this does the remains appear so real and why is it so hard to return it to the ground.

Before the funeral Mrs. Brooks had gotten word to my stepmother that she and Mr. Brooks wanted me to stand with them at the services. It amazes me that at this terrible time Mrs. Brooks would have thought to remember me. But I remember that Mrs. Brooks was that way and it should not have surprised me that she remembered that Amy meant more than life to me. But I constantly dealt with the "Ugly Duckling" syndrome and instead of feeling reassured and accepted into Amy's family as one bonded by spirit instead of flesh, I was constantly on guard for indications of fallen favor.

The funeral took place in the little Chapel of the Community Church there on Lake Fern Road, the one I had imagined so often where Amy and I would some day meet at the alter. The preacher was saying things, things that he'd torn from his heart to use as solace to relieve the pain of those in his presence. But who could hear his words? Not I. And even then, words aren't always magic.

We were sitting on the front pew only a few feet from the casket. Mr. Brooks was next to the middle aisle, Mrs. Brooks, then me. As we were ushered into the church to our places, I was in front, Mrs. Brooks had a hand on my shoulder, Mr. Brooks followed. I felt that she was guiding me, like I was her own. Her hand shook from time to time and I could feel the stressful quiver transmitted through it. I guess I thought I knew, but how could I know the terrible pain Mrs. Brooks must endure. I loved Amy deeply, as though life need not continue, but it would and I would find another life out of my youth. But for Mrs. Brooks, there was no other life. Amy was all she had, her joy and pride and fulfillment. No second chance, no hope for tomorrow. How deep into her bosom was the knife plunged?

Mr. Brooks seemed to be in a trance, seldom looking up from the floor, maybe sedated to help relieve the pain. He just stared at the floor and then at the side of the casket. He seemed to avoid looking at her beautiful face. He should have, she looked so at peace, so much resting in sleep. But why didn't he look at her? Guilt, intolerable pain, cowardice? I had this feeling that a man should be the strength for the woman, but neither Mr. Brooks or myself afforded any comfort to Mrs. Brooks. Three souls, bound by some tenuous tether, neither capable of comfort for the other.

A few moments passed and the service ended. The ushers were escorting members of the congregation to the side of the casket for a final look at Amy. Some walked by and never looked up from the floor, while others stared longingly into her face. A few would look toward Mrs. Brooks, no doubt to readily share words of healing, but there were none. There was an occasional cry out muffled under a handkerchief or scarf as the small crowd passed, one by one, each dealing with their own emotions.

As they, I too began to cry uncontrollable tears. They began streaming down my face in torrents and dropped to my shirt. My stepmother had remembered to put a handkerchief with the clothes she set out for me to wear. It was hardly sized for the enormity of my grief and lay in my hand a saturated lump.

It was very difficult not to cry out during the services. It didn't seem comprehensible that she could be dead. As the line of people ended, we moved forward to see her closely. Mrs. Brooks laid her hand across Amy's gently folded hands and took Mr. Brooks hand with the other. I heard her whisper, "Our baby."

After a moment Mrs. Brooks took my hand and pulled me close. Amy's flowing blonde hair was pulled to one side and was lying down across her shoulder to her breast. She was wearing a light summer dress with a shallow V. A thin golden chain was around her neck and the St. Christopher medal and the heart that we shared were lying in the cleft of her bosom. My hand automatically reached to my chest and I could feel mine under my shirt. Mrs. Brooks saw my hand move and knew I had realized that she had left them on Amy.

"Do you want them?" she whispered. I again remembered our vow to never remove them, I shook my head no.

She leaned over and kissed Amy lightly on the lips and stroked her cheek with the end of her fingers, fluffed the end of her hair where a strand had not lain properly, as though preparing her perfectly for her presence before God. "Goodbye precious one," she said and then motioned for the attendant to lead us out.

This was the first time I have tried to relive Amy's funeral. It brings me enormous pain to visualize this travesty of life's injustice. So horrible, so like a billion others, I won't again.

If I am only a genetic phenomenon why is my heart breaking?

Chapter #2
THE EMOTIONAL CYCLE OF GRIEF AND HATE IS NOW IN THE LATTER

I spent the next couple of days upstairs in my room wavering between disbelief, sorrow and great depression. I didn't go down to see Blue or Sam as I should have or even to eat for that matter. My stepmother would bring my food up, stand and look at me for a few minutes, shake her head and leave.

I spent hours thinking suicide and self-destruction and all sorts of ways that I could alleviate the pain without waiting for the process of time. But finally time did begin to work and I began to stare out of the window at the passing sheriff cars on their watch. I stared and thought, and stared and thought until I began to try and visualize the wreck that killed Amy. "Ronney did it. Ronney killed Amy," I said over and over to myself. "He was drunk, he killed my Amy."

As I look back I'm still amazed at how fast the emotion of hate can supplant grief, because in only a few moments, no more than an hour, I had changed from a broken, grieving child into a cunning, scheming avenger. I began to feel hunger from the days I had hardly touched my food. I was thirsty and my body began to want to move. Hate, hate!! Without even a suggestion of the word all the force of hate and revenge began creeping into my veins with a revitalization like whole blood in the arm of a dying wreck victim.

For hours I sat on the edge of my bed, staring out of the south window, toward school, toward Amy's house, toward North Florida Avenue and where the wreck happened.

I cringed with hate as I visualized the wreck and ambulance attendants carrying Amy away. I imagined blood on her face, tangled hair matted with secretions, her lifeless body lying limp across the arms of an attendant being carried up the slight embankment toward the flashing lights of the vehicle waiting along the roadside. I could see Ronney's yellow chevy, mangled, pressed against the base of the huge Royal Palm, its base bulging like a fortress, uncompassionate, unyielding.

I knew the place well, I had passed it so often on the school bus. The highway was slightly elevated there, with a row of palms growing along the grove between it and the highway right of way in border form.

My hate rose to irrational, but one thing I had learned growing up in an empty house was that cunning was superior to confrontation and I'm sure that this early training was all that stood between me and a spontaneous suicidal attempt at revenge. Oh how I yearned for revenge, the biological, and psychotic solution to all of untamed man's encroachments.

I had decided, there would be no quarter, I had to kill Ronney. I would find no peace until he was dead. Dead like my Amy. This would be all the satisfaction I would need, and the reward would be great enough for me to find pleasure and purpose in the cunning and secret planning. I would begin immediately.

But first I had to find out what was going on. I hadn't talked to anyone since the funeral. I would call Junior, make some pretense, he could be my information source while I planned the method to get Ronney.

The phone rang only once, "Stiekies", came Bills' voice. Pert and direct as usual.

"Hi, Mr. Stiekie, this is Bud. Is Junior around?"

"Bud, is that you. How you doing?"

"Oh, I'm getting over I guess. Be glad to get out of this house soon."

"Yeah, bet you will, hope they catch those bastards quick and hang'm high. Hold on, Junior's in the back."

Bill hung his head around the door that led out into the garage area of the station. I could hear him call for Junior and Junior respond. "Hi, Junior here."

"Junior, this is Bud."

"Bud," he replied with a surprised sound in his voice. "It's good to hear you. I wanted to call but didn't know whether I should or not. You know, with everything happening and all. You sure sound good though, it's real good to hear your voice. Is anything going on that I could do for you?"

"Well, first of all, you could have come by, I get pretty lonesome, you know." I said, all of this knowing that if Junior had come by even an hour ago I would have sent him away rather than emerge from my self-pity. But, now was different. Self-pity was supplanted by hate and revenge and I had to use what help and tactic was available in order to implement my plan even if it meant putting Junior on a guilt trip.

"Gee, I'm sorry. I thought your place was off-limits until they caught Moses' killers."

"Well, you could have sneaked over after dark and nobody would have known. Would they have? How would you like being cooped up all this time with no friends or anything, not knowing what's going on?"

"Okay, then, I can sneak over tonight, I guess, but I bet your stepmother won't let me in."

"Don't worry, I've got that figured out. Come up to the back of the house an throw a rock up against my window. I'll climb out and drop down to the ground and we can talk in the grove behind the house. She don't need to know."

"I'll be there a little after dark. Hope you know what you're doing. Better leave the window open, don't want to break the glass."

It wasn't long until sundown, my stepmother was cooking and the smell of pork gravy was drifting up the stairs, through my bedroom door and out the window. I figured she had made biscuits, but the gravy was the strongest smell. A little saliva was forming in my mouth. I hadn't been tempted by a smell in several days, since you know when. Even a little hunger began to twitch at my tummy. So soon had these senses become manifest after I had begun to focus the energy of my rage. Concentrating all my emotions on the implementation of my hateful plan. My plan was simple, I would at all costs, even at whatever cost to my self, kill Ronney Harper.

The implementation of the plan was a little more complex, but I dwelled on it constantly and with great excitement. It began to grow and grow as a balloon expands when inflated. I became obsessed, more nearly possessed by this overwhelming drive to kill Ronney. This one desire replaced all my logic, reason and humanity.

I didn't wait for my stepmother to call me for supper. Junior would be hiding at the edge of the grove tossing rocks or limbs up towards my window as soon as darkness provided him security, I must go on down now and rush things along before Junior gets here.

"Well, Bud," she said with some surprise, "you're down for supper on your own tonight. I'm glad, must mean you're feeling better about things by now."

"Yeah, guess I am. A little, anyway. Getting a little lonesome up there. Sure wish the sheriff would hurry up and catch those guys. Have you heard anything?"

"No, not a word. Still see that police car going back and forth, but that's all. They will though, you don't need to worry, an real soon, I bet."

"Hope so, got to get out of here."

While we were talking, she was sitting bowls of food on the table. A bowl of blackeyed peas, a bowl of rice with fried pork chops cooked in, a bowl of dark brown gravy and a bowl of biscuits covered with a dish towel.

I broke open a biscuit and laid it flat on the plate. I spooned up a large helping of blackeyed peas and covered the biscuits with them. I took out two scoops of rice and piled them on the plate. I covered the whole thing with gravy.

My stepmother eased into her chair and pulled it up to the table with a scoot and simultaneously saw the upheaval in my plate, "My goodness boy, what you do to good food is beyond me."

I was so hungry I was sure I could eat the whole thing and more. But as an empty stomach resists changing its set, in only a few bites, I was full, hungry and in pain, all at the same instant.

I apologized to my stepmother for not finishing my plate. I asked her to save it for me and maybe I would come down later and finish it up.

I pushed away from the table, she kinked her nose as the chair legs squeaked against the linoleum floor. "Sorry," I said, accented by a shrug of my shoulders. In an instant I was dis-obeying all the logic of a threatened fugitive and stood before the window awaiting the rattle of the pebble on the tin roof that Junior would toss.

Just as the darkness of the night became heavy it came, a pop and then a rattle as the small stone rolled backwards down the roof.

"Junior, that you?"

"Yeah, come on down, coast's clear."

I slid down the tin roof and dropped off the edge to the ground landing on as limp knees as I could to minimize the thud when I hit. Then passed over the trellis I would use to climb back up.

I had just slipped into the darkness of the grove and Junior rushed up as though he was going to embrace me. He stopped short and grabbed my arm in one hand and my shoulder with the other. "Damn, Bud. I sure do miss you."

"Well, won't be long now I hope," I replied. "You're a great friend for coming," I continued, stressing the friend part. I hoped I wasn't over-playing the theatrics. "Just promise we can meet here every evening so that when I finally do get released from this dungeon I won't be like a stranger in a foreign land."

We talked in whispers. I asked Junior all of the unimportant questions: How was Albert? How was Mr. Stiekie and Junebloom?. Everybody was okay, he told me, hadn't seen much of Junebloom. Nobody talked much about hunting. Maybe they'd go again when I could go.

I worked my way through what I considered trivial, but necessary conversation preparing for the extraction of the information I needed from Junior to prepare a plan to get Ronney. Finally Junior got to what seemed to be the last of the local details and stopped. We looked at each other for a moment, in silence, my heart beating a little fast from anxiety at the thought of the subject. I had to ask the questions in a manner that seemed normal or Junior might suspect my motive.

I looked at the ground as I spoke, "I guess that worthless Ronney is still in the hospital?" I asked knowing full well that he was hardly even hurt.

"No, he's not, he only went for a check-up. Hardly even hurt."

"Oh, he was hardly hurt? Man, that jerk's got all the luck. Bet his dad has grounded him good just the same."

"No, I don't think so. Somebody said they saw him in a new Chevy just like the one he wrecked. Guess his dad got him a new one."

I could feel my face flush from the raging heat that instantly filled my body. I stood speechless, my whole body trembling for revenge. But I couldn't let on. That would be even worse than the terrible news I'd just heard.

I choked back my emotions and took a deep breath, "Probably the same ole yellow as the other one and I bet he even drives back and forth to school on the same ole road just like nothing had ever happened."

"That's what I heard," Junior agreed.

That was it. That was exactly what I wanted him to do. Just keep it up like nothing had ever happened. Nothing ever happened, you'll see.

I made a big deal out of the fact that Ronney was acting like nothing had ever happened. I just couldn't believe it for one minute that he could be acting that way. Finally in his parting statement Junior agreed to check it out and let me know tomorrow night if it was true.

I pulled Junior with me over to the corner of the back porch where the trellis waited to make like a ladder for my ascent. Junior bent over and laced his finger to make a step for me to put my foot into for a boast up the trellis. "See you tomorrow about this same time?" I asked as I looked down over my shoulder from the top of the trellis.

"Yeah, sure will, you bet on it."

"Thanks Junior, I think you've saved me a death of boredom."

What ever one might think, it's anticipation that causes the mind to accelerate to a feverish pace. The anticipation of major surgery causes the mind to stress and hastens the moment to come as if it were only an instant, even though we may wish for the time to be as long as possible. Conversely, the anticipation of some great event that we desire has just the opposite effect and time proceeds at the pace of a slug. But, on the other hand, the anticipation and planning of a great plot to be executed has the effect of both. I spent hours in my room planning and visualizing the moment I would achieve my revenge and even the score of Amy's death.

Junior had investigated the comings and goings of Ronney Harper with the meticulousness and stealth of a P.I. for hire. Why he worked so hard and diligently to execute my wishes I never knew. I never even knew that he would. I never understood why anyone would make an effort to do anything for me, but people did, as though I had a strange magnetism. Like being on a mission for the King was his urgency.

After a few night visits with Junior I began to be more focused about the information I wanted him to bring back to me. More and more it was only about Ronney that I questioned him about. And more and more Junior infiltrated Ronney's crowd to trace his movements.

The final night came. I knew all that I needed to know to make and implement my plan. I had only one request to make of Junior.

It was dark now, I heard the rap of a pebble on my window. I knew that once more Junior would be waiting in the dark shadows of the trees listening for the noise of the window screen being pushed open as I crawled through the window and descended to the ground. But this wasn't a night of casual visiting. This night, more than any other, I had to be certain that I could rely on Junior to perform one more part in my plot.

In my hand I had a small sack filled with biscuits smeared with guava paste jelly that I had stolen from the supper table, a token of appreciation to Junior for a job well done (a bribe if you wish). At least a lubricant to assure that the wheels continued to turn.

"Hey, Junior," I whispered, "Anyone see you coming?"

"Of course not." You know how I am in the woods, nobody see's me unless it's my idea."

He was right. Even times that I had been stopped in the night to be questioned by a warden or a property owner, Junior would be lurking in the shadows unseen.

"Well,... OK, good."

I held Junior by the shoulder and guided him back into the grove out of range for our voices to be overheard. We squatted down on our haunches and rested our backs against the same tree. It felt good to be with Junior again. Though he wasn't intellectual and lacked heavily in the social graces, he was the kind of guy that could do things. Find his way out of a swamp on a black-dark night. Get a job and make some money on the spur of the moment. Tune up an old auto and make it run like brand new.

The paper sack made a little rustling noise as I pulled out the biscuits. I passed one to Junior and rested my head against the tree while I watched junior take the first bite.

"Damn," he said with a start and jerked his head down and spit the bite into his hand, "is that Guava stuff in there, I was expecting just a plain biscuit with butter."

I confirmed that it was and munched away in an exaggerated manner to demonstrate my taste for it.

"I think you guys are the only ones in the world that eat this stuff."

Then he began to eat the biscuit and finished the second before he indicated that he was ready to talk.

"Bad stuff, huh Junior?," I jokingly sneered.

"Tell me Junior, is everyone at the station doing OK? How about Mr. and Mrs. Brooks, are they doing OK?" I asked with a sincere yearning trying to draw Junior out.

"Well, everybody at the station seems OK. Hadn't been much talk about hunting since all this. Guess that's understandable. Heard Albert and Bill talking about Mr. and Mrs. Brooks yesterday. Said Mr. Brooks was drinkin a bunch. Mrs. Brooks just bowed up like always and is trying to keep him from falling apart. Drove by the other day, didn't stop, didn't think she'd know me, seen her sitting on the porch swinging, just looking at the trees. Hope that ain't a bad sign."

"I don't know," I responded, "If she was sittin in that swing you can bet she was thinking about Amy."

"You called her.. you know, since then?"

"No, guess not."

"How come, she sure liked you?"

"Don't know, I guess I'd just cry."

"C'mon, Bud, you can't jus think of yourself all the time. I bet that's a lonely lady. Y, they say there weren't even no close relatives to help her clean up the place, ladies from the church helped her out. You know, Bud, sometimes I think you forget that other folks got feelings to."

I wanted to lash out at Junior and tell him to mind his own damn business, that it wasn't long ago that I went to see them bury my good friend Moses. It'd hardly been a week since Amy died. What did he expect, that I didn't have any feelings either? But then I guess they all thought that since Amy was so young that we couldn't have loved each other all that much and only Mrs. Brooks had a crushed heart. But, Junior was right, life hadn't dealt me a perfect hand, but it gave me every opportunity to learn how to feel sorry for myself, and I did.

"You're right, Junior," I confessed. "I have been selfish. I plain forgot how bad Mrs. Brooks must be feeling. I'm going to get some things out of the way tomorrow and then tomorrow night I'm going to call her up and if she's not doing good I'm going to sneak over to see her. I'm going to do it even if it hurts me all the way to the bones."

Our hushed conversation continued, almost an interrogation because I was determined now more than ever to get even and tomorrow would be the day. If any of me was left then I would go to Mrs. Brooks. Then, after she knew what I had done to Ronney surely she would feel less pain because some of the get even had been done. My plan was clear in my mind. The only thing left was to make sure that the details I extracted from my stealthful agent were accurate.

I turned directly toward Junior, staring intently into his eyes searching for a weakness in the facts he had brought me. "Junior, every afternoon at 5:20 Ronney passes the Wilson fruit stand on his way from practice. You're sure?"

"Sure I'm sure," Junior retorted. "Sure within a minute or two anyway."

"And you're sure he's always driving alone. Not Peggy - Not nobody?"

"I've done told you, Peggy ain't allowed close to that car. Besides what's it to you, you got some fishy plan or something?"

"Well, let me tell you what I plan on doing - I plan on making his life pretty miserable from now on. How about this, you know that old grapefruit grove by the fruit stand, the trees grow right out close to the right edge of the road almost. I'll just be waiting for him when he comes by tomorrow and I'll splatter the side of that ugly yellow bomb with rotten grapefruit. See how long it takes the acid to eat the paint off."

"Dang, Bud, that's a hell of a plan. Count me in."

"Sorry, Junior, I've got to do this one on my own. Besides I'm going to need an alibi if he gets suspicious"

"I'd better go, he's faster than hell, being a running back on the team an all."

"No, Junior, trust me, he'll never catch me in a grapefruit grove and you know it. Besides, it won't be the same if I don't do it on my own."

The talk had become dynamic now, I was beginning to feel powerful as I began to visualize the plan in my mind. I had to stay in control because I needed Junior more than ever now, at least for one more thing. "Okay, Junior, can I count on you?"

"Sure you can. I just wish I could go along. Just in case."

"Don't worry, you can call me at home after sundown, I'll be back by then. It'll be fun telling you all about it. And then I'll sneak out to Mrs. Brook's. I'll need my cutdown. Here's what I want you to do," I was making emphatic gestures with my hands trying to illustrate the importance of Junior's part in the plan, "come to the house first thing in the morning. Come to the front door and tell my stepmother that you need to see me, ask to borrow my cut down for a few hours. Then take it to the station and make sure it's running good and fill it with gas, Mr. Stiekie will let you put it on my folks bill. But get this, bring it back by noon and instead of parking by the house, park it by the road so I can get away quiet."

"Ok, I'll have to take a half day off work, I'm running a dredge over in Scroggin swamp making house sites."

That made me a little nervous, Junior might have some notion of asking off and things could get out of whack, "Well, just don't go to the swamp tomorrow morning, they probably won't even know. Besides, I'll help you make it up latter."

I sighed a little as a sly smirk came on Junior's lips which seemed to reflect agreement.

"I'm counting on you buddy. I didn't know a guy could have such a good friend." These terms I used endearingly to reinforce his obedience. I then nodded toward the dark shadows that he had come through as his cue to depart.

It was quiet again, I leaned heavily against the tree. I began to remember the hate I had built up. It was more than an emotion now, it was a vision as well. A vision that by this time tomorrow Ronney would be dead, and it would be too late for Junior to find out that throwing rotten grapefruit at Ronney's yellow car was never in the plan from the beginning. Hate had obscured the consequences, and I sat smug and complacent knowing I would be avenged for him taking Amy from me. A strange peace had set in, as though I had already accomplished this vengeful deed. Vengeance is a powerful force and drives men beyond logic and reason and inhibits the mind from acknowledging the offsetting pain as the pendulum returns to the perpetrator. Only if the pendulum could swing in reverse and the consequences be endured first, then and only then will men learn, "Vengeance is mine, saith the Lord," and why.

I lay on my bed, my head cradled in my laced-fingers. I stared at the ceiling in the darkness. In my mind I could see my plan taking place as though it was happening. I saw every detail, I saw it over and over until it worked perfectly.

Somewhere during the rehearsal I fell into a deep, dreamless sleep. I awoke to a rap on the front door. It was early morning and Junior had arrived on schedule. He was talking to my stepmother, "Hello, Mrs. Olson, is Bud up yet? I'd like to talk to him."

"Sure can, I expect he'd like to have somebody besides me to talk to for a change. Mind you one thing though, no talk about sneaking out of here hunting, you hear?"

I was already at the bottom of the stairs when Junior saw me. I would normally have invited Junior up to my room so that we could talk in private, but my stepmother had to hear this so I met him at the door.

"Hi, Junior, what's up?" I asked, trying to appear unprepared and casual.

"Well, you know I'm dredging over in Scroggin Swamp. Sand ate up another impeller and I need to carry out a new one for the pump. I'm not sure my car would get out there, but I figure your cutdown wouldn't have no problem at all. Think I could borrow it this morning. I'd have it back to you by lunch."

Junior spent most of the time looking at the floor and twisting in his tracts like most novice liars do, but if my stepmother wasn't paying close attention she probably didn't notice anything different.

"Sure, why not. It doesn't take a key you know, just pull the knob out on the dash and hope the battery's not dead."

Junior looked up from the floor and met my eyes for a signal that he'd played the part to the end. I gave a light wink to affirm that he had.

"Well, I sure appreciate it," he drug out, "Guess I'd better head toward the swamp. Bye, Mrs. Olson."

"Goodbye, Junior, good luck with your pump. If you're here at lunchtime I'll have you a sandwich ready," she called to him as he rounded the corner of the house.

Chapter #3
THE GREATEST PLANS OF MEN AND MICE

I had never orchestrated a plan that included other events and players before. It gave a strange feeling of power as the puppeteer must have as he causes his players to twist and turn in echelon with his script. Every movement from the first to the last was burned into my mind and I could close my eyes and act out each part as vividly as if it had already come to pass. But I was possessed with a strange empowerment now. Someone was acting out the part that I had scripted for them with precision. Just like certain people have had power over other people all through history and had them march without reservation to their death, if that was the script. And, Junior was one now, separated from his independent nature, marching to my drum. I was so corrupted by this sense of euphoric power that reason and sanity had flitted away to play on another stage.

I went back up to my room to sit on the edge of my bed. To agonize over the slow passage of time. I could hear noises from below as my stepmother busied herself in the daily chores. Noises from the road as the cars passed by, they wouldn't be stopping here so I paid them no mind. I could hear noises from the dog pen. Sam was getting restless from weeks of inactivity and was pestering Blue and getting an occasional dressing down because of Blue's no foolishness disposition.

I could hear the bang-bang of an old John Deere two banger tractor off in the distance, probably moving in and out around the limbs of big grapefruit trees, dragging a shallow disk to chop up the weeds and grasses without cutting the tree roots. I wondered if it was Junebloom. Maybe he missed me? Probably not, I don't think he missed anybody. Like so many of the black people, he didn't seem to own his own life outside of his group and took friends for the moment and then left them there. Even though the law said he was as free as anybody, in his bosom he was as much a slave as his ancestors a century ago.

But, between these noises, it was absolutely quiet - no breeze to rustle the trees, no radio, no television.

Knowing Junior like I did, I figured that he did in fact have an impeller to install on the dredge pump and figured this all out so as not to lie to my stepmother. By now he would have gotten it installed and would be at the station checking out the cutdown. It probably needed a little tuning up, like cleaning the spark plugs and smoothing the carbon tips on the ignition points with a file and setting their gap with a well-worn dime. If the mechanic was around he may borrow a gauge, but probably not. If it started good and ran smooth at about half-throttle, nothing else would be asked of it or the tune-up. All that would be left would be to fill it with gas and bring it home.

I could hear the hum of the engine drawing close to the house. The motor sounded good, no sign of a miss or labor. Junior had done a good job. The loose home-made truck bed rattled as he turned off the pavement into the drive.

I heard Junior's knock on the door. My stepmother must have recognized the engine because she didn't check to see who had knocked, "Come on in Junior. I've about got the sandwiches ready for lunch."

"You didn't need to do that," Junior responded, "I could have got somethin at Stiekies."

"Well, come on in and sit down at the table, I'll call Bud."

I was already at the bottom of the steps when she called and slid into a chair at the table.

"Everything go alright, Junior?" I asked, looking intently into his eyes to intercept any signals he might have to give me.

"Yep, shur did. Got the impeller delivered and all."

Junior in his usual lack of grace, consumed the sandwich in three bites and turned up the iced tea.

"Thanks a lot for the sandwich and tea, Mrs. Olson," Junior said as he pushed away from the table. "Sure was good."

"I'm glad, let me fix you another one," she said as she backed against the counter holding a ready loaf of light bread in her hand.

"No ma'am," Junior responded, "Sure would like to, but I better get to dredging to pay for that impeller," and he moved toward the door.

"Hey, Junior," I called after him, "Don't wait until you need to borrow the cutdown again to come back, OK?"

I grabbed another sandwich and refilled my tea glass and headed back up the stairs to my room. So far everything was working pretty well. There was one hurdle, there was no way I could start the cutdown and drive off without her hearing me. I wasn't opposed to running off without permission, but she would probably alert the sheriff and I might get picked up before I got started pulling off my mission.

I thought about it awhile. It was sort of a point of stress and I can never think well when I feel stressed. I had a little time, I didn't need to be at the road side until five anyway, but I would need a little lead time to get the cutdown ready and loaded with grapefruit.

I finally thought of it. I seemed to have lost track of what was going on around, or this plan would have been obvious. It was Wednesday. She always goes to the grocery on Wednesday. She didn't go this Wednesday yet, probably because she's scared to go off and leave me here alone. I think I can make it work, but I don't want her to leave before about three or she'll get back to soon.

It was past two heading towards three when I went down the stairs. She was sitting in the porch swing enjoying the little bit of breeze that had started moving across the yard. I went out into the screened porch, about to make my most forward move and sit down beside her to play a new hand. She threw her hand up and gestured for me to stop, "I don't know, might not be a good idea for you to come out here. Do you think?"

I stopped and sat on the door step which meant that only my feet were on the porch and I was low enough that I would be hard to see.

"Bout to burn up in your room this afternoon?" she asked.

"Sure am. It gets pretty hot up there in the afternoon."

"Well, stay down here and drink iced tea. Maybe that will cool you off."

"Yeah, I think I will. It's cooler down here, alright. You know what else? I think I'll catch a nap on the couch after while."

I sat and stared out the screened door for awhile. I wanted everything calm and casual before I dropped the bomb.

When I got up my nerve I played my card, "You know what?" I said rather matter-of-factly, "What I really have missed more than anything is a strawberry 'Nehi' and some peanuts. Boy have I missed them."

"Really, I didn't know you liked them so much."

"Boy, do I. Ask anybody down at the station."

There was a little silence before she responded, "Well then, I do need to go to the grocery to pick up some things. Maybe I'll just get you one."

"Oh man," I thought to my self, "I can't believe it's going so good."

I stretched out on the couch with my head propped on a cushion, turned looking toward the front door, as if someone might be coming. But of course they weren't. I sat the large glass of iced tea on the floor beside me. I did the best I could at putting on aires of nonchalance even to the point of trying to nod off, which made time pass at the speed of the tortoise. Soon I heard the shuffle of my stepmother coming into the living room. Her purse hung on her arm and car keys in her hand. "Guess I'll go on now. What if they don't have any strawberry? Something else do?"

"Oh, no, just stop by Stiekies, he always has them."

"Well, OK. Anything else?"

"Nope, not for me."

She took a step towards the door and hesitated, turning slightly back toward me. I know she wanted to say something like don't you dare go out of the house, but after the short hesitation she turned back and went directly toward the car.

I lay still and listened to the car start and move out onto Lake Fern Road. I didn't move, almost holding my breath. I listened until it was completely out of range. I lay for a minute longer. Nothing.

I jumped to my feet, in an instant I was energized. "I may need extra time if anything goes wrong, gotta get moving now," I told myself.

I bolted up the stairs to my room to get the clothes I would need. I fumbled around in the closet until I found a long sleeve shirt to wear, in case I had to hide all night, and my sneakers. I wouldn't wear them, just take them for later. I knew that if I had to run to escape I could run better in the soft sand barefooted so that my toes could dig into the sand. And, if it works the way I planned it, I may have to run and hide for quite awhile. I found a sack to stuff my gear into. I then went to the kitchen and found some left over food - biscuits, a hunk of cheese and a can of pork and beans. Looking back, this little store of food was pretty meaningless, but it seemed important at the time, a sort of getting ready.

I dashed through the front door and out to the street where Junior had left the cutdown. I pulled the switch and the motor caught up instantly.

It felt good to be back in the drivers seat again. The peddles felt good against my bare feet. I put the ball of my bare foot against the clutch peddle, curled my toes over it, and shoved it to the floor. The gears clashed slightly as I drew the lever down into low. There was a little shutter as I released the clutch, but we were soon out on to the road and heading towards destiny.

I would not drive directly to the Wilson fruit stand, who knows who might see me. But, I knew a back way, and I would drive down through the grapefruit trees, hidden and unseen all the way to Florida Avenue where my plan would take place.

By now it should be pretty obvious that my plan wasn't to throw grapefruit at Ronney's smartaleck-looking yellow chevy. That would serve no purpose, and was not my plan from the beginning. I wanted him dead. No other punishment would do. I would do it with my cutdown.

Along the route through the grove I picked up four, ever present, fruit crates that the fruit pickers hauled the fruit from the tree to the truck in. They were made of wood and were sturdy. I placed them side by side in the cutdown bed and loaded them with fruit. The four loaded crates put just enough weight on the drive wheels of the cutdown to give it traction and thrust.

I worked my way up the highway fence that separated the fruit trees from the mown right of way until I found the opening I knew was there. It led out onto an elevated drive of two tracts to the highway. The gate had been latched with a piece of rusty wire that broke off into my hands as I untwisted it. The grapefruit trees were so large that they hung over the fence out into the right of way. I could park within a few feet of the highway edge and still be unseen by the passing vehicles until they were almost abreast of my cutdown. Ronney would surely recognize my cutdown when he saw it. But no matter, it would be too late for him to suspect what I was going to do.

It was a little before five now. I still had a few minutes before he would be passing this point on his way home from practice. I had time to think over what I was planning to do, common sense and logic would win out. I would execute the lie that I used to get Junior involved in my plan.

But I didn't. Instead, I rehearsed. I watched the cars coming by, judged their speed and estimated how close they would need to be before I raced the engine and popped the clutch. Would I hold the accelerator at full-throttle and release the clutch at the perfect instant? Would that be to much stress for the engine and better that I race the engine and release the clutch simultaneously?

Several times when no cars were in sight I raced the engine and engaged the clutch to test the traction on the rear wheels. The weight of the boxes of grapefruit was perfect and the wheels caught firmly to lunge the cutdown forward.

I looked at my watch again. Now it was a few minutes after five and I knew that from now on any car that appeared in the distance could be Ronney's.

My heart began to beat fast now. The realization of what I was about to do was beginning to sink in and in my mind I began to visualize screeching tires and folding metal. I could see the cutdown, weighted like a projectile, leaping onto the highway and crashing into the front quarter of the yellow Chevy forcing it to spin out of control and careen down the highway embankment. It would roll over and over and end over end down into the deep mire of the bar ditch. I would only look for an instant, then I would run the half a mile or so to the nearest phone and call for help. I would tell them that my accelerator stuck as I drove through the gate and I couldn't stop in time to avoid the accident. Except for a miracle, Ronney would be dead and I would have sweet vengeance for my Amy.

There he comes. The un-mistakable yellow Chevy. "Must be on probation," I thought to myself, "Never saw him drive so slow. I'd better re-think my timing. Cops must've scared him pretty bad for him to drive this slow. If I'm not careful I'll miss the front quarter."

As the car drew closer, my heart beat with increasing intensity. At one moment I remember questioning myself as to whether I should go ahead with the plan. I was not even scared. For the first time I addressed the fact that if anything went wrong I myself could be the one killed and then what. "So what," my thoughts were strong, I mumbled as I thought them through, "Don't be a coward. Don't you know Amy will be there?"

Before I could hardly complete the thought the car was on me. He must have seen the cutdown somehow because the Chevy began to accelerate. I raced the engine and popped the clutch in fast sequence or he might be beyond the point of impact. Yes, he did see me. In a glance I could see him staring directly at me. He must not have anticipated what I was going to do because he did not maneuver to avoid impact. In the instant before I leaped into his path our eyes met and he leaned toward me and with his arm outstretched toward me, his center finger curled, he shot me a defiant bird.

In my excitement I over-accelerated, the motor on the faithful cutdown revved to a screaming pitch. I popped the clutch. At first the tires only spun in the sand, but then the tread caught into the firm sand inches below the surface and drove the cutdown with great power onto the highway into the car. The instant of lost time as the tires spun was an instant I could not spare. Instead of driving the cutdown's engine into the front quarter panel I drove with power into the door panel. It was too far behind the center of gravity to cause the Chevy to go out of control. Instead it was the cutdown that went out of control. I heard the terrible tearing and twisting of the car bodies. The twisting impact caused the cutdown to spin violently and then tumble. As the helpless cutdown spun off the embankment I was thrown clear and fell in an un-conscious heap by the side of the road. I did not have to endure the stupid grin of the victorious Ronney.

And all the plans of man are carried to happy fruition in his euphoric thoughts, but only luck carries them to fruition in fact.

"VENGEANCE IS MINE, SAITH THE LORD".

Amy returns in a dream. Bud is at the edge of a coma.

"Hi, Bud," I heard the soft sound whisper through the daze and haze that pressed against my head.

I awoke just enough to make out white bed clothes pulled up to my chin. There were gadgets and gauges attached to wires and tubes running from my head and arms. People dressed like nurses were busy moving about the room watching this machine and then that. It seemed they were busy watching, but not doing much. I thought, "Why aren't they working on me, fixing something or bandaging up something."

One of the nurses walked over to the edge of the bed, she leaned lightly against it and gazed into my eyes for a minute as if looking for some sign from within. I heard her as she talked to the other nurse. Her voice sounded muffled and distant, "I'm still not getting any progress. Nothing better, nothing worse."

The other nurse called back in a voice tenor-hardened from years of watching bodies brought to her care too far gone to revive, "What's with this kid. Heard he ran his little truck right out in front of a car. Suicide you think or been drinking? These damn kids nowadays. Think they can drink like adults and get away with it. Stupid kid, to young too die. Could've killed somebody with him."

"C'mon," the first nurse barked back, "You don't know what happened, might not have been that way at all. Besides, he's not gone yet, still got vital signs."

She backed off a little still looking intently into my eyes. A moment passed by with silence. She reached both hands to the top of the sheet and rolled it down a little, gave it a little shake and tucked it back down. She was mulling over a thought and studying my face. She put her finger on my eyelid and raised it, released it after a moment and then the other. I heard her speak to the other nurse again, "Did you notice this boy's hair?"

"Nope, sure didn't. As a matter of fact I usually don't pay much attention to those details when they're in here. A bit to late for it to matter much," she responded flatly.

"I usually don't either," the first nurse replied. "Come here, look how soft and blonde his hair is." She then raised my eye lid, "Look how blue his eyes are."

"OK, he has blonde hair and blue eyes."

"Don't you remember? Just a week ago, we had a young girl, almost the same hair and eyes."

"Oh yeah, I remember now, DOA."

The first nurse's voice now turned concerned and sincere, "I would hate like hell to lose two beautiful kids in such a short time."

"What's this 'hell' stuff? Never heard you say that before."

"I don't know. All I know is I hate this job when they bring in kids for us to watch die, especially this one. He just doesn't seem to be hurt that bad. He just won't respond." She held her breath for a few seconds and then released the breath with low shallow sigh, "Think they could be related, brother and sister maybe?"

The second nurse turned and looked at her, a little puzzlement showed on her face, "Whose kin?"

"You know, this boy and that girl that was here. They looked so much alike."

The second nurse withdrew into herself as the shield from emotional involvement closed her off. Her years of experience taught her that indifference and distance was all that would allow her to cope day after day. As she spoke directly to and for the benefit of the younger nurse a sternness shaped her face, "I don't know whether they were kin or not. I don't care. It's not for me or you to know, only for me to be objective in what I do and how I care for this kid, right now. Lest if I have to pull off life support, will I be able to be objective tomorrow?"

She then turned and took the few steps it took to bring her alongside the first. She raised her arm to her shoulder and pulled her gently close, demonstrating an almost lost sign of compassion, "You know what, I've seen so many of these. Nowadays kids are so wrapped up in emotions and feelings that they cause them to do things and think things that we didn't think we had a right to think when we were that age. Least not me, anyways." She reached across the bed and laid the palm of her hand on my cheek gently raising my eyelid with her thumb, "Yep, he's in there alright, but only he can decide if he wants to come back."

The first nurse patted my cheek with her fingers, "C'mon dammit! You can do it."

The room grew dim again and I drifted away to the edge of darkness.

* * *

"Hi, Bud." This time the voice sounded more real and distinct, "It's Amy."

I looked up and there she was, as beautiful as I first remembered her. She was sitting at the end of my bed. I reached for her hand, but it was too far. It seemed that she was very close, but when I reached I could not touch her, yet she didn't seem to move away .

"Hi, Amy. I didn't expect to see you again."

"I had to see you one more time."

"What do you mean, 'One more time'?"

Amy's eyes were piercing as she spoke in a soft, hushed tone," "I just did, that's all. Bud, why did you try to kill yourself?"

"I don't want to live anymore," I responded with a tone of dejection. "Besides, I was trying to kill Ronney. Didn't you know that?"

"Yes, it looks that way to most people. But now, you can choose to live or die and you have chosen to die. Don't you want to live?"

"Why should I? You're gone. You're all I wanted to have," I said. "There's nothing else I ever wanted or had that I knew was all mine. Didn't you know how much I loved you. I don't have anything else to love, so why should I want to live. I don't want to hurt anymore. I'm tired of crying, I just want to die."

"Why did you say you <u>loved</u> me?" Amy whispered, emphasizing loved, "don't you love me anymore?"

"Yes, I do. I don't know. You're gone. How can I love you? I just see you're face and I cry."

"Bud, look at me. I still love you as much as ever. Don't you still love me at least that much?"

"Yes, I do. But how can I?"

Amy hesitated for a moment as if to allow me to think on what I had just said, "You just don't understand love. But how could you? Maybe I didn't then, either. But I do now. That's why I had to come back to you. I can tell you now and someday you will understand. Right now you won't, but someday."

"But, how can I? I can't even touch you."

"Oh my silly Bud. Don't you know that love is more than that. And bigger than that. Do you think that I could ever not love you? I gave you my heart, my love, don't you remember?"

"Yes, but..that was then," I said with puzzlement.

"Then or now," Amy said, her voice taking on an aire of a lecturer, "what's the difference? I gave it to you forever. Bud, how long is forever?", she asked.

"I don't know. Can you tell me?"

"No. Forever isn't a dimension. It's not a time."

"Amy, are you teasing me? What are you saying?"

"Bud, do you remember that time in our secret place when for the first time we kissed?

"Yes."

"And do you remember that we promised that we would love forever?"

"Yes, Amy, I do," I answered with stress.

"Tell me how it felt when we kissed?"

"It felt wonderful. I knew I would love you forever."

"Yes, I felt that way, too.

"Later on we became even closer, didn't we? You know, I always worried about you and you always worried about me. I always called on Saturday morning to make sure you didn't get hurt hunting, or sometimes you called me first to see how the football game went. I wanted you with me all the time, sometimes we just couldn't be. We agreed that we wouldn't always be together because sometimes we had things that had to be done, but we promised that we would love each other just as much when we were apart. And we did, didn't we?", her look drawing the answer from me.

"Yes, I loved you just as much, even when you were somewhere else. But Amy, it's different now. How can you love me anymore?"

"Oh, silly Bud. Do you remember the time when we were hiding from Moses' murderers?"

"Yes, I remember."

Amy looked deeply into my eyes now, as if to drive home her point, her hand raised to rest on her chest just below her neck line, "Do you remember when I held your hand against my breast?" she knew I did, "You wanted to draw it away, but I wouldn't let you."

"No you held it there, Amy."

"Did my breast feel good in your hand?"

"Nothing could be so wonderful. I think about how it felt all the time and I see your face looking at me."

"And what did you tell me just before I fell asleep?"

Again she stared at me, drawing the answer out.

I thought, and then I remembered, "I said I would love you forever." Now I knew what she meant, I wore an eternal hurt in my heart because she was not with me.

"You see, Bud, our love couldn't end even if the world tried to take it away. Love is bigger than that, bigger than life, bigger than the world you know. For each boy and girl there is one perfect love. You have to put a lot of yourself aside to find it and to nurture it. A lot of people go through life playing love. They don't really know what they're looking for so they take love from just anybody that's willing to play love with them. But it's not real, it never lasts. We were lucky, Bud, for some reason we found each other. Real love is forever."

Now she leaned toward me and looked even more intently, "Listen, my Bud, now I must tell you what you must know. If death is your choice I can't stop you. At the same time I can't promise you anything, because I don't understand that kind of death. Only this I can tell you, our love will never die. Love is eternal."

"Then what will I do. I could never love again?", I replied almost crying.

"Oh, but love is bigger than that. It's bigger than you and I. You can love again. Never like our love, that is for once - forever. But a world with no love is a worthless world. Love is all that makes life worthwhile."

"I can't. Don't say that," I blurted out.

"Quiet now, there are important things you must do. You will know what it is when it occurs. You will remember that I told you. You will remember that I will always love you."

The room became dark again, I may have slipped back into unconsciousness, or maybe I had always been unconscious.

Chapter #4
AND I WOULD REMEMER

The next morning my vital signs began to show an improvement, at first slowly and then rapidly. Through all of that time I was not aware of my improvement, nor did I have any input in the change. I suppose I was not hurt so badly to begin with. But maybe as so many have said, there is that period when life and death is truly a choice, and I chose life.

I was weak from the loss of blood, sore and bruised from the impact of the wreck, and my head hurt from the concussion when I landed head first on the shoulder of the road. There were no deep contusions, only scrapes and shallow lacerations. In other words, outside of a lot of pain I was in good shape and my young body was rebounding with good speed. In a few days I was returned to my stepmother's care and again I was to study the walls of my room.

Albert's last Chip

I was recuperating rather fast at home. The doctor who examined me from time to time marvelled at the resiliency of my young healthy constitution. As he would prepare to leave my room he would stop and turn toward me and speak admonishments, "Now, just because you're feeling better, don't do something stupid like taking those hounds out hunting before I say you can. Two stupids don't make a smart, you know."

I suppose that doctors are too busy to research the circumstances of their patients. I felt like telling him that I couldn't go outside even if he said I could, but instead I simply said "OK", not wanting to say anything that would encourage him to stay longer.

I guess young folks live in a fantasyland, because when the inevitable knocks on the door they are always surprised. And so it was the day my stepmother appeared at my bedroom door with a deputy sheriff.

She came into my room ahead of the deputy and stood by the head of my bed and turned to face him. "This man says he needs to see you in person," all the while looking intently at him as if to say one false move and you've had it.

"I'm sorry, M'am," the deputy said apologetically "but the law says that I have to deliver this summons in person."

"Well, then go ahead," she responded dryly, "But hurry up. This boy's in no condition to be disturbed."

The deputy's rigid manner revealed his training and exposure to many unfortunate situations. He handed me the summons and then a clipboard with a note acknowledging that I received it and instructed me to sign it. He apologized and was escorted out of the room by my stepmother.

No sooner had the front screen door slammed shut than I heard her coming back up the stairs. She wheeled around the corner and into my room and stood staring at me from my bedside. "What does it say?", she gasped out, "Big trouble I bet."

I unfolded the summons and threw it to the foot of the bed. She picked it up and studied it for a minute trying to make sense of all the legal jargon. Finally she found the words, "Attempted homicide," she blurted out. "You mean this wasn't an accident." She looked at me in dismay, "You mean---," and she let the sentence tail off without completion. "Oh, Son, what have you gotten yourself into?"

It had been a long time since anyone had called me son. It sounded compassionate, that she was trying to reach out to help, to penetrate my personal barrier. But she wouldn't. Amy did, but no one else ever had or would. I felt uncomfortable. Not only that someone was trying to trespass into my being, but also that I was for the moment at her pleasure.

"Oh, forget it, that's probably what Ronney told them. He can't prove it and neither can anyone else. Besides, he hates my guts because Amy --- Oh, I don't want to talk about it."

I turned over on my side to face the wall. In a few minutes I could hear her leave and I heard the systematic thump - thump - thump as she descended the stairs.

* * *

In three weeks I was to appear before Judge Harris to plea. I guess they thought I needed time to heal. So what, I could have gone today for that matter.

The day of my hearing arrived. A sheriff car pull into the drive about 9:30 AM, thirty minutes before the hearing at the Judges' Chambers. Apparently I was under house arrest, home recovery and home protection all at the same time. I didn't seem to understand the gravity of all the predicaments I had gotten myself into. I just moved as I was instructed.

I walked out to the car unassisted. The deputy met me about halfway, as if to signify that I was a fugitive that might break and run or I was a state's witness that must be protected at all times. Either way, I had gotten to the point that I really didn't care anymore. So much time had passed and so many things had happened since I was first restricted to my room that I no longer felt a risk to my person or that what was happening was real.

As I approached the passenger side of the car I saw the deputy reach for the back seat door. I passed it by and opened the front and slid in. He allowed me to close the door, but I knew he would rather I had taken a seat in the rear.

The car was clean and bright on the outside, but seemed worn and well used on the inside. It smelled of cigarette smoke and I could see cigarette holes burned into the floor. The deputy was a serious looking fellow and had already lit a cigarette. He communicated by radio with the dispatcher, and by some code indicated that we were on the way to the court house and the route we would be taking.

Just as he was about to engage the clutch my stepmother ran out of the front door hailing for us to wait. She had apparently just gotten off of the phone. "Albert will meet you up there. Now don't you go in until he finds you."

I nodded as the car pulled out onto Lake Fern Road with a bounce. The deputy displayed a bent toward heavy-footedness that is probably characteristic of all police officers. We bounced across the railroad tracts that parallel Highway #41. His hand reached for a switch on the dash and the flashing bubble gum machine on the roof began to rotate. His siren blared warning to all those in front as we sped up the highway to Hillsborough County Courthouse to see the Judge.

It's amazing that even as yet I failed to grasp the gravity of my plight. I actually found myself enjoying the ride toward the courthouse. Especially the speed and the cars peeling off to the side of the road to let the sheriff's car go by. The cool, smooth movements of the deputy as he guided the car in and out of the traffic. I was thinking maybe someday that would be a job for me. A badge, a gun, black shinny boots. To dumb and innocent to know that when the judge got through with me today, I might have a scar on my record that would stand between me and a lot of jobs.

We sped by the spot where Amy died, where I probably should have. The car slowed only slightly as the siren screamed the way clear through Sulphur Springs. Next we jogged to the right a block onto Tampa Avenue to Twiggs and right, onto Jefferson and a smooth yet abrupt halt at the back entrance of the courthouse.

I guess I didn't appear to be much of a threat to the deputy. When he came around to open my door he was fumbling with his handcuffs. But, for some reason when I stood up by the car my willowy, youthful frame didn't seem so ominous and he took me by the arm and directed me towards the door.

It wasn't until I reached the courtroom door that I remembered that my stepmother had instructed me not go in until Albert was there - as though I had any control over my destiny at this point. But, no matter, Albert was already in place, seated near the front in the empty courtroom, looking at best out of place. He was wearing his usual khaki pants and shirt. Except that these were freshly ironed, enhanced with a curious, wide beam tie with flowers, tied with an even more curious knot. All this to meet dress protocol of the court. The judge would be honored to know that the tie had probably never been worn before and probably never be worn again, except maybe at Albert's funeral.

I slid into the seat next to Albert, the deputy sat directly behind. I was looking into Albert's face as I sat, as I always did. I was examining his face to see if I could read any unspoken messages. His face was solemn, there was no shine from the gold on his teeth. It was obvious that he'd much rather not have been here and more than that, he questioned whether I was a boy having bad luck or one that caused trouble. I felt the trial had already begun and it was Albert that was the judge.

Across the room, two well-dressed men were seated, they faced each other and were talking seriously. One I recognized as Mr. Harper - Ronney's dad - the other I found out later was the county's attorney.

"All rise!" came the forceful roar of the bailiff.

I looked around to see that everyone was now standing and I stood up quickly. The talking stopped and all became serious and the courtroom was as quiet as a cavern as Judge Harris entered. If ever there was one that fit the storybook image of a county judge it had to be Judge Harris. His black robe was accentuated by his full head of white hair situated on shoulders that looked tall and strong. All of a sudden - I - the lad who could find little in life to be serious about, or authority to bow before, felt a cold chill go done his back.

The judge slipped into his highbacked, leather chair, methodically reached for his gavel and pounded the top of the desk, "Court is now in session!"

Everyone sat down, there was quiet except for the rustle of papers as the judge perused the documents before him.

"The State of Florida, County of Hillsborough, versus Bud Olson, on the charge of attempted vehicular homicide," Judge Harris read out, occasionally looking over his half-rimmed glasses, studying the audience. He paused for a thoughtful moment looking at Albert and me. Then began to speak what was on his mind, as though pre-planned, "It appears to the court that Bud Olson is not represented by council. A minor cannot represent himself in this court. And so, before I appoint a council for the defendant, I ask the State prosecutor and Mr. Newsom, who apparently is present on behalf of the defendant, to approach the bench."

Albert and the prosecutor were standing side by side looking up at the judge. Judge Harris looked stressed as he thought for words to properly sum up the situation in front of him. He looked directly at the prosecutor as he spoke, "As you know, it is highly irregular to have a defendant before the court before he has had opportunity to arrange council, besides being a great waste of the court's time. Would you like to explain to the court what's going on?"

"Well, your honor," the prosecutor said, calculating each word, "It appears in review, that the State has no testimony to refute the claim that the wreck was not attempted vehicular homicide, but was in fact an accident as stated by the defendant. We have only his statement, as it is that Mr. Harper nor his son have any statement to make. Or at least they aren't willing to make one. In view of this circumstance, the state has no case for vehicular homicide."

Judge Harris turned to Albert, "Mr. Newsom, do you have anything to say to the court?"

"Well, Bob"

The judge cut him off, "Mr. Newsom, it doesn't matter if we've known each other a thousand years, in this courtroom it is Judge Harris or Your Honor."

Albert flushed with embarrassment, he looked at his feet for a minute and then looked up, "Well your Honor, I've known this boy for a long time. We've hunted together in the swamps for coons and bobcats. Works hard on weekends for me in the groves, and you know how hard that kind of work is. Never seen him be mean or nothing like that. For a boy who's dad is gone all the time driving a truck cross country, I'd say he's pretty darn good." Albert was beginning to relax a little now after a rather shaky start. He cleared his throat and continued, "And you know he's a State's witness, been cooped up all this time, just the other day had to see'um bury his sweetheart - well how much can a young boy take without making a mistake?"

He stopped short as though his vernacular resources had ended and looked pleadingly up at the judge. For if in cards, backroom poker, where Albert had beat the judge more often than not, Albert would have been bold and boastful. But, now he had to accept the fact that the judge would be the winner and there would be no second hand or ace in the hole. Except maybe one.

Judge Harris looked out over the heads of the ones standing in front of him. There were the usual few seated around the room, mostly there out of curiosity. His eyes stopped and fixed for an instant on each person before he made his pronouncement. When he did there was no mistaking what he said, "Then, in view of the condition of this case, I declare this case dropped and further declare that no further charges will be made against the defendant with regards to this accident." Then with pomp and authority, "This case dismissed

- court adjourned." He rapped the gavel and all stood to leave. Judge Harris hesitated and turned toward Albert, "You know, a guy never knows when he'll run out of 'chips."

Albert was grinning as he turn toward me, once again I could see the lights reflect from his teeth, for only he knew what the judge meant.

The deputy touched me, "Guess I'd better get you back home. Bet your Mom's worried sick about this whole thing."

I wasn't a fugitive anymore.

We sped away from the courthouse in much the same driving style as before. In record time the car was braking for the turn into our driveway. In just that much time I was no longer a villain, charged with attempted vehicular homicide. Now I was just a kid who was under police protection for being an eyewitness to someone I didn't see.

Chapter #5
NO HIGHER AUTHORITY

I had no other cards to play now. I had exposed my hand. I executed a plan which I thought was brilliant. The rest of the world thought it was stupid. Looking back, they were right. Looking back I can see now just how stupid it was, but no one had taken the time to tell me that rage and vengeance does strange things to the brain and in fact does make the avenger stupid.

For the first few days after I was back in my room I sat and mulled over the events since I tried to kill Ronney. I had used some very important friends in a deceitful way. I had broken a trust and they were confused, as they had every right to be. Because they were honorable and unwilling to cast out a friend as worthless because of one offense, they determined that they would let this pass by without judgement or explanation. But my stepmother seemed to withdraw from me as though I were something strange and unpredictable. Like a purring cat whose talons were just under the skin, but potentially lethal just the same.

Junior hadn't been back, and I yearned for the sound of the stick on the window ledge at sundown. And Albert, I'm sure I know what he is thinking. He's questioning his judgement about me, and if he had been foolish to let me borrow the GMC to date Amy and if there is any good that can come from a kid raised without discipline and without respect for authority. I imagined I was the talk of the neighborhood. The kid whose dad was always missing and they knew he would end up this way. And there was talk, and there was speculations, but on the whole, people were more forgiving and anxious for reconciliation than I had given credit, especially to a young lad.

I was so lonely, I was so terribly lonely. There were those who reached out for me, but I wouldn't reach back. I was drowning in my losses, my sorrow, my self pity and I wouldn't reach out.

Chap. #6
A NEW BEGINNING

Maturing Is Not Always a Function of Time.

The phone had rung during the afternoon. I could catch just enough of the muffled conversation to know that Mrs. Brooks had heard what I had done, and called. I don't know whether she had called for me or not, but if she had I knew I was to have no phone calls. But the length of the conversation indicated that my stepmother was relating the details of my life as she best knew them.

Was Mrs. Brooks really worried about me, considering all the heartache she was dealing with? It never occurred to me that if I had killed myself she may have considered it her second great loss. Oh boy, how self-pity and low self-esteem can make a guy stupid. I was beginning to feel stupid as the irrationality of what I had done began to visit my mind. I wondered if Amy thought I was stupid. I wondered if she was trying to save Mrs. Brooks from any more pain.

It was nearing sundown. It hadn't been hot today, and yet the setting of the sun would be a welcome event for now I had another plan. It would be executed after dark. There would be a bright moon above the horizon not long after sundown. It would be nearly full. I often ran through the groves brightly moonlit middles, between the shadows of the trees, chasing the hounds or a crippled rabbit that I had plinked with my twenty-two. I would first run to Amy's grave and sit for a while on the mound of the fresh earth amongst the fading flowers and arrangements. We could talk, just like I sat and talked to Ole Lee after he died. I would tell her I was sorry for being stupid, that I don't ever want to hurt anyone ever again, especially not Mrs. Brooks. And if she told me what I had left to do was to look after her mother, I would start right away. I'm going to see Mrs. Brooks right away and tell her that I am going to be on my best behavior from now on and that she can count on me to be whatever she needs me to be. And then I would tell Amy that I loved her so much - that I love her so much - that I don't think my heart will ever heal. Not in a million years. . . That is what I will do - as soon as everything gets quiet and I can slip out unnoticed.

FLOWERS OF GREAT BEAUTY EMERGE FROM THE DECAYING JUNGLE FLOOR

There were busy sounds coming from the downstairs. The sounds of things being put in order so that the day could end and be put to rest. All animals and birds that I know do this. It's a flurry of energy that comes at the ending of a day - the fox paws the grasses in its burrow and circles until it meets its esoteric criteria, and there are the last calls of the mockingbirds and the Sandhill cranes. But only moments of silence, then the way is prepared and given over to the night creatures.

I peered out my window at the darkness. It was now that period between the setting of the sun and the rising of the moon, when night can seem the blackest. The moon would soon be lifting itself above the cyprus swamps and casting long shadows across the middles between the rows of fruit trees. I need to leave now before the moon becomes full up for I will need the shadows to conceal me as I traverse from grove to grove on my route to the cemetery.

It was time. I opened the screen to the window that I had slipped out so many times to meet Junior. The metal roofing over the porch that I slid down was becoming slick and shiny like a sliding board as the seat of my Levi's polished it over and over. One day my stepmother would look out of this window and it would be obvious that my room quarantine had been somewhat in-effectual. But it wouldn't matter after tonight. She could figure out whatever she wanted. I would be beyond that concern.

I had on a pair of sneakers, the same sneakers I wore when I was hunting in the swamps. The rubber soles gave me traction against the tin roofing and I scooted down to the edge of the roof pulling myself with the heels. I got to the edge and let my feet hang over moving my weight as near to the ground as possible. Then with both hands on the roof edge by my sides I pushed myself away from the roof and dropped cat like to the ground.

I knew all of the groves and the trails that would lead me to the Lutz cemetery. I could have found it on the blackest night with ease. I had to cross the highway, but in the night the traffic diminished to spasmodic. I only needed to hide in a shadow until I could see that no lights were coming.

I crossed the highway and trotted alongside it on the smooth, firm shoulder as long as I could see no car lights. But when one did appear in the distance, I moved off out into the grove and made my way to the cemetery.

The cemetery was old for a small community. It was kept fair, but not elaborate like some big city cemeteries. A big portion was covered by trees. It seemed eerie hopping the fence and making my way in the shadows among the tombstones and grave markers toward the fresh soil and small mound that marked Amy's grave. Soon I was standing in the last shadow. I was looking directly at it. The black shadows that surrounded it made it look even brighter as the moon beamed down almost from straight above.

Now, confronted by the grave, I wasn't so self-assured. I don't know what I expected, but now the whole scene didn't seem so melodramatic. But I came with a script that I had rehearsed in my head and I was going to play it out as I imagined it.

I moved out into the moonlight directly to the grave. The mound was covered with fading and dying flowers and I moved some of them to make a place to sit as I had planned.

"Hi, Amy," I said quietly, but aloud. "It's me."

I didn't speak for a minute. Maybe I thought that Amy would speak, but I knew better. Like the times I sat on Ole Lee's grave. I talked, but I really knew that I was only talking to myself. I sat silently. A whippoorwill was not far away. It called several times,

"Whip-por-will, whip-por-will". I remembered the many times that Amy and I had hidden in the shadows to be alone and listened to the nightbird make its eerie call and how we felt that there was some magic omen in its presence. But just as it began its call again, it flew away in a startled flurry.

In my mind I could see Amy's face...the smile, the little turned-up nose, her tan complexion and flowing blonde hair. I couldn't bring myself to accept that she was gone. I knew she was, but how could life be so cruel? At this age, final made no sense. I held my head in my hands and sobbed uncontrollably. The tears flowed like rain and burned my eyes. Breathing was done in gasps causing my chest to heave and quiver. I wanted to scream out, but I didn't - I sobbed. For so many years I had not so much as dropped a tear, now my heart seems to know no other emotion. I didn't want to cry, I wanted to hurt inside, like a man, I presumed, out of sight of any on looker. Was there no way to cry so that no one would know? But I sobbed, out of control, like a baby, my head buried in my cupped hands.

After a while, I don't know how long, the sobbing began to slow down. I realized that I really had nothing to say, if I could have anyway. But, I remembered that I must go to Mrs. Brooks. I must go. I had to think of someone else for a change as I promised Amy I would.. I must be strong for Mrs. Brooks, I could not run away this time. I must grow up. I must turn and face the battle, I was crouched against the cliff, I'll fight against my loss. I didn't know how to scream out for help, so, if there is anything of value to be found in me, I must let Amy rest and deal with what life has dealt me. These are the seeds of my field.

I raised to my feet and stared at the fresh mound. My hand went to my chest and there it was, the golden chain with the broken heart. I whispered a vow that there it would stay and one day I would lay next to Amy.

This seemed to be enough promise for me to move on to other thoughts. I would have to leave soon to get to Mrs. Brooks house before she would have gone to bed. It would be at least a mile or more to her house. Also, I didn't want my stepmother to realize that I was gone and alert the sheriff.

I knelt down for a minute, I turned my cheek and pressed it against the soft soil. I selected a flower, a pale pink carnation from the remaining flowers and folded it into my wallet. I forced myself to turn and walk away.

I eased back into the shadows and crouched behind a low bush as a car turned off the highway sweeping its bright lights across the cemetery. I watched as its tail lights passed out of sight. I made my way to a brushy area to cross the fence in case another car turned off of the highway. It looked clear. I put my hands on the top wire and crouched to vault over.

Out of nowhere a huge doubled fist crashed into my face. Flashes of light like lightning streaked in front of eyes, and then another. I fell backward from the fence smashing my face into the ground. I heard a 'squshing' as the blood burst from my nostrils and huge noises were screaming in my ears.

"Bury the little sonabitches face in the sand and tie'm up."

There was no doubt who had me. I'd never heard this guttural voice before, but I knew. It was Moses' killer.

Next a knee dropped onto the back of my neck. My arms were jerked behind me so hard that I wanted to scream out, but I knew that would make it only worse. Next I was jerked up to my feet by my bound arms and hair and I was looking at two large, black shadows.

"Think you're pretty damn smart, you little fart. I knew you'd get here."

They chuckled at each other. The larger one in self-satisfaction, the other in appeasement.

Mac Maston and Lew Mabrey. These were the moonshiners that killed Moses alright - Maston the killer, Mabrey the accomplice. But I couldn't know for sure. I could see where the shot came from through the swamp. But if there was a dominant one in the pair it was definitely Maston, so he was probably the one who killed Moses.

"Let's go," Maston growled, "get out of here before another ga-damn car comes round the corner."

One of them was holding the back of my pants and shoving me in front of him. We went a few feet beyond the end of the cemetery fence and I could see the rear end of an old pickup truck hidden in the brush. It looked dark and old, the license plate was smeared so that it was not legible.

Mabrey grabbed the door handle and was about to throw me in to the center of the truck seat, by the seat of my pants, when Maston grabbed his arm and swore out, "What the Ga-dam-hell you think your gonna do. You gonna sling blood over the whole inside my truck."

I was still bleeding like a 'stuck hog' as some would say. The blood from my nose had covered the front of my shirt and was still dripping with rapidity.

"Get a rag and wipe him off."

The obscured license plate and rusty truck exterior were common ploys used by moonshine runners to divert attention from the real truck whose interior was upholstered and polished clean. When Maston hit the ignition switch the motor jumped into action. It sounded large and powerful and ran smoothly. It had probably been bought especially to replace the engine that would normally have been under the hood of the old rusty thing. Then the whole running mechanism of the truck would have been rebuilt - wheel bearings, drive train, transmission - all so that even with a load of shine hidden under a tarp in the pickup bed it would outrun most of the revenuer cars, especially down the back roads.

I jerked the rag away from Mabrey and was holding it against my nose blocking the flowing blood. Mabrey flinched when I took it and clenched his fist like he wanted to hit me. Then thought better and relaxed. "You little bastard," he called me, "You're pretty young and stupid yet, but I'm gonna show you."

"Oh, shud-up," Maston bellowed at Mabrey, "Won't make no difference in the end."

There was silence in the truck as Mabrey stewed over being told to shut up. The engine purred effortlessly as we turned south onto Highway 41 towards Tampa. It wanted to move on out but Maston held it right at the speed limit. We would soon be going through Lutz. Maston knew it would be tempting for me to holler out and try to get the attention of someone I knew. "Mabrey," he said to get the attention of his accomplice.

Mabrey leaned forward and looked around me, "What?"

"You still carryin' that big nigger sticker?" he asked, making reference to a large knife that he carried in a belt sheath.

"Sure I got it. You know that."

"Well, I tell you what, jus take it out and hold it against the little farts ribs and if he makes a sound when we go through town, you jus shove it in as far as you can, don't care if he bleeds all over the cab."

I was scared now, plenty scared. I may have been brave once, young - cocky and all those. But now I was nothing but scared.

The pickup never slowed as it passed Stiekies. The GMC was at the gas pump. Albert would be inside talking to Mr. Stiekie. If it was a good day, Mr. Stiekie would call Albert to hang around at closing time because the cash drawer would be full. But only a fool would have tried to stick up Mr. Stiekie. When he was behind the counter, which is where he usually was, we all knew that there was an arsenal of weapons at his fingertips. None of us ever doubted that he would blow away half the county if they were after his money. I got just a glimpse of a light in the back of the garage, looked like Junior leaning over the work bench, dredge probably down again. I felt a clammy chill come over me as I realized that I may never see them again. They didn't know what was up. I knew they couldn't hide me forever, there was only one other thing they could do to keep me from being evidence. I could never convince them that I had seen nothing. Even if I did, it was to late now. I knew too much.

Not long ago I was prepared to let my life hang out to avenge Amy's death, but now, this seemed different. I wasn't calling the 'Shots' so to speak. To die on somebody else's terms was strange and different and I was scared - scared as hell. I just decided I didn't want to die. How did I get in this predicament? Couldn't I just be in my room?

The truck pierced the darkness of the unlit highway with the smoothness and power of a dirty gazelle. The windows were open to offset the damp, hot night air. Both Maston and Mabrey were smoking. As a matter of fact, they smoked one cigarette after another ever since the truck hit the highway. Sitting in the middle between two smokers has a lot of hazard. The smoke that converged on me from both sides of the cab was bad enough, but the hot ashes and sparks that came with the smoke made me squirm and slap as they burnt my skin. One large spark blew off the end of Maston's cigarette and landed on my cheek. Impulsively I slapped at it to get the burning, stinging coal off. Mabrey jerked around, his knife still against my side penetrated my shirt and pricked my skin pretty severely, "Watch that damn knife," I shouted at him.

He was holding the knife in his right hand, his arm crossed in front toward me. He swung backwards with his left hand and hit me in the mouth. "Keep your Ga-dam mouth shut," he screamed at the side of my head. He lifted the huge blade and shook it only inches from my nose, "Or maybe I could jus whittle off a little piece of your nose."

I sat up straight and rigid and pushed back against the seat trying to move my nose away from the blade.

"Dammit, Mabrey," Maston barked, "If you want to cut 'im up, get 'im out of the pickup first. You know I just got covers for these seats."

It got quiet again. Both Maston and Mabrey stared straight ahead, seemly looking as far down the highway as possible. They were looking for trouble ahead, like a highway patrol or a sheriff car sitting in the shadows.

Maston brought the pickup around a couple of turns, the final one, a lighted intersection. I barely make out the road sign, "Dale Mabrey." I thought to myself that it would be disgusting if such a pretty street was named after Mabrey's ancestors.

I pondered my room at home, if my stepmother had found out I was gone. It wouldn't matter now anyway, we are so far from home, nobody would look this far away. Besides, I've slipped out so often that this time wouldn't seem all that different from the rest.

We turned again, this time the sign said "Gandy Blvd." At least now I knew where we were going. You're not going anywhere but St. Petersburg on this causeway.

We were soon out on the narrow, mounded ribbon that supported the highway. It was mostly dark now, the moon had moved across the sky and could barely be seen above the distant twinkling lights that outlined the St. Pete horizon, except for the flash of light from Coleman lanterns, guarded by silent sentries holding fishing poles instead of spears.

Sooner than I wished we had crossed the causeway and were headed south down St. Pete's dark back streets, past the housing and onto a dirt road that probably was used for fisherman to access the coastline of Tampa Bay. Finally the truck began to slow. Maston looked intently along the dark roadside until the truck lights exposed an opening and a lane through the mangrove border. We turned through the mangroves, the opening so narrow that the limbs brushed the sides of the pickup. He brought the truck to a halt along side an old fisherman's camp house.

"Get 'im inside and make 'im keep his ga-dam mouth shut," Maston barked at Mabrey, "I'll check on the boat."

The camp house was built above the water on poles, there were steps leading up from the ground to a little door that was little more than screen to keep the black mangrove mosquitos from eating you up. The house was built of wood, old and bleached grayish-white from years of sun and salt spray. Under the house, hidden by branches and old boards was the boat. The house was built far enough from the water's edge to allow it to be afloat even during low tide.

"Why the hell I need to do that?" Mabrey barked back. Let's jus load up and get out o' here. I ain't gonna like it 'til we got water behind us."

"Okay, dammit. Get the ga-dam sack of food up there in the corner where I left it and we'll go."

Mabrey pushed me up the steps, held open the screen door and pushed me through. He grabbed a gunny sack off of the floor then pushed me back out the door. I stumbled and fell down the steps. With my hands tied behind my back there was no chance that I could catch myself, so I threw my shoulder down and rolled until I was lying prone on the ground at the bottom. Mabrey grabbed me by the back of my shirt and lifted me up and shoved me towards the waiting boat all in one motion.

"Get in the boat and s'down and don't get up less you want some of this," he growled shaking his clenched fist in my face.

The boat was pretty typical of a close-in bay fisherman's boat. Made of cypress planks that swelled water-tight as long as it was wet. Not too long, maybe sixteen to eighteen feet, but deep and heavy, easily big enough to handle most of the bay's roll and break. On the transom hung a weathered Johnson outboard, big enough to be twenty to twenty-five horsepower. The aluminum motor cowling was faded and pitted from the corrosive aging of the salt spray. But if this engine was akin to the truck engine, the appearance of the motor cowling was not indicative of the finesse of the engine.

I threw my leg high to try and step over the side of the gunwale of the small craft but Mabrey's shove had me off balance and I fell headlong onto the floor. Unable to catch my fall, I hit my chin hit the plank seat. I cried out from the pain, but the cry fell on unsympathetic ears.

Maston was tending the motor when I hit the floor, the noise and commotion caused him to jerk around as if I might be attempting an escape, "Good job, Mabrey," he whispered loudly, "Keep the little sonnabitch on the floor out of the way."

In the bow of the boat was the typical red, six-gallon gas can that contained the oil and fuel for the engine. A long, black hose with a coupling extended from the fuel can to the engine and Maston was tapping the engine around the side of the cowling trying to find the prongs that it connected to.

Mabrey began pushing the boat out from under the house letting it drift quietly into the open water. The fact that Mabrey was casting off the boat without even a word to Maston made him furious, which wasn't hard to do anyway. "What the hell you doing, Mabrey? I say I was ready?"

Mabrey responded with a low growl, "Gotta get this sonnabitch outta here. Don't you ever worry 'bout gettun caught?"

"I'll tell you this, you know this hose ain't no good, an if I don't get this motor going, you jus might get to swim in with the boat rope in your mouth. Better hope for a good tide."

I heard Maston swear and holler back to Mabrey that he'd found the connection prongs and the hose was now connected. "Pump that hose bulb. See if we can get this sonnabitch primed."

It occurred to me for the first time that Maston and Mabrey liked to use the same curse words. They would use the same word over and over until for some reason one of them, usually Maston, would change to another word and then it would be the word of choice for a spell.

"Okay," Mabrey said, "I got pressure on the bulb. It oughtta go."

Maston stood in the back of the boat, half-facing the engine. He pulled out the choke knob, grabbed the handle of the starter rope in his right hand, braced with his left hand against the motor and pulled the rope with a jerk. The engine popped and began running in jerks and starts with oily smoke belching from the rear. Maston released the starter rope and with a pop it recoiled into place. Quickly, Maston shoved the choke knob in against the cowling and the engine quit smoking and began to idle smoothly. Maston reached to the side of the engine and pulled the lever forward to engage the prop and the boat began to move quietly and smoothly out of the little cove toward the open water of Tampa Bay.

Lying in the bottom of the boat afforded me little visibility, but I could see the sky and some shore lights from the taller buildings. I could tell for sure that St. Pete was behind us and since the moon had sank into the horizon on the right side of the boat we must be heading generally south. The boat had become an eerie capsule in the black, silhouette-less open water. It housed three humanoids, lost in their own fears, each fearing a different force, created by a different circumstance, each with its own finale, the final scene only a curtain away.

The motor revved up a little and I began to feel the impact of small waves and breaks hit against the bow as the boat rose up at the front to meet them and drop to the basin between them. The waves against the boat became larger and more regular, I was aware we were moving further away from the shore and toward a group of barrier islands that I had known were there but knew nothing about them.

Mabrey was sitting on the bow-seat staring out into the darkness. He couldn't have seen anything even if it had been at his nose, but his intent stare would make you believe that he was searching for something. And, maybe he was. Many large ocean-going cargo ships came into Tampa Bay to unload cargo mostly from the tropical islands of the Caribbean. The wake from the stern of one of the large ships could easily swamp this little craft if it strayed within several hundred yards of it. But that was silly. The ship lights can be seen for miles out into the gulf, unless he was looking for buoy channel markers. But, going south we would soon be across the channel. Finally, he turned around on the seat and called back to Maston, "How far across this sonnabitch?"

Maston seemed to get irritated every time Mabrey asked him a question which was evident in his incomplete answers. "Gadammit,

Mabrey! S'many times you been across this channel you don't know?"

There was silence. Maston didn't bother to respond to Mabrey's question any further.

Mabrey was again staring off into the darkness. Suddenly he turned again on the bow-seat and faced Maston. "Gadammit," he shouted back at Maston, "I got a right to know." Mabrey's voice had a quiver and a barking sound like he was afraid of Maston, and afraid of the conditions all at the same time. "Gadammit, Maston. You know this bay's got a hell of a current on the tide, black as it is. How I know you ain't going straight out to sea?"

"You gaddam fart, look over the top of my head. What you see?", demanded Maston.

"Don't see nothing. It's black dark you know."

"Don't see the gaddam light on the top of that tall building?"

"Oh, you mean over there?"

"Yeah, over there. Is it straight behind the boat?"

"Yeah," Mabrey responded with a note of confusion.

"Well, as long as the gaddam-sonnabitch stays straight behind the boat we'll bump right into the east point of Mullet Key jus like we always do. Now shut your gaddam mouth."

Mabrey turned back toward the front of the boat and sulked as though he was reassessing he self-worth.

After a few minutes Mabrey turned back around toward Maston, his lingering stare belied his fear as he tried to muster up the courage to speak out, "Now you dunnit, Maston. Now you really dunnit."

"What the hell you muttering about?"

"Now you dun tol'm where were headed," Mabrey spoke up with increasing courage because he saw that Maston had made a mistake in revealing our destination.

"Mabrey, you some kind of nut? What difference it gonna make if the little fart knows where we're goin?"

"Mullet Key - Fort De Soto," I told myself. Now it was coming together. I'd never been to Mullet Key, but I'd heard of it enough. You couldn't get there by car, but it was only a few miles across the bay from St. Pete. An old military fort - big cannons to blow up enemy ships trying to sneak into the Tampa Harbor. History says it wasn't used very long. Not even one cannon fired on an enemy ship.

All that money spent building cannon bunkers and hauling in huge cannons and no ships came around to shoot at. On the other hand, maybe that's why no enemy ships came around. Just the same, by now, it would be nothing but old ruins and jungle. Little by little it began to register what Maston may have meant by 'What difference it gonna make?'

I sunk heavily to the bottom of the boat. My heart was firmly lodged in my throat and I began to say to myself, almost hysterically, "Why me?! Why me?!"

My ear was so close to the bottom of the boat that I could hear the rushing water moving against the rough underside of the cypress bottom. The slap of the small waves against the bow echoed back. The rhythmic beat of the waves caused me to hear nothing else. Until suddenly, the boat jerked, the motor crunched then stalled.

"I guess you hit Mullet Key alright," Mabrey called out. "Trying to knock out the shear pin or somethin'? Prop won't turn without a shear pin, y'know? We ain't got no more, y'know?"

If Maston hadn't been busy keeping the boat under control his rage would have caused him to take out Mabrey, but instead he needed him. "Gaddamit, Mabrey, jump out and push the boat back before a wave dumps it on the beach."

We still had further to go to get to the fort. It was around on the other side of the Key and we would have a couple of miles to go.

We rounded the east point of Mullet Key. I could feel the boat rising against a bigger surf now, we were on the edge of the main channel. The water was more open and the bang against the bow was louder and harder.

Maston called out over the noise, "What do you think? Don't seem to bad. You think?"

Mabrey responded, trying to conceal the tremble in his voice, "Keep this sonnabitch close to the shore, dammit. Never know when a big roller might sneak in on us an I'd never see the goddamsonnabitch."

Maston was trying to keep the small craft parallel to the shoreline which meant that we would be running in the trough of the waves. The boat would rise to the top of each wave as it came by and then roll and slide back into the trough. I was rolling in the bottom of the boat. I kept my feet spread to minimize the roll, but the further we went along the shoreline the larger the waves became, although in the darkness you couldn't see them. Occasionally a spray of salt water would leap over the side and shower my back. I soon found myself lying in a shallow puddle.

"How's it look up there?" Maston called to Mabrey.

"How should I know, can't see a damn thing."

"Well, keep your eyes open."

"My eyes are so open now the salt's about to burn'm up. Hell man, let's head for shore. One of them big rollers is gonna get us for sure."

"Another mile and then we'll head fur shore."

I never knew what caused a big roller like Mabrey was talking about. I could have been several smaller waves that joined up along the way, or it could be the leftover wake from a big ship that's already over the horizon. But this time stupid Mabrey was right, because I could hear the foaming of the break high above the gunwale of the boat. I could hear it because in the bottom of the boat I was shielded from all the noises of the motor. I could hear it. They could neither hear it nor see it.

I wanted to cry out a warning because the only chance a small boat would have against a large wave would be to turn into it at a quarter angle and plow over it.

The roar of the wave was loud now. Maston must have either seen it or heard it, because he powered the engine and the boat swung around to meet the wave, but too late. The wave threw the bow up and it plowed into the wave below the break. I saw Mabrey lose his grip on the sides and was tossed backwards like a stick in the surf. He stumbled and fell backward over the side, screaming for help. The boat fell upright, but the wave had broken over the side and we were loaded with water and the boat rocked dangerously.

"Over here, help, help!!" Mabrey hollered as he spit water and coughed. "I'm over here!"

Maston shut down the engine, "Where, I don't see you?"

Maston was standing, trying to steady the boat while he was searching the dark water for Mabrey.

"Over here!"

"Well, swim to the boat, I'll drag you in."

In a few minutes I could hear Mabrey bumping the sides of the boat. "Give me your hand," Maston snorted as if it was Mabrey's fault that he was washed overboard.

The boat tossed and rolled when Maston tugged on Mabrey's arm. It and the waves were uncooperative as they thrashed about. There was nearly a foot of water in the bottom of the boat now and I was on my knees to keep my head out of the water. They were so busy with their own problems that I was completely ignored. Something like an impulse came over me and almost effortlessly I slide over the side of the opposite gunwale into the water without a sound, unnoticed.

I'd never swam with my hands tied behind my back before. I'd swam lots using only my feet, but my hands were at least free and I could use them for balance. But I knew that the waves would drift me toward the shore. So, by swimming on my back, keeping my chest expanded to create buoyancy, I just might make it. I was swimming crossways to the wave pattern. I could feel each wave as it came against my feet giving me a little push and then I would shut my eyes and hold my breath as it rolled over my head. Slowly the surf began to roll louder and louder in the distance and I knew it meant I would be washed ashore soon, as the sea purges itself of unwanted debris with its indifference to the debris' condition.

Soon I heard Maston screaming over the noise of the surf at Mabrey to bail the water from the boat. I heard Mabrey scream back at Maston to get the motor going before the next roller swamps the boat and he drowns. Maston screams back at Mabrey, "Where'd the little sonnabitch go? Wash'd overboard. See im' anywhere?"

Mabrey screams back, "How you expect me to see anybody in this dark?"

"Don't matter no how," Maston responded to Mabrey, "If he goes out to sea he's gone anyway. Save us the trouble. If he makes it to the beach we'll find 'im in the morning. Can't hide long on Mullet Key."

About then my feet struck the sandy bottom. I rolled over on my face trying to get my feet under me so I could stand, but the waves would knock me forward and off balance. I was coughing from the water I had ingested and my eyes were burning from the salt as I crawled and scooted out of the water onto the beach. I lay there for a few minutes trying to catch my breath and cough the burning salt water out of my lungs. Maston had gotten the drenched motor to start. It was missing pretty bad and sputtered because of the water that had penetrated the cowling. But, it was running and it was headed toward the beach.

A fresh flow of adrenaline hit my veins and I jumped to my feet. They would soon be beaching the boat. I had no time to cover my tracks and they would know for sure that I was on the island somewhere. I didn't even know whether there would be a place to hide. There were two of them. They probably knew the island like their palms. Even if I hid, how long could I hide? These were problems to deal with tomorrow, tonight all I could think of was to run, run fast and as far from this beach as I could.

Instinctively I ran perpendicular to the beach knowing that this would put the most distance between me and my pursuers. My logic was good, but knowledge of the island was not. I was running full out, off balance because of my tied hands. I stumbled through the vines and palmetto brush, cutting and tearing my skin, falling and rolling to get my feet back under me, fear concealing the pain. In no time I began to feel the marshy muck of the mangrove fringe along the north side of the island. And before I had made any distance at all, I was already across the Key. I could have run to the right or to the left. I chose left, not because of prudence or premonition, but because I could make out a clearing that direction and hoped it would afford me some speed. I ran for the clearing, along the high, center of the Key, maybe a mile, but the adrenaline began to wane and I began to fall repeatedly. I would catch a few breaths and run again, but my legs had turned to spaghetti and in a few steps I would fall again. Desperately I half-dragged, half-crawled into a large mound of palmetto bushes and lay prone, my face in the sand. I was panting against the thundering pound of my heart as the predawn began to lighten the sky and cast a shadowy gray through the cabbage palms and into this strange and mysterious island prison.

It wouldn't be long before Maston and Mabrey would be trailing me to this clump of palmetto brush. I left the beach with my heart in my hand, my feet like lead, with no thought to cover my tracks. "What can I do?", kept running through my mind. If I were an armadillo or a gopher, Florida's version of a land turtle, I'd easily burrow to safety in the soft sand under this maize of palmetto roots.

But there would be no time for burrowing. The mumbling of my pursuers were getting closer and more distinguishable. They were so close. I didn't dare move or even breathe, but they must have been standing near the edge of the very clump I was hiding in, maybe even trying to find where my trail led away from the palmettos.

"Don't see a damn thing," Mabrey said in a whisper, "Lil sonnabitch give us the slip?"

"Slip to where? Just where's he gonna slip to?" Maston retorted. "You just go around that way and I'll take the other. If we don't cut a trail by then we'll know where to look."

The density of the underbrush was so thick that they couldn't move without rustling and breaking limbs. I listened to them move away in opposite directions.

They'd be back. They'd make their circle around the area and they wouldn't find my trail leading away from where I was hiding. In many respects they were dumb, but they would be as clever as the fox in understanding the Florida woods and finding my hideout. I knew my only chance was to run. I had to let them get as far away as they would go before turning back and then sneak out the other side. I could hear the noise as they broke through the brush getting further and further away. I knew they would turn soon...time to move. Not having my hands available to help, I slid on my belly under the low, dense, umbrella of palmetto fronds, until I was at the edge. I pulled my feet under me and slowly stood up to see above the low brush. I took one glance. I couldn't see them. I ran the opposite way.

"Maston," Mabrey shouted, "Where tha hell are you? Hear the li'l sonnabitch runnin'?"

"Go for im', we got the little sonnabitch now," Maston shouted back.

I was desperately running with as much power as I could muster. Swimming with my hands tied behind my back was not so difficult, but running requires balance as the weight of one leg moves forward and the other backward and the body twists at the waist. I ran with a hopping gait leaping over downed trees and debris all-the-while assuring myself that even with tied hands behind my back I could outrun this overweight, over-the-hill bunch. What I hadn't counted on was the size of the Mullet Key. It wasn't very big.

I broke through a thick fringe of palmetto brush and fell into a clearing. I rolled back up onto my feet and stood looking at the fort. Fort DeSoto didn't look like much, a huge mound of dirt cover by cabbage palms and palmetto brush - just a pile of sand catacombed with bunkers of concrete for storing cannon powder, artillery balls and troops. It was the only direction to go, so I headed for it.

Just as I began my dash for the fort, two hundred feet on either side, Mabrey and Maston broke into the clearing. They must have seen me simultaneously because each shouted a mixture of obscenities and threats at me at the same time. The only voice that was clear and audible was the last threat made by Maston - "Now we got you, you little sonnabitch. There ain't no where left to go."

Maston's encouragement put new flight into my feet and I sailed across the clearing to the fort. I was on the side of the fort away from the water - the side facing the channel was camouflaged with trees and brush so that enemy ships trying to slip into Tampa Bay, as early as the civil war, could be detected and apprehended. Soon Mullet Key became a major military installation with barracks, bunkers and cannons. None ever having played a major roll in any military conflict. But the side I was on was the business side. Concrete walks, nearly buried by years of blowing sand, and concrete walls, ten feet or more straight up. The walls had openings in them with steel doors. Some hung open, some were sealed shut. For me the rooms behind the doors would not have been a safe haven, but a dungeon from which I would have no escape if or when I was found. So I continued to run down the walkway alongside the concrete wall, jumping the brush and debris that had collected against the walls, but again my legs were giving out. When I jumped to clear the brush I always stumbled, often falling, the long ordeal had depleted my adrenaline reserve. I was so tired, my legs hurt, I even entertained notions of just giving up.

My only chance, though very slim, was piled right ahead of me. A cabbage palm had blown over and lay against the concrete wall, other brush and trash had blown against it to make a heap large enough for me to bury in. I heard Maston and Mabrey at the other end of the fort, Maston was admonishing Mabrey with various terms of slang to "get the lead out". I dove into the brush pile and slid under the cabbage palm and pushed in until I was pressed against the concrete wall. I could hear Maston and Mabrey getting closer. They had slowed their pace and were looking deliberately from one side to the other. They had not reached the brush pile yet, but they were close enough that I could hear their panting and heaving.

They hadn't moved from their position for minutes, apparently they suspected I was close. Finally, between deep, gasping breaths, Mabrey broke the silence, "What you think? Think he got away?"

"No! Hell, how's he gonna get away? No where to go. Who knows? Maybe in that brush pile there, I bet a guy could bury in it.

My whole body shook and my blood turned to ice water.

"Well, we gonna look?", asked Mabrey.

"No, not now. I'll stay here and watch the brush pile. You make a circle around the fort and see if you can cut a trail. Then Maston's voice took on a sinister sneer. "Well, if you don't cut a trail I'll just toss a match in that pile and watch it burn."

I heard Mabrey trudge off. I knew he would soon return having found no trail. "Why me?", I said over and over. "Why does everything happen to me?" My body was shaking from fear. This was obviously the end of the run. There was no doubt in my mind that Maston would light the brush pile and if I were in it he would get all the more pleasure. I decided I would wait until the very last second, until I heard Mabrey return and then give up. No matter what they had in store for me, it couldn't be worse than hiding in a burning bush.

It seemed that only a few minutes had passed until the heavy breathing of Mabrey's unkept body returned, "Go ahead and light'er, last place I know to look."

That was it. A sickness hit me in the stomach, I drew in a breath to call out my surrender - something touched my arm, "In here."

The dark shadow under the brush had completely concealed a doorway through the concrete wall. I could see a hand protruding from it motioning me to come through, "Come on, stupid," the muffled voice beckoned again. I twisted my body until I was lying on my stomach and slid through the opening and into a black dark chamber. Not even a crack in the concrete allowed a trace of light.

The voice slid over to the hole and moved some boxes against it. I knew I was in a concrete chamber, but it was blind dark and I

Seeds of My Field

could see nothing. But I could hear - I could hear the pounding of my heart and a loud ringing in my ears. But that was not all I heard. Coming from the outside, barely audible through the boxes I could hear the two talking. "Well, Maston, you gonna light it? What the hell you wait'n on?"

"Hell no, I ain't gonna light it. All that smoke and the coast guard'd be over here t'see what's gonin' on. Sides, if the little fart was in there he'd be scared out by now. C'mon you one-eyed turkey, I'll help find his trail."

Then there was silence, for minutes, and then it seemed like hours. Finally I couldn't keep quite any longer, "Who are you?" I asked. I was looking out into darkness. I didn't know whether I was looking at someone or whether I was alone. I asked again, "Who are you?"

"Shut up," the voice returned in a vicious, almost desperate, whisper, "Just shut up."

I could tell that the whisper was designed to disguise the real character behind the voice, but I was sure it was the voice of a young person, maybe a runaway. Right now I didn't care. I felt secure, at least temporarily. I was ready to take each moment, one at a time.

Safe haven or dungeon - I wasn't sure at this point, but for sure I had a measure of reprieve from the pair of hounds who had no mercy for my being in their plan, like a coon in hollow of a big oak tree, safe for the moment.

It was so dark and damp. I could see nothing except a dim fringe of light that came from around the edges of the box that hid the doorway that I had entered through. I could hear the breathing of the invisible person across the room. His breathing was regular and subdued compared to my own. I leaned back against a damp concrete wall. I was somewhat relaxed for the first time in hours. It must have been hours that I sat, very uncomfortable now. I shifted from one buttock to the other trying in vain to relieve the pain of the pressure of the noncompressing rubble that covered the floor.

There was no light for me to see, but I guess my rescuer must have been half cat because I could hear him moving around like he knew what he was doing. My heart had begun to slow to normal and the excitement of the being chased began to subdue enough to allow other conditions to surface. I remembered that my hands were tied behind my back, the ropes had made the skin on my wrists chafe. My hands throbbed from lack of circulation and my shoulder cramps felt like daggers penetrating to the joints. But I didn't need them on anymore, I finally had a way to get them removed.

"Are you over there? If you are would you help me get these ropes off my arms?" I asked with a pleading tone in my whisper.

Minutes passed with no response, only the breathing.

"Well, will you take the ropes off or not?" I said, this time almost demanding.

The response was not positive, "Shut up".

"C'mon," I said, "These things hurt."

"You'd better shut up or I'll put a rock to your head."

I shut up instantly. It seemed now that I had shaken the hounds only to be trapped by a demon I couldn't even see. Besides, I couldn't tell in the hushed voice whether this was a statement of emphasis or an actual threat.

There was a long silence - a pause to consider where I stood and to mourn my plight.

I heard a shuffle as he seemed to be moving closer through the darkness, "I've got some orange pieces and water. Sit still and I'll give you some if you want."

I sure did, I guess I was to scared to be thirsty until someone else mentioned it. "Okay, thanks," I whispered back.

Soon I felt a bottle being stuck to my face. I twisted my head until I got the neck into my mouth, the bottle lifted. I got three good gulps before it was taken away. I could smell the sweet smell of an orange moving closer to my face. A hand rested on my cheek and an orange segment was pushed into my mouth, and then another and another until I assume it was all gone.

The hand didn't seem big and rough like I expected. It felt small and feminine. Maybe that's why he didn't want to let me loose - to small and feeble to protect himself. Maybe then, he wouldn't harm me.

"You know what?" I said with a calculated coolness and casualness. "I don't really blame you for not undoing this rope. Who knows who I am? Maybe you could just loosen them a little. If I don't get some circulation down there soon my hands are going to drop off. Please!!"

Another minute of silence before I heard his whispered query, "What you in trouble for?"

"I'm not in trouble. Those guys are bootleggers. They think I saw something I didn't see and they're afraid I'll squeal."

"Oh sure, you think I'll buy into that?"

"Well, okay, if you don't like the truth, tell me what you will believe. I don't really give a damn." By now I'd given up getting loose and was getting pert.

"Keep your voice down, stupid," he whispered back, "I'll loosen the rope just enough to free up the circulation. Get away from the wall," he demanded. "See this rock I've got in my hand?" I couldn't see a thing. "If you try anything you'll get it."

I could feel his small hands moving down my arms finding their way to my hands and the rope. He felt up and down the rope trying to understand the knot and then began working it with his fingers. He was having difficulty getting it to free up. These dumbo's probably tied a "Granny knot". Soon I felt the knot slip. He was tugging on it to free it - then - his hand slipped and the rope flung away. There was a hushed scream of fear as he scooted away in haste.

"What the heck," I blurted out, "You're not a boy. You're a girl. No wonder you're acting so strange."

"You'll think strange when I hit you with this rock. You'd better stay put if you know what's good for you."

"Don't be so silly," I said, feeling a lot bolder now. "I'm not going to hurt you. Right now you're about the only friend I've got."

"I'm nobody's friend."

"Well, maybe you're not nobody's friend, but I'm hiding in here cause those two guys will do me in as soon as they find me. You must have reason to be hiding? Doesn't make much since for a girl to hide out here for no reason."

"You talk too much," she replied with a pronounced sneer in her voice. "Why don't you just shut up?"

We seemed to be heading toward a sibling verbal debate.

"Shut up! Is that all you can say?"

"Just shut up, okay?"

There was again a deep silence, almost as deep as the darkness. I wasn't sure whether to talk more or not. One thing, I didn't want to sit in this dark dungeon forever. Sooner or later I'd be found out.

Then in her hushed, unmodulated voice, "I can hide if I want, nobody cares."

"Nobody?"

"Nobody gives a damn about me."

I flinched at how easily curse words came from such a young sounding voice.

"That's silly," I responded impulsively, "I care, I bet a lot of people care."

"No they don't, and you don't either," she blurted back almost instantly, her voice seemed to have a sad quiver.

"Well, one thing is for sure, they're after me, not you. You could just get up and walk out of here."

"No!!"

"What do you mean 'no'?" "Are you crazy or something?"

"I'm not crazy," she screamed out.

Then I could hear a light sobbing. Something was crazy about whatever she is doing here.

"Look, I didn't mean really crazy. I just meant I don't understand. I didn't mean to make you cry."

"I'm not crying," she retorted, although it was obvious that she was.

"I'm sorry anyway."

I went on, "You know if you don't like me here you could just get up and go on out and then after dark maybe I could get away.

"No!" she fired back with anger.

"Why not?"

"No!" she said almost in a scream.

I was puzzled, but at least I had some kind of a dialogue going. She may be my ticket to escape - better keep talking.

"You know what I think? I think you've got some kind of problem. I mean, I'm in here and can't leave because those guys are after my hide - you're in here and could leave but you act like they're after you too. Doesn't make much sense."

"I'm scared of men."

"Why, you don't even know them."

"I'm scared of all men. I hate men."

She was quietly sobbing again. She didn't volunteer to talk, so we sat in silence. For some strange reason her sobbing sounded like she was pleading, not so much for help but for a resolution to some strange demon that was dwelling in her. I wasn't afraid anymore, seems there's only room in a crisis for one to be afraid at a time. Besides, some latent instinct began to tell me that I should be helping, that I should be listening.

"You know what?" I said, trying not to sound too much off the wall, "I'm not quite a man yet. Does that mean you're not afraid of me?"

There was no response so I went on, "I bet if you told your mother you are afraid of men she could help you."

"Oh, sure," she responded with great sarcasm.

"You mean your mom doesn't even care?"

Her soft crying sounded as one who cried often and long. It came from deep within. It sounded as one who was hopeless. Impulsively, not considering the possible consequences, I scooted over to her and her head fell into my lap as she continued to cry even more.

"It's okay, you know." You can cry all you want. I've been crying a lot lately, myself. But, I wouldn't let anyone see me, so I just had to cry all by myself. Sometimes, I just feel like I don't have a friend in the world anymore.

For some reason, to think that someone else might cry seemed to get her attention. I let my hand rest on her head. She didn't flinch as I expected.

"Why do you cry?" she asked, choking back her sobs.

In a short time I told her about Moses and how one of these guys shot him. And then about Amy and all that we had planned and how much we loved each other. And when I was the most lonely and insecure that she would tell me that I was important and if it weren't so she wouldn't love me so.

Before I could go on, the girl raised up. She had stopped sobbing, "You are hurt, no wonder, to have lost ones that loved you so much. No one has ever loved me. Why should I cry?"

As though it was turn about, she began to tell her story. She leaned back against the wall beside me, drew her knees up under her chin, like two chums killing time. Her low whispers were now close to my ear. Staccato now, in a monotone, almost demonic. She told me that she never knew her dad. The nearest thing she had to a dad was her mother's boyfriend who began to molest her soon after he moved in. Her mother was an alcoholic and often extended sexual favors to acquire the resources for her addiction. That when she was a small girl she would hide under the bed to not be seen and cry as she heard strange men abuse her mother. They called her disgusting names when she became to drunk to respond sexually or they would make her do perverse sex acts. And then when she became a teenager the men became more interested in her and chased her around the house until she couldn't hide or runaway. If her mother was hurting for liquor real bad she would tell them her hiding place and more than once she endured the terrible pain of accepting what her body was not matured enough for. And soon the men came looking for her instead of her mother.

I couldn't believe that such a horrible story could be true, and yet it was told with such vivid detail and sincerity that I couldn't believe it not to be true. It made me sick as my mind began to build flash pictures of ugly, dirty men. Men with no faces, pawing and pulling at this faceless young girl, her arms flailing helplessly. It was dirty, I had a sickness in my gut.

Now, even the girl sitting next to me, that I couldn't even see, seemed repulsive from no fault of her own. Like an oozing cancer or a contractible virus, I wanted to move away from her, at least enough so that we could not touch. But I couldn't, after all, I too was only a kid, in adult trouble for sure. But to this imageless female voice that came from the darkness I probably represented the only youth that she had been close to. I shifted away trying to make it seem casual and not a purposeful endeavor to get away from her. She moved until our arms were again touching.

She went on to tell that she ran away and lived along the shore, cleaning fishing boats for food and some money. When she could, she would catch a ride on a fishing boat to here and hide until her food ran out.

I asked her if her mother didn't search for her. She responded that her mother didn't care. To her she was just a liability.

"What are you going to do? You can't live here all of your life. Besides," I went on but my voice changed from amazement to confidential, "You know what happens to girls who try to grow up on the street. They wake up dead one morning."

She relaxed as I ended, "You know what?" A little more weight settled against my arm. "Sometimes I dream that I do die and I wake up in a bright light that shines and makes everything warm. Where everybody loves me and I wear beautiful clothes and I'm so clean that I smell like flowers from a meadow. I have so many friends my own age and we play and play and we're all so happy and I don't think about ugly things because there are no ugly things there and I don't remember any of the past. When her boyfriends came, I would hide. I would close my eyes and dream this dream and as long as I was dreaming I was happy and they couldn't hurt me."

"You mean, even while they were hurting you, you could dream?"

"I had to. What was I supposed to do?"

"I don't want to hear anymore," I said with a stumbling rhetoric.

"It's okay, I don't blame you. You're the first one who ever listened anyway."

She quit talking alright, but that didn't mean that the awful pictures she created in my mind went away. They caused me to flush with embarrassment and hate.

"I tell you what," my speech now hushed yet matter of fact, "If we can get ourselves out of this mess, I promise, I'll try to help get you out of yours. I don't want to read in the paper that a girl I knew was found dead in an alley somewhere."

"I want to help you, too" she whispered, "Think up a plan and I'll help."

"You don't have to help. Why risk yourself?"

"I want to, that's all," she said briskly, "I just want to."

We sat side by side, leaning hard against the concrete wall. I in deep thought. She, though I had no idea, was developing a trust and leaned heavily against my shoulder, slightly trembling, her knees drawn up tight against her chest.

"Are you cold or something?" I asked, the question not of concern but curiosity.

"Yes, I'm always cold in here when the sun starts to set."

I could see that the fringe of light around the boxes was now darker and from a different angle. It was no doubt late evening and the sun would be hanging low above the gulf horizon.

"Here, I've got a T-shirt under this shirt. You can take it. I don't need it at all."

I leaned forward and without getting to my feet took off my outer shirt and then pulled my T-shirt over my head and arms. I dropped it in her lap, and with a laugh, "Now, when the sun comes up in the morning I'll want that back. You see?"

To any other person listening to this dialogue the note of lightness in my voice would have betrayed a hint of union, but if that were the case, I didn't sense it.

Between now and darkness would be the best time for us to do what ever plan we devised and so I began to devise one. I had a plan that might work. I could see it working in my head, but so what, in my head I could leap over the moon.

"Okay," I whispered, "I think I have a plan." Then I stopped short, "By the way, you got a name?"

"Of course."

"Well."

"Well, I don't like it."

"So what, I've got to call you something," I said with a degree of irritation revealed in my tenor.

"Jesse."

"What's wrong with Jesse? Probably short for Jessica?"

"Jezebel if I know mother."

"Then I'll just call you Jesse. OK?"

"Okay, let's go on with the plan." I drew around until I was talking matter of factly into her ear. "You said you worked some on the fishing boats, right?"

"Yes"

"Can you run the motor?"

"I think so."

"Then what you will do is slip over into that brush at the edge of the fort, ease down to the edge of the water and look for Maston and Mabrey. If they're not around, push the boat into the water and let it drift out from shore a safe distance. Then start the motor and run the boat east down the island. When I hear the motor start I will know that both jerks will be distracted and I"ll run hard to the same place. I know I can outrun and outswim them so all I have to do is swim out to meet you. We'll head for St. Pete and the cops can come pick them up like monkeys in the zoo. Great plan or what?"

Jesse immediately got to her feet, "I'll go now." Then she dropped back down. With great earnesty she took my hand and held it tightly between hers, "If I don't ever see you again, I'll always remember that you cared."

With that she slid the boxes to the side and slid out of the room into the brush with the lightness and stealth of a cat.

The next fifteen minutes would seem like hours as I sat near the opening and listened for the roar of the outboard. I strained to hear, trying to visualize her movements through the palmetto brush in route to the beach.

But it wasn't the motor I heard. It was Jesse's scream. Mabrey was posted near the boat expecting that I would be the one crawling up to steal it. I slipped out of the room and crawled toward the beach. I could hear Mabrey call for Maston, "Maston, look here what I got. A little bitch trying to steal our boat."

Maston made his way over to the edge of the beach where he could see. Mabrey had Jesse's arms pulled behind her back and all her "devil may care" spunk was no match for his bulk and strength. Maston just stood looking, seemingly puzzled by this strange turn of events.

"Look, it's a damn girl - built purty good for a kid, wouldn't you say?"

"So, you caught yourself a girl trying to steal our boat. Bet she's got something to do with that boy. Tell you what, Mabrey, I'm gonna stay over here and keep a watch. You see if you can get her to talk. So you just do what you have to do."

"First thing I'm gonna do is find out what's under that T-shirt. What you little bitch, want to take it off or you need a little help?" Mabrey snarled and jerked her arm up until she screamed with pain.

I ran to the edge of the palmettos close to the beach. I could see Mabrey pulling at her clothes. Jesse screamed and swung with her free arm, but there was no way she could free herself from the grip he had. I was so disgusted and filled with rage, yet helpless to do anything. It didn't matter about getting away now. I knew I had to help Jesse, though I didn't know why.

"Let her go," I hollered, "it's me you want. That little girl's got nothing to do with all this," emphasizing the 'little girl'. "You let her go and I'll come in."

"Oh yeah," Mabrey not willing to surrender his female hostage bellowed back, "Think I'll just keep her and get you too."

He hollered for Maston, "In that Palmetto clump, go for 'im."

Maston knew that he'd never catch me in a foot race, but moved a step closer. "Say you'll turn yourself over if we release this dirty little bitch?"

"Yes, I give my word. As soon as she's clear."

Mabrey called to Maston, "We gonna let this little bitch run around free knowin' what she probably knows?"

"Shut your damn mouth. Think we can't catch her later?"

I walked away from the palmetto brush I was hiding in and moved toward the center of the clearing where I could easily be seen. Maston waited until I stopped next to a large cabbage palm with it between me and him and then he moved to a position that put him between me and my escape route. Next, Mabrey, shoving Jesse in front of him, held her arm hard against her back, alongside Maston making double-sure that if I tried to run I would have to clear them both.

Maston looked toward Mabrey to make sure they were ready in case I tried to run.

"Let her go," he said to Mabrey.

Mabrey gave Maston a quizzical look that reflected a definite I don't want to.

"Let her go, damn it. You deaf or something?"

Mabrey resisted the instruction until Maston made a move toward him, his fists clenched in preparation for a fight. Then with defiance he shoved her away hard enough that she fell spread eagle to the ground.

I held my peace until she was on her feet, "Run hard and hide. I'll find you later," I shouted the order with such force that she disappeared into the shadows in a flash.

Maston, Mabrey and me stood and stared at each other for at least several minutes. I knew I wasn't going to run. I said I wouldn't, stupid nobility, so why hurry to them.

Maston spoke first, "You coming or do I have to come over there and knock your head off."

"Whatever you say," I said staring at him in fear.

"Walk this way."

Just as I got close, both men jumped me and threw me to the ground. Mabrey dropped to the ground burying his knee in my back. He whipped a pistol out of his pocket and stuck it against my forehead, low so that I could see it from the corner of my eye. "How'd you like a piece of this?" he said in a snarling way that must have been his way of feeling mean and strong. He pushed it hard against my forehead until I felt a trickle of blood oozing.

Before he could make any more threats Maston broke in, "It's gonna be dark in a few minutes, get him in the boat and let's get out to sea a ways."

"How far's a ways?" Mabrey broke in.

"Couple of miles, anyway."

A couple of miles didn't set well with Mabrey and he protested with numerous profanities until Maston admitted that he was kidding and that even a half mile would do.

Mabrey, ready to follow instructions now, pulled me to my feet again then pulled my arm up behind my back like he had held Jesse. One thing for sure, with his weight and grip, I knew I couldn't outdo him once he got a hold on me.

He shoved me to the boat. The bow had been run up onto the sand beach and had to be turned before we could get in. Maston grabbed the gunwales about center and pushed it backwards until it floated freely, then swung it around until the rear of the boat was in front of Mabrey and myself.

Mabrey shoved me toward the back of the boat, "Get your little ass in there and don't try nothin. Might have to bloody up the boat."

I honestly believed that Mabrey would carry out every threat, nothing funny entered my head. I put my hands on the transom to crawl over. I was next to the side of the motor where the fuel hose connected. Maston had complained that the connection was worn. It looked frayed alright. When I stepped over the side I brushed against it hard, thinking that maybe it would break, but it didn't. Maston and Mabrey got in next.

"Pump the bulb. Get some fuel pressure back here so's I can get this motor kicked off," Maston said.

Mabrey had the little ball in his hand squeezing it rapidly. I looked back at the motor hoping that the strength in Mabrey's grip would explode the hose. In the twilight darkness, I could see that the hose was in tact, but a steady drip had developed and gasoline was coming from the connection, enough that there would be a sizable puddle in the bottom of the boat in a few minutes. Maston, busy keeping the boat from washing back against the beach, didn't even notice. He cranked the motor. It started, but ran sickly, not yet thoroughly dry from its previous soaking. But when the gear shift was moved into forward it pushed the boat away from the shore and out into the sea.

The wind had lain and the sea was calm tonight, there were small swells, they only caused the boat to rise and fall slightly, the motor struggled as the bow rose up to go over the top and then sped down the other side. We were moving slowly, but the motor, even with its consistent miss seemed reliable and we peered into the darkness one hundred and eighty degrees away from Mullet Key.

Mabrey was sitting in the bow seat, as usual. I watched as he began to fumble in his shirt pocket. It was too dark to see much but it had been fifteen or twenty minutes since we had left shore and I knew it was past time for him to be searching for a cigarette.

"Hey Mabrey," I shouted toward the front of the boat, "How about me a cigarette? Haven't had one since we left Lutz, you know."

"Shutup you little fart, you don't need no cigarette. Hey, Maston, the little fart wants a cigarette," he shouted over my head with a lot sneer and sarcasm.

"Well, give him one. What difference it gonna make?"

Mabrey stared at Maston with a penetration that would have made the devil shutter, but then thought better of making an issue of it. Without a word he tossed the pack at me. I held the pack and pumped it against my finger to extract a cigarette like I had seen them do in the movies. I held it in my mouth, off to the side trying to look authentic, while Mabrey fumbled in his pocket for the lighter. Finally he drew it from his pocket and tossed it toward me. It was just right, a flip top zippo, one good strike against the wheel and when it lit it stayed lit. I gave myself the luxury of an instant to go over in my head the plan. I was afraid, not knowing for sure what would happen, and knowing that if anything went wrong Mabrey had a gun and would probably use it. I stood up and cradled the lighter in my hand, not striking it but stalling for a little more time.

Maston cut in, "Mabrey, you smell gas?"

By now the bottom of the boat was covered with raw gas and the fumes were becoming nauseous. No time to deliberate, I raked the lighter wheel against my palm and it lit instantly. All in one motion I jumped onto the gunwale and pushed hard to throw myself far from the boat simultaneously tossing the lighter into the bottom of the gas filled boat. The heavy fumes of the gas filled the boat like an invisible explosive. I hit the water in a shallow dive and pulled myself down. There was only the noise of my splash and then through the dark water the flash of the flaming explosion. I could hear the muffled roar as the wooden craft blew itself apart and fell back to the sea as burning pieces of scrap.

I knew the water would be covered with burning gasoline and pieces of cyprus wood, but because of the excitement, I was short of breath and my lungs screamed for air as I pulled myself under water as far from the boat as possible. My chest began to heave and demand oxygen, I had to fight to keep from sucking in seawater, I pulled up and broke through the surface with a screaming sound as the air rushed to fill my lungs. Somehow I had swam clear of the wreckage. I turned to see what was left, but saw nothing but burning debris. I remained quiet, listening for any sound of survivors, none. I turned again toward the black outline I knew to be the trees on Mullet Key silhouetted against the starlit sky and with a long breast stroke began the long slow pull toward shore.

Chapter #5
OF SUNSETS AND DAWN

She made her way from the dark bunker. She methodically walked to the edge of the gentle sea to where the water was rolling up on to her slight ankles. Her chest was heaving as she sucked in air by the gulp between the uncontrollable sobs and the heart tearing pains that had torn at her guts relentlessly through the night, for the flash of fire, the roar of the exploding boat came echoing across the water like a blast in the face - she saw and could only assume that once again life struck her friendless. She stared mindlessly out across the sea at nothing, nothing at all. Only darkness. Only occasionally could the sounds of her sobs be heard over the quiet rippling of the water and the soft whooshing of the sea breeze. Her slender, erect body cast an eerie black silhouette against the bluish sky. My large shirt, she wore as her only contact with earthly security, blowing loosely as was her long flowing hair.

"What's left? Doesn't anyone care? Is this it? Is this all there is. Doesn't this damn world have anything for me but pain? How many times will you knock out my teeth, will you cave in my face, rape my body, steal my joy?" she screamed in raging mania above the water. Tears were flowing from her eyes. Her face was grimaced up towards the stars, her clenched fists held defiantly above her gesturing hate - futile hate.

"O God, if there's a God, why have you hated me all my life? Was I only born to delight you in my torment? What is left for you now God, you have taken the only thing, my only friend. You God, you God, damn, damn, damn. Devil - Satan, come lead me into the water, let me drown, let me live in Hell. Oh, Hell, Hell, Hell!!"

She made short jestures as though she would walk into the water, as though in some satanic madness she thought she would find her Bud waiting in the black depth of the sea, crazed to the point that death seemed her only sanctity, but so afraid, so alone.

"I must go to him, he's waiting for me. How long will he wait in the dark deep waters? I will go now, O God, Oh Satan, help me go."

She fell to her knees. The rage that had provided the courage for her a moment ago had left her. She felt the helplessness and hopelessness she'd felt so many times before. She had no power to follow her Bud.

Her crying had turned to low sobs now. There were no tears left. Each breath gave a crushing pain to her chest and she sobbed shallowly. Empty and hollow and worthless were the feelings so familiar to her. She recognized them as they crept back. She slumped deeper into the edge of the cooling water not aware of it.

A sharp pain pierced her abdomen. Instinctively she pressed it with her hand. It retreated as fast as it had come. Again the pain returned to her abdomen. She held her hand on the spot in order to keep it from returning. It was the same place that I had laid my hand to maintain a reassuring contact that night we hid in the bunker. She remembered the sweetness, the euphoric joy and security as his contact broke down her insecurity born of her first life and the hate and dread she had of all men. Even life.

The sweet memories of those short moments seemed to bring calmness. She leaned backward until her head was lying in the wet sand. The water gently rolled up the beach and carried her long hair up and then back down as it ran back to the sea. She left her hand lying on her abdomen, trying to recreate the same rushing, warm feelings when it was the hand of her man. Many minutes had passed. The warm seawater was moving up and up as the tide made its way up the shore. The ripples of the slight waves were nearly up to her face now. Soon it would cover her body. Soon it would carry another body to its waiting victims, their arms reaching up from the deep, "Come Jesse, Come on Jesse, we've waited so long Jesse. Come to us, we will love you, we will love, Come to us, Jesse."

She had given up. She was ready for the sea to take her.

Under her hand resting against her abdomen came a slight bump. "What was that," she silently asked? The bump came again in the same place. "What?"

In a moment she realized, "Is it a baby, am I pregnant?"

Slowly she began to remember the unexplainable biological changes that seemed to be happening in her and she began now to see them fall into a pattern. Yes, she was pregnant.

She jerked up to a sitting position. She stared down at her hand still holding her abdomen anticipating another tiny bump.

Conflicting emotions began to surge through her mind and body as she tried to get a grip on all of the implications of this new situation.

I will pretend that it's Bud's. I will take it with me to Bud, we will all be together, I must go to the deep to be with him."

Almost before that emotion had a chance to flee her mind, "No, I will not take it to him as a fetus in a womb. It must be in my arms, I must cradle it in my arms as I go to him. That is what he would want. I will have this baby, then I will go to Bud, then I will go to Bud."

She raised to her feet, her hand still pressing her abdomen, the other raised in defiance, "Now God, will you take him too? Will you not even let me go to Bud?"

"No, No, No," she screamed above the water, "I will not let you take my baby. It will be my Bud, I will have my Bud, do you hear me? You can't have my baby. I defy anything to take this baby. Not you, not Satan."

A sort of peace came over her. She passively looked out again into the darkness, "Bud, can you hear me Bud? I'm not coming now. I would come but I cannot. You know I want to come, I never want to be away from you, but I must wait. We're going to have a baby. I'm going to name him Bud, I know it will be a boy because it is going to just like you. He will be you, forever you. Then I will come Bud, I will come."

It was as though a transformation had come over her, a radiance had come to her. There was a peace in her voice that had never been there before. Determination and destiny had taken the place of anxiety and fear, like it has come to every mother since Eve.

"Bud, I won't have you to help me. That's alright. I will do it, I will find a way. I will steal and rob for food and hide in our secret bunker until it's time and then I will find a midwife to help me. I will find a women from the quarters who will help me. I will Bud, I can do it, I have to."

Jesse dropped back down to the sand, sitting in the edge of the water looking out, as if hoping, dreaming that somehow a person would emerge out from the water in front of her and it would be Bud.. And it would be Bud.

The yellowish hues of morning were breaking over the sand dunes behind her. She didn't seem to notice or to care. It would come up as it always came up. She neither looked forward to it before or would she now.

I stood above her at the edge of the clearing, not many feet away, watching as the sun began to light her back. My soaked tee-shirt was clinging to her, revealing a slender, willowy body. Her long, shiny black hair hung over her shoulders and what I saw was not an ugly street tramp as I had imagined but rather a well-formed, youthful body shaped into dark beauty.

The sun was casting long shadows across the white, sandy beach. Palm trees and pillars of concrete from the ruins of the old fort made shadows of ghostly giants moving about. Fear jumped into her throat as one shadow approached from behind her, the unmistakable shadow of a man approaching directly toward her, another drunk from the mainland dropped off to sober up and lost.

She pretended as though she didn't see him. How many times had she been attacked and molested by filthy, drunken men? She would wait until he was very close and as he was about to touch her she would draw up huge hands fulls of sand and throw them into his eyes and before he could clear them she would be away and hidden in the bunker that she knew so well.

Closer, closer, closer. She began to gradually dig her hands into the wet sand, every nerve stressed, every muscle tensed like a cat ready to spring.

"Jesse, it's me."

She sprang to her feet and stared in disbelief, "Bud, Bud, it's you." She fell limp into my arms. Her arms tugged to pull me close and hold me like I may try to flee. I felt excitement as she pulled her wet body against me, her small, youthful breast were firm and tingled where they touched my chest.

"Jesse, do you care so much for me?" I asked.

She didn't move her head from my chest nor release the hold of her arms. She began to sob slightly and spoke through them, "Bud," she said.

"What," I returned in a tone that sounded like I was addressing a small child.

"Never call me Jesse again. Please - will you not."

"Well, what will I call you then?"

She stood up onto her tip-toes as tall as she could and pressed he cheek against mine and turned our bodies together until we were looking at the pinkish glow of the early sun, almost in a whisper she responded, "Will you call me Dawn? I want so much for life to be all new."

It caught me off guard that this little thing that I assumed was little more than an abused tramp could have such deep feelings and I felt that old familiar grab in my throat that usually meant the beginning of a tear. I held her now. I felt the fear and trembling of her little body as she clung to me as though I was her long awaited savior from her play dream. I didn't respond for a while, visions of my own were racing through my mind, thoughts and visions from the past, how I hurt when Moses got killed, then the flowing blonde hair and deep blue eyes of Amy were there, and I remembered - I REMEMBERED - and I knew. I began to cry like a great burden had flown off my shoulder, not aloud, but I could feel the stream of tears dripping off my cheeks. They dropped on Jesse's forehead when she looked up to see why I hadn't replied.

"Bud," she whispered, more a question than a call, "Bud, are you --??"

I cut her off so not to have to respond to the question because the source of the tears was my cherished secret.

"Sure, I think Dawn's a beautiful name, it's just right."

✶   ✶   ✶   Epilogue   ✶   ✶   ✶

It was very strange how completely I understood what Amy was instructing me to do that day in the emergency room. I never looked back, from that very moment on Mullet Key beach, I knew what I would do, like I was guided by a mystic force. So from here the end ends and the beginning begins. But because you would hate me and because I hope we are friends by now, I'll tell you a little of how the beginning began.

Dawn never moved from my side. We were two lost kids on Treasure Island. We went to the side of the island facing St. Pete and dragged limbs and branches to the edge of the beach and stacked them to make a fire. On top we piled dry palm frowns, higher than my head, until I was throwing them to the top. The only minute Dawn was away from my side was when I sent her to the bunker to retrieve her cache of matches. If the fire roared large and high enough it would bring a curious fisherman or the Coastguard in to us. It did, it roared high and wild.

I backed away from the heat of the roaring fire and sat in the shade of a cabbage palm where I had full view of the open water towards St. Pete. Soon Dawn came and sat by me, she pushed up close like she had known me forever, like that was were she was supposed to be, and it was, but I don't know how she could have known. She sheepishly took my hand and held it against her cheek, "Is this okay?" she asked looking into my eyes with eyes as dark as chestnuts.

"Yes, it's okay."

A patrolling Coastguard boat saw the fire and came in close enough for me to signal help. A dingy was sent for us and we were soon on the boat. The boat captain was sure we were runaways but

I insisted with such sincerity that he radioed shore and soon found that sure enough a young lad fitting my description was missing and under police protection and that they would meet us at the dock. There was no APB on Dawn. I told them she lived next door to me and she could go home when I go.

The sheriff met us as planned and took us to headquarters to quiz me for all of the details. Finally they must have decided I was telling the truth and sent the Coastguard back out to search for bodies or debris from a burnt boat. They found everything just as I said and took me home, case closed, I was free.

I walked into the house, and straight into the arms of my stepmother. I stood frozen until she released me. I don't know why she was so concerned. I didn't deserve it. Dawn was standing about three paces behind me, reluctant to even be in the house. I introduced them as best I could, considering that Dawn didn't seem to have a last name.

"Mom," I said, I always said mom when there was a purpose, "We'd better sit down, I've got lots to tell you."

We went into the kitchen. I talked while she put drinks and food onto the table. Dawn kept easing her chair closer and closer to mine. I felt her hand touch my leg under the table and I slipped my hand down to lay on hers.

My stepmother being much wiser about the affairs of the world responded negatively when I told her I was dropping out of school for a time to work and support Dawn and the new baby. I was always able to get work in the groves and I would find a place to live and I would finish school later.

She was justifiably blunt about the fact that I hardly knew Dawn, if at all, and what we were planning to do had little chance of working out.

I told her about my mission and I knew I had to do it but I also knew that it would work out. I didn't tell her more.

I went to see Albert. He hadn't heard and looked as if he had seen a ghost as I led Dawn into Stiekies.

I began to tell him the past events. While I talked and answered questions Mr. Stiekie popped the tops from two Strawberry Nehis and poked them at Dawn and me. She looked sheepish and scared and only took small sips from the drink.

Finally Albert figured he had heard all he needed, suggested I was biting off to much for a teenager, but he did need a hand and just by chance there was that little house back of the grove that he'd throw in as part of my pay if I'd fix it up.

I thought the deal of a lifetime had just been struck and was stammering to find words suitable for the occasion.

We began to fix up the old place, Dawn and I. Dawn never ventured far from my side. When we were close, she held my arm and just looked at me. She talked very little but never ceased working and helping to prepare the house for a home, like a mother fox preparing a nest for her spring cubs.

A month or so had passed. I was enjoying working for Albert, although the pay was meager, it met our current needs.

One day while I was in the yard working on the GMC Dawn called for me to come in. She was wearing the same oversized tee-shirt I had given her. When I came in, she came close, took my hand and moved it up under the shirt. She had nothing on under it. She slid my hand under the shirt until it rested flat against her tummy. "Feel?" she asked.

"Maybe," I said, not being sure what I was supposed to feel. Doesn't it feel funny?"

It did, it had a pronounced bulge now and something in there was very active.

Dawn was shy to point of being silly, but she seemed to enjoy having at least one person in the whole world to share her secret parts with and delighted in putting my hands around on her body. Even so she often struggled to deal with past memories and the screams from her sleep told of times when her tiny body was misused and at those times I was helpless and unequipped to help her deal with horrors of the past.

I was embarrassed when Albert drove into the yard one day when Dawn and I were playing around. He seemed to ignore it and came on in.

"I've been talking to Madge." He cut it off and watched for a reaction before he when on. I knew he was talking about Mrs. Brooks, "She's needing some help real bad on her place. She pretty much let it go when…" He stopped and glanced at Dawn.

"Yeah, I guess I don't blame her much. How's she doing?"

"Well, she's trying to cope, I guess, always was strong as an ox."

"Yeah, I know," I responded with unusual sincerity.

"Well, I talked to her," Albert's voice was becoming more business like, "She's got to get some help whether she wants it or not and I said, Madge, I've got just the help you need."

I must have had question marks emblazoned on my face because Albert went on to explain.

"Bud, you've got to get over there and talk to Madge. She needs you, boy."

I didn't know the full implication of what Albert meant, but did feel some guilt because I hadn't seen her since Amy died and she did seem to care a lot for me. But I wasn't the same little innocent Bud that I was when I was going steady with Amy and couldn't believe she would want to see me now.

When I explained my reluctance to Albert it irritated him a lot and in that irritation he rebuked me, "Bud, shame on you, you think Madge ain't big enough to know how things are in this world? You get your butt over there and take Dawn. She wants to see you real bad."

The next morning, all cleaned up, Dawn and me were knocking on Mrs. Brook's front door. When the door opened, Dawn was standing just behind me, half hiding, not knowing what to expect. Mrs. Brooks stood looking at us just long enough for me to take in her appearance. Her face still looked strong and positive although the stress of the past had taken a toll. It was only a hesitation, then she hugged me like the lost sheep that had come home. Then her tears began to flow, then mine. Then, just that quick, I knew everything was okay, nothing had changed. She looked Dawn over, I could see Dawn squirm under the scrutinization. Finally Mrs. Brooks could see how uncomfortable Dawn was and responded with just the right words to make everything alright, "You sure are pretty Dawn. Bud always picked the prettiest girls."

I told Mrs. Brooks all that had taken place since last we were together. Much of it she had found out already from my stepmother. Dawn sat rigid as I told her about Dawns past, how she helped me on the Mullet Key and what we planned. I didn't tell her it was because of Amy that I would do this.

Mrs. Brooks seemed so hungry for companionship. Noon came and we carried sandwiches down to the beach house for lunch. We talked as if we were afraid to stop as if perhaps the visit would end. Soon, before I could believe, the shadows had grown long, we gathered up the lunch mess and carried it to the house. Much to my surprise, though I shouldn't have been, Mrs. Brooks had taken Dawn into the kitchen and together, side by side, they were busy chopping lettuce, dicing tomatoes and preparing the salad for tonight's dinner.

Mrs. Brooks had lost a few years from her ordeal but not her magic.

During dinner I accepted the job of caretaker of all of Mr. and Mrs. Brooks property. At first I resisted because I knew I was not prepared for such an undertaking but Mrs. Brooks assured me I could and somehow I knew if she said it that's how it would happen.

But the big undertaking was the one that Mrs. Brooks took, to love and care for Dawn. The horrors of Dawn's past didn't end as the closing of a book, nor did her fears of being instantly tossed into the realm of wife, mother and respectable person disappear. Slowly, careingly and with patience exceeding super-natural, Mrs. Brooks took Dawn under her care and taught her, as a baby taking her first steps, the very basics of etiquette and how to prepare herself for becoming a mother.

In due time, a little boy was born. Strangely, I was very proud. It seldom occurred to me that he was not my breeding. Mrs. Brooks fussed around like it was hers, like a grandchild she thought she would never have. We were one happy family. And if we were not, you would never know by our closeness and our admiration for each other.

It seemed that in no time at all the boy was up and around, at first into everything, just the way Mrs. brooks wanted it, and then at my side, my tools in his hand, his everything else in my heart.

One evening, as I was bringing the tractor up from the field to park it in the barn for the night, I noticed the moon coming up as the sun was setting, a full moon tonight. When the noise from the tractor ended I could hear Blue and Sam barking as they often did at the rising moon. At the supper table, I said I should take Blue and Sam hunting on this full moon. They'd like that. They hadn't been out of the pen in months. Mrs. Brooks exclaimed that it was a great idea. I said that I would be taking the boy. Mrs. Brooks winked at Dawn and said if I did they'd sit around the house and talk about both of us. "Right, Dawn?" she said.

Dawn agreed, but probably only because Mrs. Brooks sounded so positive about it. Dawn seem certain that every time I left her sight I'd never return.

Dawn scurried around the bedroom getting too many clothes for the kid and Mrs. Brooks dashed into the kitchen to fix too many snacks for us to eat during the night.

Mrs. Brooks had bought a pickup truck for me to use, a GMC of course. I backed it up to the dog pen, Sam was almost turning cartwheels at the prospect of going hunting. Blues emotion was a little more subdued. While Sam leaped into the pickup, Blue put his front feet onto the tailgate and almost fell backwards trying to get up, his stiff and arthritic joints unyielding.

Soon, with the little bundled fellow scooted up close to my side, I turned the GMC off the pavement and onto a familiar lane passing through Albert's grove of giant grapefruit trees and then in a short distance coming to a stop at the clearing between grove and the cyprus swamp. I turned the dogs out to begin the hunt which I was satisfied would little more than an exercise in cold trailing since neither dog had hunted for such a long time. They made their way out of site into the trees. The only sound was the splashing they made in the shallow water.

I found some dry limbs and piled them up close to a log to make a fire for us to watch while the dogs hunted. It soon blazed, casting yellowish light onto the hanging moss at the edge of the swamp. I sat down on the log and listened for the familiar sounds of the night hunt.

My little friend had grown dreary-eyed staring at the fire and was leaning against my leg for support.

It wasn't but a few minutes until Blue had struck a trail. He bellowed out as only an old, long eared bluetick can. It echoed between the swamp and the grapefruit grove, adding a little finesse to the sound. In a few minutes Sam barked, ahead of Blue by a hundred yards or so. Sam didn't bark again until Blue once again barked where Sam had barked before. This routine was to take place over and over.

The little boy said, "Dad, Blue sounds funny. It sounds like he is hurting or something."

"I expect he is hurting," I responded, "He's really old and his legs hurt a lot of the time."

"Then he really must love to hunt, right dad?"

I agreed and it was silent for a while as we stared into the dancing blaze, each dealing with our private thoughts.

Then Sam barked again, about the same distance from Blue as before.

"Dad, does Sam hurt too?"

"No, I don't think Sam hurts at all."

"Then why doesn't he go on and catch that silly Ole coon?" he asked quizzically.

"You know what I think?" Two big, round, dark eyes were now fixed on me like I was about to reveal the worlds greatest secret, "Sam and Ole Blue have been hunting together ever since Sam was just a pup and I think that Sam knows that Blue can't keep up anymore and is just waiting for him to catch up so they can get to the tree together."

A little, chubby hand reached across my lap and grasped my hand by the fingers, "You know what I think, dad? When you're too old to keep up any more, I'll wait for you too."

"I love you, Dad."

"I love you too, Son."

In the distance I heard the faithful call of the night bird. In my eyes I felt stress as tears welled around them. Nothing more from life could I demand.

And what is this strange thing we're watching, a young man and a boy with no apparent common linkage. How can one say dad and the other say son. Is dad and son not a factor of genes? And then, did we not hear one say "I love you" and did not the other respond in kind?

I say, for so long now we have been learning this miracle. Some will have found, some will still be learning and others can only love themselves.

I say, in these two, a young boy and a young man, has not the truth been found, for genes and heredity have no more to do with the truth of love than water a radiant falls. For after all, doesn't water nearly cover the earth, and yes, while some is clear and sparkling and sweet to the taste, the other stagnant and putrid.

Then what are we to conclude? Is there no peace on earth except by chance or luck.

Love is the binder of all elements, the catalyst of anomalies, a treasure greatly desired. It is as the magic lure of soft pure gold or the brilliant fire from the finest diamond. The worth of a million gold mines, the pleasure of a perfect gem.

Even if the lost treasure troves of a million Spanish Galleons buried in the warm sands of the Caribbean sea were relinquished for one man's coffer, it would bring no love.

How elusive this treasure so valuable. And if it has no measure of gold or diamonds, what then? Has it no measure?

Maybe then, not for things shall we search, but for a place. And where be that place? Many? Maybe a few, begin to search for that tiny corner, a hidden place in the far lost reaches of the heart. After all, isn't that the place that cries when love is lost, that's frequently broken. Isn't that the place of joy and life?

So, search the heart, find treasure unmeasurable, from there will love begin.

Others will find, also - to these your alliance bind. For the one who finds this treasure will pass through this life into eternity, with joy and anticipation.

* * * THE END * * *

About the Author

Okay, I was a broken home kid. If you find my writing slanted toward that sympathy it's
for reason. However, broken home certainly doesn't predispose any particular stereotype.

Show me a kid from a broken home and I'll show you a kid who has developed unique survival skills and a curious independence. That was me. Independent-curious-energetic, living with Mom my first years and then my Dad, constantly running away from one home to the other – doing pretty much whatever I thought I was big enough to handle.

Those are the years when I developed the feelings and emotions to write this book.

From those early years I went on to develop professional skills for a career – beyond that I developed skills in writing, photography – both above and below water, skiing (both kinds), scuba, fishing, hunting, hiking, horse packing, caving and exploration.

I live with my wife Dona on our Silver City, New Mexico paradise – seven grown kids – fourteen grandkids.

Printed in the United States
107652LV00004B/337-345/P